For Marga...

with all good wishes —

Eric Crozier

"CATFLAT,"

Wishaw

18 February, 1991

Assunta

ASSUNTA
The Story of Mrs. Joe

Enrico Cocozza

VANTAGE PRESS
New York / Atlanta
Los Angeles / Chicago

To the memory of my grandparents,
Benedetto and Filomena Marzella
and
Gaetano and Leonarda Cocozza

CONTENTS

Acknowledgements

Some of the incidents I have described could have happened. Most of them did.

I am deeply indebted to the following kind friends who helped me considerably in various ways when I was writing the book:

Jean Brown, Giustino Coia, Letizia Coia, Margaret Duddy, Aldo Ferri, Elisa Ferri, Lucia Ferri, Pietro Ferri, Silvio Ferri, Sarah Hislop, Theresa Murphy, Eugenio Saracino, and Robert Whitelaw.

My special gratitude is due to my colleague Sheelagh Graham, who valiantly undertook to read the original typescript and made many invaluable suggestions, guiding me carefully through treacherous waters and away from unseasonable gorse-scented landscapes.

Wishaw   15 August 1981

Assunta

Chapter One

1915—A Time for Anticipation

"Chicchiri-chí! Chicchiri-chíii!"

"Cock-a-doodle-doo! Cock-a-doodle-dooooooo!" Assunta stirred in her slumber, and the chaff mattress beneath her sighed with a muffled, crackly sound. She yawned as she opened first one eye, then the other. Trust Crestone, that loud, bullying cockerel, to rouse her just when she was dreaming she was already in Glasgow.

In her dream she had been standing with her brother, Eugenio, and his wife, Giulietta, behind the counter in their shop. It was just as Eugenio had so often described it. Large jars of delicious sweets were perched on the shelves of the gantry, while boxes of dark bars of chocolate were laid out on the counter. Assunta, tempted, lifted a bar and took a tiny bite. She was just about to relish its delightful flavour when Crestone, with his loud, shrill call, brought her swiftly back to the reality of her bedroom in Filignano on this cold February morning in 1915. Assunta shuddered under her thin blanket.

She could hear her mother, Filomena, moving around in the kitchen downstairs. The twigs in the fire she had just kindled were crackling, and Assunta listened as Filomena picked up the long, iron, blowing tube, tapped it lightly against the hearth to shake off the gathered ash at the bottom of the stem, and, placing the mouthpiece to her lips, blew three long puffs to encourage the flames. Then she shuffled lightly over to the cistern in the corner under the alcove, gingerly lowered the small pail on its iron chain until it entered the water with a dull plop, and pulled it slowly up again. She poured the cool water into a copper pitcher and placed it on a shelf where it would rest, ready to be used as it was required.

The drawing of the water from the cistern over which the kitchen had been built was a morning ritual that Filomena enjoyed, for the other women on the hill of Imperatore had to fetch their water from the well at the top of the hill, a cold task on chilly February mornings. When Filomena drew the water, she always looked carefully into the

1

pail to see that she had not drawn a live eel. Eels were kept in the cistern to ensure that the water remained fresh.

Assunta usually rose smartly at the first crowing of the cock, but that morning she lingered under her blanket, letting her thoughts wander at random over the past few years in her life. She felt that by dwelling on all the important things she had experienced, she would be preparing herself for the exciting adventure so soon to open up before her when she left her beloved Filignano to begin a new life in faraway Scotland. She was drawing her roots about her to gather together her strength so that she would be prepared for a new way of life.

She wondered what she would most miss when she found herself in this new land. Perhaps her friend Antonia with whom she often went to gather firewood or immense bundles of twigs that they carried back, precariously balanced on their heads. Antonia and she had grown up together, and, wherever they went, working in the fields or tending their goats, they exchanged confidences and secrets. In the long winter evenings, they shared each other's firesides, listening to the exciting tales of the old days that the old folk told so skilfully.

Filomena was in her element when she sat sewing by the fire, occasionally nudging her husband, Benedetto, to stir up the embers and put on another small log. Benedetto was a man of few words, but he thought a great deal as he sucked at his small wooden pipe into whose tiny bowl he would feed a glowing end of twig from the fire, as he listened to Filomena recounting her tales of brigands and kidnappings, witches and spells, murders, suicides, broken romances, and local scandals. He would glance at Assunta and Antonia from time to time, and, when Filomena was approaching the dramatic climax of some gory story, a twinkle would come into his eye to suggest that his wife, carried away with her enthusiasm, was elaborately embellishing the events she was narrating.

Although he was the elder of two sons, Benedetto had not been given an opportunity to make something of himself by his land-owning parents. The Marzellas had come originally from Vallerotonda near Cassino, and they had acquired a considerable amount of land in and around Filignano. There were two branches of the family, one having settled in a large house at Valle, the other in a smaller house at Imperatore, near the top of the hill behind the church in Filignano. Assunta's grandparents, Don Ferdinando Marzella and his wife, Donna Anna Maria, had lived in the large house at Valle.

It was by the strangest of chances that Don Ferdinando had ever married, for his parents had intended him to be a priest. As a seminarist

2

he studied diligently, coming home only at Easter and Christmas. One Easter, when he was making his way home to Valle on foot from Venafro, he was set upon by brigands and carried off to the mountains. There he was compelled to write a letter to his parents in which he explained that the bandits were holding him to ransom for a large sum of money. It was to be left at night at a certain spot under a large rock.

Ferdinando spent a few weeks in the caves with the brigands, as it took his parents some time to gather the ransom money. In the eyes of the brigands, Ferdinando, in his seminarist's clothes, was as good as a priest. So they constructed an altar from stone slabs in one of the caves and forced the boy at pistol point to celebrate mass there every Sunday. Ferdinando was so dismayed by the sacrilege he was forced to commit that when he was at last returned to his parents, he refused to go on with his studies at the seminary. His father was very disappointed by the boy's decision. Shortly afterwards Ferdinando met and fell in love with Anna Maria, and they were married a few months later.

In four years they had four children, two sons and two daughters. Assunta's father, Benedetto, was the elder of the two boys. His brother was called Daniele, and his sisters were Lucia and Anna. For some reason Don Ferdinando favoured Daniele and he was given a good education, while Benedetto was entrusted with the cultivation of their land. Daniele eventually became a tax collector. The two sisters were married off with small dowries, Lucia to a tenant farmer at Valle and Anna to a farmer at Concacasale. Both girls died young and childless.

Daniele, the tax collector, married a wealthy girl, Letizia, and they had a son, Emilio, and two daughters, Angelina and Concetta. Like his father, Don Ferdinando, Daniele was not very fond of hard work and in time, following his father's bad example, he sold off many of his holdings to pay off his debts. He appropriated more than his just share of the land and sold the best of it, leaving his brother, Benedetto, with the poorest parcels. All his scheming did him little good, for his daughters abandoned him shortly before he died. Angelina emigrated to Glasgow where she married but died young, leaving only a son, while Concetta married a widower from Venafro and met a fate similar to that of her sister. She later died leaving only a son.

When Daniele died, his son, Emilio, emigrated to Glasgow, but he rushed back to Filignano upon learning that his mother, Letizia, was at death's door. Emilio was an evil man. He had once tried to poison his Uncle Benedetto's family by smearing their cabbages with a mixture of poison and verdigris, but Assunta, who was then only a little girl, noticed the peculiar colour of the cabbage leaves, and the wicked

Emilio's plan was foiled. When he returned to Filignano, he expected to inherit a great deal from his mother, but his sister Concetta had taken the precaution of hiding the money and some jewellery in a chest of wheat grain that was stored in a small house they had let to an old lady called La Monaca.

As soon as Letizia died, Emilio went on a rampage through the rooms of the house, searching wildly for his mother's money and jewellery. When he could not find them, he grabbed his sister Concetta by the throat and made her reveal where she had hidden them. He then stormed down to La Monaca's little house, smashed in the door, terrifying the old lady, emptied the bags of flour that were stored there on to the floor, pulled the grain chest to the door and overturned it, spilling the precious grain onto the ground outside, found the money and the jewellery in two small bags, tore up the money in his mad rage but stuffed the bag containing the jewels inside his woollen vest, threw buckets of water over the flour and the grain, and finally rushed off in an insane fury.

On the following day, it became known that he had departed for America, and he was never heard of again.

All these things had happened when Assunta was very young, but she heard Filomena go over them so many times that she now felt she had lived through them. Her close relatives had been a very unsavoury lot, she thought, as she lay on, watching the sun's rays gradually creeping in through the heavy shutters of her bedroom window. Perhaps this explained why her father was such a quiet man. He had been subdued into silence by his own evil family. The wickedness had stemmed from her own grandmother. Assunta was convinced of this. Was it not a fact that Anna Maria was an *ianara*, an evil witch, as Filomena had told her so many times?

When Benedetto married Filomena, it was against his parents' wishes, for, although she was an only child, her family, the Verrecchias, had no dowry for her. They were poor peasants, scraping their small pieces of unfruitful land to eke out a bare existence. But Filomena had been a very beautiful girl. Her skin glowed, revealing vivid roses in her cheeks. Her dark, wavy hair shone with good health, and her pale brown eyes twinkled with merriment and mischief, for she was a very spirited lass. Theirs was truly a love match.

In December 1879 they had been blessed with a handsome baby boy, Eugenio. Healthy and bright-eyed, he showed early signs of intelligence, and Filomena was very proud of him. Then a sad time had begun for her. The next five children she bore Benedetto, a boy, Pietro, and four baby girls, all christened Assunta one after the other, had not

4

survived the first year of their lives. After the loss of the fifth child, Filomena was convinced that someone was putting the evil eye on her children. This was surely the evil work of a wicked *ianara*. So she paid a visit to an *ianarone,* who, it was said, had the power against all witches.

"You have a woman near you who does not wish your children to live." So he had begun. Then he continued, "It is not because she hates you that she is putting the evil eye upon them but because she feels that you are too poor to rear them."

It seemed obvious to Filomena that he could only be talking of her mother-in-law, Donna Anna Maria.

"But what am I to do?" she asked the *ianarone.*

"You have a staircase in your house," he answered, "so, when she comes to visit you again, wait until she reaches the top, then give her a push and let her tumble down!"

It seemed to Filomena that the man's recommendation was too drastic.

When she discovered that she was again expecting a child, she made a special prayer to the Holy Virgin each day. Assunta was born on the 24th of May 1895. A week later Filomena wrapped the baby in a warm, red shawl and went to visit the *ianarone* again. He looked at the infant and shook his head.

"This child will not live unless you do exactly as I tell you," he said. And as Filomena attentively listened, he went on, saying, "You will hang three bags of millet, one behind the door and the others on either side of the window of the room where the child sleeps." He went over to a drawer and lifted out a priest's stole.

"You will pin this to the back of the door under the bag of millet, and, each evening before you retire, you will recite the rosary as you sit at your fireside."

Filomena accepted the stole and handed him the fee, five lire, which she could ill afford. She followed the *ianarone*'s instructions to the letter. So Assunta, by surviving, put an end to her grandmother's evil spell. And as she grew up, she enjoyed the best of health, rivalling Filomena for her luminous beauty with her lovely auburn hair.

She attracted many suitors but did not seem to be interested in the prospect of marriage. All she wanted was to be with her brother and his wife in Glasgow so that she could earn money to send home to her parents in Filignano where times were so hard. She was now nearly twenty years of age and did not care whether she ever married or not. Besides, the very subject of marriage was a delicate one as far as Filomena was concerned.

5

Assunta remembered how, when she was scarcely seven years old, her mother had been outraged to learn from the local gossips that her son, Eugenio, who had gone to Glasgow just four years before, had found for himself a Scots girl and was seriously contemplating marriage. Filomena lost no time in selling a great portion of the wheat crop, some legs of ham, ten of her precious chickens, a gold brooch, and a necklace in order to gather together the money for Benedetto's fare to Scotland. For she was packing her husband off to bring back her worthless son. The very idea of Eugenio marrying a foreign girl!

Then, when Benedetto, who had never before been abroad, eventually arrived in Glasgow, it was to discover that there was no truth whatsoever in the rumour concerning his son. It was not a fiancée Eugenio had acquired but—a bicycle! Wheels had become his passion and now that he had bought his first bicycle, he was already looking forward to the day when he could afford a motor bike.

When Benedetto sheepishly realised that Filomena had fallen victim to exaggerated, distorted gossip, he decided he would go home as he did not take to the Glasgow air. But he had no money for his return fare, and Eugenio was obliged to find him a job selling sweets and cigarettes in a small shop in New City Road. Benedetto was a very passive shop assistant, for he did not speak a single word of English and the local girls used to come in and tease him. On one hilarious occasion, they had even tickled him, Benedetto had later confided in Assunta when her mother was well out of earshot.

On the day when Benedetto finally returned to Filignano, he first went to the house of some friends, as he was chary of facing his wrathful little wife. The lady of the house, a certain Clorinda, went on ahead to announce his return. When she arrived at the Marzella house on Imperatore Hill, Filomena was wringing clothes in a tub.

"Benedetto has just arrived from Glasgow," said Clorinda.

"And has he brought back Eugenio?" asked Filomena.

"No, he has not," said Clorinda.

"Then tell him to go back to Glasgow," said Filomena. This conversation had caused the tongues of the local gossips to waggle for many weeks.

A few months later, Filomena wrote to Eugenio telling him he was to come home at once as she had found him a suitable bride. The girl's name, like hers, was also Filomena, a good name, and her dowry consisted of a vast amount of good, arable land, three vineyards, and an orchard.

Assunta would never forget the day on which Eugenio came home. She had been only three years of age when he left for Glasgow, and her recollection of his features was very vague. The large brass knocker on the front door was hammered three times, and Assunta, opening the door, found standing before her a handsome, smiling young man of twenty, elegantly dressed in a neat grey suit. On his head he wore a smart, yellow straw hat. Two large suitcases sat on either side of him as he looked down on her with an enquiring look. Suddenly he lifted her up with his strong arms and hugged her tightly. Assunta squealed with delight, bringing Filomena in a rush from the bedroom where she had been sewing in the morning light. She threw her arms round her son's shoulders and, as the tears began to flow, repeated over and over again, "Figlio mio, figlio mio! Figlio mio bello!"

At length her weeping dissolved into joyous, merry laughter as she plied Eugenio with question after question. All this time Benedetto, unaware of his son's return, was working quietly in the orchard. Assunta was sent to fetch her father.

When the first joy of their reunion had passed, Filomena lost no time in informing Eugenio, as they ate supper, that she and Benedetto had found him a suitable wife. While his mother prattled on, singing the praises of the younger Filomena, listing all the land she would inherit, Eugenio sat and listened, smiling enigmatically. Young Assunta, studying her brother's expression, realised that his thoughts were on other things. He was obviously not interested in young Filomena.

A few days later, there was to be a *festa* at Isernia, the Feast of Saint Cosmo. It was customary on this occasion for the people of Filignano, the Filignanesi, to go to Isernia on foot. Filomena craftily arranged that they should go to Isernia along with young Filomena's family. It would be an ideal opportunity for the prospective bride and groom to become acquainted.

The two families set out early on the morning of the Feast of Saint Cosmo on their long walk to Isernia. After an hour's walking, Filomena was somewhat disconcerted to observe that Eugenio was not walking with his bride-to-be. He was chatting in lively fashion with Maria Luisa, young Filomena's sister-in-law. Where was young Filomena? She was walking and chatting with Assunta. Filomena sighed in her exasperation. Why could young people not take the advice of their elders?

Then, as they came at last into Isernia and were making their way slowly along a narrow street, they met another family from Filignano coming in the opposite direction. It was the family of Luigi and Albina Cocozza from Bottazzella, a hamlet near Filignano. There was Pietro, the oldest son, his sister Assunta, his younger sister, Giulia, and a younger brother, Antonio. The two groups paused to exchange greetings. Giulia quickly noticed Eugenio, and their eyes met for the briefest of instants.

She then turned brightly to Filomena and asked, "Zia Filomena, is this your son from Glasgow? My, what a good-looking boy he is!"

Eugenio heard the girl's excited exclamation to his mother, who received it with raised eyebrows, but he did not appear to notice. Filomena looked past Giulia and, ignoring her question, addressed herself to Albina. She had no intention of introducing her son to such a pretty girl. When the two companies parted to go on their separate ways, Giulia kept glancing back over her shoulder at Eugenio and he kept looking back over his at Giulia. Assunta's acute eye observed, and she smiled.

Strangely enough Giulia and Eugenio did not meet again at the *festa* in Isernia, although they must all have visited the fair where the prize cattle from the upper Molise were being offered for sale at one end, while at the other the ladies could admire, but not afford to purchase, the lovely, local handicraft products on display. Assunta simply loved the beautiful lace-embroidered pillows. To rest one's head on such a work of art must surely inspire beautiful dreams!

Neither did the families' return to Filignano on foot coincide, but when the Marzellas arrived back at Imperatore, Eugenio surmised that Giulia would be attending the evening service of benediction. He hastened to freshen up, put on a clean shirt and a smart tie, and gave his shoes a thorough polishing. Then, not bothering about supper, he walked smartly down the hill to the church in the piazza. Soon afterwards, kneeling at the back of the church, he saw Giulia with some of her friends just a few rows in front of him. He did not even notice that his intended, young Filomena, was also there, just a few chairs away from Giulia.

The short service seemed interminably long. At last it was over, and as Giulia passed to go out, he stood at the back of the church and caught her eye. She lowered her head but tilted it slightly in his direction as she smiled. Her large brown eyes flashed with pleasure. When Mother Filomena came out of the church with the other older women, she was just in time to see her beloved Eugenio disappearing with his new sweetheart, Giulia, on the road to Bottazzella.

She turned to Benedetto, who had just joined her, and muttered, "We have done it now!"

"Done what?" Benedetto asked.

"We can forget about your son marrying Filomena," she went on. "I just saw him disappearing on the road to Bottazzella with that girl Giulia Cocozza."

Benedetto could not suppress a grin as he remarked, "He's your son as well as mine!"

Assunta, standing with Antonia and her other girl friends, had followed the whole episode. She marvelled at the impetuous boldness of her handsome brother.

Later that evening when Filomena, Benedetto, and Assunta were sitting round the fire in the large kitchen with Antonia and another of Assunta's friends, Annella, they heard the handle of the large door turning, but it would not open as Filomena had deliberately bolted it. At the sound of the brass knocker that followed, Assunta made to go to the door, but Filomena restrained her daughter and went to open it herself. A slightly flushed Eugenio came in.

Filomena looked at him severely and asked, "Where have you been to this time, Eugenio?"

"I've been to Bottazzella, Ma," he replied breezily. Assunta, Antonia, and Annella exchanged mischievous looks. Benedetto sucked silently at his pipe. Filomena continued with her interrogation.

"What were you doing in Bottazzella, Eugenio?"

"I took Giulietta home, Ma."

"Oh," said Filomena, "so it's Giulietta, now?" And she managed to imitate the slightly embarrassed note that had crept into her son's voice when he spoke his sweetheart's name.

"And what do *you* want with Giuletta?" she went on. "You know that *she* is not for *you!*"

"What do you mean, Ma, *she* is not for *me?*" asked Eugenio, and he smiled strangely as he said it.

"She has no dowry," explained Filomena.

By this time Filomena and Eugenio, as they talked, had joined the little circle round the fire. All eyes were upon them. It was as if they were the central characters in a dramatic *festa* play that was unfolding before their very eyes. Eugenio spoke.

"Well, Ma, it's like this. You asked me to come home to get married. Now, if you still want me to marry, Giulietta is the girl for me. And if I can't marry her, then I'll marry no one else and go back to Glasgow just as I came."

At these defiant words from her son, Filomena looked at Benedetto as if to solicit his moral support, but he went on smoking his pipe, pretending he had not seen her look.

Completely at a loss, she muttered, "Well, we have done it now!" and she sighed, shaking her head. Then she continued, "Oh, well, let us get on with the rosary!" And, as she drew her large rosary beads from the deep pocket of her red flannel apron, Eugenio leaned towards her, put his arm round her shoulder, and drew her to him affectionately.

9

"Let us pray!" said Benedetto from his corner by the fire.

A few days later, without any loss of time, it was arranged to draw up a marriage contract, and the two families met in the Marzella house at Imperatore. Most of the discussion took place between the two mothers, Filomena speaking for her son, Albina for her daughter. After much bargaining and polite argument, it was agreed that Giulietta should receive a dowry of bedclothes, a bed, household linen, and some cooking utensils.

In addition she would be given a strip of land some considerable distance from Filignano. Known as Le Cisolle, the land was infertile, and Filomena knew this as she had made previous enquiries. When the name Le Cisolle was mentioned, Filomena began to mutter in protest, but for once Benedetto decided to exercise his authority as husband and father. He gave his wife such a mighty nudge with his elbow, and she was so surprised by the unexpectedness of his action, that she found herself nodding in agreement with Albina's suggestion.

An early date was set for the wedding, as Eugenio was soon to return to Glasgow. Assunta was excited by the prospect of taking part in the procession of the bride's dowry. Giulietta, already fond of her prospective young sister-in-law, had promised her this honour. The procession of the dowry was a colourful ceremony whose purpose was to parade before the whole village the various items in the bride's bottom drawer.

On a set evening, the prospective groom, having prepared a nuptial chamber in the house of his parents, sets out on foot accompanied by his friends to make his way to the bride's house. Meanwhile the bride has gathered together her closest friends, and they have helped her to fill the large wide baskets with sheets, blankets, household linen, towels, cooking utensils, crockery, and cutlery. Larger items, such as the bed, have already been disassembled and are ready to be carried, along with the filled baskets, on the girls' heads, in procession to the house of the groom.

When the groom is seen to be approaching, the girls lift their burdens onto their heads and, at a signal, the bride comes out of her house carrying a large broom and a chamber pot. Standing nearby is an accordionist and when the groom approaches the bride, he begins to play a merry tune. The bride hands the broom and the chamber pot to the groom. He places the pot on his head and carries the broom like a staff in his right hand. Then, with the accordionist at his side, he sets off to lead the long procession to his own house. The bride waits to take her place at the very end of the procession and takes up a basket containing something very special, such as an embroidered bed cover, spread out to show the beauty and intricacy of its design.

Giulietta's dowry procession caused a stir in Filignano, and a large number of young gallants accompanied Eugenio to Bottazzella. They had a double purpose in going with him. On the one hand, they were very curious to see how a comparatively sophisticated young man, who had come all the way from Glasgow, would take to wearing a chamber pot on his head. On the other hand, they were keen, when the ceremony was over, to flirt with the girls and accompany them home.

Assunta had preceded her brother to Bottazzella so that she could help Giulietta. She was told to stand on the balcony of Giulietta's house and warn the bride when the groom approached. She heard Eugenio and his friends before she could see them, for they had struck up a song, and when they appeared round the bend of the road, they were as happy as larks, their arms linked as they strode along. Eugenio was very excited, his cheeks slightly flushed, but his eyes sparkled with happiness.

Assunta ran in to tell Giulietta the groom was near. The bride in her emotion was about to burst into tears when, catching the look of astonishment on Assunta's face, she restrained herself, impulsively threw her arms round the little girl's neck, and kissed her affectionately on both cheeks. She then took her by the hand and led her quickly downstairs.

"You will walk with me at the end of the procession," she said to Assunta, "and you will carry something very special on your head."

With all eyes upon him, Eugenio, accompanied by his eight strapping lads, approached Giulietta who was standing ready with the pot in her right hand and the broom in her left. She felt no embarrassment in her excitement and when Eugenio came close to her, a wave of rapture came over her and, casting caution to the winds, she handed the pot and broom to Assunta who was standing by her side and threw her arms round Eugenio's neck. He then took the pot from Assunta and, with panache, placed it firmly on his head, took the broom in his right hand, and held it out firmly like a shepherd's staff and, surrounded by his young friends who thumped him heartily on the shoulders, made his way down to the front of the line of girls who were by now ready to leave, balancing the baskets skilfully on their heads.

People from the surrounding houses lined up on either side of the main road as the train, led by Eugenio, set off for Imperatore. The lads and the girls, accompanied by the accordionist, struck up a jolly song and the happy company proceeded on its way. The people of Bottazzella cheered heartily as Giulietta, blushing, appeared at the end of the long line along with Assunta who was proudly balancing a small basket containing a beautiful Delft wash-hand basin and jug on her little head.

As the file of girls and boys made its way along the road to Filignano, their singing could be heard in the distance and the villagers came out on to the streets to welcome them. Eugenio's appearance on the piazza gave rise to prolonged cheering, and a smiling woman came forward with a trayful of glasses in one hand and a large flask of red wine in the other. The groom was persuaded to sit for a while in the shade of the large lime tree in front of the church. The girls put down their baskets, and they were all served with wine. More flasks appeared and by the time the procession set off to climb up to Imperatore, some of the baskets on the girls' heads were wobbling dangerously. Assunta's head was the steadiest of them all as she bravely carried the basin and jug. At her age she had no taste for wine.

The wedding was to take place on a Thursday. Filomena had agreed to provide the wedding feast. She had committed herself to the extent of half of the following summer's harvest and had also borrowed money for the occasion. Two days before the marriage, the two cooks she had hired arrived. They killed, plucked, and cooked the chickens, which had been purchased from the surrounding neighbours, prepared huge quantities of tomato *sugo* for the pasta, and roasted seven large legs of mutton to feed the seventy-odd guests who were expected. Then they baked. Assunta could not remember when the round brick oven in the corner of the kitchen had been so much used. First the bread was baked, some thirty loaves. Then the pizzas. Lastly the pizza dolce and the *biscotti* and other pastries.

Assunta gave a willing hand to the two cooks, washing their utensils, and they allowed her to scrape the good things from the various basins so that she could sample in advance the delicate flavours of the beautiful cakes that later came out of the hot oven. Filomena hovered around to see that the men had all they required, and Assunta was amused when, every time they placed bread or cakes into the oven, just as soon as the iron door was closed, her mother came forward to make the sign of the cross over the door while she spoke the name of the patron saint of baking: "San Martino!" Filomena firmly believed in blessing all good things.

This was the most exciting time that Assunta could remember in her young life. At last the morning of the wedding dawned, and Assunta rose early and put on her best clothes. She wore a beautiful white blouse she had embroidered herself, for Filomena had given her an early training in the use of the needle and thread. She had a cool, blue, cotton skirt beneath her apron and white, silk stockings to set off her first pair of real black leather shoes with silver buckles. Filomena put on her best striped skirt, and a finely embroidered bodice set off her white blouse with its generous many-pleated sleeves. Her apron was black with a narrow, purple border, and on her hips she wore the traditional, vivid red, flannel cloth, known as *panno rosso,* which had given its name to the tarantella-style dance they would all be enjoying later in the day. As this was a very special occasion, Filomena also put on a pair of black shoes.

But Benedetto refused to wear shoes, even for his son's wedding. He preferred his *cioce* or hide sandals. Clean cloth puttees on his legs were held in place by long, narrow leather straps fastened into his sandals and tied firmly. But he brought out his best striped suit with its neat jacket and short trousers that fastened just below the knee. Eugenio wore his best dark suit brought all the way from Glasgow, a gleaming white silk shirt, and a smart bow tie. His black shining leather shoes completed his elegance.

At ten o'clock the groom's party, Eugenio, Benedetto, Filomena, and Assunta set off to walk to Bottazzella. Assunta carried a large bunch of fresh wildflowers, 'round which she had tied a broad, blue silk ribbon matching the one she had fastened round her auburn hair. The sun came out in all its splendour to warm them on their way. Their acquaintances called out to them with enthusiasm as they made their way along the pebbly road. When they eventually arrived at Bottaz-zella, Giulietta's elder brother, Pietro, and her sister Assunta came out to greet them. They were led into the kitchen and served with refreshments. Soon Albina and Luigi appeared, accompanied by their youngest son, Antonio, who was the same age as Assunta. He smiled at her mischievously, but she ignored him. Then Giulietta came out on to the staircase in her beautiful white satin dress, her face barely perceptible behind the short veil over her head. She was holding a bouquet of flowers around which a broad piece of white muslin had been wound.

A moment later the whole bridal party emerged led by the bride and groom, followed first by the bride's family and then the groom's. They made their way very slowly down to the main road, and some neighbours came and threw rose petals, rice, and sugared almonds. Someone threw a handful of small coins, which were quickly pounced upon by the children standing expectantly at the side of the road. When the small bridal procession, growing slowly in length as the wedding guests joined it, approached Filignano, the bells in the church tower began to peal joyfully and Giulietta, Filomena, and Albina began to weep. There was an agitated fluttering of white lace handkerchiefs, and the tearful affliction spread among the ladies standing in the

13

piazza. Giulietta and Eugenio made such a beautiful couple, their love radiating from their persons.

One of Eugenio's friends played the church organ, and the nuptial mass was punctuated with operatic themes. Giulietta's tears had dried by this time, but Filomena and Albina continued to weep. When the church service was over, the bride and groom made their way up the steps of the Municipio to sign the register.

When all the wedding guests had filed out of the church, they joined the bridal party and began slowly to make their way up the hill to Imperatore. The accordionist arrived in time to lead the whole procession, and they were all showered with rose petals thrown from the balconies under which they passed. Arriving at the Marzella house, they did not go in, but made their way directly on to the *aia* or threshing floor where trestle tables had been laid out to accommodate the guests. When they were all seated, they drank toasts while awaiting the arrival of the parish priest, Don Alfonso, for whom a place had been reserved at the head table. From the *aia* they could all look down upon the plain of Filignano, and the soft breeze stirring in the warm sunlight carried delicate fragrances from the orchards below. Assunta's eyes took in every nuance of the colourful scene as she sat by her father's side.

When Don Alfonso arrived, the serving of the meal was started. It was noon and the guests sat eating until well after four o'clock. During the long intervals between courses, songs were sung and anecdotes recounted. Toasts were made from time to time, and flask after flask of red and white wine emptied. Many of the guests kept disappearing to relieve themselves in the two small enclosures at the end of the *aia* set aside for that purpose. When the meal was over in the early evening, the tables were cleared away and the chairs arranged in a large circle round the *aia*. The ground was swept after being lightly sprayed with water from the cistern to keep down the dust.

The accordion was joined by two mandolins and a fiddle, and the dancing began. Everyone danced, and at one point, Assunta and her little friend Antonia performed a very spirited *panno rosso* that drew great applause. As the evening drew on and the sun began slowly to sink, supper was cooked for the guests, omelettes with homemade sausages and more wine. All this time the dancing continued until the couples were silhouetted in the pale blue moonlight. As Giulietta and Eugenio waltzed, the stars twinkled above them. Assunta looked at them and prayed that they would always be as happy as they were at that wonderful moment.

It was a very brief honeymoon, as Eugenio had to return to Glasgow. Giulietta was heartbroken on the day of her husband's departure. As the days passed, she grew closer and closer to Assunta and their affection for each other knew no bounds. Giulietta had a very bright, happy nature, and she was such a willing helper with the chores that Filomena soon came to realize that Eugenio had made a wise choice. The girl showed her genuine affection, and she had very winning, respectful ways. Filomena responded warmly and soon considered Giulietta as a daughter.

It would take Eugenio some considerable time to save the money for his wife's fare to Glasgow. His letters arrived regularly every week, and Giulietta never failed to shed tears when she read his warm, loving words. So the days, weeks, and months passed, and it became apparent to them all that the girl was pining for her husband. Filomena had managed to pay off all the expenses incurred for the wedding, and she began to save a little money to help Giulietta with her fare.

Then one day, a few weeks later, a registered letter arrived unexpectedly from Glasgow. The postman handed it to Filomena on the road when she was on her way home from mass. Giulietta and Assunta had gone to gather twigs for the fire, and they would not be home until noon. Filomena placed the precious letter on the mantelpiece in a prominent position. When the merry peals of laughter of the returning girls were heard echoing down the hill path, Filomena went out and sat on the two logs outside the wall of the wine cellar. The girls soon arrived and dropped their large bundles in the pen by the house.

"Giulietta, there is something for you on the mantelpiece!" called out Filomena. The girl froze in her tracks. She cast a questioning look at her mother-in-law. Filomena smiled. Giulietta beamed with pleasure and rushed into the kitchen. Assunta made to follow her, but Filomena took her by the arm and restrained her, muttering, "Let her be; this is the moment she has been waiting for."

Then they heard a loud exclamation from the kitchen followed quickly by a scream of utter delight. Assunta and Filomena went to the door and looked in. Giulietta was on her knees, tears of joy streaming down her face.

"Thank you, Holy Mother!" she prayed aloud. "Thank you, most Holy Mother, for the boon with which you have favoured me. Thank you for answering my prayers!"

So Giulietta packed her bags and left Filignano to join Eugenio in Glasgow. Assunta wept bitterly on the day of her sister-in-law's departure. Twelve years had now passed since that day. Now Assunta herself, almost twenty years of age, would soon be making the long journey to Glasgow. She brushed away the tears that had come to her eyes in recalling those events. It was time to get up. She was surprised that Filomena had not yet shouted to her to come down to the kitchen and help with the morning chores.

Chapter Two

1915—Reminiscing

When she had washed thoroughly in the basin, Assunta dressed and prepared to start the day's work. First she knelt and said a brief prayer to the Holy Virgin, then she made her way gingerly downstairs, expecting to be upbraided by her mother for being so late. A lively fire was crackling in the hearth and two *cioccolatiere,* or metal jugs filled with water to make hot coffee or cocoa, were sitting in the hot ash, but Filomena was nowhere to be seen.

Then Assunta heard her mother's voice outside as she called out, "Teeeeee-tay. Teeeee-tay!" the call she used to summon her chickens when she fed them. Assunta peeped into the bedroom. Benedetto was not there. He too had risen early and gone to collect firewood.

Assunta set the table, laying out three small bowls and spoons. She placed a few large lumps of sugar in a saucer in the centre of the table, then, moving to the cupboard, brought out a large brown loaf of bread that was already half used and cut three thick slices from it, holding it against her stomach with her left hand while she cut the bread with a large, sharp knife in her right, moving the knife inwards towards her body, but taking care to rotate the loaf so that she would not cut herself. She placed a slice of bread beside each bowl. Then she fetched a round of cheese made from goat's milk and cut off three generous pieces, placing one on top of each slice of bread.

Then Filomena came in carrying a metal basin half filled with warm goat's milk that Chiaruccia, the goat, had provided for their breakfast.

"Good morning, Sunta," said Filomena. "You will have to learn to rise earlier than this when you get to Glasgow, my girl!"

As she said this, she smiled, glancing approvingly at the set table. Despite a certain stubbornness in her nature, her Sunta had grown into a good girl and could be relied upon to work hard. Assunta went out to fetch eggs from the henhouse and as she was returning, carrying the warm eggs in her apron, she saw Benedetto striding down the hill path. He was balancing a small tree trunk on his shoulder.

"Good morning, Ta!" she called out to him. "That's a heavy load you have there. You're just in time for breakfast."

Benedetto glanced over to acknowledge her greeting and called out, "I'm ready for it, to be sure."

When they were sitting over breakfast, Filomena gave Assunta her orders for the day. She should take Chiaruccia to the wood at the top of the hill and gather twigs after completing her morning chores. When the breakfast dishes had been washed and put away, Assunta went round to the goat pen to let out Chiaruccia who greeted her with that peculiarly quiverish, throaty sound that goats make when they say "Good morning!" There was a strong bond of affection between Assunta and Chiaruccia, for the goat had once saved her life.

About two years before, she had taken the animal with her one day when she was going to hoe the strip of tilth land they owned at the far end of Imperatore. Old Zia Peppina was also there, working the adjoining strip and when it was noon, they sat down together on a large flat stone under a tree to eat their bread, cheese, and dried figs. Chiaruccia was behind Assunta, nibbling at some short grass. As the two women chatted, Chiaruccia suddenly gave out a curious sound, "Tooooorrr! Toooorr!" that Assunta had never heard her make before.

"Oh," said Zia Peppina, "that goat has seen something. Look behind you, Sunta, and see what it is."

When Assunta turned her head, it was all she could do to refrain from screaming, for there, just a metre away by a tree, was a large black snake, its thin, glistening body erect and its evil-looking head poised ready to strike.

Zia Peppina saw it at the same instant, and she said in a low voice, "Don't move, Sunta!" Then she rose gingerly to her feet and lifted a large stone.

"When I throw this stone," she said quietly, "I want you to move quickly."

But before she had time to carry out her plan, Chiaruccia took action. The goat butted Assunta in the back, knocking her forward. Then Zia Peppina threw the stone, missing the snake by several centimetres. Assunta leapt to her feet, threw herself into Zia Peppina's arms, and together they scampered away. When they looked back, they saw that Chiaruccia had calmly resumed her nibbling by the tree. The snake had disappeared.

Chiaruccia followed Assunta everywhere, and some evenings she would remain in the kitchen until late. One evening they were all sitting round the fire ready to recite the rosary when the goat came forward and, pushing her head through between Filomena and Assunta, made a place for herself in the family circle. Filomena had the rosary beads in her lap, and she held them up as she made the sign of the cross. The beads rattled slightly before being lowered again into Filomena's apron.

The sound attracted Chiaruccia who must have thought the wooden beads were small, tasty acorns. As Filomena sleepily began to recite the prayers, Chiaruccia moved her head over and, taking one end of the beads in her mouth, began slowly to nibble. The goat had already swallowed several of the beads when Filomena, feeling a slight tug from the animal's head, looked down and was horrified to see what Chiaruccia had been up to. A little tug-of-war followed, and Filomena at last managed to extract the badly chewed beads from the goat's throat.

Benedetto, who had watched the whole performance with a certain irreverent glee, observed, "I see we now have a praying goat in the family!" Chiaruccia was firmly led away to her pen outside before the family prayers could be concluded.

On another occasion Assunta had gone for the day with Antonia to work in the fields, taking Chiaruccia with her. Filomena had prepared a small basket of food for the girls. It contained bread, ham, grapes, and figs. When they arrived at the fields, the girls decided to gather twigs and sticks to carry home in the evening when they had finished hoeing. Chiaruccia showed great interest in their basket, sniffing it from time to time, so they decided to place it well out of the goat's reach. They hung it on a high branch of an oak tree and went on with their work.

When they moved some distance away, Chiaruccia nimbly stood on her hind legs, stretching herself as much as she could and, leaning against the trunk of the tree, she nudged the basket with her snout until it slithered along the branch and finally fell to the ground. Having eaten all the food that fell out of the basket, Chiaruccia proceeded to eat the figs that still lay inside. She squeezed her head in to reach the last fig and it stuck. Try as she might by shaking it, the basket refused to be dislodged. The goat then calmly made her way to the spot where the girls were still gathering twigs.

Assunta and Antonia were at first amused by the sight of Chiaruccia with the basket stuck on her head. Then it dawned upon them that all their food had been eaten. Antonia held the goat by the rear while Assunta tugged at the basket until she managed to remove it. Chiaruccia looked very pleased with herself. In her eyes they could see that vaguely faraway look that is particular to thieving goats.

"What are we going to do now?" asked Antonia. "We can't possibly go home so early without doing the hoeing."

By this time they were decidedly hungry. Fortunately they were not far from Zio Donato's vineyard, so they went along and picked some grapes. Assunta then climbed up a fig tree and threw down some figs to Antonia who caught them in her apron. The girls ate so much fruit that next day they had a severe bout of diarrhoea.

Let it not be thought, however, that Assunta even dreamed of punishing Chiaruccia for her naughtiness. She loved animals too much to be cruel to them. And Assunta had many pets. The trouble was that she became too attached to them, and when some of them were due for slaughter she was heartbroken. Many a tear was shed over the loss of a pig in January or a pet cockerel at Easter.

One of her favourite pets was the little donkey she called Piccirella. When Benedetto was not using the donkey to carry grain to the mill at Venafro or to help him with the transport of heavy logs, Assunta would borrow Piccirella and visit her girl friends at Valle. The manner in which she mounted the animal was rather special. She would climb on to a dry stone wall and bid Piccirella to come close. The donkey would obey, but sometimes she would not stand close enough.

"Nearer, Piccirella, nearer!" commanded Assunta, and the animal would do as she was asked. Assunta would then lower herself on to Piccirella's back, and they would set out for Valle.

The happy moments she had experienced with her various pets were flitting through Assunta's mind as she strode up the stony path followed closely by Chiaruccia. When she arrived at Antonia's house, the upper half of the front door was open to let light into the kitchen. Assunta looked in and called for her friend.

Soon they were on their way up the hill and as they were approaching the crest, they turned to look back down on Filignano, while Chiaruccia happily chewed the short grass at the side of the narrow path. They could see the plain surrounded by hills rising gradually, each of which had its own little cluster of houses. Far away on their left, they could see Collemacchia and in the opening between that hill and Monte Pantano the Mainarde mountains in the far distance, their peaks covered perennially with snow.

Before them the campanile of the church at the foot of the hill gave an indication of the position of the piazza, and the upper, bare branches of the immense lime tree could just be seen. Beyond the row of houses flanking the main road rose the old mountain of Filignano. It was not high, but its long ridge extended for a fair distance. That ridge had been the site of the old village, called originally Fondemano, said to have been destroyed by an earthquake several centuries before.

During the nineteenth century, just before the rise of Garibaldi, the area had been infested by bandits.

Assunta and Antonia often wandered over the face of the mountain, and near its base they once came upon an old building buried in rubble. In the old roof, there was a small square opening, and they knelt to peer down through it and saw heaps of human bones. Skulls leered up at them with their empty eye sockets. The girls made a hasty retreat from the gruesome place.

When Antonia and Assunta had walked a short distance, they came to the wood where they began to gather sticks, tying them up with long, narrow, pliable twigs into big bundles. They sat down to rest and began discussing Assunta's impending departure for Scotland. Then, seeing the disused well near the edge of the wood, they were reminded of the sad destiny of a girl who had come from Glasgow. Her name was Antoniella, and she had been born in the Scottish city to which her parents had emigrated from Filignano. But when Antoniella was seven years of age, her father had fallen into poor health and they had come back to the village from Scotland.

Antoniella grew into a beautiful girl, and a young builder called Alfonso began courting her. Carried away by their passion, they became incautious and soon Antoniella found that she was carrying Alfonso's child. The young man promptly did his duty and married the girl, bringing her to his mother's house after the quiet wedding. Soon a handsome baby boy was born, and they called him Alfredo. But Alfonso's mother could not bring herself to like her daughter-in-law, and, as time passed she began to taunt the young woman for having seduced her son. It was a constant torment for Antoniella, all day when Alfonso was at work, to have to listen to her mother-in-law's bitter reproaches. But the old woman said nothing when Alfonso was at home. So Antoniella knew it would be useless to complain to her husband, for he adored his mother and would never have believed her capable of cruelty.

A day came when Antoniella could no longer put up with her mother-in-law's insults. Leaving little Alfredo behind, she put on her shawl and rushed out of the house. She was making her way up Imperatore Hill in a state of utter despair when she met an old lady called Ernestina.

"Zia Ernestina," she said, "I have a great favour to ask of you."

Ernestina noticed how agitated the young woman was. "What is the matter, Antoniella?" she asked, "and where are you going in such a state?"

"Never mind where I am going, Zia Ernestina," said Antoniella,

21

"but I want you to go at once to my mother's and tell her she is to collect my baby from my mother-in-law. Tell her that she is to look after little Alfredo." And Antoniella rushed on. Ernestina called after her to come back, but Antoniella did not heed the old woman and ran up the hilly path to the wood.

Ernestina called out, "Antoniella, for the love of God, don't do anything silly!" But Antoniella was already out of earshot.

Ernestina, panicking, began to call out for help, but no one in the houses nearby appeared to hear her. She went up to several doors and pounded on them with her fists, but no one answered. Then, as she turned, she saw Alfonso rushing up the hill towards her. He had gone home at noon for his meal, and his mother had told him about his wife's very odd behaviour.

"Alfonso, Alfonso! Hurry, Alfonso! The well, the well!" screamed out Ernestina, her eyes now blinded with tears. Alfonso ran up the path to the well, followed slowly by old Ernestina. Then, when the old woman was approaching the crest of the hill, she heard Alfonso in the distance call out like a madman when he reached the well and looked into its depths. Under the cool, clear water, his dead wife's open eyes were staring up at him. The well was closed and never used again.

Assunta and Antonia pondered over this sad tale. It had caused a stir in the village, and Alfonso's mother had been branded as a murderess and shunned for many a long day by the women of Filignano. Little Alfredo was brought up by Antoniella's mother, and Alfonso left Filignano and emigrated to America. His mother never heard from him again. This was her punishment.

As the girls spoke, they heard the school bell ringing in the piazza. It must be eight o'clock. The bell brought back memories of the mischievous days they had passed in school when they were young. They were very spirited girls and sat together at the back of the small classroom, but each day they were made to sit apart for their chattering and their boisterousness. Assunta had been in the top three of the class, the other clever girls being Concettina, daughter of the postal officer and another Assunta, whose father was a local builder.

The teacher, Donna Maria, was very strict and often used the long cane she carried to discipline the children. Antonia and Assunta had received many a whack on the head from an irate Donna Maria. But the lady did take a special interest in those girls who showed promise. As the annual visit of the school inspector was soon due, she set Concettina and the two Assuntas some special work to be done in order to impress the important official.

One morning Donna Maria discovered the girls had not done the extra homework they had been set for the previous evening. Now the normal school hours were from eight o'clock until noon. This allowed the pupils to get on with their work in the fields or tending their animals in the afternoons. When the church bell rang out at noon, Donna Maria dismissed all the children, but the two Assuntas and Concettina were told to remain behind. The teacher then locked the door of the schoolroom.

"Now my girls," she said, "you are going to remain in school today until you have done all the work you should have done last night. I am going home, and I shall return to let you out at three o'clock. I hope this punishment will teach you a good lesson."

She then let herself out and locked the door behind her. Now the schoolroom was situated in the piazza on an upstairs floor of a partly disused old house. When Assunta did not return home at the proper time, Filomena became uneasy because she could not leave the house to go to the fields with food for Benedetto and some helpers.

Soon Assunta could hear her mother's voice calling out from the balcony of the bedroom. "Suuuuuunta! Suuuuuunta! Where have you got to, Suuuuuuuuunta?"

By this time the two Assuntas and Concettina were starving, for they had not eaten since seven o'clock in the morning. Assunta knew they must make their escape. She went over to the window at the far end of the room and threw it open. Looking out, she saw what appeared to be a large mound of straw directly underneath. She turned to Assunta and Concettina and said, "Right, girls, if you want to go home, follow me!" and without further ado she climbed on to the window sill and jumped down on to the straw heap.

But the straw was only a thin covering over a large mound of manure. She suddenly found herself waist-deep in the filthy stuff, but, before she could call up to warn the others, they had jumped and found themselves also immersed in dung. It was three very foul-smelling miscreants who found their way home that day. When Donna Maria returned to the schoolroom in the afternoon, she was appalled to discover her pupils had escaped. Her cane was never so well used as it was on the following morning when the three naughty girls, accompanied by their mothers, were ushered into the stern presence of the teacher. And although all three had already received a good smacking at home, Donna Maria was requested to add her share of physical punishment. From that day they never failed to do their homework.

Assunta and Antonia had always enjoyed the same tomboyish activities, laughed at the same things, worked well together, and helped one another as much as possible. On that fresh February day, as they sat at the top of Imperatore Hill, Assunta promised her friend that she would write to her regularly from Glasgow.

"Will you send me something special one day from Glasgow?" asked Antonia.

Assunta knew that she was alluding to the lovely present Giulietta had sent her the previous summer. The Feast of the Eighth of September had been drawing near when a parcel arrived from Glasgow for Assunta. It contained a most beautiful two-piece suit in pale blue. The skirt had fine pleats, and the jacket was beautifully tailored. There was also a lovely, light-blue, silk blouse and neat, brown, leather shoes with fine grey silk stockings. A complete outfit for a special occasion!

On the morning of the feast, it was a very proud Assunta who walked down the hill to church with Filomena, Benedetto, and Antonia. She was careful where she placed her feet as she walked, so as not to scratch the precious shoes. After mass, when the congregation spilled out into the piazza to form a procession, Assunta became the target of admiring and envious glances from all the village girls. Aware that she was causing a stir, she enjoyed the moment and, when the statue of the Madonna was brought out to be carried round the village, she deliberately lingered on the church steps so that she and Antonia found themselves at the very end of the procession winding its way slowly through the narrow streets.

It is usual in such processions for the men to be separated from the women. So the women followed the Madonna, and the men tagged on to the end of the column of women. Just as Assunta and Antonia passed the men, who had gathered to follow, she was greeted with a great deal of whistling and admiring Ahs and Ohs. Although she blushed, she felt greatly flattered, realising she must really be attractive to solicit such admiration.

Once she was in Glasgow, Assunta thought, she would save and buy a lovely dress for Antonia to arrive in time for the next September feast.

The morning was drawing on, and it was time for them to go home. They lifted their large bundles of sticks, placed them on the rolled towels on their heads, and set off down the hill. A strong wind had arisen and, as they reached the broad steps leading down the last part of the slope, a tremendous gust came down behind them and lifted them simultaneously down two steps with their bundles still on their heads. It happened so unexpectedly that, after the first shock, they were convulsed with laughter and dropped their bundles. The wind swept them down the hill in front of them. Chiaruccia, who was following them, stopped in her tracks to look down at the strange scene as if to say "They must be going crazy, these two!"

That same evening, as they sat round the fire, Assunta asked Filomena to tell them stories about the old times.

"Shall I start with a sad one or a funny one?" asked Filomena.

"Tell us a sad one first," said Antonia, "so that if we weep too much, you can stop our tears with a humorous one."

At this juncture Benedetto rose and, moving to the table, poured himself a generous glass of red wine, drank it down, and returned to his corner by the fire.

"Have you quenched your thirst sufficiently?" asked Filomena in a slightly impertinent tone.

"Be quiet, woman, and get on with your sad story!" said Benedetto. Filomena looked at the girls, raised her eyes heavenwards, sighed, and then began.

"Not long ago, in 1911 to be precise, something very tragic happened in Venafro. There are two families in that town called the Feliciottis and the Armieris. The Armieris are very well-to-do, professional people, great owners of property, very wealthy. The Feliciottis own a restaurant from which they make a good living, but they could not by any means be considered to be wealthy.

"Now the Feliciottis had a lovely daughter called Giuseppina, a real beauty this girl, and the second son of the Armieris, a really handsome lad called Michelino, saw Giuseppina in church one Sunday and fell in love with her right away. He followed her and her mother when they left the church and noted where they lived and had their business. He made a point of walking frequently in that part of the town and one day, naturally, Giuseppina, going out to do some errands for her mother, caught the admiring glance of the young man as he walked past. It dawned on her that this was the same young man she had seen from her window one evening as he walked slowly up and down on the opposite side of the narrow street where she lived. That same evening she stood, sheltered by the heavy curtain of her bedroom window, and glanced across the street. Yes, there he was, walking up and down, just as he had done before!

"As Giuseppina continued furtively to look, the young man suddenly raised his head and seemed to be looking directly at her window, almost as if he knew she was standing there behind the curtain. She drew back instinctively, at the same time experiencing such a palpitation she thought she was going to faint with excitement. That night Giuseppina could not sleep, and next morning she could not eat her breakfast. As usual, she went to market on her errands and bought vegetables, fruit, and cheese, and she was just making her way back to the house with a heavily laden basket on each arm when she heard a step behind her. She knew at once it was the young man and she quickened her pace, but he caught up with her and said in a strange voice, that could not conceal his great emotion, 'May I help you, signorina, with your baskets?'

"In ordinary circumstances Giuseppina would have severely rebuked any young man who dared to make such a suggestion, but before she realized what she was doing, she handed him one of the baskets and murmured, 'Thank you, sir,' for the young man was dressed like a signore in the finest of clothes.

"As they walked the short distance to her house, he plied her with countless questions. What was her name? What did she do? Did she have any admirers? Did she love music? Giuseppina, under his spell, answered all his questions and then she bravely asked his name. As they arrived at the door of her house, the young man, Michelino, barely had time to ask breathlessly, 'May I call on you?'

"She could not give him an answer, for at that very moment her mother came out on to the balcony and, seeing her daughter in the company of a stranger, at once beckoned to her to come in. Giuseppina hurried upstairs and, ignoring her mother's angry 'Who was that young man?' she rushed to the window and looked out, but Michelino, alas, had already gone. Giuseppina then told her mother frankly all that had occurred, for she had been brought up always to speak the truth. Her mother smiled when she mentioned the name Armieri, because she knew that her daughter had no hope of being associated with any young man from that illustrious family.

"In the evening, when Giuseppina and her sister, Adelaida, were sitting sewing by the fire, there was a gentle knock on the door downstairs. Their mother, Carmela, opened the door to find young signor Michelino Armieri standing with a small bouquet of violets in his hand.

" 'I hope you will forgive me, signora, for being so bold,' he said in a quiet voice, 'but I was wondering whether signor Feliciotti and you would be so gracious as to permit me to call upon your lovely daughter, signorina Giuseppina?'

"Carmela was flattered by the young man's polite approach, and she bade him come in. He was shown into the downstairs living room and asked to wait while she fetched her husband from the restaurant next door. Antonio Feliciotti was surprised when his wife asked him to go through and meet Signor Michelino. When they had introduced themselves and shaken hands, he asked the young man what were his intentions regarding Giuseppina. Moreover, would the Armieris ever give their approval to Michelino's courting someone beneath his class? Michelino assured Antonio that his intentions were serious, since he had fallen in love with Giuseppina the first time he had set eyes upon her. He would be only too pleased to speak with his parents that very evening if only signor Feliciotti would give his consent for him to call upon Giuseppina.

"Feliciotti could tell that the young man was in earnest. Michelino's sincerity shone out from his eyes and was there to be heard in the very inflection of his voice. Feliciotti had a sentimental nature, and he was the last person in the world to stand in the way of true love. Yet he insisted that he could not give his formal approval until the Armieris gave their consent.

"Michelino handed the violets to Carmela and asked her to give them to Giuseppina. He then left, promising to return on the following day, if that would be convenient. They assured him that it would.

"You can imagine how moved Giuseppina was when her mother handed her the flowers and informed her of the conversation that had just taken place downstairs.

" 'Why did you not ask him to come up?' she said.

" 'All in good time, Giuseppina,' said her mother, 'all in good time, my dear.'

"When Michelino consulted his parents, they were not pleased. How could he, training for the profession of lawyer, even consider the possibility of such a marriage? Michelino began to realise that he would never convince his parents. Downhearted and crestfallen he made an apologetic appearance before the Feliciottis on the evening of the following day and, upon their earnest advice, agreed with heavy heart to abandon the idea of courting Giuseppina. As he was departing he looked up at the balcony and caught a glimpse of Giuseppina's little hand dejectedly waving a white handkerchief.

"As the days passed, Adelaida could see that Giuseppina was pining for Michelino. She took pity on the young lovers and devised a plan to permit them to meet in secret. Every Wednesday afternoon the two sisters visited their aunt, who lived at the other end of the town. Now Adelaida had observed that Michelino was in the habit of sitting reading his newspaper every morning at the café in the piazza.

"One morning, when it was her turn to do the marketing, she stopped to speak briefly with Michelino at the café, introducing herself as Giuseppina's sister. She told him to be at a certain spot on the road to her aunt's house at three o'clock on the following Wednesday. So, every week on Wednesday the lovers met and went walking on a quiet country road outside the town, while Adelaida went to visit her aunt, making excuses for Giuseppina's absences, saying her sister had a chill or a headache.

"But the aunt grew suspicious, for she saw her niece at mass every

Sunday and she looked well enough to her. She came one Thursday to the Feliciotti house to enquire why Giuseppina had not come with Adelaida on the previous day. When the girls' deception was thus discovered, there was an angry scene between them and their parents. On the following Wednesday, neither Giuseppina nor Adelaida appeared when Michelino went to the usual trysting place.

"Now Giuseppina's bedroom was at the front of the house while Adelaida's, at the back, overlooked an orchard where they cultivated vegetables, such as potatoes and beans, and fruit, such as grapes, plums and cherries. Adelaida, a born conspirator, came up with another plan. She arranged with Giuseppina that every night when their parents, who slept downstairs, had retired, the girls would exchange bedrooms. Then Michelino could use a ladder to climb up to Adelaida's bedroom and meet his sweetheart there. But Michelino did not at first approve of this daring plan, since he had certain scruples and had no wish to compromise the girls. In the end, however, his love for Giuseppina prevailed over his conscience.

"Each night, when the old people had retired, Michelino climbed cautiously up the ladder and spent a romantic hour whispering the tender secrets of his heart to Giuseppina. But they never went beyond the bounds of propriety, and kissed only when Michelino departed, for they still hoped they could somehow overcome the opposition of the Armieris and one day be married. As time went on, the intensity of their passion grew and Michelino, knowing they could no longer restrain their ardour, decided to tackle his parents again. But his request again met with a stern refusal. On that same day, Michelino made a special purchase in the local pharmacy.

"Late in the evening, Giuseppina welcomed Michelino in her sister's bedroom.

"Next morning when Adelaida awoke, she was startled when she realised she was still in her sister's bed. Giuseppina had not come to her as she usually did after Michelino's departure. Adelaida tiptoed along the landing to her bedroom and tried to turn the handle in the door, but it was locked. She tapped lightly on the door panel. Not a sound could be heard from the room. She screamed and ran downstairs to call her parents, muttering incoherently in her excitement. Antonio went up and banged on the door. When there was no reply, he put the full force of his shoulder against it and burst it open. There on the bed lay the young lovers, locked in their last embrace. In their despair they had swallowed poison.

"A weeping Antonio made his way to the Armieri house to break the tragic news. Shocked and grief-stricken, the Armieris realised too late how true the love of the two young people had been. The families arranged a double funeral, and Giuseppina and Michelino were laid side by side in the same grave.

"Now custom decrees that when a marriage takes place, the groom's parents should visit the bride's, bringing gifts. This happens usually when the happy couple are on their honeymoon. As a mark of respect, the Armieris decided to fulfil the old custom. They came one day to visit the Feliciottis, laden with gifts, fine wines, liqueurs, and sweetmeats. The Feliciottis received them graciously, and the old people embraced with great emotion. A week later the Feliciottis called upon the Armieris with gifts and were warmly received. The friendship between the two families has continued to this day, thus ensuring that Giuseppina and Michelino are united in their love in Heaven, for Our Lord is merciful and has surely forgiven them for taking their own lives."

When Filomena finished this sad tale, she sighed and dried her eyes. Assunta and Antonia blew their noses while Benedetto grunted and went on sucking his pipe. The girls then rose to prepare cocoa, and when they were all sitting, sipping the hot, brown liquid, Filomena began to tell another story.

Chapter Three

1915—Amusing Memories

"Have I ever told you the story of the two eggs?" Filomena asked Assunta and Antonia.

"I don't remember that one," answered Assunta.

"Oh, do tell it, Zia Filomena!" said Antonia.

"Very well," said Filomena, "it's a good story and it can teach us a useful lesson."

Then, taking a sip of cocoa, she began.

"This story concerns someone you know. I am speaking of Zia Maria from Franchitti. You know how poor she is, and she lives by herself in her tiny house. The little she earns by sewing is not enough to keep her and so, twice a week she goes visiting, hoping that her friends will give her some food to help her along.

"One day, a few weeks ago, she went to see her niece Angelina. She was given a lovely meal of pasta and beans, and when she was going away, Angelina gave her two eggs. That same morning Zia Maria had been visiting her old friends Giorgina and Palma, and they had given her a bottle of wine, some dried beans, and some potatoes. She put the two eggs along with these provisions into her round basket and, placing it firmly on her head, set off for home. Now Angelina had suggested that Zia Maria could make herself a nice omelette with the two eggs for her supper, but, as the old lady walked along, balancing the basket precariously on her swaying head, she began to think aloud.

" 'Well, now, I already have two hens at home and one of them will soon be brooding. I know what I shall do! I shall place these two precious eggs under the hen. She will patiently brood over them and hatch them out. Yes, that will be wonderful, for I shall then have two lovely, little chicks. Oh yes, and then when they grow up, I shall have four hens altogether, and no doubt they will lay lots of eggs.

" 'Ho, ho, I'll be able to sell my eggs and by and by I shall have saved enough money to buy a piglet! I think I'll call him "Porchetto," and I'll feed him with the best acorns I can gather in the woods. I'll collect food scraps from my good neighbours and feed him with the potatoes Giorgina and Palma always give me. My, my! How happy I'll be when I see Porchetto getting fatter and fatter as the weeks pass. But I must be sure not to get too fond of the little beast, and when I sell him off for slaughter, just imagine how much money I shall have! Goodness me! I shall be really rich, and everyone will have to respect me, and when they meet me on their way home, the men will touch their caps, and the ladies, out of respect, will bow to me and call out: "*Buon giorno*, Donna Maria!" and won't I be proud just then!'

"And, as 'Donna' Maria said these words, she bowed to her imaginary admirers, tilting her head slightly forward. Out plopped the eggs from the front of the basket, breaking on the pebbles at her feet, as the basket itself quickly followed, scattering wine, beans, and potatoes all over the place."

Antonia and Assunta could not help giggling at the sad story of Zia Maria's lost eggs, for they had often heard her talking to herself as she walked along with her basket on her head.

Filignano was a village rich in what today we call "originals," people with very individual personalities and a very unique outlook. Assunta and Antonia naturally knew all the local "characters," and they loved to hear Filomena's accounts of their misdemeanors. So Assunta took it upon herself to prompt her mother into telling them the story of Giambattista Panecotto.

"I don't know whether I should go into that story," said Filomena. "It's not exactly a moral tale, you know."

"You're just dying to tell it," said Benedetto, "so, do get on with it!" Filomena threw him a reproachful look as she began:

"As you know there lived in Filignano a few years ago a young man nicknamed Giambattista Panecotto who, as a result of a nasty accident, lost his right arm. As he was unable to work normally, he had to be supported by his parents, who, fortunately, were quite well off. But they both died when he was still a youth, and a couple of years later he married, since he required a good woman to look after him. His wife, Filomena, was from Collemacchia, and she was a good worker, so things went well for a while. In time they had two children. The first, a boy, they called Francesco, and the second, a girl, was named Lucia.

"But times grew hard, and money became scarce so, one day, Giambattista turned to his wife and said, 'I shall have to do something to try and earn some money. Listen, I have an idea. There are two girls I know from Cardido who play the accordion very well. They have been travelling around the local villages, playing their instruments and earning a fair amount of money. Now, what I was thinking was this:

If you don't object, I would like to set out with those girls and we could travel far and wide and make a small fortune. We could go to all the big towns and cities over in Italy and might even get as far as Turin. Naturally I would send you some money every week.'

"When Filomena heard her husband's promise to send money regularly, she was naturally won over by his plan and readily gave her consent.

"Giambattista approached the two girls, and they were delighted by his proposal, for they had often wanted to travel farther afield but lacked a protector. Although Giambattista had only one arm, he was a sturdy man in every other respect and the girls had complete confidence in him. So the three of them set off on foot, the girls playing their accordions and Giambattista playing a tambourine with his one arm, just to make his small contribution to the entertainment.

"Well, they began to earn a great deal of money and every week, as he had promised, Giambattista sent money home, and Filomena was happy. Then, as the weeks and months passed, when they stopped overnight at an inn or a hotel, he began to share his bed with one of the girls, Florinda. Soon she bore him a baby girl, whom they devoutly christened Elmerinda. Now the other girl, Denisa, was jealous and resentful of the attentions Giambattista had been paying to Florinda and one day she said to him, 'Why can't you also sleep with me? If she is good enough for you, what's wrong with me?'

"Giambattista, being very generous at heart, could not turn a deaf ear to such an appeal, and soon Denisa gave birth to a baby girl whom they called Margherita. So they were, all five of them, extremely happy, Giambattista sleeping with Florinda and Denisa in turn. Perhaps I should have said before that Giambattista, despite his disability, was an exceptionally handsome man.

"Several years passed and the girls Elmerinda and Margherita grew up and began to contribute their share to the musical act that they performed in the town streets to delighted audiences. The girls were lovely, graceful dancers. And all this time, Filomena kept receiving money regularly from her husband. Although she was aware of vague rumours regarding the increase in numbers in her husband's performing company, she did not allow this to worry her, as she was really very broadminded and tolerant, a very understanding lady, in fact.

"Then one day the urge came over Giambattista to go home to Filignano. Yearning for his roots, he felt homesick. After travelling down the length of Italy, he and his two other families arrived unexpectedly and when Filomena opened the door, she was surprised to see how many of them there were. But, as Giambattista stretched out his left arm to hand his wife a large wallet stuffed with notes, she welcomed them all with great warmth. Beds were quickly purchased and three bedrooms arranged in rooms that had lain empty, one for the young girls, Margherita and Elmerinda, and one each for their respective mothers. Filomena suddenly became aware that her years of loneliness were over, for she now had a houseful of people, all of them helpful and cheerful, so harmony prevailed in the augmented Panecotto household.

"One Thursday when I passed the house, I saw Filomena sitting out on the porch sunning herself. I sat down to chat with her and, in the course of our conversation, I asked, 'Tell me frankly, my dear friend, as one Filomena to another, where did you get the courage to let all those people into your house after so many years?'

" 'What was done was done,' said Filomena Panecotto, 'and there was nothing I could do to change it. Besides, he arrived with a considerable amount of money, and, in these days, as you well know, that is not a small matter.'

" 'But how do you manage to put up with it? I mean, does he now sleep with *you,* Filomena?'

" 'Oh yes, he comes to bed with me every night, but he turns his face to the wall and pretends he is asleep. Then, when he thinks *I* am sleeping, he creeps stealthily out of bed and disappears into one of the other bedrooms. That does not worry me, you know, for I am getting past that sort of thing. With a man it's different. Besides, all that matters is to keep up appearances and he does give me my place by coming to bed with me first!'

"Now, as you know, the people of Filignano always like to have the last word in these matters. The other day when Giambattista Panecotto was out having his evening stroll, I overheard two worthies in the Piazza remarking, 'Just imagine, Giambattista Panecotto has only one arm, but he has three wives. Lord knows, if he had two arms, he would need half a dozen, would he not?' "

Assunta and Antonia chortled as Filomena ended the story of Giambattista Panecotto, the one-armed Casanova. It was getting quite late, and Assunta decided to accompany Antonia the short distance up to her house for a breath of air. As the girls went up the pebble-littered pathway, they went over Filomena's story and laughed again at the sheer naughtiness of it. Antonia then recalled the amusing incident some time later when Giambattista's son, Francesco, had decided to marry.

The girl of his choice was from Collemacchia, and her name was

Cecilia. On the day of the wedding, the bride and groom made their way to the house of the groom's parents and, as neither Giambattista nor his legal wife, Filomena, were churchgoers, in view of the circumstances of his domestic arrangements, it was decided to revive the old custom of the bride's arrival at the groom's house. When the bride arrived at the door of the house, her mother-in-law would come out and hand her a large palm leaf and say, "Welcome, my new daughter, and accept this palm leaf from my hand. Now you must leave behind all your bad habits in your own home and bring only your best service and good behaviour to my house!"

The ceremony went well up to the point when Filomena uttered the traditional words to her new daughter-in-law. At this moment, however, Cecilia, who was inclined to be somewhat outspoken, looked into the house and saw the large number of her father-in-law's two other families. So, instead of answering, "Oh, my new mother, I shall do as you bid and shall try to please you in all ways," she smiled sardonically and, winking at her husband, Francesco, said loudly, "I'll just do whatever the hell I like!"

The unexpected audacity of the girl's reply did not offend Filomena. On the contrary she admired her bold wit, appreciating the subtle allusion to her own husband's little peccadilloes. She threw her arms round Cecilia's neck and welcomed her warmly to the house of many families.

Next morning Assunta rose early, and Filomena was surprised when she came through to the kitchen to find the fire already kindled, the water drawn, the table set, and the cocoa brewing. Filomena was going to miss Assunta when she went off to Glasgow. Despite Filomena's severity, tempered always by Benedetto's leniency, Assunta always felt close to her mother. They had shared so many experiences.

When Assunta was still a baby, Filomena had left her with her grandmother one day when she was going to gather firewood. It was forbidden to collect wood on the forest land, which was the property of the commune. Filomena's search for wood was difficult, and she was tempted to venture into the forbidden forest where she quickly put together a sizable bundle and, placing it on her head, made to go home. Suddenly the forester loomed before her on the path. He took note of her name and reported her at the office of the clerk of court.

A week later Filomena found herself standing before a stern magistrate, charged with stealing wood from the forest of the commune. When asked why she had taken it, she had no defence except to explain that she could not find good wood anywhere else and she required it really desperately or they would die of cold in her house. The unfeeling magistrate fined her the impossible sum of twenty lire or seven days' imprisonment. Not having the money, Filomena chose imprisonment. She explained she could not be separated from her young child who was still being breast-fed. Benedetto's irregular offer to go to prison in his wife's place fell on deaf ears.

A sympathetic jailer was moved to pity when he saw Filomena trying to nurse her child in the communal cell of the local gaol and, after questioning her regarding the nature of her offence, he arranged each night under cover of darkness to have her brought with the child to his house nearby, where a small room was placed at her disposal and the jailer's wife brought her a plate of soup and some bread to eat. Thanks to the jailer's compassion, Filomena and baby Assunta spent their nights in comfort while the daylight hours were spent in the cell. Thus Filomena paid her debt of seven days in prison for stealing a small bundle of firewood.

If there was one thing Filomena could not tolerate, it was bad language. When Eugenio was a little boy, he was the innocent victim of an incident involving him in swearing. By nature he was quiet and inoffensive, and he had never before been in trouble. But one day, on his way home from school, he passed some workmen on a scaffold beside a new house that was being built for the doctor. All the men knew Eugenio, and they called down to him. The boy nimbly climbed the scaffold and joined his friends for a few words. Now two of the workmen, Raffaele and Nicandro, were a mischievous pair. From the platform on the high scaffold, they could look down on the people walking past on their various errands. Sometimes someone would pass for whom, for some reason or other, they harboured a particular dislike. So they had a bright idea.

"Look here, Eugenio," said Nicandro, "we want you to do us a favour. When certain people pass below, you should call after them and swear at them."

"Oh, I could never do that," said Eugenio. "My mother is very strict about swearing. Why, she doesn't even allow my father to swear, even if he is angry!"

The men laughed heartily at the boy's remark. Then Raffaele saw Giambattista Panecotto coming along the street. He nodded to Nicandro and winked and, at a signal, the two rogues grabbed Eugenio by the legs, turned him upside down and held him precariously over the edge of the scaffold, ready to drop him over if he did not do as they said. The poor boy, terrified, complied and a moment later Giambattista Panecotto heard a young voice above him calling out, "There you go, old Jimmy, you randy old one-armed fool. How are your three wives, you dirty old bugger?"

Fortunately, Giambattista had gone a little deaf and did not hear the boy's insults. Later the local moneylender, don Cicciotto, heard a young voice above him call out:

Don Cicciotto, hard as nails,
Stores his victims' money in pails.
Mean old bugger, hard old skinflint,
Show him your money!
See how his eyes glint!

But hard behind don Cicciotto came don Alfonso, the parish priest, and when he heard the commotion, he looked up and saw what was happening. He called up to Raffaele and Nicandro to stop their nonsense and let the boy down or he would climb up the scaffold himself and box their ears.

A scared, badly shaken Eugenio was making his way home up the hill to Imperatore. Unknown to him, more trouble was awaiting him at home. Don Filippo, the teacher, had taken it upon himself to call upon Filomena and complain about her son's misdemeanours. Over a glass of wine offered by Filomena, who was honoured by the teacher's unexpected visit, don Filippo pompously began, "I am sorry, signora Marzella, but you will have to do something about your son. He has developed a foul mouth and has been shouting slanderous insults at people for the last hour. You will have to take him in hand when he comes home. A sound thrashing is what he needs."

Filomena could not believe her ears. *Her* Eugenio did not swear! But Don Filippo had barely finished when the door was knocked and there was don Cicciotto, puffing and blowing, also come to complain about Eugenio's insults.

"Is this possible?" Filomena asked Benedetto, who had been sitting all the time quietly listening in his corner. He did not answer his wife. He merely shrugged his shoulders.

"I can assure you it was definitely your son," said don Cicciotto.

"No doubt about it, it was your Eugenio," added don Filippo. And they went away, muttering to one another and shaking their heads.

Poor Eugenio, coming up the hill, met the two old men on their way down and they threw him a withering look as don Filippo muttered, "You'll be for it when you get home, my lad. Oh yes, you'll be for it." Eugenio hurried on, fearful of what awaited him.

When he got to the door of the house, it lay ajar. He stepped inside. Filomena was standing holding a large stick in her right hand behind her back. Benedetto was still in his corner.

"Where have you been until this time, Eugenio?" asked Filomena in an angry tone.

"I was down where they are building the new house for the doctor," said Eugenio, and his voice was unsteady.

"And why were you swearing at the people who were passing?"

"I wasn't swearing."

"Yes, you were, my boy, and there are witnesses," and, as she said this, Filomena thumped the poor boy over the head with her stick.

"This is from me," she said, "and now your father will deal with you," and, turning to Benedetto she added, "See what you can do to deal with this swearing boy!"

Benedetto, cornered, obviously unwilling to mete out punishment to his son, suddenly exclaimed, "Oh, let the bloody boy swear in peace, woman!" Filomena, taken aback by her husband's reply, dropped her stick.

"Now tell us what really happened, Son," said Benedetto to Eugenio. By the time the boy blurted out his sad story, Filomena was thoroughly ashamed she had doubted him in the first place.

She picked up her stick, put on her shawl, and marched down to the doctor's house where the two culprits, Nicandro and Raffaele, were still working. There they were, stooping to shovel some lime, their backs to her. She set about them quickly, whacking them over the head and shoulders with her stick while she whipped them with her sharp tongue until their ears smarted. They dared not even dare to defend themselves, as she was a small woman. They hung their heads in shame and mumbled weak words of apology. Filomena felt the honour of her boy had been restored, and Eugenio was warned never again to speak to those scoundrels Raffaele and Nicandro.

Assunta knew her mother was a remarkable woman, particularly when she was roused by some injustice. She knew how to fight for her rights. Hard times had made her very shrewd, and she had no patience for anyone who came begging. Not that she could refuse anyone who was in genuine need. She just had no time for loafers or scroungers. She even considered travelling musicians going from door to door through the village to gather food delicacies at feast times as good-for-nothings. Even the pipers who came to play the novena at Christmas were only tolerated. When, as a girl, she had been in service to one of the local rich families, notorious for its meanness, she had been shown a valuable method of cheating the poor pipers.

The custom was that when they had played the novena, they were invited into the kitchen where the serving girl offered them a plateful of wheat grain and some Christmas doughnuts to put into their canvas bags. Filomena learned that you could put two or three doughnuts on top of the grain and at the very moment of pouring wheat and doughnuts into the bag, a clever piece of legerdemain could be executed. By ringing the doughnuts round the middle finger of the hand and rotating the plate at the moment you poured, the grain fell into the bag while the doughnuts, concealed by the plate, could be retained on the finger. So, every Christmas when the pipers arrived to play, they might receive a few grains of wheat from Filomena, but never, unless her finger slipped, any doughnuts. She had to work too hard for what she had, to want to give it away.

Near the piazza was the house of the goldsmith whose wife, donna Marella, loved to sun herself on the porch every afternoon. One day Filomena had made several trips to carry firewood and each time she passed in front of the goldsmith's porch, donna Marella, gave her a long, interested look. When Filomena passed for the seventh time, balancing the wood on her head, donna Marella felt compelled to say something, intending to be condescendingly polite.

"Filomena," she called out. "I have been asking myself where you get the strength to carry all that wood. Just how do you do it?"

Filomena was incensed by the patronizing tone in the woman's voice. She turned her laden head and shouted, "And how do you manage to do what you do, Signora, sitting on your bottom all day fanning yourself, while other good women must work for their living?" Donna Marella never again spoke to Filomena.

Yet, when Assunta was very young, Filomena had been wet nurse to Gemma, donna Marella's little daughter, as it was beneath the dignity of such a lady to breast-feed her own child. Filomena badly needed the five lire that donna Marella paid her every week. In those days it was customary to suckle young children even when they had started to walk. Donna Marella's Gemma and Assunta were of the same age. When it was breast-feeding time, Filomena would sit on a low stool in the kitchen and with the two little girls standing in front of her, suckle them both simultaneously. Donna Marella would have her cook prepare the richest chicken broth for Filomena so that her milk would be good.

Now Assunta began to be envious of little Gemma who was always beautifully dressed, and she resented having to share her mother's milk with the other girl. One day when Gemma was brought by donna Marella's maid, Assunta went up to her and said, "Go away, you are not going to get my mother's titty today. Go home and get your own mother to give you her titty."

"But my mother's titty hasn't any milk," said Gemma in a plaintive little voice.

"Well, if you want Mamma Filomena's milk," said Assunta, "then I must have a lovely dress and a nice apron just like yours!"

Filomena and the maid had been eavesdropping, and they were very amused. The maid must have reported the little girls' conversation to donna Marella, for in no time Assunta's wardrobe was greatly increased. Assunta was astonished at the clarity with which she could recall such incidents from her childhood. She could even remember the colour of the first dress from Donna Marella, her favourite colour, blue. With this happy thought, she closed her eyes and fell asleep.

Chapter Four

1915—Murder at Valle Noce

As Filomena had promised Assunta that she could go to the market at Venafro on the following day to buy the things she required for her journey, Assunta rose at Crestone's first early call. Antonia had managed to get her Aunt Rosa's permission to go with Assunta. When Filomena and Benedetto came through, breakfast was already on the table.

Benedetto remarked, "There's a lot of noise in this house today." Over breakfast he looked at Assunta and asked, "Planning to spend all your mother's money, are you?"

"We can't have her going to Glasgow with empty cases," said Filomena.

Leaving her mother to clear up, Assunta pulled her headscarf over her head, tied the ends under her chin, and went off to fetch her friend.

When she knocked at Antonia's door, it was Zia Rosa who answered it. The old lady screwed up her eyes, for she had very poor eyesight and did not at first recognize Assunta. But she knew Assunta's voice when the girl spoke and welcomed her into the kitchen to wait for Antonia, who was still dressing. In the corner of the kitchen was Zia Rosa's goat, Cerasola. Seeing the goat brought a smile to Assunta's lips, for she remembered something funny from the previous summer.

Zia Rosa had employed some day workers in her field, ploughing and sowing, and was preparing some cabbage soup for their supper. Now, when Zia Rosa prepared a large cabbage for her soup, she separated the tough outer leaves from the inner tender ones. The tough leaves were for the goat. When the time came to add the cabbage leaves to the ham stock in the *pignatta,* or earthenware pot by the fire, Zia Rosa, in her shortsightedness, picked up the wrong leaves. So Cerasola had a choice meal of the tenderest cabbage leaves that day, while the poor field workers, when they returned from their labours that evening, were rewarded with a very indigestible mess. To add insult to injury, since Cerasola had also been nibbling at the tough leaves before they were put into the soup, some of her loose goat hairs had fallen on them and had consequently found their way into the *pignatta*. The workers went home hungry that evening, as they were not very partial to tough cabbage goat's hair soup!

Little did Assunta know, as she sat at Zia Rosa's fire recalling the cabbage soup farce that only a few months later, sitting beside that very fire, the old lady was to meet a tragic end. She would always sit there with her rosary beads in her lap, enjoying the glow of the embers, and, as her eyes slowly closed, her lips would continue mechanically to form the words of the prayers. In this way she would gradually sink into a slumber, praying all the while.

It was Antonia who was to write to Assunta a few months after her arrival in Glasgow telling her the terrible details of Zia Rosa's death. Apparently Antonia had been delayed one evening when she was out visiting Filomena and Benedetto. She had left her aunt sitting happily by the fire, and Cerasola had been put out in her pen for the night. When she came home, she was horrified to find the old lady lying face downwards in the fire, her clothes burned into her shoulders, her face a mass of terrible burns. She had probably fallen into the fire in trying to retrieve the rosary beads that had slipped from her lap while she dozed.

Antonia appeared, neatly dressed for their journey to Venafro. Both the girls wore their aprons, for they carried the small towels in their apron pockets that they would later roll into round neat mats to place on their heads upon which they would carry the purchases. Soon on their way to Venafro, the girls enjoyed the walk as it was downhill almost all the way. When they were approximately halfway on their journey, they saw a small white marble cross set against a hillock by the side of the road. Neither of them spoke, keeping a respectful silence until they drew level with the small monument. Then they knelt and prayed. The cross marked the spot where an old man had been murdered in very cruel circumstances. After praying, the girls resumed their journey, but neither of them made to speak. They were both thinking of the grim story of Rosa the Devil Woman.

This old woman had lived in Bottazzella and had the reputation of being an *ianara* so that everyone shunned her, and as she grew older she became more and more bitter and resentful. It was whispered she could cast evil spells upon her enemies, though no one had actually proved this. One man in particular, Marco Ranni, was convinced that Rosa had blighted his projects by putting the evil eye upon them. If he happened to meet her, she would leer at him in sinister fashion. He had a long spell of bad luck, three poor harvests, one after the other.

Then some of his animals died of mysterious ailments and, to add to his misery, his wife, Annabella, went into poor health.

Thoroughly dejected, he happened to be going home one day when he again found Rosa on his road. He was sure she glared at him as he went past, and a moment later he distinctly heard her cackling. His anger rising, he turned and followed her. When he caught up with her, he seized her by the shoulders and spun her roughly round. Now Marco was a mild-mannered man but, standing face to face with this old witch, who, he was convinced, had done him so much harm for no apparent reason, his voice coarsened and he shouted, "If you do not stop this nonsense, woman, I warn you I shall kill you!" Then he gave her a good shaking to frighten her and, turning on his heels, left her. Rosa, terrified by the suddenness of his attack, was left speechless.

That same evening she was visited by her sinister nephew Nerone, who, it was said, was in league with her and helped her to carry out her evil doings. He was a large, broad, powerful man with the mentality of a child. He did not shave regularly, and the dark stubble on his chin together with the swarthiness of his complexion made his dark, blue-green eyes shine out with a wicked expression from his squarish face. When Nerone went to see his aunt in the evening after dark, neighbours passing the door had often heard their voices raised in what could only be devilish incantations. On this particular evening after her encounter with Marco Ranni, Rosa had specific instructions for her obedient nephew.

"Listen, Nerone," she said as he tucked in to a large bowl of *polenta,* "I was brutally set upon today by that rogue Marco Ranni. I am determined to have my revenge and only you, Nerone, can help me." She paused and then, fixing her gaze upon him, said slowly and deliberately, "I want you to kill him!"

Nerone dropped his fork on the table and looked at his aunt. Then he picked it up, put another forkful of *polenta* into his mouth, and spoke.

"That is easier said than done. How on earth am I to kill him? He's not just a goat, you know, that I could kill with a well-aimed rock. If you were to ask me to kill a pig, why, that would be easy. But to kill a man? How am I to do that and get off with it?"

Rosa smiled reassuringly as he went on eating. She sat down opposite him and, waiting until he put a large forkful of *polenta* into his mouth so that she would not be interrupted, went on saying, "I happen to know that he will soon be going to the mill at Venafro. Now, he is not in the habit of going in the early morning. In fact he usually sets out in the middle of the night with his laden donkey so as to arrive first thing in the morning to catch the first milling. By the time he reaches Valle Noce, halfway to Venafro, it will still be quite dark. You can lie in wait for him there and surprise him."

As she slowly said all this, she poured Nerone a large glassful of good red wine and smiled. He seemed to be under her spell as he slowly nodded.

About two weeks later, Marco Ranni set out when it was still dark, leading his donkey charged with two large sacks of wheat down the winding road to Venafro. Stars shimmered in the dark sky above, and Marco, who had slept uneasily for two or three hours before his departure, for he had been a prey to strange dreams of violence, had the very odd sensation that he was slowly floating down the white road. He could hear the soft clippety-clop of the donkey's hooves, but his own steps were inaudible. Then his feet became leaden as if they did not wish to take him on his slow journey down to the mill. And still he had this strange feeling of drifting along. The road gradually levelled off, and he was aware that he was approaching Valle Noce. He would stop there for a time to rest the donkey.

The man and the donkey slowly left the road and walked on to the grass. At that very instant, a huge, dark form loomed up in front of Marco. Two mighty hands tightened round his throat like a relentless vice. As his head fell back, his right hand dropped the rope with which he had been leading the donkey. For the last time, his dimming eyes beheld the stars above. Then he sank into his last sleep.

Nerone was panting with the exertion of his foul deed. Marco Ranni lay lifeless at his feet. The donkey stood beside the crumpled heap of its master's body. Nerone took to his heels, screaming, "What have I done for you, Zia Rosa, what have I done?"

At that very moment, Rosa awoke from the heavy slumber into which she had fallen after Nerone's departure. Her flesh crept, and she sensed a malevolent presence in the bedroom. The stifling air seemed to be charged with the stinging odour of sulphur. Then she saw at the foot of her bed a dim, greenish glow. It grew in intensity and all at once, through it, she perceived a demon riveting her with his evil, malicious eyes. Her voice rose in a high-pitched scream, awakening the neighbours. But they did not rise to come to her aid, for they knew that she was possessed. Her screams continued to echo in the small courtyard, for the bedroom window was wide open.

When Doretta Donato, who lived directly opposite, was forced to rise to close her shutters in order to blot out the old woman's blood-curdling screams, she was transfixed as she stepped to her window. Across the courtyard she could see a bright green glow in Rosa's bedroom. The green slowly changed to red and then back to green. As the alternating red-green glow rose and fell in brightness, so did the volume of Rosa's terrible, haunting shrieks. Doretta crossed herself and hurried back to bed, pulling her sheet over her head.

Some time afterwards, still unable to sleep, she heard a terrible pounding on Rosa's door and rose in time to see the downstairs door being opened to let in Nerone. That was the last anyone ever saw of the big man, for his aunt must have given him the money he required to run away and escape the consequence of his heinous crime.

Marco Ranni's body was found in the morning at Valle Noce, the donkey, weighed down with its two sacks of grain, standing patiently beside it, nibbling at the grass. All sorts of rumours and speculations were whispered round the village. Only very gradually was a picture of what had occurred pieced together. Someone had seen Nerone setting out for Venafro shortly after Marco Ranni's own departure in the night. Another, returning to Filignano from Venafro after an evening of drinking in the local cantina, was sure he had seen Nerone hiding in the undergrowth not far from Valle Noce. But it was Doretta who had witnessed the strange lights in Rosa's bedroom and the old *ianara* opening the door to her nephew in the early hours of the morning. Nerone's unexplained disappearance at the very time of the crime was too coincidental to be without significance.

But it was what happened at Bottazzella in the few weeks following Marco Ranni's death that confirmed everyone's suspicions regarding Rosa's association with the Devil. Night after night she was heard screaming in her room while her double shadow created by the flickering light of two candles trembled against the wall as she paced to and fro, demented. She did not eat and became very frail. Then one morning, covering her head and shoulders with a black shawl, she came out and made her way slowly to the piazza in Filignano. There she went into the joiner shop of Emilio Coia. She was seen to hand him a quantity of money as she whispered certain instructions. Emilio stood back from her and seemed to be measuring her with his eye.

A week later Rosa's neighbours were startled to see the joiner's cart arriving at her door with a dark, oak coffin. Helped by his apprentice, Carluccio, Emilio carried the lugubrious box into the house. As the old witch was nowhere to be seen, the neighbours thought at first she had died suddenly during the night, but a moment later she herself came to the door to show Emilio and Carluccio out.

That night Rosa's house was unusually quiet and a bold lad named Luigi, dared by his companions, placed a ladder beside the bedroom window and climbed quietly and stealthily up. When he was level with the window, he leaned carefully to the side and peered into the room.

He nearly toppled off the ladder at the sight that met his eyes. There, in the centre of the room on the floor, lay Rosa fast asleep in her coffin, her sickly, yellow features lit by the shaky flames of four candles placed round the coffin. Later Luigi swore that in the farthest corner of the room sitting on a low stool he saw the Infernal Spirit himself. The Devil's green eyes flashed, and at that very moment Rosa let out a piercing cry. In his haste to get down the ladder, Luigi missed his footing and fell on to the ground with a mighty crash, pulling the ladder over with him. His friends rushed to help him to his feet, and then they all scuffled away in confusion, leaving the ladder lying in the courtyard.

The only person who showed any compassion for old Rosa was Giulietta's mother, Albina. She nursed her in her last illness. It was indeed from Albina that Filomena had learned the whole story of Rosa's eccentric behaviour. Albina had insisted on the coffin being removed to an adjoining room and made Rosa lie in her bed. When the old woman became delirious during the night, she would sometimes scream. When she merely talked, she went over all the details of her plot to have Marco Ranni murdered and told how she had been haunted afterwards with visits from the Devil. Fearing she would not even be permitted to be buried in a coffin because of the monstrousness of her crime, she had ordered the village joiner to make her one. Once it was delivered, she was drawn to it and could not resist sleeping in it. She could never close her eyes in bed. In the coffin, even if the Devil came into her room, she felt temporarily safe.

When Rosa died she was buried in unconsecrated ground. So she paid the penalty for the murder of Marco Ranni.

After buying two large suitcases and a few small items of clothing at the Venafro market, Assunta and Antonia made their way back to Filignano. They did not linger at Valle Noce but hurried on, leaving the creepy spot behind them. Although Assunta was saddened by Marco Ranni's tragic end, within herself she felt even sorrier for old Rosa. The old woman had been driven to the dreadful deed, a victim of the superstitious ignorance of people who ignored and despised her because she happened to be different. Going about her business, troubling no one, she never stopped to speak to anyone.

Then, when it was reported that her nephew called on her every evening, tongues began to wag. Perhaps they drank too much and tried to sing, their unmusical voices creating the impression of evil incantations. Perhaps Rosa had even heard someone referring to her as an *ianara*. An evil seed planted in an impressionable mind can grow into a monstrous thing.

Yes, Assunta was sure this was how it had come about. Rosa had gradually assumed the character attributed to her by petty, cruel, uncharitable people. As the evil within her grew, she actually believed she saw the Devil. So it was not Rosa and Nerone who were responsible for Ranni's murder but the insensitive, irresponsible spreaders of idle gossip. Assunta wondered if these people realised how wicked *they* were.

Chapter Five

1915—Assunta and Benedetto

As they were sitting round the fire after supper, they were startled by the mournful tolling of the church bell. The clapper, hand-held, struck at regular intervals, dong ... dong ... dong ..., announcing the death of an old person. Had it been the second of the three bells with its slightly higher pitch, the death of a younger person would have been made known, while the smallest bell with its tinkling ring told everyone that a child had been called to Heaven.

"It must be Zia Mariuccia from Cerreto," said Antonia. "I heard this morning at church she was sinking."

So they all knelt on the stone floor of the kitchen while Filomena intoned some prayers for the repose of Zia Mariuccia's soul. But they were not greatly moved by the old woman's death, as she was only casually known to them.

"I shall never forget the funeral of old Zio Donato," said Filomena.

"Is this your way of cheering us?" asked Benedetto.

"Well, it's a story with humour of its own," said Filomena, and, nudging her husband with her elbow to let him know she would brook no interruptions, she began.

"Many years ago in Cerreto, there lived a couple called Donato and Mezia who, although married for many years, had not been blessed with any children. They owned a great deal of land, so Donato decided to draw up a will, bequeathing it to his nieces, Dolfina and Elisa, his sister's daughters. Then old Zio Donato fell ill and died. His nieces, in view of the inheritance, decided they would give their uncle a grand funeral. They sent to Venafro for a band and hired a special hearse to make a good show.

"The people of Filignano had never witnessed such a spectacle. The band, numbering twelve players, played a solemn funeral march as it preceded the glass-enclosed hearse surmounted by three large wooden angels painted in gold and drawn by four large black horses wearing harnesses decorated with black-and-white plumes and silver accoutrements. Inside the hearse the expensive oak coffin containing

47

Zio Donato was covered with wreaths and bouquets of fresh flowers. The funeral cortège was followed by a weeping company on foot. There were six or seven members of the family, the others being paid mourners hired for the occasion to swell the ranks.

"Leading the lamenting company of mourners were Mezia, Donato's widow, and his two nieces. Now Dolfina was a young lady who believed in attacking her tasks with enthusiasm. She was not blessed, however, with a good sense of timing, nor was her musical ear in any way outstanding.

"In any well-conducted funeral procession done on a grand scale, there should be moments of quiet solemnity when only the muffled strains of the band's instruments can be heard. Then, when the band stops playing for a time, the mourners may tastefully raise their voices in lamentations and shed tears to demonstrate the extent of their grief.

"But Dolfina chose the wrong times to express her sorrow. So, when the weeping company fell silent as the band took up another solemn piece of music, Dolfina suddenly began to scream, 'Oh, band, band, why do you bother to play? Can't you see my Uncle Donato is dead and cannot hear you!'

"And as she repeated these wailing complaints over and over again, they rose above the band's music, rending the air like an inharmonious dirge rising to the proportions of a hysterical scream. The effect was so incongruous that it provoked some laughter among the paid mourners. I leave you to imagine what a farcical spectacle poor old Zio Donato's funeral turned out to be. The band's instruments were thrown out of tune by Dolfina's shrieks, and the mourners lost all control and began to fall by the side of the road convulsed with laughter. For months afterwards many a naughty girl working on Filignano's hilly slopes could be heard mimicking the ill-timed cries of the hapless Dolfina."

As she lay in bed that night before falling asleep, Assunta recalled another funeral story that she would never have dared to repeat at home. It was a story she had heard from Antonia's Aunt Rosa. There was a village near Filignano called Selvone that had a certain reputation. It was fortunate in having a large number of beautiful girls. Unfortunately they were not very fond of work and had taken to entertaining gentlemen to earn their living. Now Antonia had a young cousin, Salvatore, who often went to Selvone on business. One day Assunta and Antonia met Salvatore on his way home from Selvone, and they boldly asked him about the rumours they had heard concerning the lovely young ladies of that village.

Salvatore could not help smiling at the audacity of the inquisitive girls and answered them as tactfully as he could, saying, "Well, it's like this, *ragazze*. Selvone consists of one long *contrada* that wanders up a fairly steep hill. Now, if you were to stand at the foot of this long, narrow street and look right up at the houses on either side, and if you could imagine that a pretty girl lived in each house, you could safely say to yourself, pointing to every second house: 'This one is and so is that one, this one is and so is that one!' "

"Is what?" Assunta and Antonia chorused.

"A pretty girl who hates work and prefers to sell her charms to some amorous gentleman!" said Salvatore with just a shade of embarrassment in his voice.

"He means a trollop!" said Assunta mischievously to Antonia, and the girls burst into merry peals of laughter and walked on, leaving a blushing Salvatore standing like a fool.

Later they questioned Zia Rosa about Selvone, for she had relatives in that ill-reputed village. Zia Rosa could tell a saucy story with a twinkle in her eye. Moreover, she enjoyed doing this, so she lost no time in telling them the tale of Sofia. It appeared that Sofia was one of those beautiful girls who had taken to "entertaining amorous gentlemen," but, after a few years, she tired of this sordid way of life, and when one of her regular clients proposed, she accepted and married him. They settled down and were very happy, but Sofia did not have any children.

Then, quite suddenly, Sofia's husband, Marco, took a chill and died. She could not honestly say that she was grief-stricken, for their marriage had been one of mutual convenience, but she was sorry to lose him, for he had been kind to her. So she decided to give him a proper funeral. Suitable arrangements at a reasonable price were made, and Sofia decided, out of respect, to go through the performance of the sorrowing widow, as all decent, bereaved wives should. Perhaps it was her recently acquired respectability that she was wanting to preserve.

As Marco's coffin was being carried to the church, Sofia, dressed in black, with a dark veil over her head, walked behind it, her eyes streaming with tears. Now and then she would lift the veil, dab her eyes with a black lace handkerchief, and call out disconsolately, "Oh, my husband, beloved companion, oh, Marco. How am I to live without you? Oh, Marco, Marco, what is to become of me?"

And the older women, following in the procession, cast sidelong glances of approval at one another as if to say, "Sofia is doing her part very well."

When the line of mourners approached the piazza, Sofia remembered it was market day and some merchants had already laid out their wares by the side of the road. As she slowly walked behind her husband's coffin, Sofia glanced at the fine things on display, laid out on sheets on the ground. She saw some lovely leather shoes and one pair in particular excited her fancy. The shoe merchant was standing by his wares and, as Sofia drew level with him, she paused, raised her veil and, pointing to the shoes, asked, "How much are you asking for those shoes, my good man?"

The woman directly behind Sofia was so shocked when she heard what the widow was asking that she gave her a nudge and observed, "You are really forgetting yourself, my dear. This is no time for pricing shoes!"

Brought back to the tragic reality of the moment, Sofia checked herself with a heavy sigh and called out, "Oh, companion, companion, oh, my beloved Marco, I am so sore with grief I don't know what I'm doing. For a moment I even forgot you were dead." Then, annoyed with herself for being such a hypocrite, she turned to the woman who had nudged her and hissed in a low voice, "I am putting *one* in his grave, but it won't be long until another *hundred* will have sampled me!" Thus, at one stroke, Sofia cast aside her mask of respectability and returned to her old profession.

Assunta could never understand why girls made such a fuss over men. She and Antonia seldom discussed boys, although they were both sought after. They were not yet inclined to encourage anyone seriously. On one occasion when Assunta was fifteen years of age, she and her young friends had broken into an impromptu dance in the neighbours' house next door. There were six girls and six boys and the son of the house, Fiorentino, played the accordion.

One of the boys tried to engage her in conversation in the piazza after benediction, but Assunta brushed him off with a few polite words and a diffident smile. He was a handsome fellow with dark hair and bold, grey-blue eyes, but she felt the expression she saw in them was rather fresh, to say the least. Now, as they danced a lively *panno rosso,* they enjoyed the jumping rhythm of the dance, and the brisk pace brought colour to their young cheeks.

As the dance gathered speed to the beat of the music, the daring Davide suddenly placed his right arm round Assunta's waist and, drawing her close to his body, he spun her round and round and away from the other dancers. Then his hand slipped down to her thigh, and he squeezed it. As Assunta broke away, she swung her right arm upwards and hit him such a mighty slap on the face that she sent him spinning. He lost his balance and collapsed against the wall at the far side of the room.

Assunta bolted down the stairs out into the yard across to her own front door, which she quickly opened and, still panting, brushed past her mother and rushed upstairs to her bedroom. When Davide had partly recovered from the shock of Assunta's assault, he followed her and, coming to the Marzellas' front door, raised the brass knocker and let it strike upon the small brass plate underneath. Filomena answered the door.

"Where is she? Where is she?" Davide asked frantically.

"Who is *she?*" asked Filomena.

"Assunta! Assunta!" said Davide, his lips trembling in his excitement.

"*She*'s gone upstairs to her room," said Filomena. "But what has happened and why do you want to see her?"

"She hit me a terrible slap on the face, and I can't understand why she did it!"

"Oh," said Filomena, with an amused note in her voice, "I am sure *she* must have had a perfectly good reason," and with these words she promptly closed the door in Davide's face. By the time she had done this, Assunta had crept downstairs again in time to hear her mother's last remark. Filomena turned and, catching the amused expression in Assunta's eyes, they both dissolved into cries of laughter.

"My family has gone mad," said Benedetto in his corner by the fire.

The morning after Filomena told the story of Zio Donato's funeral, Benedetto rose exceptionally early and, calling Assunta, asked her to accompany him to the Cisolle fields. It was too early in the year to start sowing, but a fair amount of hoeing required to be done. Benedetto was perfectly capable of doing all this preparatory work himself, but he thought of asking Assunta to accompany him so that they could spend the day together. Filomena prepared a large basket of food for them, and they set out on their two hours' journey as the sun was rising. Assunta balanced the basket on her head while Benedetto carried both the hoes they would be using, shouldering them like a pair of rifles.

Although Benedetto was inclined to be taciturn by nature, there were times when he had told Assunta a favourite story. Where Filomena preferred the melodramatic accounts concerning local people, Benedetto went back to the simple moral of the fable. So, when they had left Filignano well behind, Assunta asked her father to tell her one of his favourite fables. Benedetto always took life at an easy pace. Never to hurry was part of his way of life. He cleared his throat, slowed his step and then began, "A fox once struck up a friendship with a toad. The fox was amused by the way in which the toad leapt here and

51

there. The toad admired the great speed with which the fox could run. They were always complimenting one another. One day, the cunning fox suggested they should have a race along the broad top of a drystone wall. The fox said he would offer the prize, a fine chicken he would steal, knowing that the toad could never match his speed. But the toad devised a plan to outwit his cunning friend. He had a twin brother who was identical to him in every detail. So, before the start of the race, he arranged for his brother to be waiting at the end of the wall. At the appointed time, the race began and, of course, the fox raced along the wall at high speed and was just about to reach the end, leaving his hopping friend well behind.

"At that very instant, the twin toad popped up and, looking the fox boldly in the eye, exclaimed, "I have won, Foxie."

"The fox looked at him and observed ruefully, 'You say you have won, but you don't seem to me to have the face of a runner. You're not even out of breath!'

"Just then his friend the toad came hopping up to see the effect of his ruse on the fox. The two toads and the fox looked at each other and laughed. But the fox had the good grace to admit that his friend had outwitted him, so the three of them sat down and shared the chicken."

Before Assunta had time to comment upon the fable, Benedetto went on talking. He reminisced, going over the important family events of the preceding years.

"Do you remember the year when you and I went to Montecassino?" he asked.

"Of course I remember," said Assunta.

Every year Benedetto liked to make a pilgrimage to Montecassino, and he always went alone. But every time he went to the Monastery of St. Benedict, Assunta suffered a mishap of one sort or another. One year she had a nasty fall that left her covered in bruises. On the following year, she sprained her ankle. When Benedetto was next preparing to set out on his annual pilgrimage, Assunta begged to be allowed to go with him. As it was a very long journey on foot, her father was not too keen. But Assunta was insistent, and at length he consented.

So father and daughter set out on their long trek to the monastery. They passed through Laguno, Mastrogiovanni, and Monterotondo, and it seemed to young Assunta that the road was endless and they would never arrive. She did not wish to admit she was tired and kept walking bravely at her father's side. When they finally arrived, they were both very ready for the meal they ate in a local trattoria. After eating they sat on a bench and rested. Then they set off for the mountain. When they reached the base, Benedetto pointed to the monastery near the summit and indicated the long route they would have to take, walking up the winding road stretching before them. Assunta's spirits sank.

"As we proceed on our way up the mountain, Sunta," said Benedetto, "we shall come to three different chapels. Saint Benedict, you understand, had three sisters. They were always pestering him to allow them to go with him to the top of the mountain where he was building his monastery, praying and studying. Since they were so insistent, he finally agreed on condition that they would not look back on the town as they climbed. If they dared to look back, they would be punished.

"But human nature being what it is, they had been climbing for barely an hour when the first of the sisters, unable to control the urge that came over her, glanced back over her shoulder. She was immediately paralysed. They left her there and continued their journey to the monastery but, before they could reach it, the two others sisters had also succumbed and had looked back, and each was paralysed like the first. Later three chapels were built, each marking the spot where one of Saint Benedict's sisters had looked back."

Benedetto's story had a comforting effect upon Assunta, although it described such unpleasant contingencies. She was encouraged to go on climbing but never looked back, lest she too might suddenly be paralysed. So they came to the three chapels, pausing and praying at each of them. When, exhausted, they reached the top of the mountain in the evening, Assunta was enchanted by the beauty of the setting.

A large hall had been set aside where the pilgrims could spend the night before going back down to the town on the following day. Monks brought large bales of straw and empty mattress slips so that the pilgrims could make beds for themselves. The number of slips was unfortunately limited, and some of the people had to bed down on the straw. Assunta and Benedetto, being among the last to arrive, slept on the dried corn stocks. She enjoyed the fragrance and sank into a deep sleep.

They rose early in the morning and went to confession and mass in the beautiful church. There they met a cousin, Concetta, who had arrived before them on the previous evening. Despite her refreshing sleep on the straw, Assunta was still very tired and she told her father she doubted whether she would be fit to walk back all the way to Filignano. Her legs were very painful and her feet badly swollen. When they arrived back at Cassino, Benedetto put the two girls on a horse-drawn charabanc that would take them back to Filignano. He was obliged to walk as he did not have sufficient money for the three fares.

So Assunta and Concetta travelled back on the charabanc. The roads were very bumpy and the springing hard so they were jostled and shaken from side to side quite mercilessly.

When a very weary and sore Assunta appeared before Filomena later in the day, her mother could not help observing that she was no better after her trip to Montecassino than she had been on the previous years with her accidents. Yet, despite the discomfort, Assunta had really enjoyed her father's company, sharing a unique experience.

Here they now were together again on a much shorter journey. When they came to the two large fields, they lost no time in starting to hoe. They worked side by side, and the work was hard, for the earth was very stony. The sun rose high in the sky and by and by, they had covered almost half the area of the first field. It was almost noon, and they decided to eat in the welcoming shade of a large oak tree.

Assunta laid out the food and poured some wine for her father. They ate in silence, breathing in the acrid redolence of the freshly turned earth. The day was mild for February, the sun continuing to shine brightly in a pale blue sky. When they had eaten, Benedetto stretched and leaned against the tree trunk while Assunta tidied up and packed the little food that was left back into the basket. Assunta then sat for a while at her father's feet and he decided to tell her the following story:

"There is a true story that has always haunted me. Lately it has been running through my mind very frequently, and I don't know why. It concerns events that occurred many years ago, but I can remember my mother telling it more than once. There was this peasant who had two sons. His wife died and when the boys grew up, one of them made a good marriage and left the house. So father and son were left on their own and they worked hard, getting on well together, though they did not possess very much land. Then the son decided it was time for him to marry.

"He brought his wife to live with him and his father in their small house. For a time all went well. Then the children began to arrive. In a few years, the family numbered seven, all trying to live in a house that was too small for them. The woman began to resent the presence of her father-in-law who, by this time, was so old that he could not even do a full day's work in the fields. She persuaded her husband that he would have to get rid of the old man.

"So the son approached his father and spoke to him as kindly as he could, saying, 'I am sorry, Father, but you can see how things are. Times are hard. We have had two bad harvests. There are so many mouths to feed, and there is not room for all of us in this small house now that the children are growing up. I'm afraid you will have to go, Father.'

" 'Where can I go, Son?' asked the old man.

" 'Just you leave that to me, Father. I'll see to it that you won't starve,' and as he spoke, the son lifted the old man, who by this time was unable to walk steadily, onto his back and carried him several kilometres until they were approaching another village.

"Just outside the village, the son put his father down on the ground, saying, 'I'll just leave you here, Father. You are very near the village, and you can make your way there in your own time. You will find the villagers here very kind and they will take pity on you. Someone is sure to take you in, and you will get food and shelter. They will look after you, for they have the reputation here of being compassionate to helpless, old people.'

" 'You are leaving me here to beg, Son,' said the old man.

" 'Yes, Father, and I am very sorry,' said the son, 'but you can see I have no choice.' Then the son began to cry, and he put his arms round the father and held him close for several moments.

" 'It's all right, Son,' said the old man. 'Dry your tears. I understand and I forgive you. Good-bye, and God bless you.'

"So the son left his father sitting on the ground and slowly went away. When he came home, his wife was very pleased with what he had done, but he could not bring himself to speak to her for several days. Time went on, and the unpleasant business was eventually forgotten.

"The four children grew up, and the eldest son married and left the house. Then the two daughters found good husbands, and they too were settled in their new lives. The mother took ill and died, leaving her husband and the youngest son to look after themselves. All went well with them for a year or two. Then the son married, and he brought his pretty wife to live with him and his father.

"Soon they were blessed with twins, both boys, and as the years passed, times grew hard yet again, and the son's wife began complaining that the old man had become a burden as he was no longer fit to work. Food was scarce and they were barely able to exist. He would have to take the old man away somewhere. So the old man found himself one day being carried on his son's back and, as they made their way along the dusty white road, he recognised many spots where he himself had been obliged to rest when he carried his own father.

"Eventually he saw the village in the distance where he had abandoned his father, and there was the very spot where he had put him down on the ground. But his son kept walking and was about to pass the place when the father said, 'This is far enough. You can put me down here, Son.'

"'Oh no, Father,' said his son. 'I can carry you right into the village and arrange for you to stay with someone, for the people here are known to be kind.'

"'No, no, I insist that you put me down here, at this very spot,' said the old man.

"'But why do you wish to be put down here, Father?' asked the son.

"'Because this is the very place where I left your grandfather so many years ago,' said the old man, 'and now the circle is complete.'"

Assunta dried the tears from her eyes.

"Oh, Father," she said, "you can rest assured that Eugenio and I will never forsake you and Mother."

"I am well aware of that, Sunta," said Benedetto, "but your mother and I are going to miss you very much."

Then, seeing that his remark had brought the tears to her eyes again, he handed her a hoe and suggested they get back to work. Shortly afterwards when his hoe had struck a large stone, he turned it over and exclaimed, "This is as large as the stone of Monte Sacco."

"I've never heard of it," said Assunta.

"When my brother and I were quite young," said Benedetto, "we decided one day to climb Monte Sacco. When we came to a rocky spot, there was a huge stone lying in our path. As we came up to it, we could read some words that someone had inscribed on top of it. They read:

I AM THE STONE OF MONTE SACCO

and farther down in the same large letters

HAPPY WILL BE THE ONE WHO TURNS ME OVER.

Naturally we immediately thought of treasure or money, for, as you know, the brigands used to hide out in the caves of Monte Sacco, and they would often bury their hauls and mark the spot with a large stone.

"So we pushed and heaved at the stone until the perspiration dripped from our brows, and at last, with a mighty effort, we managed to turn the stone over. You can imagine our surprise when our eyes met another set of words on the underside reading:

NOW I HAVE BEEN TURNED, I CAN GO BACK TO SLEEP."

Assunta's eyes sparkled with merriment, and Benedetto was glad to see he had cast off the spell of sadness created by his previous story. She now took it upon herself to tell her father one of the stories she and Antonia had heard from Zia Rosa. It was supposed to have happened during Lent and concerned a shepherd they knew by the name of Nicola.

This boy had a weakness. He could not help lifting things and putting them in his bag, whether they belonged to him or not. Nicola lived in Cardido, but he did not like going to confession in his own village, preferring Filignano where the priests did not know him so well. When he came to Filignano just before Easter to make his confession, he was told, when he arrived at the church, that the priest was ill. So he went round to the priest's house and knocked on the door. It was answered by the housekeeper who told him don Alfonso was unwell and still in bed. Nicola explained he had come all the way from Cardido. She went upstairs and told the priest who agreed to hear the young man's confession in his room.

On the previous day, the housekeeper had removed dried sausages from the kitchen pulleys and had placed them in a basket under the priest's bed, as she had not had time to preserve them in pig's fat in large earthenware pots. She would do that when she had time.

Nicola, his shepherd's cape wrapped around him, was shown into Don Alfonso's bedroom. The priest bade him kneel by the bed and prepared to listen to his confession.

"Bless me, Father, for I have sinned," began Nicola, but he felt slightly nervous away from the shelter of the confessional where he was used to reciting his sins, and his hands began to wander under the bed and came upon the basket of sausages.

"I have had lustful thoughts six times. I swore at my mother ten times. I argued with my father eleven times," Nicola went on, and his right hand came upon a stick of sausages that had dried into a stiff hook at one end. So he slipped the hook over his left arm under the cape and continued: "And oh, Father, I stole some sausages. I had impure thoughts when I last looked at Maria Luisa, my older brother's young wife."

Then, having hooked another two sticks of sausages over his arm, he went on, "And oh, Father, I stole some more sausages."

The performance continued until he had hooked almost all the sausages over his arm, and each theft confessed was interspersed with his lustful longings for the pretty girls in Cardido. Then, when he had stolen the last of the sausages and his left arm was beginning to ache under their weight, Don Alfonso lost patience and remonstrated with him, "My son, stealing is a pernicious sin, and you keep telling me over and over again that you stole sausages. Why can't you tell me all at once how many sausages you actually stole and get it over with?"

"But, Father," said Nicola, "I just take them as they come!"

Then, since by this time his left arm was really painful, he finished his confession, leaving his right arm free to make the sign of the cross as he rose and left to recite his penance in church. His broad cape amply covered the stolen sausages, and the housekeeper did not appear to notice the increase in his bulk as she showed him out.

Shortly after the shepherd's departure, she went up to the priest's bedroom to fetch the basket. When she looked in and saw they had almost all disappeared, she began to scream, "The sausages, the sausages. What have you done with the sausages?"

Don Alfonso looked into the basket and said, "Ah, now I know why that scoundrel of a shepherd boy kept repeating that he stole sausages. Go to the church at once, for he should still be doing penance, and bring him back to me. I'll deal with him myself!"

But Nicola had decided he would recite his penance on the road back to Cardido, and he was already well on his way when the housekeeper looked into the empty church. Oddly enough, from that day Nicola preferred to go to confession in Cardido.

Benedetto smiled when Assunta had finished reciting her scandalous little story. The sun was beginning to set, and it was time for them to go home. They had completed the hoeing in one field, and Benedetto was satisfied that, in spite of all the talking they had done, their work had not been hindered by their tongues. So, Benedetto, who so rarely spoke, surpassed himself by telling Assunta yet another tale on their way home.

It concerned a young man who had fallen in love with a very beautiful girl called Iolanda. Each morning on his way to the joiner's shop where he worked, he would see her watering her geraniums at the window. Her family was well-to-do, and she was used to her little luxuries. When the young joiner, whose name was Carluccio, made bold to request her hand in marriage, Iolanda agreed to become his wife on condition that she would not have to do any housework. She just wanted to be a lady. Carluccio readily agreed, promising he would do all the chores himself before going to work. Moreover, he would do all the shopping and even the cooking. The young couple were duly married and moved into the joiner's charming little house.

Iolanda took her pet cat, Baldassare, with her to keep her company during the day when Carluccio was at work. So each morning Carluccio set out for work after kindling the fire, giving his wife her breakfast in bed, washing the dishes, and setting a *pignatta* of cabbage to cook slowly by the kitchen fire. He put a nice piece of lean ham in to flavour it and set the pot at the right distance from the embers where it could gurgle quietly all day, not requiring any attention from his young lady wife.

Now Iolanda was fond of needlework, and she liked to sit in the warm kitchen, sewing away as she hummed a little tune to herself, while the cabbage bubbled contentedly in the *pignatta*. One afternoon Baldassare padded quietly into the kitchen and, after sidling up to his mistress so that she could stroke him and give his ears a little scratch, turned his attention to the *pignatta* as he could smell the ham cooking in it.

Purring loudly to soothe his mistress, he went over to the fire, gingerly placed one paw on the rim of the *pignatta*, while with the other he knocked off the little metal lid. His lady mistress glanced at him and tut-tutted, but she made no attempt to move from her comfortable chair. Then Baldassare smartly thrust his paw into the *pignatta* for a mere fraction of a second so that he could not possibly be burned, and with admirable dexterity extracted the ham, which fell with a wet plop on to the tiles. The lady of the house followed his manoeuvre with one eye while keeping the other on her sewing.

At last the ham had cooled sufficiently, and the greedy cat quickly gobbled it. Then he sat on the warm tiles and grinned over at his mistress.

"Ah, Baldassare," she called out to him, "it's a good job for you that I am a lady and cannot stoop to certain menial tasks or I would be right over beside you and give you a good kick for what you have just done, you naughty pussy!"

Baldassare's *pignatta* recalled another and, without pausing, Benedetto went on to talk about it. The anecdote concerned the Valentes at the time when Domenico the tailor was making clothes for the whole family. It was the custom for the tailor to work at his client's house for a few days when a big order was involved so that the mistress of the house could see that the work was being done to her satisfaction. The tailor, naturally, ate with the family while he was there.

One morning Amalia Valente decided to have cabbage for the evening meal. She put a fair quantity of water into the *pignatta* after putting in the shredded cabbage leaves and the ham, and then she added a small handful of salt. Domenico observed her preparations as he sat by the kitchen window sewing. Amalia then went out to feed her hens and get on with other work outside. Then Amalia's husband, Antonio, came in, greeted Domenico, went over to the *pignatta*, lifted the lid, and put in a small handful of salt.

Domenico thought nothing of this and quietly went on with his work, his skilful needle neatly stitching the material in his hands. Antonio then went out. Shortly afterwards the daughter, Maria, came into the kitchen and, after drinking some water from the copper pitcher on the small table, she noticed the *pignatta* by the fire, went over to it, lifted it, and gave it a slight shake to mix up the contents. Then she put it down, lifted the lid, and put in a small quantity of salt.

This time Domenico began to wonder why they were all putting salt into the cooking cabbage.

Ah, he thought, *it must be some form of devotional ritual for a special intention. Oh well, since I am temporarily one of the family, I too might as well participate.*

He rose from his chair, put down his sewing, went over to the *pignatta,* gave it a slight shake and added his small handful of salt.

The rest of the day passed quietly, and at last Amalia and Maria came into the kitchen. Maria set the table while her mother took a large basin into which she put several slices of bread. Then, having placed the basin on the table, she took the *pignatta* from the fire and poured the contents over the bread. Antonio arrived with his two sons, and in no time they were all sitting round the table ready to tuck into the cabbage.

It was Antonio who was first to taste it and he let out an exclamation, "What's happened to the cabbage? This is a mess of salt!"

"But I only put in a small amount this morning," said Amalia.

"So did I!" said Antonio.

"And I!" said Maria.

And the apologetic voice of Domenico, who had not yet come to the table from his chair by the window, echoed, "Me too!"

"Do you mean to tell me," said Amalia, "that you watched us all putting salt into the *pignatta,* and, not only did you say nothing, but you then added some yourself?"

"But I thought you were all performing some kind of family devotion," said poor Domenico. So the salty cabbage was thrown out for the pigs, and they all had bread and cheese for supper.

Benedetto just managed to finish the cabbage story as he and Assunta arrived in front of the house. It was ajar and from the kitchen there wafted out the delicious smell of cooked cabbage!

"Good heavens!" exclaimed Benedetto, grinning at Assunta. "Let's hope your mother has not been performing devotions today or we shall be having bread and cheese for supper!"

Chapter Six

1915—Last Dreams in Filignano

For some reason Assunta found it difficult to go to sleep that night and when she did fall over, fitfully, she was a prey to the strangest dream. She seemed to be haunted by the people who figured in her mother's stories, many of whom Assunta had known when she was younger, and she saw them vividly and spoke with them. One in particular persisted—a sad young man called Peppino. His had been a tragic fate.

Peppino's father, Giacomo, had married three times. His first wife, Maria, had presented him with two daughters. When she died, shortly afterwards, he remarried and his second wife, Carmina, brought two boys into the world, the younger of whom was called Peppino. When Carmina, after a brief illness, also died, Giacomo married for a third time but his third wife, Nunziata, did not bear him any children.

As Peppino was only a child when his mother, Carmina, died, Nunziata took to the young boy and brought him up as if he was her very own. She saw to it that he was always well fed and cared for, scrupulously clean, and that he attended school regularly. He was very successful in his school work, being diligent, and endeared himself to the teacher because of his happy nature, often going about his tasks singing to himself. When he left school at twelve years of age, the teacher saw to it that he was apprenticed to a suitable trade.

Peppino decided he would be a cobbler. His employer, Renaldo, was very pleased with his young apprentice, for the lad showed an eager aptitude to learn his trade. Moreover, Peppino attracted many clients because of his cheerful disposition when he sat singing quietly to himself at his last.

The months and the years passed happily for Peppino, and he had taken to composing his own melodies while he sat each day making his shoes and boots. He hummed the tunes over and over again. It then occurred to him that he should purchase a musical instrument. The one that most appealed to him was the clarinet.

So Renaldo gave him some time off and the lad, now sixteen years of age, went to Naples and bought a fine clarinet. He came back full of the joys of life and brimming over with new music, for he had already been practising on the instrument on the charabanc bringing him from Venafro to Filignano. Peppino was obviously going to be a great composer. He learned to read music and was soon able to write down the tunes coming into his head while he worked. His clarinet lay on the small table beside his last. He would swing around, carefully pick up the instrument, and play some new melody.

Many of the lads of the village who were musically inclined began to cluster round Peppino. Some played the cornet, others the trumpet or the trombone or the accordion. There were several flautists and drummers, and two of them could play the violin. Encouraged by Peppino and his new music, they formed a small orchestra of about twenty players, and in the summer evenings they would gather on the loggia at Peppino's house and practise until the sun went down. No one objected to the fine music as it echoed down the hill to the piazza.

And it was indeed in the piazza on the Feast of the Madonna on the eighth of September that Peppino and his orchestra played in public for the first time, exciting the eager admiration and spirited applause of the people of Filignano who were utterly delighted to have their own orchestra. Peppino announced the melody he had composed for the occasion on his clarinet and, as the other instruments took up the theme, the Filignanesi heard such mellifluously enchanting sounds as they had never before encountered in their lives. They marvelled at the gay tunes in waltz time setting their feet a-tapping and soon most off them were dancing by the large lime tree that offered its cooling shade on the brilliant, hot day.

Then the tempo altered as Peppino intoned a plaintive little tune that swelled gradually into a warm, passionate air, expressing the sheer joy of living and the warm-blooded, heady enthusiasm of youth. Yet within it there was just a hint of sadness, enough to infer a bitter-sweetness evoking the sympathy of the young people who recognised in it the mysterious nuances of their own yearning, while it simultaneously struck warm chords of nostalgia in the hearts of their parents and grandparents. A wondering, almost incredulous witness to her stepson's artistic success on this splendid occasion, Nunziata shed tears of pride and joy.

The fame of Peppino's orchestra spread rapidly among the surrounding towns and villages. They found themselves playing at *festas* in Venafro, Montaquila, San Biagio, and Monterotondo. The volume of Peppino's musical compositions grew as he felt inspired to write something new, and he was happy in his fulfilment. Apart from the great satisfaction he derived from expressing himself in his music, he was now earning good money, which he gave willingly to Nunziata to compensate her for all she had done for him in the past. Yet, ironically, it was through Nunziata that his rapture was to be of brief duration.

One day she was going to work in the fields some distance from home, and she asked Peppino if he would be good enough, when he came back from work, to bring in the hens, as it would probably be dark by the time she returned to make the supper. In the late afternoon, when Peppino came home, he took out his clarinet and began to compose. He liked to sit on the loggia in the shade of the fig tree. From there he could see the hens pecking contentedly near the house. As the sun began to set, he remembered he had to gather them in, so he put away his clarinet and his music sheets and went down to the road.

Some of the hens had wandered up a few of the pebble-covered steps, and Peppino went up to shoo them down to the yard where he would guide them into the henhouse beside the pen. He walked softly past them, taking care not to frighten them and as he came round behind them, he raised his arms and stamped his feet lightly on the ground to urge them forward and down. But as he came to the edge of a step, his right heel slipped. He lost his balance and came down with a dull thud, the bottom of his spine receiving a sharp, jarring jab as it struck the keen, hard rim of the step.

Peppino felt a fierce spasm of pain shooting up his spine, and he let out an anguished cry that sent the chickens fluttering down to the yard in front of the house. Then he gingerly drew himself up until he was sitting on the step. Leaning forward he rubbed the bottom of his spine with his right hand, but the acute throbbing of the pain brought tears to his eyes to his bewildered shame. Then, when he tried to rise, his legs would not hold him and he fell back. He sat there in agony until it was almost dark when Nunziata, climbing the road to the house, was puzzled to see him in the distance sitting on the step while her hens were still wandering around the front of the house.

With his stepmother's help, Peppino managed to hobble painfully into the house. When Giacomo returned, she sent him at once to fetch the doctor. It took the doctor an hour to come as he had not finished his supper when Giacomo called. He gave Peppino an injection to ease the pain and advised him to stay in bed for a few days. But the weeks passed, and still Peppino was unable to rise from his bed, although the pain was not so acute. The doctor advised he should be taken to Naples to be examined by a specialist.

The journey was very sore on poor Peppino as he was shaken and jolted in the charabanc. He was so worn out by the time he saw the specialist that this worthy gentleman arranged for him to spend the night in hospital after his medical examination. The consultant's diagnosis was not favourable. Peppino should have been sent to him months before. Now complications had set in, and the professor could not see any hope for a cure. Peppino might show slight signs of improvement for a time, but the severe inflammation at the base of the spine would recur. Peppino pled with the professor to perform an operation, but it was unsuccessful. The poor young man was brought home in a litter and carried up to his bedroom.

Giacomo moved his bed up to the window so that he might look out and enjoy the passing of the seasons. Peppino was not downhearted. Nunziata nursed him with motherly affection, and his friends who had played in the orchestra came to visit him frequently. They talked of him getting better soon so that they would all play together again. Peppino would look at them and smile with a faraway expression in his eyes whenever they mentioned the word "orchestra," and he would nod his head from side to side.

As time passed, many of his friends moved away to play in bands throughout the region. Some of them had given up their trades to play in Peppino's orchestra and, having sampled the pleasure of a professional life, were unwilling to go back to being joiners, builders, or labourers.

One morning Peppino asked Nunziata to bring his clarinet and place it on the table by his bed. For a few days, he did not touch it. He would just eye it wistfully and sigh. But one evening as Nunziata was coming down the hill to the house carrying water from the well, she heard Peppino's clarinet in the distance. The sad air he was playing described the desolation in his heart. Nunziata knew then that so long as he played alone in his room, he would continue to be dejected. She spoke to one or two of his musician friends who had gone back to their trades in Filignano after Peppino's accident and, in the evenings after work, they gathered often in his room, bringing their instruments and trying to cheer him up by playing his best melodies.

So summer and autumn passed and when winter came, Peppino's window had to be closed to keep out the biting, icy winds and the stormy rain. At last came spring to bring him new hope and his window was opened to welcome the sunshine, the fragrance of the blossoms, and the singing of the birds that entranced him in the early hours of the dawn as he lay awake. Peppino began to improve though he could not rise from his bed, and each day the sound of his clarinet grew stronger. Now and then he would compose a new melody and write it down. Soon the table by his bed was weighed down with new works.

The bright spring welcomed a radiant summer and during the long hours when he was alone in his room, Peppino conferred with nature's elements through his open window. The birds came to know his music and when he played a new motif, they would join in, adding their own trilling variations to Peppino's theme. He now realized happily that he had found another orchestra, and they played to appreciative audiences of old people, too wearied with age to work, sitting on their doorsteps, charmed by the delightful sounds drifting over the gulley from Peppino's window and the trees nearby where his feathered instrumentalists sang of the joys of sunshine and blue skies, of wheat ripening in the fields, and fruit swelling on the trees.

As the summer passed, Peppino felt more fulfilled than ever before, and his happiness was reflected in his eyes despite the angry pains he had begun to feel again ever since the first brown leaf, blown lightly through his window to land gracefully on the white lace cover of his bed, came to proclaim the coming of autumn. One evening young Assunta, coming home laden with her usual large bundle of twigs, paused in her tracks when she heard Peppino's clarinet on the other side of the gulley that separated Imperatore from the western slope of the village.

"This is my last song," the tune seemed to be saying, "and I am resigned to my awful fate, for I know I shall not see the spring again." The birds outside Peppino's window had hushed their strains to a low warbling.

Peppino put down his clarinet and sighed. Nunziata brought his supper, but he could not eat. She called Giacomo and they set chairs by the bed and sat with him. He looked at them and smiled weakly. Then he spoke in a surprisingly firm voice.

"Dear Father, dear Mother, you know that my time is running out. I have a favour to ask of you. When you put me in my coffin, I wish to have my clarinet with me, by my side. I also want all the music I have written to be buried with me, for I want to take everything I have created with me. I hope you don't mind, but this is something I have to do. I want you to know how much I love you both for all you have done for me. Now you must grant my last wish so that I can die happy."

Peppino died in the early hours of the following morning. His clarinet and all his musical compositions were buried with him, just as he had requested. There was no music at his funeral, for no one could match the music he was taking with him.

Assunta awoke crying. In her dream she had heard Peppino's last song. Now she lay back and asked herself why he had wanted to take all his music with him. Everyone had wondered about this. Stranger still, although many had enjoyed his fine melodies, no one could actually remember them now, though only a few years had elapsed since his untimely death. A moment before she had really heard his song in her dream. Now she was awake, the tune eluded her. Then the answer to the mystery suddenly came to her. Peppino's music was not really of this world. It belonged to another. Those privileged to hear it had been granted a moment of the bliss awaiting us beyond this life. This was the explanation. Comforted by her discovery, Assunta drifted back into sleep.

Through a pink mist, she saw herself when she was a very young girl hurrying to church to hear the result of the Christmas lottery. Each year a fine crib was offered, an enchanting object that would be a credit to the house of the girl fortunate enough to win it. The infant Jesus lay in the manger watched over by Mary and Joseph. Around them were the animals and in the dark-blue sky painted above the stable shone the bright star to guide the Three Wise Men with gifts for the Holy Child.

Assunta was kneeling expectantly at the back of the church when don Alfonso made the important announcement.

"This year the Christmas Child will go to the house of . . . " and he paused, looking round at the sea of eager little faces. As he continued to speak, Assunta knew he was going to call out her name just a second before he said, "the house of signorina Assunta Marzella."

She was utterly delighted by the great privilege and conscious of the envious glances of her young friends. At the end of the service, the priest came up to her and handed over the precious crib. Antonia helped to carry it home, and her parents were overjoyed when they arrived. A space was made on the shelf in the niche on the landing of the staircase leading upstairs to Assunta's bedroom. There the crib was arranged so that the Holy Child, His parents, and the animals could be seen to advantage. Benedetto cut some straw into tiny pieces and placed it along the front. Filomena hung a little oil lamp on a hook at one side of the niche, the bright silver star in the blue sky glimmering as it reflected the flame of the lamp.

Then Benedetto decided to make a special case that would house the entire scene. After taking measurements he decided it would be better to entrust the making of the case to a proper craftsman. So he went to Emilio the joiner, and two days later a fine case with a smooth, glass panel in the front was delivered. A little door at the back opened on hinges, and through it the figures and pieces could be placed inside. Benedetto made another small stable and placed it on one side of the case. Two small toy horses occupied it. On the other side of the case, he constructed a small stall to accommodate the cow. Then he hung the blue-sky background with the star above the new case, creating an impressive dimension behind it. Candles were fixed on either side of the niche, replacing the oil lamp, and when they were lit, the whole scene glowed.

When Filomena's mother, Nonna Vittoria, called, she was entranced by the splendid crib her granddaughter had won in the Christmas lottery. She went down on her knees in front of it and prayed to the Holy Child. After her first visit, she kept returning every day to spend some time praying before the crib. When she had finished her prayers, she would gaze with pride upon the infant Jesus and say in her quivering sing-song voice, "Oh, the Holy Child, the Holy Child has come to the house of my little granddaughter Assunta." And she would repeat the words over and over again in a shaky voice that betrayed her reverent emotion. Filomena would then call her down to have something to eat.

After her meal she would rise from the table and make her way slowly back to the crib. This time she would not kneel and pray but look at it and repeat, "Oh, the Holy Child, the Holy Child has come to the house of my little granddaughter Assunta." Then she would lean forward and kiss the glass panel, crossing herself before turning to come down the steps. This was the only time in her life that Assunta won a lottery. She heard Nonna Vittoria's voice echoing "The Holy Child" into the distance of a happy time that was past as she slowly awoke to Crestone's call.

Chapter Seven

1915—The Journey to Glasgow

The time for Assunta's departure for Glasgow was imminent. She viewed the prospect of her journey with a mixture of eager anticipation and uneasy apprehension. Going about her tasks in the house or outside, she paused frequently to linger over objects or features that in some particular manner appealed to her. She was imprinting on her memory the whole setting of her home so that she could picture it fully when she thought about it in Scotland.

Assunta was endowed with an aesthetic susceptibility that fed on the vivid impressions her keen eye perceived. She was sensitive to the beauty surrounding her. Her eye registered the subtly varying colours in the patterns of the landscape while her ear was open to the natural music emanating from it in its different moods. Each season brought its own sounds and hues, and Assunta readily absorbed their configurations. They became a part of her inner being and whenever she tried to envisage places still unknown to her, she relied upon them as points of reference.

Eugenio had described the Scottish landscape, yet, in her mind's eye, she imagined its hills to be similar to those of Filignano but covered in pink-and-white heather, for her brother had brought her two sprigs of the lovely shrub, one pink and the other white, and she had treasured them in a small vase in her bedroom. She could not really imagine what Glasgow was like. The only city she had ever visited was Naples. Eugenio told her the buildings in Glasgow were darker and higher. It was, according to him, a very noisy place.

One evening as Filomena was preparing supper in the kitchen, Assunta was dusting in her parents' bedroom. She put down the cloth and stepped on to the balcony to look down on the village. The sounds of activity came up to her, and she inhaled the homely fragrance of the woodsmoke drifting up from the chimneys. Down in the piazza, noisy urchins were playing and their shrill voices rent the air with piercing cries. Behind their youthful clamour, Assunta could hear the steady, rhythmical whining of the joiner's saw, then the banging of his hammer as it struck the nail heads. The old women sitting round the base of the lime tree were gossiping or praying and their murmuring voices mingled with the tones and vibrations that hung suspended in the evening air. On the right from some house came the whimpering of a child while from the left in the far distance of Collemacchia she could hear the faint tinkling of sheep's bells.

She leaned heavily on the iron rail of the balcony and began slowly to sway from side to side as a simple melody Filomena had taught her when she was very little rose to her lips. She hummed it softly, and it awakened a whole stream of memories filling her with the sheer joy of being alive. As she intoned the little tune, she stepped back into the bedroom, breathing in its many evocative odours. In the far corner was her mother's large wooden chest filled with the good wheat grain in which she liked to preserve her eggs. Assunta went over and lifted the heavy lid. She ran her fingers through the grain, enjoying the sensation of the hard, cool smoothness of the little seeds as they trickled across the palm of her hand. The earthy aroma of the wheat recalled the autumn harvest days when they all worked feverishly under a blazing sun.

As she closed the lid of the chest, she became aware of a different perfume. Filomena kept her dried vegetables and fruit on large wooden trays supported by trestles. There were raisins, figs, prunes, and dried marrow rings laid side by side, mingling their musty smells. Above the trays hung two large garlands of spicy hot peppers. Their prickly, pungent scent made Assunta sneeze, interrupting her tune. Then Filomena called out from the kitchen. Supper was ready.

Antonia arrived after supper to accompany Assunta and her mother to the evening service of benediction. The girls linked arms as they walked down the cobbled road to the piazza while Filomena followed at a slight distance, envious of the youthful spring in their step as they skilfully avoided tripping over the loose stones. There were no seats in the church, only unanchored chairs and when the members of the congregation were not sitting on them, they would kneel on the slabbed floor, using the seats as elbow rests. Assunta's thoughts strayed during the service, and her eyes fell on a large broad flagstone that had once been the entrance to a crypt beneath the church. As she recalled the circumstances in which the crypt had been sealed, she shuddered.

Many years before, a plague had raged in Filignano. It was the dreaded cholera that mowed down the villagers, so many, in fact, that it became impossible to bury them in individual graves. So communal graves were dug in the cemetery, but eventually the Filignanesi could not cope with the speed with which the horrible disease claimed its victims. So the crypt under the church was opened and the bodies, just as they were, without winding sheets, were thrown into its depths. The stench rising from the place was abominable, and large bucketfuls of lime and phenol were poured in. When the bodies were still warm, they were quickly carried to the church and dropped through the square hole into the dark crypt. At the end of the day, the heavy flagstone was pulled across to seal in the foul odours.

When the epidemic was raging at its worst, many poor people were lowered into the crypt before they had actually expired. A young girl, who had been the last to be placed there one evening, must have revived after the sealing stone had been pushed into place. She instinctively took off her apron and rolled it into a head mat. Then, placing it on her head, she clambered to the top of the heap of corpses and tried hard to push up the slab. The space between it and the mound of bodies was so small that she was forced to squat. In vain did she try to push the stone up. Overcome by the stench of putrefaction and the fumes from the lime and phenol, she swooned and died. On the next day, when the slab was lifted to deposit more bodies, the poor girl was discovered immediately beneath the stone, wedged in her squatting position with the rolled apron still on her head. The priest was so horrified when he learned of the girl's dreadful ordeal that he had the crypt sealed immediately and forbade further burials in the church.

A young girl had been cut off at the very threshold of her life in pitifully gruesome circumstances. Now, so many years later, Assunta was about to find a new life in a strange land. Her lips formed a prayer of gratitude. Then she prayed that God would protect her on her long journey and bless her dear parents and Antonia.

When they came home, Benedetto had already retired for the night as he had worked a long and weary day. Antonia decided to go home and, as she was about to leave, she spontaneously threw her arms round Assunta and gave her an affectionate hug. Then Filomena decided she too would go to bed. Assunta sat for a short time at the fire, stirring the embers with the long metal blower. Then she made her way upstairs and, after a further brief prayer, slipped into bed. She fell asleep but some time later she stirred, feeling another presence in her bedroom.

The blue light of the moon filtered in through the curtains outlining Filomena's silhouette as she sat quietly on a chair at the foot of the bed. Assunta's head on the pillow was in the shadowed part of the room, and Filomena did not see her daughter's eyes opening for an instant before she closed them again. Assunta could hear her mother's whispering voice reciting the Our Fathers and Hail Marys of the Rosary, which, for once, had not been said at the fireside downstairs. The whispering ended, and Assunta lay with her eyes closed, breathing regularly to simulate sleep. She heard her mother rise and quietly replace the chair in the corner of the room. Then she came close to the bed and stood for a while, looking down at her daughter. Assunta could feel her mother's protecting aura slowly enveloping her and she succumbed to the comforting sensation. She fell fast asleep unaware of the moment when Filomena left the room.

In the early hours of the morning, Assunta was rudely awakened by a deep rumbling that seemed to be coming from the very depths of the earth. Her bed rattled and the whole house vibrated. The air seemed to be charged with an unnatural heat, the atmosphere heavy and stifling. By the time she leapt out of bed and ran barefooted downstairs, the noise subsided. She met Filomena and Benedetto in the kitchen, and they were just as scared as she was. They heard cries outside.

"Terremoto! Terremoto! Earthquake! Earthquake!" But by this time all seemed normal, and the house stood steady as a rock. They dressed quickly and went outside to look around. The wall of the outhouse they used as a cellar at the opposite end of the small courtyard had shed some of its plaster, and it lay in a dusty heap at the base, but the wall itself was intact.

People were swarming all over the place and calling out to one another to exchange impressions, but the houses were undamaged and soon they all disappeared indoors. Later that day they heard that a little town near Rome had been badly damaged by the earth tremor.

Benedetto had arranged for Assunta to travel in the company of Celestina Coia who, with her two young boys, Mario and Pascalino, was going to rejoin her husband, Giuseppe, in Glasgow. In the afternoon Assunta, accompanied by Antonia, walked to Collemacchia and visited Celestina to confirm the arrangments for their early morning departure on the following day. As Celestina would have had to walk from Collemacchia to the piazza in Filignano with her boys and her luggage, Assunta and Antonia offered to take her two large cases and deposit them for the night with her sister, who lived near the piazza. The girls' offer was gratefully accepted, and soon they were on their way to Filignano balancing the heavy suitcases on their heads.

The rest of the day was spent in packing Assunta's own luggage, and Filomena saw to it that every square centimetre of space was used. She put all the foodstuffs into a single case, a leg of ham, a bag of maize, dried figs, homemade sausages, black puddings, goat's milk cheese, and three freshly baked loaves of bread. Eugenio loved his mother's bread, and she knew he would think of her when eating it. Benedetto did not go out that day but sat dejectedly on the double logs outside the wine cellar while Filomena, Assunta, and Antonia bustled to and fro.

The hours passed quickly, and soon they were all sitting round the supper table enjoying a meal of cabbage and beans. When the dishes were cleared away, they sat round the fire. Assunta and Antonia excitedly discussed the journey that would start next day, and Assunta promised she would write a detailed description of the trip when she arrived in Glasgow. When they came to recite the rosary, their voices were charged with emotion as they made the responses. Soon it was time to say goodnight. Antonia went home and Assunta made her way upstairs to sleep for the last time in her little chaff-mattress bed.

It seemed she had barely closed her eyes when she was awakened by Crestone. She got up smartly, and Filomena had already heated a large pot of water for her to have a good wash before putting on her clothes. She wore a warm, brown skirt and over it a blue, long-sleeved blouse under a traditional black-velvet bodice. Filomena had embroidered a lovely blue headscarf for her daughter, and from her old clothes chest she drew out a fine, white woollen shawl. When Assunta was dressed, her warm, brown stockings and silver-buckled black leather shoes completed the picture of a beautiful young *contadina* in her Sunday best.

When the church bell was ringing matins, Assunta stepped out of the house followed closely by her parents. By the time Antonia appeared to help carry the luggage, Assunta had already said good-bye to Chiaruccia the goat and Piccirella the donkey in their pens. The neighbours came to their doors. Some waved and called out their good-byes wishing Assunta well, while some of the older women ran out to embrace her, their loud kisses resounding as they smacked Assunta's cheeks. Then something extraordinary happened as the group made its way down to the piazza.

Doors opened and young girls, all friends of Assunta and Antonia, joined them. By the time they arrived at the piazza, there must have been fifty of them and there were still others awaiting outside the small Municipio. The horse-drawn charabanc was already standing there, and Celestina was with her two boys and some relatives.

Assunta felt an odd tugging at her heart and her excitement rose. Her eyes blurred with tears, and she had to dab them with her handkerchief. Filomena held on to her daughter's arm as if she could not let her go. With the cases deposited in the charabanc, the moment of departure came all too soon. Assunta kissed Antonia, then she embraced Benedetto who stood silently, never speaking. Filomena blessed her daughter. Then, overcome by her grief, she clung to Assunta and wept. It was Benedetto who gently separated them and, taking his daughter by the arm, led her to the charabanc. The vehicle moved away as Assunta and Celestina, Mario and Pascalino looked back at the large crowd of weeping friends who slowly receded into the distance. When the charabanc turned the corner of the road, Assunta caught a last, fleeting glimpse of Filomena, a small, dark, sad little figure pitifully fluttering her handkerchief in farewell.

When they arrived at Venafro, they were met at the station by Celestina's friend Signor Grimaldi. He had been on holiday for a few weeks and would be travelling with them to Glasgow where he had his business. He smiled reassuringly when Celestina introduced Assunta, and she was comforted by the thought that they would have an experienced guide on their journey.

Soon they were on the train, and Signor Grimaldi lifted their luggage on to the high racks in the compartment. Assunta wondered at the narrowness of the racks fearing that, at the first sharp bend, the cases would come tumbling down on them. As the train gathered speed, she marvelled at the rapidly changing scenes speeding past her eyes. It was an exhilarating experience, and it helped to distract her thoughts from the sadness of leaving her parents and Antonia.

When they arrived in Naples, the train sat for twenty minutes in the busy station. Assunta was astonished by the vastness of the place. The constant coming and going of large numbers of people on the platform, well-dressed ladies and gentlemen, peasants, soldiers in uniforms, railway officials, vendors wheeling their trolleys laden with rolls, fruit, and large twin metal urns from which they served cups of hot coffee. Signor Grimaldi left the train to purchase rolls and coffee for his travelling companions and handed them up through the compartment window. When he joined them with his own cup in his hand, Assunta took the small bag in which she was carrying her money and her papers and offered to pay for her share of the breakfast, but Signor Grimaldi would not hear of such a thing and Assunta, embarrassed by his kindness, thanked him profusely.

When they finished eating, she collected the cups from them and bravely got off the train and took them back to the trolley. All the time she was on the platform, she was scared that the train would suddenly move away and leave her behind and she raced up the steps when she returned to the carriage. As the train set off again, Assunta whispered to Celestina that she was needing to go to the toilet. She had heard there were conveniences on trains but had no idea where to go. Celestina warned her boys to behave, then beckoned to Assunta to follow her.

In the corridor they were unsteady on their feet as the train swayed and lurched. As the toilet was very small, Celestina went in first while Assunta waited, holding onto the window rail. Then Celestina opened the door for Assunta and showed her in. Assunta was a little dismayed by the noise and reverberation in the tiny compartment, but her need was by this time desperate and as she sat she was reminded of the jogging that had shaken her all over when she had ridden on a mule from Filignano to Santa Maria Oliveto. The little adventure being over, the ladies made their way back to the compartment where Signor Grimaldi was reading a newspaper and the boys had fallen asleep.

At noon they came to the outskirts of Rome, and again Assunta was astonished by the beauty of the fine buildings that swept past. But when the train drew into the immense station, a sad scene met their eyes. The platforms were crammed with refugees from the town that had been partly destroyed by the earthquake on the previous day. Assunta was very moved to see these poor people clinging to the little that was left of their personal belongings. Women carried babies while their husbands had bundles slung over their shoulders and suitcases in their hands. Old ladies were squatting on the ground, weeping silently over their lost homes.

A guard came on to the train to announce that there would be a considerable delay because of the disaster. Passengers for the north would have to alight and wait for further instructions. So they gathered all their luggage and joined the hordes of homeless people on the platform. Since it was very early in the afternoon, Signor Grimaldi suggested they could deposit their cases in the left-luggage office and take a short stroll in the city, but neither Celestina nor Assunta were very keen to accept this suggestion. They imagined a train would arrive miraculously at any moment to permit them to proceed on their journey.

But their hopes were frustrated, and they spent the rest of the day and the following night in the station. Assunta, so used to getting out and about, found the long wait tedious and exhausting. The little group sat despondently on their cases, dozing occasionally, but ready to hear the announcement of their departure. Signor Grimaldi, a charming man, did his best to uphold the morale of the travellers, joking with the boys and teasing Assunta for wearing her traditional clothes for the journey.

The morning wore on, and they had breakfast in the station. Many of the displaced people had now gone, and the station was becoming less congested. At last an announcement appeared on the large notice board stating that the train for the north would leave at noon. Soon the train drew in, and they gathered their luggage again.

Once on their way, Assunta took time to enjoy the varying landscapes through which they were speeding, and she could not stop marvelling at the sheer beauty of the scenery.

My country must be the most beautiful in the world, she thought, as she looked out. She caught fleeting glimpses of Pisa and Florence, cities she had obviously heard of but never seen, and now her ear informed her that the Italian spoken by the passengers who came on to the train at these places was very refined. This was the language she had studied in school, and Signor Grimaldi and Celestina were rather amused to notice, as they proceeded northwards, that Assunta's accent was becoming ever more cultivated. She was a natural mimic and could not resist imitating the pronunciation and intonation of the speech of these northerners.

Leaving Milan and Turin behind them, the landscape became more rugged and high mountains loomed around them. The train climbed higher and higher, and they drew in to the frontier town of Modane. Assunta had fallen into a light sleep, exhausted by the vastness of the world racing past the train window. When the train lurched to a stop, the jolt brought her back to wakeful reality. The door at the far end of the corridor was opened and a voice called out, "*Passeports, passaporti,* passports!"

Signor Grimaldi told the women to bring out their passports for inspection, and they sat waiting as the customs officers made their way slowly along the passage, stopping at each compartment. When they came to theirs, Assunta knew at once they were not Italians, recognising the nasal sound of the French language she had often heard spoken by Filignanesi home from Paris on holiday.

The customs officers looked at Signor Grimaldi's passport and found it to be in order. Next they examined Assunta's and politely returned it. When they came to inspect Celestina's, one of the men frowned, shook his head, and then told her that it was not in order. Signor Grimaldi, who knew a little French, intervened and, after exchanging a few words with the officer, turned to Celestina and explained that her passport had not been properly stamped by the Italian Consul in Rome when it had been issued a few weeks before. The date of issue did not appear. In these circumstances there was nothing for it but to return to Rome.

Celestina's eyes opened wide when she heard this pronouncement.

She put her hands to her head and began to cry, "Back to Rome? Back to Rome!"

Then, turning to the customs officers, she addressed them in Italian, "Back to Rome? Back to Rome! But *who* is going to take us back to Rome?"

At this the tiny voice of Pascalino, who was sitting in a corner, piped up, "The lame chicken!"

At this unexpected solution to the problem, borrowed from a child's nursery rhyme, Celestina, Assunta, and Signor Grimaldi burst into nervous laughter. The Frenchman, intrigued by the sudden change of mood, turned to Signor Grimaldi and asked him to translate. When he told the officer what the boy had replied to his mother's frenzied question, he and his fellow officer began to laugh. He took the passport away and returned shortly afterwards, saying he had taken the liberty of date-stamping the passport himself. So they did not have to rely on the services of the lame chicken after all and continued on their journey.

Their passage across France seemed interminable, and the small company of travellers became wearier and wearier. The children became very listless, and Assunta spent a great deal of time telling them stories and playing guessing games with them. As Assunta talked, Mario would sit and listen with wide-open eyes, while Pascalino, who had taken to sitting snugly on her lap, would gradually close his eyes and drift off to sleep. The train stopped frequently and once in the middle of the night, Assunta fancied she heard thunder in the distance. Signor Grimaldi told her it was more likely to be gunfire.

They arrived in Paris on a cold, grey morning, and the buildings they saw seemed dull and drab compared with those in Italy. Assunta found it hard to attune her ear to the nasal, throaty sounds of the French language. But there was one thing she liked in Paris—the wonderful coffee and the light, crisp croissants they bought from the station trolley. She tried quite unsuccessfully to pronounce the word "croissant."

On the journey from Paris to Calais, Signor Grimaldi tried to teach the ladies some useful phrases in English to prepare them for their arrival in Britain. Assunta felt she had a potato in her mouth when she found herself repeating, "Good morning! Pleased to meet you! I do not yet speak English. Yes, please? No, the boss is not in!" and other indispensably useful phrases that Signor Grimaldi pronounced in random, inconsequential order. As a result of this well-intended but rather impractical method, Assunta was later to find herself in some rather embarrassing situations. But if they served no other serious purpose, the English lessons did help to while away the tedium of the journey.

They arrived in Calais in the late afternoon. There Assunta was obliged to part with her luggage for the first time. Her suitcases were entrusted to a French porter who gave her a numbered metal disk by which she would recognize him by the same number on his cap once on board the ship.

This was the most exciting moment of the journey for Assunta, Celestina and the children, for they had never before in their lives been on a boat. Assunta remarked upon the dark grey of the sea water. In Naples the Mediterranean had been bright blue. Amidst the hustle and bustle on deck, they finally found their luggage and paid the porters who politely tipped their caps. The sea was reasonably calm, and Assunta enjoyed the sharp tang of the sea air in her nostrils. The slight roll of the boat was comforting. They went below to the toilets but were nauseated by the smell of food and beer being served in the dining room.

They hastened back on deck to enjoy the freshness of the ozone and the spray rising from the sea as the boat cut through the water to the heavy throbbing of the engines below. Assunta was astounded at the vastness of the waters. She had imagined it all quite differently when she heard it described as The Channel. Nearly an hour later, Signor Grimaldi pointed to the famous cliffs of Dover. Their chalky-grey outlines came nearer and nearer, and soon they were in Dover.

Now Assunta heard English being spoken all around her as porters swarmed on to the boat to collect luggage. Again they went through the ritual of numbered metal disks. When they stepped on to the gang-way to disembark, Assunta began to sway slightly. At the bottom of the gangway, when she took her first step on to the firm soil of England, it seemed to roll beneath her so that she was obliged to take Celestina's arm to steady herself. At that moment she felt she had severed the last connection with Filignano. This was a different ground she was treading upon, separated from the continent of Europe by a vast expanse of grey water.

The porters brought their cases to the customs shed where they were asked to open them for inspection. When Assunta revealed the foodstuffs carefully packed by Filomena, the strong odour of cheese was too much for the officer, and he quickly closed the case and marked it with a white cross in chalk. The train now waiting for them seemed small in comparison with the one upon which they had travelled from Rome. The luggage racks seemed even more precarious. Then Assunta began to feel embarrassed by the curious glances that her clothes excited among their fellow passengers.

There were two young soldiers sitting opposite who could not keep their eyes away from her. She decided they should be put in their place. When she and Celestina rose to go to the toilet, she looked at them as she passed and said loudly, "No, the boss is not in!"

The poor soldiers were quite bewildered by her words but there was no mistaking the menacing tone in which they were uttered. When the ladies returned to the compartment, the soldiers had disappeared.

As they journeyed on to London, Assunta took a good look at the English landscape. The grass seemed greener, but the sky was overcast and soon it began to rain. The steady patter of the raindrops on the window and the quiet rhythm of the train in motion made her drowsy and she was roused by an English voice calling out. "London, Victoria! London, Victoria!"

From Victoria they took a cab to Euston to catch the London-Glasgow train and, although the taxi journey was not long, Assunta took time to admire the broad London streets. They drove past a large imposing palace, and signor Grimaldi told them it was the residence of the royal family. By the time they were seated in the train at Euston, it was early evening. They were early and had the whole compartment to themselves but as the evening wore on, the train became crowded and by the time they departed, passengers were standing in the corridor. Signor Grimaldi had bought rolls and sandwiches. Assunta found these somewhat tasteless. They seemed very white and doughy, though she liked the flavour of the cheese filling.

As the blinds had been drawn, they had no chance to see the London suburbs. They settled down in their seats for the night and fell asleep, awakening when the train stopped briefly at the various stations on the route. Then, early in the morning, Assunta was awakened by Celestina to be told they were now in Scotland. Since the lights had been extinguished, the blinds had been raised and Assunta looked out on the vague outlines of the countryside through which they were passing. She caught her breath when she realized that very soon she would see Eugenio and Giulietta.

Her eyes looked in vain to see the hills covered with pink-and-white heather. The land was flat, and here and there she could see cows grazing in green fields and curiously long-shaped farmhouses with grey-slated roofs. What struck her most was the apparent colourlessness of the buildings that appeared when the countryside gave way to the blotted, ravished setting of industrial Lanarkshire with its dark bings. Smoke rose into the air all around them, and the flaming furnaces of the foundries lit the darkly clouded sky with crimson tints. It was a very dramatic spectacle.

At last the train began to slow down as it approached the bridge over the Clyde and drew into Glasgow Central Station. They took down their luggage and stood ready to alight when the train stopped. As they had been at the back of the train, when they stepped on to the platform, the ticket barrier seemed a mile away. Porters offered to carry their cases, but they were disregarded. Assunta forgot the presence of her fellow travellers as she looked eagerly ahead, trying to see Eugenio. They surrendered their tickets and passed through the gate into the main area of the station where the overpowering noise assailing their ears was almost unbearable, for the train had been full and the clamour of the passengers' voices mingling with the puffing and hissing of the locomotives created a veritable cacophony. Assunta's heart began to pound as she looked round in vain to see Eugenio and Giulietta.

Then, as she stopped to put down her heavy cases, she felt a light tap on her shoulder and, turning round, suddenly felt her brother's arms around her. He kissed her warmly on both cheeks before handing her over to Giulietta. By this time Celestina had also found her husband and signor Grimaldi, his wife, and his son. This emotionally moved group of people standing in the centre of the station formed a small island of joy amidst the swarming tides of travellers hurrying past.

When Assunta had said good-bye to signor Grimaldi, Celestina, and the children, Eugenio took her cases and led the way to the tram stop in Union Street. She could not take her eyes off her brother and her sister-in-law. How smart he looked in his city clothes and how elegant Giulietta was in her beautiful hat adorned with feathers. Vehicles were passing to and fro on the busy road while the trams rumbled past. The pavements were crowded with people going to work, most of them women of all ages. When their tram arrived, Giulietta took Assunta by the arm while Eugenio lifted the cases and put them on a broad shelf on the rear platform. There were only two long rows of seats on the bottom deck of the tram, and passengers sat facing one another.

Giulietta chatted away in Filignanese, asking for news from home. Eugenio sat smiling, noticing that Assunta, in her peasant garb, was attracting much interest from the passengers opposite. When Assunta saw the broad grin on his face, she wondered what was amusing him.

He turned to her and Giulietta and observed, "All these people think my sister has been to a fancy dress ball!"

Although Eugenio's café was in Byres Road, the house in which he and Giulietta lived was up three flights of stairs in a tenement building in Argyle Street, just round the corner from Radnor Street.

79

The stair walls were tiled and as they climbed, Assunta thought her brother must indeed be prospering to be able to live in such a fine place. Giulietta went on ahead of them to open the door and when Assunta and Eugenio arrived, breathless on the third landing, Giulietta was already inside putting on the kettle for breakfast. She came into the lobby from the kitchen as they stepped in and took Assunta's shawl. Then they went into the kitchen where the table was already set.

At one end, beneath the window, was a large iron sink with one cold-water tap. A coal fire glowed in the hearth, set in what appeared to be a broad iron stove with an oven. The iron kettle sat on a ring over the fire. Assunta had never seen a kettle before and was intrigued by its ingenious shape. How easy it would be to pour from such a utensil. She was also surprised to see a bed in a recess at the other end of the kitchen.

"This is where you will sleep, Sunta," said Giulietta. "It will be very cosy for you, but you will have to rise early to kindle the fire in the morning. But here I am already telling you what to do when you have barely arrived!" and she smiled.

Over a good breakfast of well-baked rolls and tea, the women chatted away while Eugenio listened and smiled when Sunta described her impressions of the long journey. There was a great deal of laughter over Pascalino's lame chicken at the French frontier.

Then it was time for Eugenio to go and open the shop, so he turned teasingly to his sister and said, "You had better slip into something less colourful before you come to Byres Road or you will be turning the eyes of all the eligible young men in the area."

Giulietta and Assunta started to unpack the cases, and Assunta was amused when her sister-in-law hung the homemade sausages on the kitchen pulley. The large ham was placed in a cool cupboard along with the dried fruit while the three loaves that had been baked in Filignano were placed in a large enamelled bread bin.

"We shall have to get you some warm clothes," said Giulietta. "Tomorrow you and I shall go shopping in Sauchiehall Street." Assunta had no idea where Sauchiehall Street was, and she was tickled with the idea that Giulietta should assume so soon that she was familiar with the street names in the city of Glasgow.

By this time Giulietta had placed two large pots full of cold water on the coal stove in preparation for Assunta's wash. Then she drew out a large zinc bath from beneath the kitchen bed and set it out in the middle of the floor quite near the fire. An hour later Assunta was having her back scrubbed as she enjoyed her first Scottish bath.

By mid-morning they were on their way to Byres Road on foot. There was a beautiful park on their right. Giulietta told Assunta it was called Kelvingrove. Assunta repeated the odd sounding words as her sister-in-law spoke them, "Radnor Street, Sauchiehall Street, Argyle Street, Kelvingrove Park!" stumbling over the difficult sounds.

They crossed a bridge over the "River Kelvin" and when Assunta looked up on her right, she saw the fine buildings of the university. They seemed immense. All the while the noisy trams trundled past and people were coming and going. No one stared at her now, for she had put on a warm blue dress Giulietta had given to her to wear and a smart grey coat with a lovely fur collar. They had enjoyed trying to find Assunta a suitable hat from Giulietta's large collection, for she wore her hair in a middle parting, with her long auburn tresses wound round in a large bun on the nape of her neck. In the end Giulietta came upon a blue velvet beret with a tassel, and she placed it neatly on Assunta's head. She looked and felt very smart as she walked along by Giulietta's side.

They turned into Byres Road, and Assunta read the numbers on the shop doorways, anticipating the moment when they would arrive at number 108. It was soon there, and they found themselves in front of a wide doorway flanked by high, broad windows on either side. Later she was to understand the strange words she saw on the windows: WILLS' GOLD FLAKE & THREE CASTLES on the left and FRY'S 300 PRIZE MEDALS CHOCOLATE on the right. The main sign above the shop read THE CONTINENTAL CAFÉ.

When they entered they found Eugenio in his shop jacket behind the counter, serving customers with sweets and cigarettes. Assunta was surprised to see the very jars of sweets and boxes of chocolate bars that she had seen in her dream in Filignano. On the right hand side of the café, seats were fixed against the wall with long, slender tables between them. Oval mirrors on the wall above them gave an air of spaciousness and grandeur that she found very impressive. Her brother must indeed be rich to own such a place.

Giulietta then took her into the backshop, which consisted of two large rooms. The one on the left served as a store and workshop, and in it a broad, white sink sat squatly beneath a high window. The room on the right was set out as a kitchen with a black metal coal stove and just beside it in the corner, a gas stove. In the centre, surrounded with chairs, sat a solid, square table. On the right was a wooden chest of drawers painted dark green. Against the wall facing the door was a long mirror, and beside it a broad wardrobe in the left-hand corner completed the furnishings.

They hung their coats in the wardrobe, and Giulietta brought out overalls and handed one to Assunta to put on over her dress.

"For the first few days, I don't want you to do anything, Sunta," said Giulietta. "Just you watch me as I go about my chores, and you will learn how we do things in Glasgow. You are not in Filignano now, my dear, and you will have to get accustomed to different ways of doing the work."

Then she prattled on, "Now the first thing I am going to do is prepare our midday meal. As a special treat, we are having pasta today. Just you watch me!"

And Assunta followed her sister-in-law's every move as she set a large pot of water to boil on the gas stove. When the water was bubbling, she added salt and then the long strands of pasta. In the meantime the *sugo* she had prepared on the previous day was already heating slowly in another pot on the other ring. Then she took a large oilcloth and laid it out on the table and from a glass-doored cupboard took plates, cups, and saucers and laid places for three. She took knives, forks, and spoons from a drawer and set them out beside the plates.

"Now, Sunta, when the pasta is cooked, we have to drain it thoroughly. We don't leave water in the basin as we used to do in Filignano so that we could steep the stale bread in it and save pasta. All that is behind you now. Here we drain the pasta."

And as she busily spoke, she took a large white, enamelled colander and placed it on the ledge by the sink in the other room. When the pasta was ready, she lifted the large, steaming pot through, and, placing the colander in the sink, poured pasta and boiling water into it. Then she lifted the colander by its side handles to shake the pasta and drain off the last of the water, but at that very moment disaster struck. One of the handles broke off, and all the pasta tumbled into the sink. Giulietta looked at Assunta in dismay.

Unable to contain herself at the helpless expression on her sister-in-law's face, Assunta burst into gales of laughter, exclaming, "So this is how you cook pasta in Glasgow! You throw it into the sink when it is ready!" By this time, embarrassed as she was, Giulietta too was laughing. Eugenio, hearing the commotion, came through from the shop to see what mischief they had been up to. The pasta was put in the waste bin and a fresh lot cooked.

When they had eaten, Assunta helped Giulietta to clear the dishes away. Then she sat at the table and wrote two letters, one to her parents and the other to Antonia, describing all the details of her journey to Glasgow. Giulietta then took her to the post office in Byres Road where the letters were posted without delay.

The rest of the day was spent in the backshop where Assunta began to familiarise herself with the contents of the cupboards. She helped Giulietta to prepare the evening meal. Then she went and sat for a time in a corner behind the counter, observing how her brother dealt with the customers' needs. Eugenio showed her British coinage, and she learned to distinguish a farthing from a haepenny, a penny, a sixpence, and a shilling. By eight o'clock Assunta was starting to yawn, and Giulietta decided to take her home, leaving her husband to close the café much later.

When Assunta lay cosily between the sheets of her high bed in the kitchen alcove, Giulietta bade her goodnight and extinguished the gas mantle above the fireplace. Assunta drowsily reviewed her long journey to Glasgow from Filignano. Then, quite inexplicably, tears came to her eyes although she did not feel unhappy. She wept herself silently to sleep and dreamt she was back in the house on Imperatore, going about her chores under the watchful eye of Filomena.

Chapter Eight

1915—The Continental Café

In the weeks that followed, Assunta very soon adapted to her new way of life. Her mental and physical resilience combining with her natural curiosity made it easy for her to condition herself to a daily, unpredictable routine and soon helped her to establish relations with the many people with whom she came into contact. In the morning she was always first to rise. After kindling the fire, she would put the large kettle on to boil, make her bed, and tidy the kitchen, working quietly so as not to disturb Eugenio and Giulietta, still asleep in their large bed in the room. Then she would have a good wash in the basin in the sink. It took her fully ten minutes to brush her lovely auburn hair when it fell down over her shoulders, and she could follow the strokes of the brush in a square mirror hanging by the side of the sink.

By the time she had dressed, the large kettle would be boiling on the stove ready for her brother's toilette. He always tapped on the door before coming in, then he would greet Assunta in English with a hearty "Good morning!" This was the signal for Assunta to leave and go through to have a chat with Giulietta. Sometimes she would take a cup of tea, which Giulietta enjoyed in bed. Assunta then sat on the edge of the bed while her sister-in-law outlined their plan of work for the day. On some mornings Eugenio would leave before them and go to the shop, and they would remain to clean the house. On other days they set out together and occasionally, on wet mornings, they might take a tramcar from the corner of Radnor Street to Lawrence Street in Byres Road.

As soon as the shop was opened, Eugenio would begin stocking the shelves behind the counter, while Assunta swept and scrubbed the floor on her knees. Giulietta prepared breakfast in the backshop, grinding coffee beans in a large, twin-wheeled grinder. When the coffee was ready, Assunta would hop over to the baker's to buy three crisp morning rolls. Eugenio loved a thin slice of Filignano ham in his roll, while the ladies preferred a plain roll and butter with their coffee.

After breakfast, as they went about their other chores, the three of them would break into song and anyone passing the open door of the Continental around nine o'clock could enjoy a varied selection of Italian songs. As there were not many customers at that early hour, it was an ideal time for Eugenio to instruct his sister on the prices of cigarettes, tobaccos, and confections. He loved to play-act and would take the part of the customer while Assunta, as herself, served him politely. The cash drawer was built into the underside of the counter, and she enjoyed picking out the small change from the round, wooden, bowl-shaped compartments.

In those days ginger beer or "stone ginger," as it was called, was usually made on the premises. The stone bottles were placed, ready to be used, on a shelf behind the counter. A small amount of ginger-flavoured syrup was poured into each one. Soda water was then added and the bottle shaken slightly to mix the ingredients before the stopper, held by a metal clip, was firmly put in place. The soda water itself was prepared in a large barrel rocked on a noisy contraption operated by foot pedals. This part of the process never failed to amuse Assunta. She thought her brother cut a ludicrous figure sitting on a low stool operating the pedals. He looked like a cyclist without a bicycle.

One day she was helping him with the making of the stone ginger while Giulietta was working in the backshop.

"You look as if you were rocking a cradle," said Assunta.

"Oh, be quiet, Sunta," said Eugenio, but she went on teasing and giggling. Eugenio let go of the barrel, got up and, grabbing his sister, gave her a good tickling. She escaped from his grasp and scampered into the backshop, followed closely by Eugenio. They circled the table three times before scurrying back to the counter.

"Behave yourselves," called out Giulietta, "you are both quite mad!"

So they settled down again. Now, when Eugenio started to agitate the barrel, he had to do it for four minutes without stopping. Assunta took advantage of this and resumed her teasing. Eugenio, in a singsong voice, called out loudly to Giulietta in the backshop, "If you hear my sister screaming, don't come and help her, for she is insulting me, and she is for it, she is!"

As he sang these words, he unexpectedly released the barrel on its rocker and made to catch Assunta, but she evaded him and ran wildly into the backshop hotly pursued by her brother. There he caught up with her and, grabbing her by the hair, gave her two sound smacks on the cheeks for her impertinence. Giulietta was dismayed by this show of violence, but Assunta screamed with laughter.

There was never a dull moment with Assunta around, her tom-boyishness being boisterously matched by her brother's mischievousness. Giulietta would shake her head and remonstrate with them for disturbing the peace of the Continental Café.

Eugenio acquired a fine motor-bike with sidecar. This replaced the humble push-bike that had caused him so much trouble with Filomena a few years before. So that he and Giulietta could get out occasionally, he saw to it that Assunta served regularly behind the counter. Soon he would be able to leave her in charge of the shop. One sunny evening early in April, he turned to her and said, "Sunta, I'm going to leave you in charge for half-an-hour or so while Giulietta and I go for a wee run to Anniesland."

She was not too keen, but he pointed out that the experience would help her to increase her self-confidence. As soon as he and Giulietta departed, Assunta took up her position at the counter.

Now, among the regular customers were a rather bold group of young men, all of them around eighteen years of age, and they loved to play the fruit machines after buying their glass of lemonade or stone ginger. The leader was called Davie, a very handsome lad, and it was he who had been so impetuous as to wink at Assunta on more than one occasion. She had ignored this, of course, since audaciously flirtatious young men must be kept in their place. It had been indeed Davie who, soon after her arrival from Italy, asked Eugenio, loudly enough to let her hear, "Eugene, who *is* this lovely young lady you now have in the shop?"

And Eugenio had wittily replied, "My father's daughter!"

When Assunta had worked out her brother's reply, she wondered what he meant by it. Then she challenged him when Davie had gone.

"What do you mean by telling that boy I'm your father's daughter? Don't you want anyone to know I'm your sister?"

She had no sooner uttered the question than the whole point of the joke dawned upon her. Eugenio grinned broadly when he saw the perplexed expression on his sister's face change to one of amusement.

When Eugenio and Giulietta had departed for Anniesland, Assunta was not very pleased as she saw Davie arriving with his friends. She served their drinks, and they began to play the fruit machines. When he realised Assunta was in sole charge of the shop, Davie began to tease her. Turning to his companions, he remarked loudly, "If you ask Miss Marzella for a packet of cigarettes, she understands perfectly and gives you the correct change. But just you try to converse with her and she will cut you right away with an innocent 'Me no understand.' "

The boys laughed boisterously at Davie's remarks, and Assunta's cheeks flushed with anger, but she ignored them. They began to bang the machines, making a great din and Assunta was frightened. When the noise showed no sign of abating, she decided to take action. Rummaging in a drawer in the counter, she came upon a large screwdriver.

She could not remember the exact word for this effective weapon, but, grasping it tightly in her fist as she advanced upon the boys, she shouted, "If you don't get out of the shop right now, I'll stab you with this schooldriver!"

"A schooldriver? What's a schooldriver?" laughed Davie, and at the same instant Assunta dropped the weapon on the floor, grabbed him by the scruff of the neck, and propelled him forcibly to the door. Then, giving him a mighty heave, she threw him on to the pavement where he landed face down. His friends edged gingerly past a wrathful Assunta. As Eugenio and Giulietta drew up, they were just in time to see Davie lifting himself from the pavement and making a hasty run with his friends round the corner of University Avenue.

Greatly amused, Eugenio turned to Assunta and said, "I told you that you could manage perfectly well on your own!"

In spite of this somewhat violent interchange, the boys endeared themselves to Assunta, calling to apologise on the following day with a large bunch of flowers. Later that year they were to come and say good-bye when they left to fight in France.

Although she was well aware a war was going on, it did not seem to Assunta that great sacrifices were being called for in 1915. The voluntary meatless days patriotic citizens were asked to have amused her, for back in Filignano they had only eaten fresh meat a few times a year on the occasion of special feasts. Then, in comparison to the heavy work she had done in Filignano, her working day in Glasgow seemed child's play.

Eugenio read out the war news from the newspaper every day, sometimes giving his wife and his sister a short reading lesson, using the paper as a topical textbook. While it was not necessary to translate the words into Italian for Giulietta, he often had to explain their meanings to Assunta. Some comparatively sophisticated words gradually crept into her vocabulary, words such as "U-boat, blockade, conscription," making her feel very knowledgeable. But the real horror of the war being fought was still outside the range of her experience, and, although she listened to descriptions of military actions and Eugenio's detailed explanations of them, she could not really picture them accurately in her mind's eye.

Having his business in the West End of Glasgow gave Eugenio a certain prestige among his compatriots. He and his wife were frequently visited by the Filignanesi in Glasgow and Lanarkshire, and the large backshop made an ideal reception room. Giulietta was an excellent baker, and she and Assunta prepared all sorts of delicacies to serve with coffee or tea, which their guests enjoyed. Although married eleven years, Eugenio and Giulietta did not have any children. To compensate for this, they often acted as godparents for the children of their many Italian friends.

When such an event occurs, a new, very close relationship is created, not only between godparents and godchildren but also between the parents of the children and the godparents themselves. They use the term *compare* or *commare* in addressing one another, while the godchild, if he is a boy, is called *patino,* and, if she is a girl, *patina.* These same terms are used by the godchildren in addressing their godparents.

Often a whole family would arrive at the Continental, father, mother, and perhaps two little girls and a boy, and the first few moments were spent in exchanging the formal greetings.

"*Gesú Maria, compa', Gesú Maria, comma'*. Jesus and Mary, *compare,* Jesus and Mary, *commare.*" To which Giulietta and Eugenio would both reply,

"*Gesú sempre, compa', Gesú sempre, comma'*. Jesus always, *compare,* Jesus always, *commare.*" Then the children's voices would chime out with the same greeting, "*Gesú Maria, pati', Gesú Maria,* pati'."

And again the godparents would reply, "*Gesú sempre, pati',*" the shortened form, "*pati',*" standing for "*patino*" or "*patina.*"

This little ritual would then be followed by a great deal of fuss when Eugenio lifted the children one by one and kissed them smackingly on both cheeks. The visitors would then retire to the backshop with Giulietta for tea or coffee and a good chat, while Eugenio and Assunta took it in turn, between customers, to look in and exchange friendly greetings. The children eventually found their way into the counter where they would be presented with a few sweets or a bar of chocolate. On warm days they might even have a pokey hat, a small cornet of ice cream the top of which would be smeared with a slight dab of raspberry flavouring.

Assunta never ceased to be astonished at the large number of visitors who flocked regularly to "Byres Road." This was the term adopted by their friends.

"Where shall we go today? Let's go to Byres Road!" they would say. The main social function of the week was the gathering in the backshop on Sunday evenings when the shop was closed earlier than usual. The Filignanesi took it in turn to entertain there. As they worked intolerably long hours, their backshops became their homes. That was why they really looked forward to Sunday evenings when they would gather to share a well-cooked meal, and when the ladies retired to wash the dishes, sew, knit, and chat, the men settled down to a good game of cards, generally *scopa* or "winner takes all." This was their social life.

Assunta soon became acquainted with many of the Glasgow backshops, and she marvelled at the number of Marzellas, Coias, Cocozzas, Ferris, Franchittis, Mancinis, and Valerios who had come from Filignano and settled to an entirely different way of life in Scotland.

One day in early summer, they were visited by friends from Lanark. The Bandinis were accompanied by their daughter, Maria, and their niece, Giulia. These attractive young ladies were very smartly dressed. Maria wore a two-piece costume consisting of a full skirt over which a long jacket sat neatly. A fine, white lace collarpiece sat loosely round her neck ending in two long flaps falling elegantly over the lapels of her jacket.

Giulia was wearing a well-shaped grey skirt, the seam of which was decorated with cloth-covered buttons. Above the skirt a long-sleeved, white silk blouse set off her lovely complexion. Both girls wore their hair swept over the crown of their heads, but while Giulia's ended in a large bun at the back, Maria had boldly had hers bobbed. As Assunta admired the young ladies, she thought, *What a contrast to my own hair with its old-fashioned middle parting.*

Although she was not a mirror-gazer, Assunta's attention had been drawn to her hairstyle in a family photograph taken shortly after her arrival in Glasgow. In the group consisting of Eugenio, Giulietta, and herself with Giulietta's older brother, Pietro, his wife, Erminia, and their two children, Angelina and Alberto, Assunta, to her annoyance, had been placed in the centre standing next to Antonio, Giulietta's younger brother. Assunta did not care for Antonio. She sensed that Giulietta had planned the pose of the photograph as she would have welcomed a match between Assunta and Antonio. The displeasure on Assunta's face could be clearly seen in the photograph, and Eugenio laughed heartily when he saw it.

Now, to add to Assunta's embarrassment, Giulietta brought out the horrid photograph to show it to the Bandinis. As they all looked at it, Maria and Giulia happened to glance up at Assunta and saw on her face an exact replica of her expression in the photograph. They could not restrain their spontaneous laughter and Assunta, quickly sensing what had happened, joined them in their mirth.

From that moment the three girls became good friends, and they were soon sitting together in a corner discussing plans to improve Assunta's appearance. Giulia was going to Lanark to spend a week with her relations. Would it not be grand if Assunta could also go with her? The three of them would have a jolly time. Maria impulsively threw the question at Eugenio when he looked in to greet his friends. While Giulietta did not seem to be keen on their plan, Eugenio thought it would be good for his sister and readily gave his consent.

The anticipation of a short holiday, the first in her life, gave Assunta some sleepless nights. But one sunny morning she found herself with Giulia on the train to Lanark. This was her first real outing, a great adventure, and soon, when they left behind the drab outskirts of the city, she saw green fields and trees, and in the far distance low hills. To be sure, she had been hoping to see those elusive pink-and-white heathered hills, but they still evaded her. The journey took just over an hour, the train stopping frequently, but at last it puffed and strained its way into Lanark station where Maria was smilingly waiting to welcome them.

Years later Assunta was often to look back on her holiday in Lanark with nostalgic feelings. It was there she gained the first vivid impressions of the beauty of landscape that was essentially Scottish. Her first surprise was the sheer size of the Bandinis' house above their shop in the High Street. She and Giulia had a room to themselves, and the bed was the most comfortable in which she had ever slept. And the generous hospitality of their hosts extended beyond the range of their house and kitchen. They arranged to borrow bicycles so that the three girls could make excursions into the surrounding countryside. Assunta soon mastered the bicycle and, since she was so strong, she could easily outrace Giulia and Maria. One day they cycled to Biggar, and Assunta was quite charmed by the town with its lovely houses and picturesque little shops.

Her bond of friendship with Giulia and Maria grew each day, and they were very happy together. But the week flew only too rapidly past and on the morning of her last day in Lanark, her hairstyle was changed by Maria and Giulia. The broad centre parting was dispensed with, and her hair was swept back loosely and tied in a bun at the back. Not only did the new style set off the line of her features to better advantage, but it actually seemed quite strikingly to increase her height. Then, to add to her joy, Maria presented her with delicately fashioned, gold earrings, and Giulia gave her a lovely gold ring. In the afternoon they made their way to the local photographer's studio and had their pictures taken together.

Giulia said mischievously, "We'll see whether you come out frowning this time!" In the evening Eugenio and Giulietta wondered who the elegant young lady was who walked into the Continental fresh from her adventures in Lanark.

The month of May came in with a few mild, sunny days. In spite of the sunshine, Assunta saw that people were going around with troubled faces. After nine months of war, a certain strain was beginning to be felt. Then on the 7th of May, the liner *Lusitania* was sunk by a German submarine and over a thousand people were drowned. Assunta was horrified by the photographs of the bodies on the Irish beaches she saw in the newspapers. At the Sunday meeting in the Continental backshop that week, the men were less inclined to play cards. They talked about the war at great length, imagining what would happen if Italy were to enter.

"I will volunteer immediately!" said Antonio, Giulietta's brother, as he smiled at Assunta.

Just like him to be so boastful, she thought. *We'll see what he will do if Italy does come into the war!* Within herself she almost hoped he would go so that she would be rid of his unwelcome attentions. It did not occur to her just then that Eugenio also would have to go.

The days passed and soon it would be her twentieth birthday on the 24th of May. She was hoping to invite Giulia and Maria for a little celebration with Giulietta's consent. But her plan was to be upset. On the 23rd of May, Italy declared war on Austria, having previously agreed with Russia, France, and Britain to cooperate with them against their enemies. The small Italian colony in Glasgow was thrown into a state of great excitement. But neither Eugenio nor Antonio made any move to volunteer at first.

Eventually, when applications began to arrive at the Italian Consulate in Glasgow, it was discovered that the procedure for volunteering was long and complicated. Those who applied generally received temporary certificates of exemption from military service. It was not until provisions were made by the Military Service (Conventions with Allied States) Act in 1917 that a regular flow of Italians in Scotland began to return to Italy to do their military service.

Italy's entry into the war threw Assunta into a state of alarm. She was terrified lest Austria should invade Italy. The fact that her parents lived so far in the south of the country did not ease her anxiety. The few letters arriving from time to time from Filignano grew more and more precious and, although Antonia invariably assured her that all was well, her heart remained troubled and anxious.

As the summer wore on, the routine in the Continental changed.

The shop opened at the earlier hour of eight o'clock and closed at ten, but the law was then changed to permit a "carry-out" trade from ten until midnight. Business was bad, however, as many commodities were by now becoming scarce. Fortunately Eugenio had good trade connections, and he was able to obtain enough supplies to keep the shop turning over. But it became a matter of urgency to make as many small economies as possible.

When they took the tramcar each morning from Radnor Street to Byres Road, the fare was one haepenny each. Thus it was costing one shilling and ninepence per week to travel from the house to the shop and back. Eugenio suggested they should walk every day as the weather was reasonably good and they would benefit from the fresh air every morning and evening. To save pounds you had to start by saving haepennies. That was obvious to anyone with good sense.

One evening it was still quite light when Giulietta and Assunta set out to walk back to Argyle Street. Eugenio remained behind to sell a few more sweets and cigarettes from the little hatch he had built in the side of the shop window. The ladies decided to walk up University Avenue, past the university buildings, and then made their way slowly round to the bridge running over the Kelvin in Kelvingrove Park. By the time they turned into the road leading to the bridge, it was already getting dark. Now Giulietta always carried her umbrella, no matter where she went, no matter what kind of weather was expected.

As they walked along, they became aware of a man's step not far behind them. Giulietta stopped while Assunta went on a few paces and, when she looked back to see why her sister-in-law was no longer beside her, she heard a man speaking to her. Then she heard Giulietta say, "We have not come here for pleasure, but for our own convenience, and we are not what you think we are!" and, as she spoke, she struck the man over the head with her umbrella. The man scampered away. Assunta did not know whether to laugh or cry. She was so astonished by Giulietta's behaviour.

When her irate sister-in-law caught up with her, breathless with indignation, Assunta asked, "What was all that about?"

Unguardedly, Giulietta replied, "He was looking for clicks."

"Clicks? What are clicks?" Assunta asked innocently.

"I'll tell you another time," said Giulietta. "I think you are still too young to know about certain things!"

But Assunta was not as simple as Giulietta thought, and she realised the man had made an improper suggestion. A smile passed across her face. After this incident they stopped taking the route through the park and walked down to Argyle Street every evening by the main road.

As the days were warm, there was a great demand for ice cream at the Continental. The freezer in which it was made had not yet been motorized, and it was very hard work for Eugenio. The metal container was packed round with chipped ice and salt in a round barrel-like sheath. A handle was then placed in a slot on the rim of the container so that it could be revolved by hand. A metal blade on a wooden shaft was dipped into the slowly freezing mixture, and the hardening ice cream on the sides of the container was scraped off and mixed with the softer cream in the centre.

The basis of ice cream in those days was fresh milk, sugar, and a suitable custard powder or corn flour. Vanilla pods were often used to flavour it, and the boiling of the mixture was done in the backshop in a large copper-bottomed boiler holding up to ten gallons. It took two persons to lift the boiler down from the gas stove so that the cooked mixture could be tipped into zinc pails. At busy periods it was not unusual to have a dozen or more pails of the ice-cream mixture stacked on the shelves in the working backshop. When the mixture had cooled, clean linen towels were placed over the rims of the pails to protect it from dust or flies.

Assunta, with her tremendous strength, was of great help to her brother. She could lift the pails effortlessly on to the shelves, scrub out the copper-bottomed boiler until it sparkled, then carry the pails of ice-cream mixture to the freezer as they were required. On really hot days, the freezer hardly ever stopped and Eugenio was often exhausted by the end of the day. Assunta gradually took over a great deal of his work, operating the hand-turned freezer herself. Giulietta, who was inclined to to be more delicate, was unable to undertake heavy work of this kind.

With the coming of autumn, the ice-cream season became less intensive and other delicacies such as hot peas, or pea braes, were more in demand. Assunta was always amused when large numbers of children appeared on Saturdays to spend a haepenny on a pea brae. A spoonful of cooked peas was placed in a Bovril cup, and the pale grey-green water in which they had been cooked was added to fill the cup. This was served with a spoon and a saucer, and salt, vinegar, and pepper were added if requested. Not many of the Continental customers asked for coffee in those days, their favourite beverages being Bovril or Oxo or tea. The hot, meaty drinks were usually served with two or three water biscuits.

By this time Eugenio had opened a second shop in New City Road, putting Giulietta's brother, Antonio, in charge of it. Antonio slept in the back shop and there he also cooked for himself, only coming to Byres Road for a meal on Sunday evenings when he closed early.

The subway vied with the trams as an excellent and reliable means of public transport. Assunta had never been on the subway, and one day Eugenio took her to the shop in New City Road. They took the train at Hillhead and alighted at Cowcaddens. She did not particularly enjoy her first experience of going underground but had to admit that it was very practical since they seemed to arrive in no time even though the trains were then cable operated.

When they walked into the shop in New City Road, they found a strange young man behind the counter. Antonio had not been expecting a visit from his brother-in-law and was apparently playing cards with some of his cronies in a house nearby. It was just as well that Eugenio sent the young man to fetch Antonio, for he was quite drunk when he appeared, supported by his young friend, half an hour later. Eugenio was very angry and gave him a thorough dressing-down. After this incident Assunta noticed that Giulietta never again mentioned the possibility of a match between herself and Antonio.

Antonia's letters reassured Assunta in the knowledge that her parents were well and contented. The harvest had been a good one, and Antonia had been very helpful to Filomena and Benedetto. Assunta bought the dress she had promised and sent it to Antonia in good time for the Feast of the Madonna on the 8th of September. Soon it would be Christmas, and Antonia promised Assunta that she would spend a great deal of her time with the old people during the festive season. It was about this time that Antonia's Aunt Rosa met with her fatal accident when she fell into the fire, and Assunta was shocked to learn of the old lady's horrible death.

Christmas and New Year in Glasgow were a new experience for Assunta. Eugenio had managed to buy a good stock of confectionery, and they were kept busy serving customers who were buying gifts to fill their children's stockings. It was an icy season, and Assunta was obliged to wear extra clothing and long woollen stockings to keep warm behind the counter. From Lanark the Bandinis sent an enormous capon for their Christmas dinner, and Giulietta cooked it carefully in the gas oven. Assunta attended her first midnight mass in Scotland on Christmas Eve. After closing the shop, they went home, put on their best clothes, and went to St. Peter's in Partick for the service. The singing of the carols moved Assunta deeply, and she felt very homesick for the house on Imperatore where her parents would be already asleep at that hour.

But when they stepped out of the church shortly after one o'clock in the morning, the first few flakes of snow were beginning to fall. On their way back to Argyle Street, she felt she was walking through an enchanted landscape as the tiny snowflakes flickered down in the light

94

of the streetlamps. Soon a thin carpet of white stretched before them on the pavement, and their steps were muffled. Arriving at the close entrance, they stamped their feet and shook their clothes before going upstairs.

Next morning when Assunta rose to look out of the kitchen window, an unusual brightness met her eyes. She marvelled at the snow-covered rooftops and the back courts covered in a white mantle endowing them with an unwonted air of purity. They ate their Christmas dinner early in the day so that they could open the café in the early afternoon, and Giulietta surpassed herself with the meal. She had taken the time to bake a fine pizza dolce and those delicately flavoured crisp egg biscuit bows fried in olive oil, which they called *nocche*. Eugenio opened a bottle of red Italian wine, and their eyes were shining by the time they had finished eating.

New Year's was quite a different occasion. There was no closing of the shop then. It was the busiest period of the winter season and remained open all day on Hogmanay (a word that Assunta found very amusing) right up until three o'clock in the morning on New Year's Day. Their stocks were practically cleared, and Assunta had the experience of dealing with dozens of clients in varying stages of intoxication. But there was no unpleasantness. On the contrary Assunta found the Scots to be more outgoing, warm, and friendly than she had ever imagined they could be.

Shortly before midnight all went quiet and the shop was deserted. Eugenio explained that the Scots would be awaiting the stroke of midnight in one another's homes to wish each other a Good New Year. Then he brought out a bottle of Strega and poured some into three small glasses. He handed one to Giulietta, another to Assunta, and took the other himself.

He pulled out his watch and as the hands met at midnight, he said in English, "A Happy New Year!" and then in Italian, *"Buon inno e buon anno e buon Capo d'Anno!"* and, raising his glass, invited the ladies to drink. But he had not warned his sister how potent the liqueur was, and a moment later Assunta was spluttering helplessly as the hot syrupy liquid burned her throat. She rushed to the sink, grabbed a tumbler, and poured herself some water from the tap. It all happened so quickly that by the time Giulietta and Eugenio reached her she was already gasping with relief as the cold water soothed her hot throat.

"What a way to bring in the New Year, Sunta!" exclaimed Eugenio when he saw the tears running down her cheeks. Then he added, "And it's nothing to cry about!" whereupon they all began to laugh and warmly wished each other a Happy New Year in 1916.

Chapter Nine

1916 to 1918—A Time of Stress

The year 1916 brought harder times. In January came conscription, and many of the young men frequenting the Continental came to say good-bye as they went off to do their military duty. Assunta knew she would not see some of them again and was sad when she saw them leave. But she was glad there was still no sign of Eugenio going away to serve his country. Now that Italy was a war ally, the Italians in Scotland were viewed with a new respect.

Then an event occurred that was to add greatly to their prestige in the eyes of the Glaswegians. The Italian government arranged a tour of the principal cities in Britain by a *carabinieri* band. When the concerts to be given in Glasgow were imminent, a wave of excitement swept through the Italian families in the city and Lanarkshire, and many a young Italian girl's heart fluttered in anticipation of seeing a band of handsome men in splendid uniforms performing for their benefit in the city's halls.

It was a quiet morning when Eugenio read the small announcement in the newspaper giving details of the first performance in St. Andrew's Halls. Assunta broke into a broad grin when she heard it.

"What's so funny, Sunta?" asked Eugenio.

"The word *'carabinieri'* reminds me of one of Mother's funnier stories concerning a particular *'carabiniere.'*"

"I don't recall hearing it," said Eugenio, "and, as we don't appear to be having any customers today, perhaps you would like to tell it to us over a cup of coffee?" And he glanced hintingly at Giulietta as he said this. She soon made some coffee, and they all sat down in the backshop to enjoy Assunta's story.

She began, "What I am going to tell you happened many years ago in Naples. The story concerns a certain Palombino who had married Minuccia. They had a fine little boy, Pascalino, who was five years of age. But Palombino had started shift work and was constantly working at night, and Minuccia began to feel neglected. A local *carabiniere* with an amorous disposition, learning that Palombino was at work every night, began visiting Minuccia late in the evening. She would cook him a good supper and, after putting young Pascalino to bed, invited the *carabiniere* to share hers and in this way dispel her loneliness for the better part of the night."

At this point in Assunta's narrative, Giulietta looked at Eugenio and tut-tutted, but he merely smiled and told Assunta to go on, which she did.

"One evening when Pascalino had been put to bed early, he grew thirsty and, rising to go through to the kitchen for some water, was just in time to see the *carabiniere* taking his mother by the hand and leading her into the bedroom. *How strange!* thought the boy, then, having quenched his thirst, he went back to bed and fell asleep, thinking no more about it.

"On the following morning, the boy rose early and went out to meet his father, who would be returning just then from his night work. As he took his father's hand, Pascalino looked up at him and asked, 'Tell me, Papà, are *carabinieri* human beings?'

" 'Are *carabinieri* human beings?' repeated Palombino with an incredulous note in his voice. 'But why are you asking me such an odd question, Son?'

" 'Oh, I was just wondering,' said Pascalino, 'because you see, Papà, every evening when you go to work, a *carabiniere* comes to our house, and when he has had his supper, he takes Mamma to bed!'

"Pascalino's ingenuous revelation brought an abrupt end to the *carabiniere*'s amorous interlude with Minuccia!"

Giulietta could not help smiling at the naughty tale of the bold *carabiniere,* and Eugenio remarked, "It's the smart uniform that turns the heads of the ladies. I had better keep a special eye on the two of you when the band arrives next week!" Then, since customers continued to remain elusive, they sat on and Giulietta took up the theme.

"Since we have been hearing about an unfaithful wife," she said, "here is a story my mother, Albina, used to tell."

"Oh, do let us hear it!" said Assunta, eagerly.

"Your sister is becoming quite incorrigible," said Giulietta to Eugenio. Then she began her story.

"There was a shepherd from Cardido called Nicola who had been married for several years to Carmela Pizzulli. They had no children and in the lonely nights when her husband was on the hill watching his sheep, Carmela had taken to sharing her bed with a number of the local young men who took it in turn to spend the night hours with her. Carmela's incautiousness attracted the attention of a nosey neighbour, and this good woman took it upon herself one day to inform Nicola of his wife's infidelity.

"So, one evening, Nicola set off as usual to tend his sheep and, shortly afterwards Carmela opened her door to young Filippo, the butcher's son, whose turn it happened to be. But Filippo had no sooner sat down to eat his supper than there was a loud knocking at the front door. Carmela ushered him hurriedly into the bedroom, told him to hide in the wardrobe, locked him in and, concealing the key in the pocket of her apron, answered the front door.

" 'Why are you back so soon?' she asked Nicola.

" 'It's going to be a stormy night,' he replied as he walked into the kitchen, glancing here and there, 'so I thought I would have a night indoors for a change.'

"Then, seeing the table was set for two, he enquired, 'Were you expecting someone?'

" 'Oh no,' said Carmela hastily. 'I thought I would set up the table tonight to save me a little time tomorrow. I have also been cooking.'

"Nicola smiled wryly at her flagrant lying and turned to go into the bedroom.

" 'Where are you going?' Carmela called out.

" 'To bed of course!' said Nicola, and he added maliciously, 'You can join me when you have finished cooking for tomorrow!'

"When he entered the bedroom, he heard a distant creak coming from the inside of the wardrobe. Smiling grimly, he slowly undressed and called out to Carmela, 'Are you coming to bed or not?'

"She came warily into the bedroom and, her heart pounding, took off her clothes. Nicola watched her movements through half-closed eyelids, and he observed how flushed she was in the flickering candlelight as she put on her nightdress, glancing frequently in the direction of the wardrobe, before blowing out the candle and getting into bed beside him.

"A deep silence fell upon the room as they lay on their backs pretending to sleep. Now and then a resonant creaking was heard inside the wardrobe, and Nicola suddenly called out, 'We'll have to be doing something about those woodworms in the wardrobe!'

"Carmela gulped and murmured weakly, 'Yes.'

"She was very agitated, and a cold sweat was making her shiver. So, three unhappy people, two in a bed and another crouching in a cramped position in a wardrobe passed an endlessly weary, sleepy night. Every so often the woodworms in Filippo's bottom gave him a cramp, and when he tried to shift, the whole wardrobe grated discordantly and Nicola bellowed, 'Damn those woodworms. I can't get to sleep for them!' while Carmela moaned in despair.

"At the first glimmer of dawn, Carmela slipped out of bed and quickly dressed while Nicola still pretended to sleep, snoring softly on his back. For a madly delirious moment, she thought of unlocking the wardrobe door there and then to release her hapless young lover and let him steal past her sleeping husband, but Nicola seemed to read her thought and he opened his eyes wide and asked, 'Up so early? Have you not slept well, Carmela?'

"Thoroughly demoralised, she mumbled something about kindling the fire and went into the kitchen.

"In the meantime, Filippo, who had not eaten since noon on the previous day, was suffering the sore pangs of hunger, in addition to other physical discomforts.

"He heard Nicola calling out to his wife, 'Carmela, bring me something to eat. I have decided to spend the day in bed as the wet weather seems to be persisting. The rest will do me good.'

"And Carmela moaned audibly in the kitchen. Her lament was echoed by a deep sigh from the wardrobe, and Nicola smiled sadistically to himself.

"He spent the entire day in bed, rising only to relieve himself in a pail. The muffled sounds from the wardrobe grew ever more intense and desperate, and Carmela kept making excuses to come into the bedroom. Through it all Nicola lay back contentedly, pretending not to hear the sounds from the wardrobe and enjoying every moment of his wife's torture.

"Night came again and Carmela was obliged to lie down again by her husband's side. She had not eaten all day and was in a state of complete mental and physical exhaustion. Yet she still did not dare fall asleep and lay listening to her husband's steady breathing and her lover's groans as the torturing night wore on.

"In the early light of the morning, she glanced over and saw a trickle of steaming urine issuing from the slit between the bottom of the door and the solid base of the wardrobe. This decided her. She rose at once and fetched the key from her apron pocket. When he heard her moving, Nicola sat bolt upright in bed, but she ignored him and made straight for the wardrobe door.

" 'I see you have noticed the wardrobe is leaking, Carmela,' said Nicola, but she had already unlocked the door by the time he said this. A dishevelled, snivelling, desperate, wide-eyed, foul-smelling Filippo emerged limping painfully, and he turned to them and screamed in a hysterical voice, 'PANE! PANE!—BREAD! BREAD!' before hobbling out of the room to the kitchen. He reached the front door, opened it, and rushed out leaving it wide open. Then he disappeared down the street followed by the derisive laughter of Nicola who was standing at the front door in his red drawers."

Eugenio and Assunta pretended to be shocked by Giulietta's scandalous story, but she realized right away they were teasing her.

The *carabinieri* band descended upon Glasgow the following week, creating gay havoc among the unmarried Italian girls in the city. They gave several concerts to packed audiences in St. Andrew's Halls and each evening received a standing ovation. Eugenio went twice. First he took Giulietta, then Assunta who was delighted by the stirring music. The smart young men came on to the platform in their dress uniforms, the twin rows of brass buttons on their tunics gleaming brightly while the brass badges on the front of their *tricorni,* or three-cornered hats, matched the shine on their handsome, tanned faces. Their neat, dark collars ended in two flaps on their necks, and each flap carried a gold star. Before beginning to play, they raised their hats to the audience before removing them. Every number was greeted with thunderous applause.

Assunta recalled the bands in the piazza in Filignano, and her eyes moistened.

As the members of the band were free during the day, they were to be seen in the streets of Glasgow in their khaki uniforms, with heavy boots and leggings. This gear was topped by their spectacular *bersagliere* hats, broad-rimmed with a large brass badge in the centre above the forehead and an impressive array of feathers on the right. They smartly carried gloves as they strode through the streets, causing a stir as they paused to look at the shop windows.

The romantic young Italian girls lost no time in persuading their parents to allow them to invite the young men to their homes for a generous midday meal. They were generally invited in pairs and then seated conveniently beside the charming eligible daughters of the family. For once the strict observance of the custom of chaperoning was overlooked, and every afternoon Kelvingrove Park became the setting of romantic walks and humorous interludes. Many of the girls could speak only the dialect of their parents and consequently found it difficult to communicate with the *carabinieri* who spoke Italian.

A report of a rather farcical episode was soon circulating round the Italian backshops in Glasgow. Two sisters, who had better remain nameless, invited two *carabinieri* to their house for lunch and in the afternoon went out walking with the young men. Now, one of the sisters spoke Italian, as she had been studying, and had no problem in conversing with her companion. The other sister knew only the odd word of dialect, and some of the expressions in her limited vocabulary range were not exactly polite. It so happened that she became separated from her sister and her escort. So there she was walking through the shaded pathways of the park in the company of a good-looking *cara-*

biniere whose charm was matched by his audaciousness.

First he took her gently by the hand as they walked, and she thought nothing of that. Then, as they drew near a broad tree with large, overhanging boughs, he forcefully led her into the shade, pressed her gently against the trunk and, placing his hand where it ought not to have been, made to implant his lips upon hers.

At this she panicked and in an outraged tone came out with the first expression that came into her mind in order to let him know that he was much too rakish for her. She meant to say, "You're much too cunning for me!" but the expression she used was equally effective in dialect or in proper (or improper!) Italian, and, translated not too literally, expressed the following delicate sentiment: "You're a crafty little bugger, aren't you?!" which, coming so unexpectedly from her dainty little mouth, knocked the passionate wind completely out of the young man's sails, bringing the romantic interlude to an abrupt end.

The Battle of the Somme began in July 1916, dragging on in a series of battles that continued until the end of the year. Supplies became ever more scarce, and at times there was very little to sell over the counter at the Continental. But milk was still reasonably plentiful, and they could make ice cream, although sugar was not easily come by and limited the quantity that could be made. The effects of conscription were now being felt, and women went into the factories in ever increasing numbers. Munitions were being manufactured in Glasgow, and sometimes tragic accidents were reported in the daily papers. On the Glasgow tramcars, conductors were being gradually replaced by conductorettes wearing long tartan skirts.

In these harder times, Eugenio, Giulietta, and Assunta found they had more leisure hours when they could sit and talk about the old days in Filignano. Filomena had sent a large flask of good olive oil and Giulietta decided, one quiet afternoon, to bake a few pizzas. While she and Assunta were busy making the dough and rolling it out on the table, Eugenio kept popping in and out of the backshop.

"Was Zia Nicolina still making her good pizzas when you left Filignano?" he asked Assunta.

"Yes, she was," said Assunta, "and what is more, she was still refusing to give any to her friend Mariuccia, although they visited one another often enough. The feud between them was still going on."

"What caused this disagreement?" asked Eugenio, and Assunta thought she had better tell the whole story.

"It all started one day when Zia Nicolina was baking her bread, and Mariuccia, seeing the oven chimney smoking, decided to look in on her friend later in the day, hoping to be given a nice piece of tasty pizza. But, a few days before, Zia Nicolina had taken umbrage because of some tactless, silly remark Mariuccia had passed and she was in disgrace with the old lady. Besides, Zia Nicolina was really exasperated with Mariuccia since she made it a habit to arrive at the house at the very moment when she was lifting the pizza out of the oven. Oil was very scarce that year, and she could only afford a small pizza for herself, baking it first to test the heat of the oven before putting in the loaves to bake.

"As Zia Nicolina had been predicting to herself, just as she removed the pizza, Mariuccia knocked at the door. Zia Nicolina put the hot pizza on the settle by the fire and quickly covered it with a large, dark cloth. Then she let Mariuccia in and smartly sat down on the pizza, spreading her skirt widely over the seat.

"As Zia Nicolina had overlooked three loaves that she had forgotten to put into the oven, Mariuccia did this for her, making the sign of the cross over the oven door and saying 'San Martino' three times. Then she came over to the old lady and, sniffing significantly, asked, 'Have you been baking a pizza, Zia Nicolina?'

" 'Not today,' said Nicolina, 'I have no oil.' Mariuccia guessed that the old woman was sitting on the hot pizza, for her face had grown quite red and she was perspiring, and she kept fidgeting uncomfortably on the settle. Mariuccia sat down opposite her on a chair and chattered away about this and that, while Zia Nicolina perspired more and more, wishing that Mariuccia would go away.

" 'Would you like to change seats with me, Zia?' said Mariuccia. 'You seem to be too warm by the fire.'

" 'I'm all right here,' said Nicolina. 'I'll just stay where I am.'

"So Mariuccia and Zia Nicolina sat on for another quarter of an hour, and the old lady was in torture. At last, when Mariuccia thought Nicolina had been sufficiently punished for her greed, she rose to take her leave. Zia Nicolina rose painfully from the settle to see her neighbour to the door. As Mariuccia was going out, she turned to Zia Nicolina and said rhymingly,

> '*I* am going as I have come,
> But *your* pizza has burnt your bum!' "

That afternoon, when the pizzas had all been baked, Eugenio decided to take his sister for a short trip on his motorbike and sidecar while Giulietta took her turn to look after the shop. He drove past Anniesland and took the road to Milngavie. The trees had already donned their autumn coats and the leaves, many of which had fallen by the side of the road, lay in small heaps of varied hues from yellowish green to russet and brown. The air was clean and crisp, and Assunta felt a rare tingle in her cheeks as they drove through Milngavie and took the road to Aberfoyle. Soon the hills rose before them, silhouetted against a pale blue sky flecked here and there with light, wispy clouds.

Suddenly on her right, Assunta saw a tall tree standing impressively by itself high up on a rock shelf. It seemed to be growing out of an immense boulder at a slight angle and stood there precariously yet boldly against the sky, throwing out a proud defiance to the world as it seemed to proclaim: "This is where I have chosen to grow and here I shall remain as long as I can, even though I have to contend with the elements on my high perch!"

Then, as she looked along the length of the rock shelf, she suddenly perceived a hill just beyond it, and, miracle of miracles, it was covered in pink heather! She could not restrain the delighted, joyous exclamation that rose to her lips and called out to Eugenio to stop. Then she leapt out of the sidecar and went running across the road, through a gate and along a narrow path that led to the hills. *My sister has gone mad,* thought Eugenio. He sat down by the side of the road and lit a cigarette.

Assunta was gone fully half an hour before she returned, her arms filled with pink heather. She hugged it to her and breathed in its dry fragrance, and, turning to Eugenio, said, "We can go home now!" This was a glorious experience for Assunta and by the time they turned and were on their way back to Glasgow, she knew she had fallen in love with Scotland, irremediably and irrevocably.

The winter passed and in April 1917 America entered the war. By this time compulsory food rationing had been introduced in Britain, and it was no longer possible to make ice cream. Sugar was in very short supply. The only sweet lines they could get to sell in small quantities were the chocolate jelly fish, which sold at the inflated price of one shilling per quarter.

Eugenio grew restless and talked of leaving for Italy to do his military service. Giulietta was not pleased at the prospect of his going but accepted it with resignation, knowing it was inevitable.

For the first time in her life, Assunta was able to read a great deal. There were novels that Giulietta devoured and then passed on to her. Her range of romantic concepts was broadened by her reading, but she found it difficult to be as sentimental as Giulietta who often wept over the melodramatic episodes or sighed at the beauty and tenderness of the love scenes.

Oddly enough, it was about this time that Assunta was besieged by suitors. They came in all shapes and sizes, shopkeepers and commercial travellers, and they were all promptly despatched and sent about their business. Assunta was not yet ready for romance or marriage, even though the ambience of the Continental might be more propitious to those pleasant states since Eugenio had bought a graphophone, an instrument producing music from cylinders. The café echoed with the narrowed voices of famous operatic singers or the thinned tones of large symphony orchestras whose broad, rich strains had been compressed on to these tiny cylinders.

In this year of great scarcity, one family business was still thriving in Glasgow. The Minicellis, mother, two sons and a daughter, were Italian warehousemen. They stocked vast quantities of edible commodities as well as tobacco, cigars, and cigarettes. They were suppliers to most of the small cafés owned by Italians in the Glasgow area and were doing such good business that they now employed travellers to collect orders that were quickly delivered by horse and cart.

Arturo, the younger of the two sons, would sometimes call personally to take an order at the Continental. He was very attracted to Assunta and made some preliminary, polite advances. Although Giulietta would have been delighted to advise her obstinate young sister-in-law, as the time was ripe, to encourage the young man's interest, Assunta remained cool and rather aloof.

Then one afternoon a new young traveller called from the Minicellis, and Eugenio took him into the backshop for a cup of coffee while they talked business. The young man listed the commodities available and wrote down in his order book the quantities Eugenio wished to purchase. On this occasion there was a special offer on Swan Vestas matches and just as Assunta came into the back shop, she heard the young traveller's voice utter the words "Swan Vestas." There was something in his intonation that attracted her attention, a sort of velvety, musical quality she had never heard in a man's voice before.

As she glanced at the speaker for an instant, his large, dark brown eyes rose to meet hers. She at once sensed a strong attraction and when he smiled to reveal strong, white, even teeth, she nodded politely before going about her work. That was all that happened, but it was enough to kindle the hopes of the young traveller whose name was Giuseppe Cocozza.

When he got back to the Minicelli warehouse at the end of his journey, he was having a chat with Arturo, with whom he was on very friendly terms, and he mentioned he had seen the loveliest auburn-haired Scots girl at the Continental.

Arturo laughed, "That was no Scots girl, Giuseppe. She is Assunta Marzella, signor Marzella's sister."

"That's great," said Giuseppe, "for they come from Filignano, my native village in Italy. I wouldn't mind approaching that young lady seriously, for I find her very attractive."

"You can put that idea out of your head right away, my dear chap," said Arturo, "for I have aspirations regarding Miss Marzella myself."

"Oh," said Giuseppe, "I couldn't have known," and, being a decent fellow, he immediately tried to put the auburn-haired Miss Marzella out of his mind.

Nevertheless, when next he called at the Continental, a few weeks later, he thought he detected the glimmer of a welcoming smile on Assunta's face when she saw him coming in. By this time Giulietta and Assunta were on their own, as Eugenio and Antonio had both gone to Italy to do their army service. So it was Giulietta who received Giuseppe in the back shop and gave him the order, and he had to admire her great gift for bargaining. When she left him for a moment to attend to some matter in the shop, Assunta came in to put on the kettle.

"Are you missing your brother?" asked Giuseppe.

"Yes, we are," said Assunta. "In fact, we are feeling rather lost at the moment without him."

"I wish I could be of help," said Giuseppe, "but I too am leaving for Italy next week. This will be my last call. Arturo Minicelli left two weeks ago. Did you not know this? Do you think you might allow me to write to you, Miss Marzella, when I am in the army in Italy?" Giuseppe spoke rapidly for fear that Giulietta would come back. Assunta could not help smiling at his impetuous questioning.

"You can write to me if you wish," she said, "but I won't promise to reply."

Then Giulietta did appear, and Assunta lifted the tray she had prepared and made her way back into the shop. When Giuseppe took his leave, Assunta was behind the counter and he threw her a warm smile. She acknowledged it with the same brief nod with which he had been favoured before. Then she regretted not having spoken to him again before he left, when it dawned on her that she might never see or hear from him again.

The days dragged when they were not busy, and Assunta and Giulietta grew closer in their affection for one another, missing the comforting presence of Eugenio. His letters arrived regularly to their great delight. He was stationed in Bari, a driver in the Third Squadron of Aviators. He was happy as he could use his mechanical knowledge to advantage. He had been to Filignano on a short leave, and all was well with the old folks.

Antonio also wrote to his sister from time to time. He had been promoted to Sergeant Major in the Italian Infantry. Giulietta began to have feelings of national pride in the realisation that both her husband and her brother were serving their country. Then, one day, Eugenio wrote telling them of the sad death of Arturo Minicelli. He had not been killed in action but had died of pneumonia.

Shortly afterwards a letter in a strange hand arrived one day for Assunta. Even before she opened it, she knew it was from Giuseppe. He wrote in formal terms, telling her of the death of Arturo Minicelli. Then he went on to express the wish that she might find time to write to him and let him know whether there was any hope that she might reciprocate the strong feelings he now felt he had for her. She showed the letter to Giulietta who smiled when she read the flowery phrases with which it ended. But Assunta did not reply to the letter.

Christmas and New Year passed, and they were now into the year 1918. Another letter arrived for Assunta. Giuseppe expressed his disappointment at not having been favoured with a reply to his first letter and earnestly appealed to her to write him a few lines. His language had a strong, poetic quality, and Assunta found it rather embarrassing to let Giulietta read it. It was she who pointed out, however, that it was Assunta's duty to reply.

"It would be very discourteous of you not to do so," she said, "and besides, it is our duty to encourage our men who are fighting for us."

So Assunta took pen and paper and wrote Giuseppe a very short note, thanking him for writing and expressing the wish that he was well. She assured him that Giulietta and she were both in good health, and she hoped his family were also in the best of health. She signed the letter: "Yours sincerely, Assunta Marzella."

When Giuseppe read the lukewarm phrases in Assunta's letter, he attributed her reticence to shyness and determined to break down the barrier of her coolness with passion. When her friend Giulia came to visit, Assunta confided in her and read out Giuseppe's letters.

"He sounds very sincere," said Giulia. "I think he is really in love with you, Sunta."

"Time will tell, Giulia," said Assunta.

Although Giuseppe's letters continued to arrive every week, becoming more and more passionate, Assunta only replied every month, expressing the usual platitudes about her health and his health and

106

the health of all their relations. What really annoyed Assunta was that Giulietta insisted on reading Giuseppe's letters to the many visiting ladies, and their tittering and significant glances in her direction irritated her to the point of exasperation.

Then one day in September, shortly after Bulgaria had asked for a truce, thus suggesting that an armistice was imminent, two strange ladies appeared at the Continental. One was in her late forties and dressed in black, while the other, who looked like her daughter, was less than twenty years old. The girl reminded Assunta of someone. As the older lady began to speak, Assunta realised they were Giuseppe's mother and sister. When they had introduced themselves, Assunta blushingly led them into the backshop where Giulietta was busy preparing a modest meal. She introduced the ladies.

The mother was signora Leonarda Cocozza, and her daughter was signorina Irena. Signora Leonarda explained that her son Giuseppe had worked, as a boy, in the small café business at Parkhead Cross, owned by her eldest son, Antonio. Giuseppe had recently written to say he was corresponding with signorina Assunta Marzella, and, as business was quiet, she and her daughter had decided to pay a friendly visit. All the time Leonarda spoke, her eyes scarcely left Assunta and she was painfully aware of small waves of hostility coming in her direction from the lady in black. Irena, on the other hand, was all smiles and charm. She did not speak but listened intently to her mother while turning now and then to smile at Giulietta and Assunta.

Signora Leonarda was a widow, her husband, Gaetano, having died when he was still young. Their small house was in Collemacchia, where most of the Cocozzas came from, although she herself was a Capaldi. Her son Antonio was already married and was the father of two children, Alberto and Dalfina. For that reason his military service had been delayed, but he was leaving for Italy on the following week so she and Irena had thought of coming to the Continental before he left. As Leonarda went on talking, Giulietta listened politely but Assunta made excuses to absent herself to do some little chore in the other backshop or to serve someone at the counter.

Giulietta invited the ladies to share their meal and, while they were eating, Leonarda plied Assunta with all sorts of questions. How old was she? How long had she been in Glasgow? How long had she known Giuseppe? How often did Giuseppe write to her? How often did Assunta reply to his letters? And she ended this barrage of questions with, "Has Giuseppe asked you to marry him?"

Assunta was so enraged that her cheeks flushed and she answered sharply, "There is no question of marriage between me and your son, signora, since I scarcely know him, and besides he does not really interest me. If I have written to him, it was out of politeness and merely to do my duty in upholding his morale as he is a soldier."

Signora Leonarda's eyebrows rose slightly at the girl's insolence, but her reply seemed to satisfy her and she made her departure shortly afterwards with Irena. She thanked Giulietta for her hospitality and invited her, should she ever be in the proximity of Parkhead Cross, to call in and visit.

When they had gone, Giulietta turned to Assunta and smilingly observed, "You would have a real tartar of a mother-in-law in that lady, don't you think?" Assunta shrugged her shoulders and determined to dismiss Giuseppe Cocozza from her mind for good.

But Giuseppe's letters continued to arrive. When Giulietta was present, Assunta pretended that she was not interested in them, leaving them unopened on a shelf in the backshop. But one afternoon when her sister-in-law had gone out on an errand, Assunta looked at the four unread letters and, no longer able to resist, she opened them. Reading them chronologically, she became acutely aware that Giuseppe's disappointment at her failure to reply was growing into anguish, and this made her feel guilty and wretched.

"I understand my mother and sister came to visit you," he wrote, "but since then I have not had a single line from you, Assunta. Did something happen when they came to see you? Why this terrible silence? Do you realise what you are doing to me? Can you imagine the tortures I am suffering when I cannot know what you are thinking?"

Assunta swithered. Her first impulse was to write to him at once, reassuringly. Then she recalled his mother's inquisition, and her indignation came to the surface.

She took pen and paper and wrote briefly, "I think you should stop writing to me. I don't think your mother approves of me. I could not really take to your mother. There is something about her that scares me," and she ended, "Don't write to me again until the war is over."

One day in November, as she stood behind the counter, Assunta was startled to hear the ringing of chimes from the university. She went out to the door of the shop followed closely by Giulietta who had also heard the joyous sounds through the open window of the backshop. Now they could hear hooters from factories in the distance and sirens from the ships on the Clyde. Crowds began to gather excitedly in Byres Road, and the happy cries of "The war is over!" echoed from corner to corner. People embraced warmly and danced with elation on the pavements. Assunta could not believe that the Scots could be so expansive. They swarmed out from houses in their dozens. In no time the road was blocked with hundreds of people, all cheering and singing, their cries broken by the impatient clanging of the bells of the tramcars trying to make their way along the road.

Then a sound of distant thunder was heard, and everybody looked up to the sky. A flight of aeroplanes approached and flew past to announce victory. Now a special edition of the *Glasgow Herald* appeared as if by magic in the hands of many of the bystanders, the caption "VICTORY" boldly emblazoned on the front page. Melodeon players made their way through the crowds, while here and there the reedy sound of the pipes could be heard.

Giulietta hugged Assunta, and Assunta hugged Giulietta, and they wept with joy. Then Giulietta broke all the rules and closed the shop. When they had hastily eaten, they locked up and made their way home on foot through the milling crowds. It was getting dark and when they came to the corner of Byres Road and University Avenue, their eyes were drawn to the left. They beheld hundreds of small, flickering flames coming down the road in four long lines. Assunta had never before seen a torchlight procession. Down they came, hundreds of students, each carrying a flaming torch, their voices raised in jubilant singing. Then Assunta began to feel faint and held on to Giulietta's arm.

"What's the matter?" Giulietta asked.

"I don't feel very well," said Assunta.

They walked slowly all the way to Argyle Street through throngs of people hysterical in their elation. Everywhere there was a great deal of noise. Everyone was mad with joy. At last, with much effort, they reached the third landing on the stairs, and Assunta slumped on to her knees. Giulietta, alarmed, unlocked the door and, helping her poor sister-in-law to her feet, led her into the lobby. Assunta saw the blur of the kitchen door as she lost consciousness.

Chapter Ten

1918 to 1921—Courtship and Marriage

For the first time in her life, Assunta was seriously ill. She had fallen victim to the dreaded Spanish 'flu, which swept through Glasgow during the last months of 1918. For three weeks she was confined to her bed in the kitchen, nursed by Giulietta and Giulietta's sister-in-law, Erminia, wife of Pietro, whose business was in Maryhill Road. Occasionally Giulia, her closest friend, would come and sit with her. When she tried to brush Assunta's hair, it came out in handfuls. As she could not eat, Assunta lost weight. But her sound constitution stood her in good stead and by the end of the third week, she began to eat again. Giulietta prepared nourishing chicken broth, and soon Assunta was able to get up for short spells and sit in the chair by the fire. She had lost most of her hair and looked quite pitifully drawn and pinched.

Soon it would be Christmas again and, although she felt very miserable, her hopes rose with the realisation that Eugenio would be returning from Italy. And Giuseppe too. Giuseppe too? The thought made her sit up. What was she doing thinking about that young man? Then she had to admit that for some time he really had occupied a special place in her affections. She realised she had been very harsh with him. But she was not yet completely ready to give him encouragement in his suit. He must prove to her that he really loved her.

As the war was over, Giuseppe took her at her word, and his letters began to arrive again. She acknowledged every second letter, though she never betrayed her feelings for him. She now discussed the weather as well as the state of their health. It was now February in 1919.

One day, looking in the mirror, she noticed that her hair, which was slowly growing back, was changing colour. It was losing its auburn tints and settling into a definite brown. It was a dismal winter. They were plagued with yellow fog, and the whole city was shrouded in dark, shadowy dirt. Assunta felt it was a pall of deep mourning for the three and a half million young men who had given their lives on the battlefields of Europe. Davie and his mischievous young friends had all perished in France. She would never see them again. And when those soldiers who had survived began to come home, disillusioned by the horrors of the carnage they had witnessed, their attitudes were changed.

One day in mid-February, Giulietta was overjoyed to receive a postcard from Eugenio. It had been posted in a little town called Culoz in France and read, "My dear, here I am in a little town where I also stopped last year. We have travelled well so far and are hoping to reach Paris this evening. My love to you both, Eugenio."

All day Giulietta was wildly excited at the thought of seeing her husband again. There was no news from Antonio, although he had written some weeks before to say he would be spending some time in Filignano where he had met a charming girl, Vittoria Ferri, whom he intended to marry. Assunta was particularly pleased by Antonio's news.

Then, one happy morning at the end of February, Eugenio arrived in Glasgow. Assunta found him unchanged by his experience. He had trimmed his moustache, and this made him look very smart. He was now in his fortieth year but did not look a day over thirty. Losing no time in getting the shop re-organized, one of his first jobs was to motorise the freezer. The days of hard hand-turning had come to an end, and the age of electrification had begun. To celebrate his return, he bought a beautiful gramophone. Its large horn gave it a certain impressive elegance, and it was placed in a prominent position on an extension of the counter that Eugenio built himself. Soon he began to make weekly purchases in the shop where he had bought the gramophone, just a few doors up Byres Road, and his record collection rapidly grew.

Assunta heard the voices of Caruso, Melba, and Destinn, and the range of her musical appreciation broadened. The orchestral pieces she particularly liked were the overture from *William Tell* (whose fast section never failed to accelerate the pace of her work), and Gounod's ballet music from *Faust*. One afternoon Eugenio excitedly brought in a record of Bach's *Toccata and Fugue in D Minor* made by a famous American symphony orchestra. This was a different kind of music. It seemed to describe the tragedy of the war they had just come through, but it ended with strong feelings of hope for a better world.

On her twenty-fourth birthday on the 24th of May 1919, Assunta received a long, affectionate letter from Giuseppe. He was about to be demobilised and for that purpose he was to travel to Rome. Now that he would be returning to Scotland, the time had come for him to marry, as his brother Antonio was moving from Parkhead to Airdrie to open a new business. His mother and sister would be carrying on with the shop at Parkhead, but Giuseppe felt he would like to have a business of his own. Now he wished to know what were Assunta's intentions? Did she find she had any feelings for him, and, if so, would she consent to marry him?

Assunta did not like making quick decisions. She replied suggesting that, since he was so desperate to find a wife, and since he was to go to Rome, so near Filignano, he might care to spend a short time in his native village where he would find just the right young woman to make him a good wife. She was sure there must be dozens of attractive girls in Collemacchia who were just dying to marry someone who would bring them to Glasgow. When Giuseppe read Assunta's words, he was at first astonished and puzzled. Then, when he read the letter again, he saw red. What did she mean by giving him advice of this sort? How dare she tell him what to do! He would teach her a lesson once and for all. This spirited young lady would have to be tamed, and he was the very chap to do it.

Early in July one morning, Assunta glanced up from the newspaper she was reading as she leaned on the counter to find herself looking into the dark-brown eyes of Giuseppe, eyes in which she saw smouldering anger and indignation mingled with a certain astonishment when he saw the changed colour of her hair. Before she even had time to speak, he drew her letter from his pocket and, waving it under her uppity, proud nose, said loudly, "How dare you write me such a letter, Assunta Marzella! Don't you have any feelings for anyone but yourself? Are you quite determined to break my heart?"

Assunta could not resist smiling at his passionate outburst. She looked at him calmly and asked in a quiet voice, "So you did not go back to Filignano after all?" As she said this, the mischief in her eyes made them sparkle, and she went on smiling. Giuseppe, as quick-witted as she, realised at once what her game had been, and he broke into an embarrassed grin.

"Yes," said Assunta. "I was really testing you, but now that I know your intentions are serious, I am quite willing to marry you when my brother gives his consent."

By this time Giulietta was beside them, and she overheard the last part of their conversation. She smiled and invited Giuseppe right away into the backshop to speak with Eugenio. Then she went back to Assunta and scolded her.

"Shame on you, Sunta, for keeping the poor boy hanging for so long. Take my advice and accept his proposal without further ado. I hear he is buying his own shop and has saved a great deal of money. He is also a good worker and besides, he's not bad-looking, you know!"

As Giulietta prattled on, Assunta thought, *Yes, he now has all the desirable qualities that she values, but she doesn't yet realise the most important thing for me is that he really loves me and now, at last, I am sure I too love him.*

After an earnest talk with Giuseppe, Eugenio was well satisfied that this young man would be a good husband for his sister. He gave his consent on condition that the marriage would not take place until Giuseppe had proved his new business was going to be profitable.

So a longish courtship began, for it was to take Giuseppe more than a year to prove to Eugenio that he would be able to support Assunta. He bought the goodwill of an old café in Garscube Road and set about fitting it out. He installed a fine, mahogany counter, wide, comfortable seats with long, marble-topped tables, and the walls of the shop were lined with beautiful oval mirrors in carved mahogany frames. The new fittings were set off by a really splendid terrazzo floor to make his café one of the best appointed in the area.

Giuseppe was a young man who liked doing things in style. There were no half measures with him and when he wanted something, it had to be of the very highest quality. To that end no expense was spared, and his hard-earned money was spent very freely.

He had a very captivating manner with the ladies and soon endeared himself to Giulietta, showing her great courtesy, respect, and civility. He also expressed himself well when he spoke and could turn a good phrase to excellent effect. He was naturally witty, and this added greatly to his charm. Assunta felt rather proud when he began calling once a week to take her to the pictures.

In those days the rules of chaperoning were strictly adhered to among the Italians in Scotland. No matter where Giuseppe and Assunta went, they were always accompanied by Giulietta or Giuseppe's sister Irena. Sometimes, as a special concession, Assunta's friend Giulia was allowed to go out with them. Giuseppe introduced Assunta to sophisticated pleasures she had never been permitted to enjoy before, going to the theatre as well as the cinema, having tea in Glasgow's fashionable tea rooms, and one day he took her to the Art Galleries where they admired the paintings of the masters. He often jokingly referred to himself as "Romeo with his two Juliets" when they were chaperoned from place to place.

Giuseppe's mother and sister often came to Byres Road, and the slight hostility Assunta had sensed from her future mother-in-law seemed to vanish as the weeks passed and they came to like one an-

113

other. She grew especially fond of Irena, and the two of them would often sit in a corner of the shop and have a good chat.

Giuseppe had rented a small room and kitchen house in Burnside Street, just round the corner from the café in Garscube Road. There Assunta and Giulia spent many an afternoon with Irena washing and cleaning, dusting and ironing. This little house was soon to be Assunta's first home of her own in Scotland.

But just when all seemed to be going well for them, out of the blue, Giuseppe contracted rheumatic fever and he was confined to bed for several weeks. The shop at Parkhead had to be closed while Leonarda and Irena took turns at nursing the invalid. Assunta and her friend Giulia kept the café open in Garscube Road. By the spring of 1920, Giuseppe was again on his feet and, although he had been badly shaken by his illness, his cheerful disposition soon set him right.

Giulietta's brother Antonio had married Vittoria Ferri, and he soon afterwards brought his lovely bride to Glasgow. They opened a café at the top end of Garscube Road, calling it "The Thistle Rest." Assunta was very attracted to Vittoria with her warm, friendly personality, and they soon became good friends.

As 1920 was drawing to a close, Eugenio being pleased with the profit Giuseppe was showing in his shop, the date for the wedding was fixed for the 20th of January, 1921. Giulietta and Eugenio decided to make the wedding a great social occasion. More than a hundred guests among their Italian and Scottish friends were invited.

Although Assunta's engagement to Giuseppe had not been formally celebrated, she now wore the ring her fiancé had bought her on her twenty-fifth birthday. It was on that very day he had impulsively kissed her for the first time after placing the ring on her finger, although Eugenio, Giulietta, and Giulia were all present in the backshop. It had been a very brief kiss, but the moment their lips met, Assunta felt a strange, new, warm spark kindling in her heart, and a wave of love for Giuseppe swept through her, awakening strong desires she had never dreamt existed. The blood rushed to her cheeks, and the small company were amused by her blushful embarrassment.

When Giulietta had bought the white silk material for Assunta's wedding dress, she handed it to Mrs. Wiseman, a local dressmaker who was a good friend of the Marzellas. Under her skilful fingers, a beautiful dress was created. Oval-shaped pearls were sewn into the rucked neckline, and at the front of the dress from the waist hung two broad silk ribbons, each ending in a fringe over which three more pearls had been sewn. The dress had elbow-length sleeves ending in a double frill to cover the cuffs of the long satin gloves the bride would wear on her wedding day. The long, flowing veil was purchased separately and would be held in place with a simple head-dress intertwined with lily-of-the-valley simulated in wax with a small sprig of real white heather at either end.

Giuseppe insisted upon buying the white satin shoes with slightly raised heels and the white silk stockings that would complete the bride's ensemble. Each of the shoes had a flower motif held in position at the centre by a round matching pearl. Mrs. Wiseman also made the white satin dress to be worn by the bridesmaid, Irena. She too would be wearing a short veil. Giuseppe asked his good friend Giorgio Capaldi to be best man.

Christmas and New Year were not particularly exciting for Assunta that year as she looked forward to her wedding day. Apart from the sheer joy of marrying Giuseppe, she was relishing the prospect of seeing her parents and Antonia again after six years, for Giuseppe had decided they would be honeymooning in Italy. She could hardly believe that so much time had passed and marvelled at the speed with which her marriage had been settled.

Wedding presents began to arrive early in January 1921. Eugenio and Giulietta bought Assunta a very fine mahogany bedroom suite, and it had already been delivered to the house in Burnside Street. In addition, Eugenio opened a bank account with the Glasgow Savings Bank in his sister's name, depositing the magnificent sum of fifty pounds.

Assunta constantly shared her delight at all the wonderful things that were happening with her friend Giulia. Then, early in January, tragedy struck at Giulia's family, and her younger brother, Alfredo, contracted diphtheria and died within a few days. This sad death cast a deep shadow over Assunta's happiness, and she wept bitter tears when Giulia clung to her after the boy's funeral. She felt so much for her friend's bereavement that she even considered postponing the wedding, but Giulia would not hear of this.

"I shall not, of course, be attending your wedding, *cara* Sunta," she said, her eyes moist with tears, "but there is a favour I would like to ask."

"Anything, anything you want, *cara* Giulia," said Assunta.

"Could I have the privilege of dressing you on the morning of your wedding?" asked Giulia.

"There is no one I would rather have than you, Giulia," said Assunta.

So, early on the morning of Thursday, the 20th of January, Giulia arrived at the Marzellas' new house in University Avenue, into which they had moved a few weeks before. Situated just round the corner from the Continental, it was a comfortable top flat with two bedrooms, a large living room with a recessed bed, a kitchen with a bed in an alcove, and a large bathroom with toilet, wash hand basin, and bath.

Assunta was just emerging from the bath when Giulietta opened the door to Giulia. They all went into Giulietta's bedroom where the gas fire glowed warmly, and Assunta was soon dry and ready to be dressed by her friend. Giulietta left the two girls to go through and attend to Eugenio. While Giulia was dressing Assunta, neither of them spoke. But when she had finished, the tears soon welled from her eyes, and the girls threw their arms round each other's shoulders and stood there silently weeping. Giulietta, popping her head round the door, beheld a very sad picture.

"Come, come, girls," she called out, "dry your tears. This should be a happy day. We don't want to cloud the bride's eyes!"

As she spoke, the doorbell started to ring, and she hurried away to answer it. Assunta and Giulia went through to the parlour where two lovely bouquets had already arrived from the florist, one for the bride and the other for the bridesmaid. When Giulietta answered the door, it was the groom himself, delivering his sister Irena. He exchanged a few hasty words with Giulietta who assured him his bride was up and well and already dressed, but, under no circumstances, could he see her.

Waiting for him down in the taxi was his best man, Giorgio. They were both very well turned out in their black, tailored suits. Giuseppe wore a high, twin-peaked, starched collar over a white silk shirt and a fine, grey silk tie. From his waistcoat dangled a gold chain with a large ruby on the end. His white cotton gloves matched the spats he was wearing over his black, patent leather shoes. The gleaming whiteness of the tip of the white silk handkerchief peeping out from the breast pocket in his coat competed perfectly with the white carnation in his buttonhole. Giorgio wore a more conventional shirt with which the white bow-tie he was sporting went well. The carnation in his buttonhole was pink.

As it was too early to go to the church, the groom and best man went on a brief tour of the city centre. They discussed business prospects for 1921, the unsettled state of the country, the alarming early signs of unemployment. It occurred to Giuseppe that he was perhaps being extravagant in planning a long honeymoon, but he thought it might be a very long time before they could afford another holiday. Giorgio agreed. Then it was time to be at St. Peter's, and they stepped out of the taxi just as the sun parted the clouds with which the day had begun. As they went up the steps into the church, Giuseppe looked up at the sky and smiled. It was going to be a fine day.

From the moment Eugenio led her from the taxi inside the church and up the long aisle, Assunta came under a strong enchantment. She seemed to move lightly up to the altar where Giuseppe and Giorgio were waiting. Irena walked close behind her and took up her position beside Giorgio, while Eugenio, having conducted her to Giuseppe's side, stepped back and joined Giulietta in her seat. Some of the people in the church who were not wedding guests imagined it was going to be a double wedding when they saw Irena also wearing a veil.

Assunta was overwhelmed by the beauty of the setting. The altar had been decorated with fresh flowers, the candles glowed softly, and the organ was quietly singing. The fatherly face of the old priest was comforting and when he spoke, she made her responses without effort. Soon she felt Giuseppe taking her hand and, as he placed the ring neatly on her finger, their eyes met beamingly. As soon as the priest had uttered the final words of the wedding ceremony, Giuseppe raised her veil and leaned forward to brush his lips delicately against hers. Her happiness brimmed over, and two tiny tears made their way slowly down her cheeks.

The pale January sun shone down upon them as they stepped out of the church and made their way down the steps to the waiting taxi. Giorgio threw handfuls of small coins for the eager children who scrambled forward to pick up what they could. Assunta felt their smiling little faces were blessing her, and she put her hand to her mouth and blew them a kiss. Some of the children cheered, and Assunta waved to them, gratefully. As the taxi drove away, she noticed many of the guests were already getting into their taxis.

What a lot of people have come to my wedding, she thought, and all the time Giuseppe tightly held her hand in his.

As they travelled along Dumbarton Road to Sauchiehall Street, the movement of the taxi caused the confetti on their shoulders to fall silently onto the floor. Irena and Giorgio sat opposite the bride and groom, and Irena kept murmuring over and over again, "What a lovely wedding! What a lovely wedding!"

Giuseppe had had the foresight to arrange for a full photographic session at Romney's and there he was photographed with his bride, and then a full group showing the principal members of the young couple's families was taken. Assunta and Giuseppe sat in the centre of the front row. On Assunta's left Alberto, her new nephew, sat beside his mother, Genevina. On Giuseppe's right was Dalfina, his little niece, and next to her, Mamma Leonarda. Directly behind Leonarda stood

117

Giorgio with Irena, then Eugenio and Giulietta and, at the end of the back row behind his wife and son stood Antonio, Giuseppe's brother.

Their guests were awaiting them at the Charing Cross Halls, and, after the bridal party had retired briefly to a side room to freshen up, they came out to be congratulated. They moved round the lined-up guests, shaking hands and exchanging a few polite words. Everyone was finely turned out, the ladies unaffectedly fashionable in their long dresses and neat silk gloves, many of them wearing small corsages of vari-coloured carnations, the men shining and smart in their dark suits with their carnation buttonholes. When the five-tier wedding cake had been cut and the champagne served, they all filed into the dining room for a splendid five-course meal.

Assunta ate very little as she heard many toasts being made in the distance. Telegrams were opened and read out. Eugenio made a short speech in which he sang the praises of his sister. Then Giuseppe rose to say a few words of thanks. By this time the strains of a little orchestra could be heard filtering through from the adjoining suite, and the bride and groom went through to open the dance. As she enjoyed the first waltz with Giuseppe's arm around her, Assunta had a strong sensation of everything and everyone fading away around them. She and Giuseppe were dancing alone in a hall of mirrors, and she felt she could go on dancing with him until the end of time.

Later, as she sat beside signora Leonarda, her mother-in-law turned to her and said, "You have made my son very happy by marrying him today. When I first met you, I had some doubts about you because you gave me the impression of being a haughty and proud young lady. But I can see now you will make my son a good wife, and I am sure you and I are going to get on well together." Assunta felt such a glow of affection at Leonarda's kindness that she turned and kissed her warmly on the cheek. Giuseppe came up to them at that very moment.

Delighted by Assunta's gesture, he exclaimed, "I see you two are getting on well. Come, Mamma, let's you and I show this company how a good Italian dance should be performed!" and, turning proudly to the guests, he announced in Italian, "Ladies and gentlemen, my mother and I will now dance for your pleasure. We hope that, after the first round of the dance, you will all join in."

Then, as he had doubtlessly primed the leader of the orchestra beforehand, the first bars of a lively tarantella quickly followed his words. Signora Leonarda rose smartly to take her son's arm and when they reached the centre of the floor, they broke into a lively dance with a great deal of hand-clapping and hopping, hooping and hooting. The long, white silk scarf Leonarda was wearing over her black satin dress

118

swirled with the rhythmical, jerky movements of her body. Soon the dancing couple were joined by Irena and Giorgio, Giulietta and Eugenio, and many others while Genevina sat with Assunta and admired the lively nimbleness of the dancers.

Assunta's thoughts went back to the many times she had danced the *panno rosso* in the open setting of the *aia* beside the house on Imperatore, under a full moon after a long day of harvesting. She dreamily recaptured the strong scent of the freshly cut wheat, and the woodsmoke drifting over the open fires where the workers were grilling sausages. In a few days' time, she would again be breathing the pure air of Filignano. Would she find it much altered? Would her parents and Antonia find her greatly changed?

Her reverie was broken by the sound of a familiar voice raised in song. Giuseppe, so full of himself in his happiness, was singing a favourite Neapolitan song, a daring one to be sure, and, his eyes fully upon her, he continued, "Oh Mari, oh Mari, how sleepless my nights over you. If I could only sleep one night with my arms entwined around you!" and the guests tittered good-naturedly at the emphasis Giuseppe placed on the second line of the song. But he sang well and was rewarded with loud applause.

Thus encouraged, barely pausing for breath, he launched into "A vucchella" — "Enchanting little mouth," moving closer to Assunta's chair with each line he sang. She became very ill at ease as he moved closer. Then to add to her disconcertion did he not bend over and kiss her fully on the lips, just as he finished the song! For a brief instant, she thought she was going to slap him as he had really gone too far this time, but his kiss evoked such enthusiasm among the guests who came out spontaneously with cries of "*Bravi gli sposi, che bravi gli sposi!* Well done, our newly-weds, well done!" that her anger quickly subsided into pleasure and she smiled at the guests, acknowledging their praise. The groom's songs inspired others to sing, and the Charing Cross Halls echoed with Italian and Scots songs.

Now it was nearly nine o'clock and time for the departure of the bride and groom. Assunta changed into her travelling clothes, a warm woollen suit with brown, wool-lined boots over which she wore a brown coat with a dark fur collar. The honeymoon couple began to take leave of their relatives and friends, and there was much hand-shaking, hugging, and kissing. Leonarda broke down and had a good cry when her son and Assunta came to take their leave.

Eugenio and Giulietta accompanied them to the station where they were to take the overnight train to London. Soon they were all aboard, and Giulietta went through the motions of dabbing her eyes with her handkerchief while Eugenio grinned and told them not to get up to any mischief in Paris. He said, "Don't eat any meat there unless you fancy a bit of horseflesh. Stick to chicken, and you will be all right."

"Don't forget to go to Bottazzella," said Giulietta, "as my mother has not been too well of late."

Eugenio and Giulietta alighted as the train was about to depart. Then, as they both smilingly looked up from the platform, Assunta said, "Thank you for all you have done for me. I shall always be in your debt."

Eugenio smiled and muttered, "Forget it. It was nothing."

The guard blew his whistle, there was much puffing and blowing from the large locomotive, and as the train suddenly lurched into motion, Assunta and Giuseppe, leaning out of the narrow window in the corridor, banged their heads together, as they waved to Giulietta and Eugenio. When they should have been looking reasonably earnest, they were in fact convulsed with laughter. Eugenio and Giulietta grew smaller and smaller as the train progressed along the platform before they disappeared completely as it took a bend in the line. Giuseppe pulled up the window, using the broad, leather strap, then, rubbing the side of his head as he turned to his wife, he smiled and exclaimed, "Alone at last!"

Chapter Eleven

1921—Honeymoon in Filignano

On their long journey to Filignano, the newlyweds stopped in Paris for two days. Giuseppe had spent some time in the city on his various journeys to and from Italy, and he loved it. After a choppy crossing from Dover to Calais, they boarded a French train and arrived in Paris on the evening of January the 21st. They booked in at a small hotel in Montparnasse that Giuseppe knew. After settling in, they went out and had a meal in a bistro around the corner, avoiding steaks following Eugenio's advice.

There was a nip in the air when they came out, so Giuseppe hailed a taxi. They went on a leisurely tour of the city, and Assunta enjoyed the brilliance of the illuminated signs they saw everywhere. It was nearly ten o'clock, and the streets were very animated with people going hither and thither, gazing into the colourful shop windows, making their way into theatres and cinemas. Giuseppe told the driver to stop outside a cinema that was showing a Charlie Chaplin film. The large letters **CHARLOT** promised an hour of laughter. They were amused, because they could not understand the French captions, but had no difficulty in following the adventures of the little bowler-hatted tramp.

An hour or so later they were walking over one of the many bridges crossing the Seine. The air seemed milder on the Left Bank and they sat down at a café and sipped warm lemon tea. They did not talk much, having by this time fallen into that sweet silence of lovers engrossed in each other in which they communicated with a swift or lingering look and the smallest of gestures. Giuseppe scarcely let go of Assunta's hand. So they sat for an hour watching the people walking past, and musicians came on to the café terrace playing accordions. At the corner of the street, an old man was selling roast chestnuts over a hot stove. Assunta had the clear, vivid impression of life being enjoyed at an intense level in this beautiful city.

Next morning they rose early and enjoyed a good breakfast of creamy coffee, crisp fresh, fluted bread with butter and marmalade, and hot croissants that melted deliciously in their mouths. They then went on a tour of the city, first taking a taxi to Notre Dame where they admired the beautiful façade of the cathedral from the Place. Later they found themselves walking along the banks of the Seine, intrigued by the large number of small bookstalls where so many second-hand books were on offer.

"The Parisians must read a great deal," observed Assunta.

"You must remember there are thousands of students studying in Paris," said Giuseppe.

In the distance they could see the Eiffel Tower. They slowly made their way to it. The streets were bustling with people going about with a purposeful air, ladies in elegant outfits, mustachioed gentlemen in warm coats with fur collars. Everywhere, on street corners, on the bridges, artists with their easels were trying to capture on canvas the vibrant truth of the moment their eyes beheld. They did not seem to mind if one stopped to study them at work, and Assunta was intrigued to see the street scenes emerging on the canvases under the deft strokes of their brushes. The weather continued to be fine and eventually and inevitably, having taken two lifts, they found themselves at the very top of the Eiffel Tower looking down on the variegated pattern of the most beautiful city Assunta had ever seen.

"I believe I could live here," she said.

"Too late for that now, Sunta," said Giuseppe. "It's Garscube Road for us when we get back!"

They spent the next day exploring the city and walking along the banks of the Seine. In the evening after dinner, they left the hotel and made for the station where the train for Rome was leaving at midnight.

Following the sophisticated delights of Paris, Rome seemed somehow more provincial to Assunta. The streets and piazzas were well lit, but they did not match the brilliance of Paris. Giuseppe was amused by the number of clergymen they saw everywhere.

"This is truly the City of Priests," he commented. They were also aware of the tremendous amount of human noise assailing their ears as they sat eating at a trattoria. There was no doubting they were now in Italy, surrounded by their voluble, loquacious fellow countrymen. Next morning they took the train for Venafro, arriving shortly before noon. Once out of the train, Assunta was enveloped by the fragrance of her native air. She breathed it in, happy to be so near home. On the taxi to Filignano, she recognised the various spots on the road she knew so well.

There was not a cloud in the pale blue sky as they came into the piazza. Unloading their luggage, they remained unrecognised at first by the curious few standing around. They had not bothered to wire, so they were not expected just then. Giuseppe went into the post office and asked the lady in charge if they could leave their luggage with her for a short time. But when he came out, in some mysterious manner, the news of their arrival had already reached Imperatore, and he saw Antonia and two other girls hugging and kissing his wife. Then, without further ado, the girls went into the post office, carried out the three suitcases and, after shaking hands with Giuseppe, lifted them on to their heads and began the climb to Imperatore followed closely by the newlyweds.

People appeared at doorways to greet them warmly, and old women rushed out to embrace the bride and wish the young couple well. Their progress up the hill was interrupted more than once while the call was heard echoing over and over again, "Assunta Marzella has arrived from Glasgow with her husband, Giuseppe!" Then there were prolonged ohs and ahs when the couple came into view. Their fashionable clothes were much admired, and Assunta was congratulated for choosing such a handsome chap to be her husband. Giuseppe beamed with each new compliment.

At last they came to the large oak door of the house. But there was no sign of either Filomena or Benedetto. Assunta raised the large brass knocker and let it fall three times. At the third, dull knock, she heard a sound on her left and Chiaruccia, the goat, now very much older, came clumping over from the *aia*, whimpering rather than bleating, to greet her long-lost mistress. Assunta fell on her knees and put her arms affectionately round the animal's neck. Giuseppe and the girls smiled. Then Antonia hurried to the edge of the *aia* and slithered down the short slope to the vegetable plot where she found Filomena hoeing at the hard earth.

When she heard that Assunta had arrived with Giuseppe, she dropped the hoe and left it lying on the ground. Then she scurried up the slope with Antonia, wiping her hands on her woollen apron as she hurried along. Assunta turned in time to see her mother, who seemed to have grown smaller, rushing towards her in a series of short, uneven steps, her lips trembling with emotion, her eyes already glistening with tears. They threw their arms around each other and wept. Again and again they embraced, unable to believe they were really together again, and Filomena could not contain the little cries of happiness that rose to her lips from time to time. Then Assunta introduced Giuseppe, and he threw his arms around the little lady, almost lifting her from the ground in a warm hug.

"Come in, come in, all of you come in!" said Filomena as she opened the door and showed them into the kitchen. Then she rushed to fetch a jar of wine and some glasses, and Assunta helped her to pour the wine.

"How wonderful you look and how smart you are, Sunta!" said Antonia, who could not get over the astonishing change in her friend.

"I wonder where that father of yours has got to?" said Filomena. Her question was answered by Antonia who had seen Benedetto walking up the hill to the wood earlier in the day.

"Then we shall not see him until supper time, I fear!" said Filomena. So they all sat down round the kitchen table and drank the wine, and Filomena brought out some *biscotti* she had baked, and she plied Assunta and Giuseppe with eager questions about Eugenio and Giulietta, and Glasgow, and the wedding, and their journey, and why they had taken so long to come home.

The girls then carried all the luggage upstairs to Assunta's bedroom where a double bed had been installed for the happy couple, and they helped Assunta to unpack, while Filomena got busy downstairs in the kitchen preparing the evening meal, enjoying her first long chat with her new son-in-law.

At the first opportunity, Assunta could not resist taking a short walk round the house. Everything seemed to be as she remembered it. Beside the pen outside where Chiaruccia was kept, a sty had been constructed and a fat, grunting pig looked up at her inquisitively as she stood there.

"What's your name, pig?" she asked, and her question was answered by Antonia who was close beside her.

"That's Porcone," she said, "and I am afraid he is to be slaughtered next week." Assunta thought it was just as well she had not come home sooner, for she would have become too attached to the pig and would have been heartbroken to see him killed.

Filomena then appeared with a basinful of acorns for the animal and suggested, "Why don't you and Giuseppe take a walk up to the wood and bring your wandering father home?"

So the bride and groom set off up the stony road and, as they passed Zia Adelaida's house, that worthy lady came out to congratulate them on their happy marriage, and she insisted on having a kiss from the groom as well as the bride. They had walked some distance and were near the wood when they saw Benedetto emerging with a large tree trunk over his shoulder. He had stripped it of all its branches and as he walked along, bending under its weight, it swayed up and down on his shoulder.

He was so intent upon balancing it that he did not see them and was about to pass when Assunta called out, "What's the matter, ta', don't you recognise your own daughter just because she happens to be with her husband?"

Benedetto came to a sudden halt when he heard Assunta's voice. The tree trunk fell to the ground with a dull thud and went rolling down the slope a short distance before coming to a halt against a boulder. Then, as he turned round, he felt Assunta's arms round his neck and her kisses on his cheeks. He forgot his usual reserve and returned her greetings warmly. Then he stepped back, smiled, and took a good look at his daughter. Assunta introduced Giuseppe, and the two men embraced with feeling. Giuseppe went down to the tree trunk and lifted it with difficulty on to his shoulder, ignoring the mess that the loose bark made of his jacket.

So, the three of them walked down to the house to be greeted with Filomena's cry, "What's this, Benedetto? Your son-in-law has just arrived and already you are shifting work on to him!" And she tut-tutted when she saw the marks on her son-in-law's good jacket.

That evening, as they sat round the fire after supper, Assunta felt a special glow and satisfaction in seeing that the family circle now included Giuseppe. As expected, after the rosary, Filomena could not resist telling one of her stories. Seeming to address Giuseppe in particular, as she looked at him, she began.

"When Assunta was only a tiny girl, Antoniella Ciabotto fell in love with Pacifico Cocozza, an excellent cobbler. Theirs was a whirlwind courtship, and soon they were married and settled in Pacifico's little house. All went well at first, but after a few months Pacifico took to meeting his friends in the local cantina on Sundays. There they played cards and drank. Antoniella spent the day at her mother's and went home early in the evening to make Pacifico's supper.

"One Sunday Pacifico drank more than usual, which was very incautious on his part. By the time he left the cantina to go home, it was getting dark and, unsteady on his feet, he tottered and lurched here and there. In his bemused state, he thought he would take a shortcut as he did not want to annoy his wife by being late. So he staggered off the road and cut across a *pastino*, or tilth, and jumped over a dry stone wall. But the wall was higher than he thought, and he landed face down on some boulders on the other side. He felt a sharp jab of pain in his bladder, and, trying to rise to his feet, found he could not lift himself. He was not far from the house and he called out in agony to Antoniella.

"When she heard her husband's cries, she rushed to his aid but

125

could not lift him. She ran for help, and the hapless Pacifico was carried into the house and laid on his bed. All this time he never stopped screaming with pain, and the sweat was running out of him. The doctor was sent for but, after examining Pacifico, he shook his head and suggested that Antoniella should send for the priest. In his fall, Pacifico had burst his bladder. So that is the sad story of a cobbler who drank too much," Filomena concluded, her eyes still upon Giuseppe.

"I feel there is a warning somewhere in this tale for me," said Giuseppe, turning to Assunta, "but I would ask you to inform your dear mother that I am not a boozer!" and they all smiled at his boldness in putting his mother-in-law in her place.

"That's a very gloomy story to be telling these young people on their honeymoon," said Benedetto to his wife. "Can't you tell us something more amusing, woman?"

"I'll try my best," answered Filomena, and, patting Giuseppe on the shoulder to assure him she was not seriously getting at him, she went on.

"Once in Naples there was a lovely young woman called Serafina who used to stand at street corners selling pizza. So she was a *pizzaiuola*.

"One day when she was selling her delicious pizzas, a young street minstrel called Gerardino came passing by, his guitar cradled in his arms. He paused to admire Serafina's beauty but said nothing and went on his way striking up a happy song. On the following day, he made a point of passing near the same corner, and this time he lingered so that it was obvious the love songs he was singing were for the benefit of Serafina. When her eyes turned to him, he thought he saw in them a welcoming expression. When he finished his recital and picked up the few coins thrown in his direction, he went up to her and bought a pizza.

"Then, squatting on the ground beside her, he asked, 'Do you mind if I eat my pizza here, beside you?'

" 'Not at all,' she said, and, lifting a flask of good red wine with a glass over its mouth from beneath the little table she used as a stand, she offered it to him, saying, 'Here is good wine to wash it down.'

"With such encouragement from the *pizzaiuola*, Gerardino lost no time in pursuing his suit, and shortly afterwards they were married. Just before the wedding, Serafina asked him what he could offer by way of security if she married him.

" 'I can offer you only my guitar and my little house,' he answered, and since he seemed so earnest and sincere as he said this, she did not have the heart to turn him down.

"Once they were married, Gerardino was too proud to allow her to continue plying her trade selling pizzas. He insisted she stay at home while he wandered round the streets of the town singing his love for Serafina, trying to earn enough to support her. But times grew hard, and although the people liked listening to his songs, very few could afford to toss the odd coin on the ground. Serafina's meagre savings were soon used up. There was no money in the house to buy food and other necessities. Since there was little to do, Serafina would sit at the window and watch her husband when he walked past, singing.

"One evening as he did so, he sang out to her, 'Serafina, Serafina, what have you prepared to eat?'

"And she sang gaily back, 'There's nothing in the house, so you can nibble at your feet!'

"And he: 'Well, I told you, Serafina, all I had was my guitar!'

"And she:

'And your house whose little door is now very much ajar,
For the tasteless wind of hunger is blowing very cold,
And you'll starve to death, my sweet, before you're very old!' "

When Filomena finished reciting the rhyming end of this bitter-sweet story of the Neapolitan lovers, Giuseppe assured her that he would see to it that her daughter would never lack food.

On her way to Bottazzella next morning to visit Giulietta's parents, as she had promised, Assunta walked through favourite spots on the high road from which she could look down and admire the plain below. The trees were bare, the air crisp, but the mild sunshine offered comforting warmth. She swung the small towelful of *biscotti* Filomena was sending to Albina from side to side as she made her way along the stony road.

But when she arrived at Bottazella, she was dismayed to see how ill Albina was. She was being nursed by Giulietta's sister, Assunta, who had left her family in Santa Maria Oliveto to come to her mother's assistance. She was worried as she had now been away from home for three weeks. Her three children, two boys and a girl, were at an age when they needed constant supervision. Assunta offered to help by returning on the following day when she would stay with Albina for a week and let the other Assunta get back to Santa Maria. It would be a good opportunity for Assunta to repay in part Giulietta's kindness to her in the past.

Then she would be in Bottazzella when they killed the pig and would miss that unpleasant business. When the pig was slaughtered, neighbours had to be called in to help with the processing of the meat, the making of sausages, and the salting of hams. She remembered being subjected to this ordeal every year when she was young. It was Alessandro Marzella, Zia Adelaida's son, who actually killed the pig. The poor animal's hind and fore legs were bound firmly with thick ropes. This was when the shrill screaming of the poor victim started, and Assunta would stuff her ears with wool to shut out the distressing cries.

Four strong men then lifted the struggling creature on to a heavy wooden table so that its head hung over the edge at one end. The men held the pig firmly down while the slaughterer inserted the long, sharp, pointed knife into the animal's neck as his screams grew more frantic and desperate. Women stood ready with large tin basins to catch the gushing blood, and as the flow of red, steaming liquid increased, so did the pig's cries gradually diminish to a pitiful whimper until at last, with a final shuddering of his whole frame, he became inert and finally still. When Alessandro was satisfied that his victim had expired, the carcase was carried to a cool room where it was suspended head downwards from a stout beam, a basin being placed under the head to catch the last drop of blood. Assunta never failed to shed tears at this gory spectacle, and the sound of the poor creature's screams rang in her ears for many days afterwards.

When the carcase had been hung for a couple of days, those neighbours who were skilled with the knife, were called in to help with the quartering. In the meantime a large portion of the pig's blood had already been used to make *pappone,* or blood porridge. A large cauldron was set over the open fire and the blood, thinned slightly with water and salted, was placed in it. When it began to heat, maize flour was added, a handful at a time, and all the while the mixture was stirred as it slowly cooked and thickened. Certain aromatic ingredients were added such as pine seeds, orange peel, and herbs. Filomena even added raisins. When cooked, the *pappone* could be eaten hot, or cooled to be fried later as it was required.

Only a small quantity of the pig's blood was used for this seasonal dish. The rest was left aside for the making of *sanguinacci,* or black puddings.

When the pig's carcase had been quartered, those parts that were to be salt-cured were wrapped in cloth gauze and left hanging for a few more days. The rest of the meat was cut up to make sausages. The entrails were thoroughly washed and the liver and kidneys set aside to be chopped up. The meat, liver, and kidneys to be used for the sausages were not minced but cut by hand with sharp knives into the tiniest of pieces and put into separate metal basins. Salt and black pepper were added as well as crushed hot peppers and herbs. The guts were then cut into suitable lengths, tied at one end and stuffed with the seasoned meat, liver, or kidney. The congealed blood was cooked with a small quantity of maize flour, seasoned, and then stuffed into the washed lengths of gut.

When the sausages and the *sanguinacci* had been made, they were ready to be preserved. The usual method was simply to hang them on pulleys in a cool, dry place until they dried. Another was to melt some of the pig's lard and pour it over the newly-made sausages in a *pignatta*. When the fat solidified, it preserved the sausages. Those who had pure olive oil to spare would use this same method, substituting oil for lard.

The salt-curing of the hams was a long, laborious process. Having been placed on a heavy table, the hams were rubbed all over with coarse salt. This rubbing went on for two to three hours. Deep, narrow incisions were then made in the hams with special knives, and fine salt was inserted and pushed in with spikes. Then the rubbing process was resumed until the hams were well and truly salted. Cured in this way, the hams would not be ready for eating for several months while they hung in the cool, wine cellars.

Giuseppe was sorry to lose his bride for a week while she went to look after Albina, but he realized it was her duty to do so. He promised to visit her at Bottazzella every evening after helping Filomena and Benedetto with the various chores at Imperatore.

Assunta swept and cleaned the Cocozza house, washed the bed linen, which had to be changed every day, cooked the meals, and helped to feed the animals. Albina and Luigi were very grateful for the young woman's help. In the evening when Assunta and Luigi sat by the invalid's bed to keep her company, Assunta prepared two large braziers and set these on the floor to keep the room warm and comfortable. The nights were cold, and she made Luigi wrap a warm blanket round his shoulders while she kept on her woollen shawl. Giuseppe came and sat with them every evening, keeping on his coat. The old people wanted to know everything concerning their daughter in Glasgow, and Assunta needed no great encouragement to prattle on, to the delight of Albina and Luigi who absorbed all the details of her accounts.

Albina began to show signs of improvement and one evening near the end of the week Assunta asked her to tell them about the family's journey to Russia many years before.

Albina began, "In the last year of the last century, the year 1899 to be precise, we had an exceptionally bad harvest. There we were, Luigi and I, with six hungry mouths to feed and the prospect of a grim winter before us. Giulia was then fifteen, Pietro thirteen, Assunta eleven, and Antonio six years of age. I had always wanted to see a bit of the world, countries beyond the northern frontier of Italy, for I had an aunt who had travelled all over Northern Europe and she had even been to Russia, coming back laden with wealth and wonderful tales about that unusual country.

" 'Why don't we go to Russia?' I said to Luigi. 'Not for good, only for a year or two. We could earn a great deal of money and come back rich.' For Giulietta could play the accordion and Assunta could dance. The boys could sing and Luigi played the violin. I too had a tolerable voice.

"We left our house and land in the care of my cousin Maria and her husband, Alberto. They would plant the crops in our absence and take the benefit themselves. We sold off all our animals and set off bravely on foot, making our way very slowly to the north of Italy. Our performances took place in village piazzas and town squares, and we earned a fair amount of money. Sometimes we would spend the night on a farm, sleeping in a warm stable. If we had a good day, we would stop at an inn and enjoy a nourishing meal before sleeping on comfortable beds. We proceeded slowly and did not reach the Italian frontier until early spring. By this time we had saved enough money to pay for our train fares. So we began our long journey by rail, stopping off here and there to perform in strange places, just as our fancy took us.

"It was one of the happiest times in my life. How good it was to awaken each morning in a different place with new faces, strange tongues, odd customs, and unusual varieties of food. We had no difficulty in making ourselves understood as the language of signs is international, and, since we were able to pay our way, there were no obstacles to our progress. Our music was much appreciated, no doubt seeming exotic to foreign ears. The people of Poland warmed to us, and we found them kind and sympathetic. They are a very religious people, and they practise the real charity of Christianity with sincerity.

"The autumn of 1900 found us in Russia. I could not hope to describe to you the extraordinary landscapes of that exceptionally wonderful country. And the people. When we appeared before audiences of countryfolk, we could feel waves of affection coming over to us. And what hospitality! Comfortable rooms with enormous beds to sleep in, warm, appetising food, and such tasty bread! The Russians love fairs, and often we would find ourselves at a country fair in some village. Hundreds of peasants would flock there to sell their produce and purchase clothing and household utensils. Moving from place to place, we came to some areas where there was poverty, and there we earned nothing.

"By this time we had purchased a small covered cart and a horse, and we could travel from village to village more quickly. It was very comforting to spend the nights in huts heated by stoves fed with logs. Giulietta had bloomed, and often Luigi and I had to ward off the interested attention of the handsome, sturdy, young Russians whose eyes flashed in her direction. Sometimes in our wanderings we came to the immense house of some nobleman. When we arrived, the servants would show us to a comfortable hut where we could live for a few days, on the understanding that we would make ourselves available in the evenings to entertain the guests in the house.

"Giulietta's contribution to the entertainment became more and more special as the months passed. She would pass her accordion to Assunta and perform a gipsy dance with a tambourine. If the performance was being given indoors, she would throw off her shoes and dance barefoot, her lithe little body bending and twisting to the wild rhythms beaten out by dozens of hands clapping in unison. Large sums of money were showered upon us, and our stock of useful materials kept growing. Sometimes the lady of the house, charmed by her dancing, would present Giulietta with a large bolt of silk or satin or velvet. At one palace she was presented with a gold locket on a gold chain.

"Presently it became apparent that the little cart we had could not hold all the things we were collecting. So Luigi bought a larger one, and it was so roomy we could easily sleep in it when the nights were not too cold."

While Albina was speaking, Assunta realised that the old woman's recollection of her journey through Russia was already shaded with that nostalgic aura that we confer upon those periods of our lives we later realise were the happiest. There were no details in her descriptions, no regular progression or chronology. She was simply recalling the highlights of a unique experience.

She went on, "Weeks and months passed as we led our nomadic way of life. In winter the heavy snow hampered our activities, and we preferred to spend that season in the cities where we could lodge cheaply and limit our performances in the open air to short periods in the evenings when we could busk outside theatres or town halls where functions might be taking place. To be sure Luigi and I were not too happy about that sort of thing as we considered it to be a kind of begging.

"So we came to the spring of the year 1902, and Giulietta was now a young woman, Pietro a handsome young man of fifteen, Assunta already fourteen, and Antonio no longer a child at nine. It was time for us to be making our way homewards. On the way back, we naturally passed through towns and villages we recognised. We did not hurry, lingering in those places holding some special attraction for us either because they were beautiful or because the people were exceptionally kind to us.

"One day when we were playing in a Polish market town, a young man with fiery eyes and a neat beard came up to me after the performance and indicated he would like to paint Giulietta. He would pay a good fee, and his studio was just round the corner. Although I was just a little suspicious of his intentions, I agreed. Leaving Luigi, Assunta, and Antonio at the cart, I took Giulietta and Pietro with me and followed the artist to his studio. There he made Giulietta pose on a high-backed chair while we sat and watched as he skilfully sketched her before starting to paint.

"I had never seen an artist at work in his own studio. It was a fascinating place, well-lit as the sun shone through a glass roof. Paintings were piled against the walls, most of them portraits of men and women of all ages. There were also some landscapes that had an other-worldly quality I found attractive. His use of vivid colours was very pleasing. I mention this episode because it was so unique.

"After painting for several hours, he asked if we could return on the following day when he hoped to finish all the work he required before completing the painting without his model, as he realised we would have to be moving on. Next day I took Luigi, Assunta, and Antonio along, leaving Pietro at the cart. I wanted to give them also a glimpse into the special world of the artist. He did not object to their presence, and soon we were witnesses to a kind of artistic miracle. A very beautiful Giulietta emerged upon the surface of the artist's canvas. To this very day I regret we could not stay to see the painting finished. The artist paid me generously, and we took our leave gratefully. Giulietta was amused by the whole episode but now, so many years later, I often wonder if her portrait is famous and perhaps on display in some Polish museum.

"As we made our way homewards, we began to sell most of the lovely things we had collected, keeping only a very few in our suitcases, for we would have to sell the horse and cart and take the train. When we at last stepped on to the train, a great joy seized me as I realised we were coming home rich. Just as my aunt had done. This time we did not travel down the length of Italy on foot but went directly to Naples on the train. On the charabanc from Venafro to Filignano, our happiness knew no bounds. With the large sums of money we had earned, we refurbished the house, bought new furniture, purchased some more land, and all went well with us. Even now I look back with nostalgia to those lovely years abroad."

Albina was not exhausted by her long narration, and Assunta observed that the feverish flush had gone from her cheeks. She was getting better. By the time Albina's daughter returned from Santa Maria two days later, the old lady was getting up and doing light chores around the house. Assunta said good-bye and went home to Imperatore to find that Giuseppe had made plans for an excursion to Naples.

They arrived in Naples on a Friday near the end of February. Although Assunta had been in the city before, it had always been on business of one sort or another. Filomena had once swallowed a fish bone that stuck in her throat. Since the Filignano doctor had been unable to dislodge it, they had to go to Naples to consult a throat specialist. The bone had been removed in less than it takes to tell. Filomena begrudged the expense and hurried back to Filignano to give the doctor the benefit of her mind. On that brief visit to Naples, Assunta had merely glimpsed the sea.

Now, with Giuseppe, there was time to wander round seeing the sights. They stayed in a small hotel overlooking the large piazza in front of the railway station and in the morning, after breakfast, they took a *carrozza,* or horse-drawn carriage, for a drive along the coast. It was a mild, sunny morning and the sea was greyish blue. Here and there they heard the voices of fishermen raised in song. The rest of the day was spent in sightseeing, and in the evening they went to the theatre where they enjoyed a variety spectacle describing the history of Naples. The show was crammed with music, dance, and mime. When they got back to the hotel, Giuseppe announced they were going to Capri next morning.

Rising early for breakfast, an hour later they were sailing across the Bay of Naples to Capri. The sea was deep blue and the water sparkled. Soon they saw the silhouette of the enchanted isle against the azure skyline. Disembarking at Marina Grande, they took a *carrozza* up to the town of Capri where they booked in at the Pagano Vittoria Hotel. It was off-season, and they had no problem in obtaining a splendidly large bedroom with a lovely view of the sea. Assunta found the landscape of the island not dissimilar to Filignano, although the houses were brighter, being mostly whitewashed. She was enchanted by the lovely setting. Somehow she felt very much at home there. This feeling was strengthened when they walked up to Anacapri and all the more when she saw goats in the narrow streets.

Together, Assunta and Giuseppe, explored every corner of the island. From the heights of Mount Solaro, they looked down upon the Faraglioni that had guided ships there in ancient times. They visited the ruins of the villa of Tiberius, notorious for its primitive erotic rites and orgies, although the guide assured them many of the accounts given of these unpleasant events were grossly exaggerated. Immediately beneath the site of the villa, tiers of cultivated land indicated the presence of a small Capri farm. As they slowly made their way down the road, they saw two barefooted women carrying pitchers of water on their heads as they made their way to a small white house nestling against the side of the hill. Children were playing with a ginger cat and a short, darkly tanned, barefooted man, wearing a brightly coloured kerchief on his head, was busy chopping wood. A wizened old woman was cutting long grass to feed the cow.

Assunta and Giuseppe were delighted with this scene of lively activity, which made such an effective contrast with the deserted setting of the stark ruins above. It was a superb location for a small farm, perched so high, overlooking the deep, blue sea in the near distance. In another time and in different circumstances, Assunta thought, she and Giuseppe could have led a fine life on just such a farm, breathing in the pure Mediterranean air and enjoying the benefit of the bright sunshine. Soon they would be returning to the rigours of Scotland's climate to start a new life together so different in pace from the leisurely life of the Capri farmers.

After a few days, they returned to Naples and decided to spend the night in a small inn in the heart of the city. The proprietor indicated he had an excellent kitchen and could he expect them for dinner that evening? They agreed to sample his cooking. Later, as they were walking through the narrow streets bustling with people, Giuseppe felt a man jostling against him as he went past, but the man excused himself and Giuseppe thought nothing of it. Assunta saw a lovely musical box in a shop, and they went in to purchase it. When Giuseppe felt for his wallet to pay for the box, he was horrified to discover it was gone. Dejectedly they went back to the inn and told the owner what had happened.

Signor Alfonso, for that was his name, seemed quite unperturbed by their sad account, and he told them to sit down and start their meal. Above all they were not to worry, for he would sort out their little problem. They sat down, but had no appetite for the first course. Then signor Alfonso came up to them and asked them to describe the man who had brushed against Giuseppe in the street, and could they possibly describe the street where it happened? They did their best to recall the man's appearance and dress, and the locality where Giuseppe had been robbed.

Assunta and Giuseppe then proceeded half-heartedly to sip the excellent soup. By the time they had finished it, signor Alfonso came in again, sat down beside them, and produced three wallets.

"Which of these is yours?" he asked a wide-eyed Giuseppe. All agog, poor Giuseppe could not believe his eyes when he saw his own wallet sitting between the other two. Signor Alfonso handed it to him muttering, "Of course, the fool could not have known you are my guests."

Giuseppe asked, still bewildered, "But how have you been able to trace my wallet in such a short time, signor Alfonso?"

"Ask no questions, and you will be told no lies, my dear signor Cocozza," said the smiling signor Alfonso, "but when you go back to Filignano, tell all your friends, if they want to come to Naples and walk the streets safely, they must come and stay at my little inn. Now, enjoy your meal!" And he went off to the kitchen with a twinkle in his eye.

Back in Filignano they found themselves in the middle of the windy season of March, and the Marzella house, perched so near the top of the hill, echoed with the noise of banging shutters and prolonged, fluted, moans in the dark hours. After a particularly noisy night, when Assunta tried to rise in the morning, she felt strangely light-headed. Filomena came to her assistance, and when a worried Giuseppe wanted to fetch the doctor, his mother-in-law called him back.

"We don't need the doctor to tell us what the trouble is," she said, throwing him a significant look, "for you are the culprit this time. If I am not mistaken, you are going to be a father." Giuseppe's anxiety quickly turned to joy, and had it not been for Filomena's restraining presence, he would have thrown his arms round his wife there and then.

Assunta smiled, although she still felt wretched, and, catching her husband's eye, said, "I am sure it will be a boy."

She now adopted a completely new attitude to life. A strong feeling of responsibility for the child she was carrying made her more cautious in her actions than she had ever been before. Filomena, observing this change in her daughter, promptly told her to stop being so foolish. She should be as active as she possibly could.

"If you want your child to be healthy," she said, "the answer is hard work." And she began to order her daughter around as she had always done when Assunta was a girl.

The trees were soon covered with buds in the early days of April announcing the coming of spring. With these signs came good news, for Assunta's friend Antonia had fallen in love with a charming young man, Pompilio Marzella. It would not be a long engagement, for Pompilio, a thrifty fellow, had already saved enough money to pay their fares to Scotland, where they would be going to make their fortune.

Giuseppe went each day with Benedetto to the fields where he helped his father-in-law to turn up the soil in ridges and furrows. Then they would sow the seed. Next they moved into the small areas of tilth land to hoe the brown earth and plant vegetables. Giuseppe enjoyed the company of his father-in-law although Benedetto seldom spoke. They understood one another as they worked side by side, and Benedetto respected Giuseppe for his eagerness to help. Giuseppe also enjoyed the physical exertion, which sharpened his appetite and made him look forward each evening to the simple, wholesome meals Filomena prepared.

Early in May, Antonia and Pompilio were married. It was a very simple wedding, for they had to save every *centesimo* for their new life in Scotland. Although Antonia was obviously radiantly happy, Assunta felt a little embarrassed and somewhat ashamed when she compared the austerity of her friend's wedding feast with the extravagance of her own, and she made up her mind to help Antonia and Pompilio in Glasgow as much as she could. A few days later, they all four left for Scotland. Filomena was not as upset by Assunta's departure as she had been in 1915 because she knew that her daughter now had security and would surely come to visit her when she could.

On the journey to Glasgow, Assunta relived much of the excitement of seeing new places through the eyes of Antonia and Pompilio, for it was now their turn to marvel at the wonders they saw. But the journey seemed strangely short, and on a chilly morning in May they arrived in the Central Station at Glasgow.

Chapter Twelve

1921 to 1924—Garscube Road

Anyone walking down Cowcaddens to Garscube Road in May 1921, soon had the impression of entering a lively quarter of the city. At the road junction where New City Road led to St. George's Cross, the clock in the tower of the Normal School looked down on busy tramcars and horse-drawn vehicles. People went about their business with an enthusiastic air, and the shops near the subway station of Cowcaddens, grocers, butchers, jewellers, and outfitters, all side by side, were well stocked to supply the needs of their frequent customers.

The Normal School with its grounds occupied the entire corner on the left hand side, and beyond it in Garscube Road a long line of three-storied tenements stretched into the distance. On the right where Cowcaddens ended with the Grand Cinema, a broad, open space with green patches and trees arranged symmetrically to surround a large, iron fountain, announced the presence of the Phoenix Park, beyond which lay warehouses, small factories, and whisky stores. Small as the park was, it nevertheless created an impression of spaciousness for the tenants who looked down upon it from the windows of the tenement directly opposite.

It was in this very tenement that Giuseppe and Assunta had their café. It was flanked on either side by interesting little shops. On the left, beyond a close, was Simpson's fruit and vegetable shop. On the right was a little newspaper shop where crockery, household articles, and toys were also stocked.

This wee shop was owned by a delightfully polite, very elderly lady by the name of Mrs. Welsh. In her long, black dress with spotlessly clean starched cuffs, and a lace collar that matched the brightness of her white hair, Mrs. Welsh was one of the distinctive personalities of the quarter. Hers was more than a mere shop. It was a haven of comfort for the local housewives, for there they could discuss their problems and leave with good, practical advice.

Assunta soon made friends with her shop neighbours, and they welcomed her into the community with warmth. She soon began to feel at home. Working by Giuseppe's side in the shop gave her great joy. She admired the clever way he had with his customers. Curiosity to see the "new folk" in the café brought many in for a first purchase. Giuseppe made sure they would come back by giving generous measure and serving everyone with a smile.

Assunta, less inclined to smile as frequently as her husband, gradually fell into his ways, for, when he saw her toiling away with an impassive expression on her face, he would go up to her, raise her chin with his hand, and look into her face, imitating her serious look. Then his eyes would gleam with mischief, and he would break into a broad smile, prompting her to follow his example. When she did so, if there was no one around, he would kiss her impulsively on the mouth. More than once they were caught in this romantic situation, and the word soon travelled round the area that the young couple in the new café were love birds. This accounted for the curious looks they received from new customers.

One day a mature lady with a kindly face asked Assunta, "Are ye' settlin' in, hen? How dae ye like Gerscube Rooaad?" Assunta, who had never experienced the affectionate sound of the word "hen" at the Continental in the posh West End, was more than delighted to assure the lady she was very happy to be in Gerscube Rooaad.

The people in the district were obviously not very well off. Older women wore shawls instead of coats. Most of the men wore caps. Anyone wearing a soft hat or bowler was assumed to be a bill collector or a factor and was consequently regarded with suspicion or hostility. In the warm summer days, many of the children ran about barefooted to save their shoes. But there was a warm, sympathetic spontaneousness and a natural kindness in these good people that endeared them to Assunta.

Except on Saturday evenings! For it was then they were plagued with tipplers stumbling out of the pub on the corner. They would make their tottering way into the café and slump onto the seats to order Bovril or hot peas. Some insisted on singing as they waited to be served, others leaned their heads, heavy with alcohol, on their arms on the table surface and fell asleep. Some even slid helplessly on to the terrazzo floor where they lay in troubled unconsciousness until closing time, catching pneumonia. Giuseppe had a hard time rousing these boozers and helping them to the door where they usually collapsed again on the cold pavement outside.

It was the children who came in for their penny pea braes at dinner time or their haepenny pokey hats after school who appealed most to Assunta. She had a particular soft spot for those who went habitually barefoot in their worn clothes, with their grubby little faces and their unkempt hair. They were the ones with the liveliest eyes and when she thought Giuseppe was not looking, she would stick a small sweet on top of the ice cream to be rewarded with a warm, "Oh ta, missus."

Perhaps it was because her own child was growing within her that she felt such affection for these poor children. And on hot days when the sun shone down and the children paddled in the Phoenix Park fountain across the road, she could hear their shrill voices raised excitedly like the piping of sparrows as their sounds travelled across, broken occasionally by the thunder of the tramcars hurtling past.

The summer was busy, and soon, Giuseppe, seeing how Assunta in her condition was beginning to find the work too much for her, arranged to employ a girl to help in the shop. She was Irish, and her name was Bridget. Only recently had she arrived from Ireland. Hardworking and clean, she was a good help and really earned her ten shillings per week, working long hours behind the counter as well as helping Assunta with the heavier domestic chores in the backshop. It was obvious she had lived in poverty, as she was very thrifty.

One autumn day Assunta decided they would have soup, and she sent Bridget to the butcher's for a large marrow bone. The girl offered to make the soup herself, and soon the delicious aroma floated out into the counter from the backshop.

"We are going to have Irish broth today, Giuseppe," said Assunta.

"That will make a nice change from minestrone," said Giuseppe. For the next three hours, they were kept busy while Bridget worked away in the backshop, cooking the soup, washing pails, dishes and dishcloths. Then who should arrive but Giulietta for a short visit, and the moment she entered she started sniffing and remarked on the appetising smell. Then Bridget announced the soup was ready. Giulietta and Assunta took some. It was excellent and Bridget beamed with pride as the ladies complimented her. Then Assunta's eye happened to stray to the shelf above the gas stove and there, to her surprise, she saw the large marrow bone used for the soup stock, sitting in a large plate.

"Why have you kept the bone, Bridget?" she asked.

"It will do to make soup again tomorrow," said the girl.

"I've never heard of that before," said Assunta.

"How do you mean?" asked Bridget.

"Well, all the good will have been boiled out of the bone today!"

"Oh no," said Bridget, "back in Ireland my mother always uses a bone at least three times."

"We live and learn," said Assunta, winking at Giulietta.

139

"Yes," agreed Giulietta, "and you are going to save a lot of money if you leave Bridget to make the soup!"

Giuseppe, who had followed the whole conversation from the back-shop doorway, observed, "It's high time someone started economising to make up for the free sweets Assunta gives away to her wee ragamuffins in the shop!"

Bridget proved to be one of the best assistants Assunta had in the years they spent in Garscube Road.

One day, late in September, Assunta had a visit from Antonia and Pompilio. Things had not been going well for them in the shop they had rented. They decided they would not settle after all in Glasgow. Pompilio had a brother in Paris who had set up his own business making accordions, and he was doing so well he required Pompilio's help. The news was a disappointment to Assunta, for she did not wish to lose her friend. Two weeks later Assunta and Giuseppe were waving a tearful farewell to Antonia and Pompilio as their train rolled out of the station taking them to a new life in Paris.

After Antonia's departure, Assunta found herself drawn more and more to Antonio's wife, Vittoria, since their shop was only ten minutes' walk from Giuseppe's café. As Assunta's time drew near, Vittoria became a daily visitor. Antonio and Vittoria had no children. One day Vittoria asked Assunta if she and Antonio could be the godparents of her child. Assunta readily agreed.

The month of October was cold and bleak and, as it drew to a close, it was evident that the baby would soon be born. Giuseppe, anxious that all should go well, insisted that Assunta should remain in the house at 7, Burnside Street. Leonarda and Irena came every day from Parkhead to help. Giulietta also came when she could get away, and Giulia, Assunta's close friend, was there every afternoon. She was certainly not being neglected.

When Giuseppe rose on the morning of the 6th of November, he knew that the child would be born that day. He waited until Leonarda and Irena arrived before going down to the shop. Then, as soon as Bridget came in, he left her in charge and went back up to the house. By this time Giulia, Giulietta, and Vittoria had also arrived, and they advised him to call the midwife. Shortly after he left, Assunta went into labour. The midwife, timing her arrival perfectly, came an hour later. There were no complications and at five past two in the afternoon, Assunta gave birth to a noisy baby boy.

Leonarda hurried down to the shop to tell Giuseppe the good news. He was beside himself with joy and rushed back up to the house. The smiles of the ladies congratulated the proud father, and Giulietta took him in to see his son. Assunta, exhausted, smiled weakly as he approached the bed. Then he saw a little bundle in her arms and a tiny brown face with a remarkably prominent nose and a small mouth emitting piercing cries of protest for coming into the world on such a cold day.

"Here is your noisy son," said Assunta quietly, "and what are we going to call him?"

"With a voice like his, he is sure to follow in Caruso's footsteps," said Giuseppe, "so we shall call him Enrico."

Later in the day, Assunta raised herself slowly onto her elbow and looked over the edge of the cot at her son. He had settled down and was sound asleep, recovering from the adventure of being born.

I wonder what he will do with his life? she thought. And she resolved there and then that she would never stand in his way. Whatever he chose to do, she would help him as best she could, but she would let him grow in his own way. With a new feeling of wonder, she realized it would be a constant pleasure for her to see him developing. And she and Giuseppe would provide for him with good food, a fine education and, above all, guidance in the appreciation of the fine things in life. In this hopeful frame of mind, she closed her eyes and fell asleep.

Several times that night, the new parents were awakened by the shrill cries of their hungry son wanting to be fed.

"This son of yours is a glutton!" said Giuseppe when he rose for the third time to hand the child to its mother's breast.

"He's just like his father," said Assunta.

In the morning, Leonarda, who had been staying overnight, was feeling unwell, and she went home to Parkhead. Giuseppe said he would send Bridget for Vittoria so that someone could sit with Assunta. When Giuseppe had gone, Assunta lay and dozed. She awoke some time later, it was mid-morning. There was no sign of Vittoria, the fire was well down, the doctor would be calling around noon, and, as she looked around the room she thought the floor could do with a good scrubbing. . . .

Bridget opened the door of the house to let Vittoria in. They had been delayed, as Antonio was out when Bridget arrived at the shop, and they had been chatting until Antonio returned to let Vittoria away.

"We're here, Mrs. Cocozza," called out Bridget. Then, as she went into the bedroom, she let out a scream of dismay. Assunta was lying on the floor beside a pail of soapy water, a wet floor cloth in her hand. The baby was screaming hungrily in his cot. The two women managed to lift Assunta on to the bed, alarmed to see the blood staining her white nightdress.

When the doctor examined Assunta, he gave her a terrible row for her incautious behaviour. She was told to remain in bed for at least two weeks. In the evening her temperature rose, and next morning when he called again, the doctor shook his head and muttered, "Childbed fever." He suggested she should be removed to the hospital at once but Assunta refused.

"Well, I won't answer for the consequence if you disregard my advice," he said, as he went away. Assunta was nursed by her good friends for several days after which she began to show slight signs of improvement. A week later she was able to resume feeding the baby. But she was to reap the unpleasant reward for her indiscretion later.

The child was christened Enrico and brought home in splendour by his doting godparents, Antonio and Vittoria. From the moment he was given the name, he stopped crying and settled down serenely to give his parents peace at night. Leonarda was not pleased by the choice of name. She had wanted the boy to be called after her, Leonardo.

"He was not born to be an artist," explained Giuseppe to his mother, "but some day he will be a great singer."

"What foolish pretensions," Leonarda muttered, under her breath.

Soon Assunta was able to get up, but she was not yet well enough to venture down to the shop. Christmas would have been boring for her but for the visits of Giulietta, Erminia, Vittoria, and Giulia. Eugenio made such a fuss of the child every time he came to Burnside Street, and spoke to him as though he were already grown up. The remarkable thing was that the child listened intently when his uncle spoke to him. Assunta had to admit that she was delighted with her little son. Already, from the moment he opened his little, brown eyes, he showed precocious signs of being well aware of the world around him and every time the face of a new visitor loomed down upon him in his cot, his small right hand stretched out instinctively to accept the silver coin being proffered while a gleam came into his eyes as he smiled in gratitude.

"That child is already aware of the value of money," said Giuseppe one day.

"Which is more than his father can claim," said Assunta.

The spring of 1922 brought many innovations. When Assunta took the subway to Hillhead one afternoon, she carried baby Rico in his warm woollen shawl. As she arrived at the Continental, there was great excitement in the backshop, for Eugenio had just installed a wireless set and one could listen to local broadcasts from the new BBC studios in Glasgow. It was a great novelty hearing the announcers introducing musical items as one listened through the headphones.

142

Assunta marvelled at her brother's skill, for he was able to install the most complicated electrical gadgets and make them function properly.

As they sat drinking tea, and taking it in turn to listen to the wireless in the crowded backshop, baby Rico was much fussed over as he was passed from visitor to visitor. After tea, Giulietta opened a large, deep drawer in which she kept linen and sheets, put in some cushions and then laid the baby on these so that he could have a little nap. She and Assunta then retired to the counter for a little tête-à-tête, leaving Eugenio with the visitors. They drew up two chairs and sat down.

"Are you happy, Sunta? Now that you have a son?"

"Yes, I think I am, though, to tell the truth, I don't yet feel as strong as I would like to feel."

"You were very foolish, doing what you did, scrubbing the floor that morning."

"Yes, I know that now. I suppose I panicked when I realised the doctor would soon be there and the floor was in such a state."

Then Giulietta changed the subject.

"I would like to ask you a favour, Sunta, but I don't know if you would approve."

"Just ask, Giulietta, and you will find out."

"When the little boy starts to walk, would you bring him here sometimes and leave him for the day, with Eugenio and me?"

"Now why are you asking me to do that, Giulietta?"

"Well, in the first place, Sunta, I don't think Garscube Road is the ideal place for the child. You have such scruffy people in that area, and their language can be very coarse. Then, Eugenio and I miss not having children of our own, and it would give us a great deal of happiness to have the child here with us for a day now and then."

Assunta smiled, saying, "I respect your second reason, Giulietta, and I shall certainly let you have the boy from time to time. But I must tell you that although you may find the Garscube Road people coarse and scruffy, I have had nothing but kindness and affection from them." Giulietta accepted Assunta's observation with good grace.

At that very moment, Assunta Coia arrived with her children, Letizia, a charming, beautiful girl of fourteen, Josie, a sturdy, curly-haired little boy of ten, Elisetta, who had roses in her eight-year-old cheeks, and Antonietta, who, at six years of age had large, solemn, brown eyes set in an oval, pretty little face. Giulietta and Eugenio were the godparents of all these children. Assunta Coia took great pride in them, and they were always beautifully dressed, the girls wearing lovely silk ribbons in their long hair.

Giulietta smiled and welcomed them announcing loudly: "Here come the lambs of St. Anthony!"

They were then conducted to the backshop to join the other visitors while Assunta remained in charge of the counter. "The lambs of St. Anthony!" she mused, knowing right away why Giulietta had described her godchildren in this way.

Back in Filignano when the lambing season started, a prize lamb was always selected and presented to the parish priest to be kept for the feast of St. Anthony on the 13th of June. A day or so before the feast, the lamb was carefully washed and decked out with vari-coloured ribbons while a small holy picture of St. Anthony was attached to its back. Two men then led the lamb from house to house, making a collection of wheat grain in the large sacks they carried. The large quantities collected in this way were then given to the priest.

On the feast of St. Anthony, the grain was sold in front of the church, thus implementing the church funds. As Assunta was picturing the feast in her mind, Josie Coia wandered into the counter, sat down on Giulietta's chair, and fixed his large eyes upon her. She offered him a sweet, which he eagerly accepted. No sooner had he swallowed it than he rose and made his way back to the backshop to listen to the wireless.

Assunta was amused by the boy's serious air, and she recalled an amusing incident Giulietta had told her about him. It had occurred two years before when Josie still had difficulty in pronouncing the letter 'r' so that when he felt hungry he was 'hungwy,' and if a bell rang for others, it 'wang' for Josie. At that time the Coias had rented a shop in Parliamentary Road, and the little boy liked taking up a stance in the shop doorway where he solemnly observed the passersby.

One day, clad in his good velvet suit, he was playing with his hand windmill, holding it in his right hand. Nature calling, he made his way to the toilet, unbuttoned the fly of his trousers, and did his duty. He had unbuttoned his trousers with his right hand while he held the windmill in his left, but, after relieving himself, he passed the windmill from the left to the right hand again, not thinking to button up his trousers. He then walked calmly round to the shop door and took up his position on the step. Shortly afterwards, not at all aware of the slight draught in front, he was fiddling away with his windmill when an old man, who had a special regard for Josie, happened to pass.

He noticed Josie's little exposure and called out, "Hello, Josie. I see your beer shop is open!" and Josie, raising his right eyebrow slightly, but never deigning to look down at the little opening, stared the old man straight in the eye and with sombre dignity replied, "Why don't you come in fow a dwink?"

144

When Assunta came back to Garscube Road, Giuseppe had good news for her. The factor had called for the shop rent and told him there was a house for them in the same tenement as the shop. It was a two room and kitchen house with an inside toilet and was a considerable step up for them from the house in Burnside Street where they had to share the toilet with three other families. They would have to move within the week. That was the good news. The bad news was that Bridget's mother had been taken seriously ill, and the girl would have to take the overnight boat back to Ireland. But her friend Rosie would be willing to help out while Bridget was away. Assunta realised that Giulietta would be looking after Rico much sooner than she had expected.

The flitting took place a few days later, after Assunta, helped by Rosie, had scrubbed the new house from end to end. It was three stairs up, and the view from the bedroom windows was pleasant as they looked out over the Phoenix Park, while from the kitchen, one could peer into the back court, that magical no-man's-land where the children acted out their fantasies in singing games on sunny summer afternoons. Assunta, Giuseppe, and Rosie had the new house in good order in no time at all. And all this time, baby Rico was being thoroughly spoiled by his doting aunt and uncle at Byres Road. When, one morning, Rosie appeared to take the child home, Giulietta was very disappointed.

Spring gave way to summer, and the warm weather helped the ice-cream trade. Assunta was constantly at work behind the counter, and the baby was often left alone for long periods in his pram in the back shop. Parisio and Assunta Coia at that time were "between shops" and living in a house in College Street. Not owning a business of their own, they were willing to offer their service, if required, for a small remuneration. Giuseppe invited the Coias to help him and Assunta.

This left Rosie free to look after the baby. Bridget had failed to return from Ireland, and Rosie had now been taken on permanently. Apart from being a good worker, she had a good way with the customers when she was not looking after Rico. She particularly enjoyed the ritual of putting on records on the large-horn Gramophone, which had become such a prominent feature of the café.

She could also deal effectively with the mischievous children who, when they thought she could not see them, fired peas into the gramophone horn with their peashooters. They had overlooked the mirrors, which gave Rosie a full reflection of their misdeeds. She would descend upon the miscreants, confiscate their weapons until they had finished supping their pea braes, and then, before returning their peashooters, she would make them each in turn climb on to a low stool, carefully stretch their arms deep down into the round mouth of the horn and

145

retrieve the peas they had so accurately fired into it.

When Rosie took her half-day holiday every week, she went to visit her mother, taking baby Rico with her. The baby had the dark skin of his father, and his black hair, growing in curls, set off the dark brown of his eyes. One day, with the baby warmly wrapped in a shawl in her arms, she was standing waiting for the tramcar when two men walked past. They glanced at Rosie with her fair skin and light red hair. Then they looked at the child she was holding. She heard the first man say to the second, "Huh, a white wummin wi' a black man!" When she came back from her mother's, she told Assunta and Giuseppe what she had overheard at the tram stop.

Assunta turned to Giuseppe and said, "I always thought your ancestors came from Africa!"

It was Providence that brought the Coias to help Giuseppe and Assunta in the late summer of 1922 for, shortly after they started, Giuseppe was struck down with another attack of rheumatic fever. He became desperately ill, and Assunta required all her energy to nurse him. Rosie took the baby almost every day to Byres Road. Sometimes wee Josie Coia would offer to take the child out in his pram over to the Phoenix Park. Josie became very attached to the little boy and when Rico began to take his first, tentative steps, it was Josie who encouraged the child and helped him. Assunta was very grateful for the warm-hearted help the Coias were giving her, and she was never to forget it.

Giuseppe was confined to bed for a considerable time, and it was not until the spring of 1923 that he was able, with the aid of a walking-stick, to make his way down to the shop again. By this time Assunta was beginning to wonder whose child Rico was, for more and more of the time he was with his aunt at Byres Road. Giuseppe's recovery was well timed, for the Coias had to relinquish their help, as Assunta Coia was expecting another child.

So Giuseppe decided to employ a full-time assistant, an Italian lad by the name of Fonzino. Young Rico was left to his own devices during that busy time, and he often wandered into Mrs. Welsh's shop where the old lady let him play with the toys. Sometimes she would let him have a broken one to take home. He would also pay regular visits to Simpson's fruit shop where Nancy and Susie, the shopgirls, entertained him in the backshop and gave him an apple or an orange.

Rico had started speaking when he was just over a year old, but there were some sounds he found hard to pronounce. Like his older friend Josie Coia, he had problems with the 'r' sound, which came out as a 'v,' while 'l' became 'w' or was not pronounced at all. So Mrs. Welsh became Mrs. Wesh. When he went into her shop, the old lady enjoyed his chattering as he played with the toys. Sometimes he would remove the price labels from the cups and saucers, stacked on low shelves, and re-arrange them. This created complications but Mrs. Welsh bore them with good grace. Then, if she gave him a broken toy, he would hurry away to show it to his mother.

When Assunta asked, "Who gave you that toy?" he would reply, "Wesh."

One day he walked in with a toy train that was quite undamaged. Surprised, Assunta asked him, "Who gave you this train?"

He boldly replied, "Vico!"

The little rascal had helped himself when Mrs. Welsh was too busy to notice what he had been up to. There and then Assunta marched the culprit into Mrs. Welsh's shop and made him hand back the toy, and she apologised profusely. Mrs. Welsh was amused.

Rico also paid regular visits to the Simpsons returning with apples, oranges, and cabbages. But he always answered truthfully when his mother asked who had given him the fruit or the vegetables. Giuseppe was eventually obliged to ask Mrs. Welsh and the Simpsons to discourage his son by giving him nothing. But one afternoon Rico appeared with a Teddy Bear in one arm and a cauliflower in the other, and Giuseppe lost his temper and gave the boy a good smacking on the hands. Nevertheless Rico continued to misbehave.

On a bright day in late summer, Assunta was working in the backshop when, through the open window, she heard the strains of a mouth organ being played in the back court. Itinerant musicians were a regular feature of the back-court entertainments in those days. They would start at one end of the road and work their way through the various back courts, earning a living in this way, depending upon the generosity of the housewives throwing them a penny or a haepenny from the open kitchen windows that looked down on to their asphalt stage.

It was the tune that the mouth organist was playing that attracted Assunta's attention, and she paused for a moment as she washed her dusters to listen. It was the melody of "O sole mio." Then she heard a piping baby voice taking up the tune, singing the Neapolitan words. The voice was indeed very familiar. Surely it couldn't, yet it must be! She placed a chair by the window, climbed on to it, and looked out.

There was Rico, with his little arms outstretched and his shiny little brown face raised to the windows above, singing away to his heart's content. The old man playing the mouth organ kept glancing at the child, astonished, for the little voice was in tune, and he suddenly

147

realised he was not playing the melody but accompanying the song! When the song ended, pennies and haepennies came tinkling down, and some of the women at their windows were heard to applaud. Rico helped the old musician to gather up the coins, and they were just about to start an encore when Assunta arrived and, taking her son's arm, led him gently but firmly away.

The child had been sensitive to the beauty of Italian melodies even when he had lain in his cot listening to Assunta's lullabies. Then, when he began to walk, his attention turned to the gramophone and when Rosie put on the records, he would listen attentively. He particularly liked the Caruso records, which were so popular with Giuseppe's older customers. Giuseppe would often find him perched on a low stool in the backshop imitating Caruso. He even reproduced the low strains of the orchestral introduction with a subdued "Pu pum, pu pum," before launching into the song. Naturally, Giuseppe encouraged him, for he still cherished the hope that one day Rico might be a great singer.

He was not keen, however, that the boy should play the gramophone in the shop. So he bought Rico a small toy gramophone and a few miniature records. Rico would sit contentedly on a rug in the backshop and play his little records for hours on end. Although he was too young to be able to read the labels on the records, he could nevertheless tell by their colour and other signs comprehensible only to himself which records were which. His two favourites were "Uncle Joe" and "Beaver Meh." These were played incessantly.

One day when Assunta had gone to the "steamie" wash house with Rosie, Giuseppe and Fonzino were on duty behind the counter. Rico, in the backshop, was playing his records. "Uncle Joe" was followed by "Beaver Meh," and "Beaver Meh" was followed by "Uncle Joe" and this monotonous recital went on and on until Giuseppe, not a little exasperated, went in and told Rico to play something else. Giuseppe was in a bad mood that day as he had lost some money on the horses. He had no sooner got back to the counter than his ears were assailed again with the strains of "Uncle Joe." This time he lost his temper.

Rushing into the backshop, he stopped the gramophone, lifted the record on the turntable and another, and smashed them to pieces on the floor. Then, realising he had behaved rather strongly, he paused in the doorway and looked down to see what effect his violent outburst was having on his son. Rico sat calmly on the rug for a time, ignoring his father completely. Then he rose, picked up the pieces of the shattered records and examined them carefully. He dropped them on to the floor, looked at his father, and threw him a disdainful look. He then clasped his hands behind his back, began to pace slowly up and down the whole length of the backshop, pondering all the while.

Suddenly, as he drew level with his father he stopped, turned to him and said, "So, Giuseppe, you have broken 'Uncle Joe' and you have broken 'Beaver Meh'? Well, you can just go to hell!" Giuseppe was so confounded by this severe dressing-down from his son that he retreated to the safety of the counter where, upon telling Fonzino what had just happened, they both dissolved into convulsive laughter. Rico refused to speak to his father until the two broken records were replaced.

Assunta and Giuseppe soon realised that they had a son to be reckoned with. Although he seemed outwardly to be pliable, it became obvious he had a mind of his own and would brook no interference with his activities. Eugenio appreciated the boy's questioning mind and encouraged his sensibility to music. At Byres Road he was allowed to play his uncle's gramophone. Despite Assunta's remonstrations her brother continued to undermine the little authority she had over her son. And Giulietta positively spoiled the child with fine clothes.

The winter of 1923 to 1924 passed without incident. Things seemed to be going well, but in the spring of the year Rico took ill. It was the expected scarlet fever. The weeks passed, and the boy did not seem to be making a good recovery. He was pale and listless and very prone to colds and chills. The doctor's advice was sought. He advised a change of air, not sea air, just good, country air. Someone advised Giuseppe to try Eaglesham. It was not far from Glasgow, and it would help Assunta also to have a break for a couple of weeks.

Rosie travelled with Assunta and Rico to help with the baggage, and they found themselves at the door of a boarding house in Eaglesham one morning in June. The landlady showed them into a bedroom on the ground floor and, when they had unpacked, Rosie stayed to lunch before returning to Glasgow. Assunta then took Rico into the bedroom. To her dismay she saw dozens of cockroaches crawling all over the floor. She took the child by the hand, whisked him quickly out of the room, and called the landlady to inform her she would be leaving immediately to return to Glasgow. The landlady assured her she would attend to the problem.

"It's a lovely day, my dear," she said, "so why don't you take your little boy for a nice, long walk, and I promise you that by the time you come back there will not be a single black beetle left in the room."

Assunta took the lady's advice and went for a long stroll, enjoying the fine, country air, but she was still having doubts when she returned two hours later. But the landlady was as good as her word. Assunta pulled back the bed and looked at the carpet beneath it. No cockroaches. She peered into every corner of the room. No cockroaches. There was

149

a strong odour of some kind of disinfectant but nothing else. That night she rose several times and switched on the light, but she could not see any of the unpleasant insects in the room. Rico slept soundly in the large double bed beside his mother.

After the bad start to the holiday, all went well. The sun shone and they were able to take full advantage of the good Eaglesham air. Giuseppe came twice to visit them, and they enjoyed walking in the countryside. Rico's appetite improved day by day, and by the end of the fortnight he had lost his pallor.

In the early autumn, a letter from Filignano informed Assunta that Filomena was unwell. Giulietta was anxious to go back to Filignano to visit her own mother so it was suggested that the three of them, Assunta, Rico, and Giulietta, should travel together. They left on the 3rd of September and arrived in Filignano in good time for the start of the annual feast. Filomena was on her feet within three days of their arrival. She took great delight in her naughty grandson but kept a tight rein on him and would not always let him have his way. He grew to respect his grandmother and obeyed her without question. So Rico spent his third birthday in the home of his grandparents in the healthy atmosphere of Filignano. When Giulietta, Assunta, and Rico came back to Glasgow on the 29th of December, Giuseppe and Eugenio were overjoyed to see how well they looked.

Chapter Thirteen

1925 to 1928—Good Times and Bad

After the problems and setbacks of 1924, Assunta and Giuseppe settled down to what they hoped would be better times in 1925. Their circle of friendly customers widened and Giuseppe, dropping the Italian form of his name, came to be known to everyone as Joe. Assunta accepted this change. She enjoyed the comforts of her new house and her neighbour Mrs. Sneddon, a widow, had two little boys who played with Rico in the back court. The only cloud in Assunta's sky was the change she noticed in Joe after her return from Filignano.

He had always enjoyed betting. Now he was seized with an obsession to gamble every day. Every morning he went in to Mrs. Welsh's shop to buy the *Noon Record* so that he could study form. Then he would carefully write out his bets, and the bookie's runner would call to collect the lines. Sometimes he was lucky and won a few pounds. More often than not he lost. But he was stubbornly determined to make his fortune on the horses, come what may.

Assunta tried to reason with him, but in vain. He could not control the urge that overcame him when he studied the *Noon Record*. After a time she left him alone. She had learned long before to count her blessings. Joe did not smoke and drank only in moderation. Although he had an eye for a pretty girl and teasingly flirted in her presence with the young lassies who came into the shop, this did not worry her in the least. She knew Joe loved *her* and she could trust him. But she worried when he lost large sums of money on the horses.

Joe also had a passion for football. Having lived in Parkhead, he supported Celtic and spent long hours talking football with his friends Jake and Barber. Jake, who was unemployed, spent a great deal of his time in the café, and Joe often sent him on errands, rewarding him with a small packet of Woodbine cigarettes. Then there was Joe's bow-legged pal Barber who was a handyman, doing odd jobs around the shop when Fonzino was busy with other things. He lifted the heavy pails of ice cream mixture that were still too heavy for Joe after his illness. Since Joe was a little stiff on his legs, Barber or Fonzino climbed the steps to stock the shelves, or washed the shop windows with a long, soapy brush dipped in pails of hot water.

But Joe would not allow anyone to dress the shop windows but himself. He had a flair for unusually compelling window displays, and one day he was inspired to surpass himself. In one window reserved for the cigarette display, he constructed a castle with empty cigarette packets. Children passing by lingered to observe his progress as they saw the castle gradually rising against the blue-sky background of coloured crêpe paper Joe had pinned to the back of the window.

In the afternoon he started the arrangement in the other window where he was going to place his pièce-de-résistance, a large framed photograph of the Celtic football team he had obtained from a footballer friend who played for them. The photograph was placed prominently on a stand in the centre, while sweets and chocolates were arranged around it in small, open bowls and baskets. Beneath the photograph was the following legend in bold letters printed on a board: "GOOD SWEETS AND CHOCOLATES FROM JOE'S WILL HELP YOU PLAY THE GAME!"

Jake arrived as Joe was putting the finishing touches to the window.

"You're just in time, Jake," said Joe. "Come out and tell me what you think of my windows. See if you can find any faults."

So Jake and Joe went out to examine Joe's handiwork, and Jake carefully appraised the cigarette packet castle with an approving: "Uh huh!" Then he went over to the other window, hummed and hawed for a time, finally turning to Joe and saying, "Well, Joe, you have done a good job, but you can rest assured, aye, you can set your mind at peace, if a motorist goes driving past your windows at sixty miles an hour, he'll no' see ony faults!"

During the following week, Joe had some luck with the horses, winning a considerable sum of money. He bought an ice-cream cart and a fine, high-stepping pony, which he promptly named Nellie. The business was now expanding. Assunta's work increased, for on hot days, having to keep both the shop and the cart supplied with ice cream, she had to boil the ice-cream mixture more than once in the course of a day.

Their profits soared, and Joe opened two new savings accounts in the Glasgow Savings Bank in New City Road. One was a joint savings account in his own and Assunta's names. Since Rico would be four years of age that year, he deposited twenty pounds in the boy's name, five pounds for each birthday. Every year thereafter he would always deposit five pounds in Rico's account on his birthday.

So Assunta spent the whole summer in the shop. Rico was sent often to his aunt's. Then, early in July, just before the start of the Glasgow Fair Holidays, Assunta began to feel that something was wrong. She had a sixth sense when trouble was imminent, and on this particular afternoon it manifested itself in a malaise making her almost sick. Leaving Rosie and Fonzino in the shop, she made her way upstairs to the house. She climbed the stairs quickly, barely pausing for breath and just before reaching the third landing, she knew she would find the house door open. And indeed it was, wide open. She was afraid to enter, so she turned to her neighbour's door and knocked. No answer. She knocked again, more loudly. Then she heard the key turn in the lock, and the door was opened slightly.

"What is it?" Mrs. Sneddon asked, and there was a slur in her speech suggesting she had been drinking.

By this time Assunta was in tears and she said, "Oh, Mrs. Sneddon please help me. Someone has forced the door of my house, and I am afraid to go in."

Mrs. Sneddon's door opened wider to reveal her standing in her nightdress, a half-filled glass of whisky in her hand. She stepped in to the landing and looked at the open door of the other house.

"I don't think a kin help ye, hen," she said, "a'm no' very well the day. A think ye better go fur the polis." She turned on her heel, swayed into the house, and closed the door behind her.

Assunta was by now beside herself. But she plucked up courage and stepped into the house. The doors of the rooms were all open. Clothes were lying all over the place. Drawers had been ransacked or emptied. Then she saw the door of the large wardrobe had been forced. She rushed to the toilet and was violently sick. She felt her house had been defiled. She did not know what had been taken and at that moment she did not even care. What upset her was the realisation that someone, a stranger, had entered her house and rummaged through her personal belongings.

Then anger took hold of her. Had she entered the house carrying a weapon and surprised the intruder, she would have been capable at that instant of striking him; yes, she could have killed him. Closing all the doors, she hurried back down to the shop. There was a policeman walking up from the bottom of the road. She hurried to him and blurted out her story. Then she ran into the shop and told Rosie and Fonzino what had happened, and, asking Fonzino to accompany her, went back up to the house with the policeman.

When Joe returned at tea time, he was shocked by the news of the burglary. He hurried upstairs where the house was being thoroughly examined by two policemen and two plain clothes men. Assunta was trying to cope with their many questions. Mrs. Sneddon was also questioned but could offer no information. All the police investigations led to nothing. Joe had not insured the house, and Assunta lost her jewellery, two good coats, and a canteen of cutlery. Joe discovered his two good suits and several pairs of shoes had been taken. New locks were fitted to the door, but Assunta could never be happy in that house again and a few weeks later Joe asked the factor for another in the same building. Early in 1926 they moved to one near the New City Road end of Garscube Road. Joe then took out a burglary insurance policy.

Assunta and Joe now adopted a very hard working routine. In the summer season, there was no relaxation for them as they earned good money so that they could afford to provide the best of everything for their son. The shop never closed, but Joe saw to it that they each in turn had one half-day off. Rosie would visit her mother, taking Rico with her. Fonzino would go to the cinema and then visit his family in the south side of Glasgow. Assunta invariably went to Byres Road and occasionally to Parkhead to visit Leonarda and Irena.

Joe, like Fonzino, loved the cinema, and he would spend most of his half-days at the pictures. He was moved by the great silent film dramas, one of his favourite actresses being Billie Dove. But the film that caused the greatest stir was *Ben Hur*, starring Ramon Novarro, and Joe went to see it several times as it was shown for a few weeks. The sequence that most captivated Joe was the famous race of the charioteers. It inspired a Sunday morning event in Garscube Road that was to be the talk of the district for a long time.

The ice-cream parlour nearest to Joe's café was owned by the Ziggi brothers. There was great competition between them and Joe and the Ziggis had two horses and carts to sell their ice cream in the area. Early on Sunday mornings, before loading their vehicles to go on their rounds, the two Ziggis and Joe would take their ice-cream carts to the Round Toll where they would line up. At a signal they would go charging down the entire length of Garscube Road, racing like Ben Hur. They placed bets with one another. Joe invariably won with his high-stepping pony.

The inhabitants of the Garscube Road tenements rose early to watch the race of the "Charioteers" from their front windows. It became a weekly event causing much speculation as well as engendering a fair exchange of cash when bets were placed among the dwellers in the tenements, Joe being a regular favourite. But Assunta did not approve of this childish activity, and she put down her foot. The Sunday morning race of the ice-cream chariots was abandoned.

Meanwhile at the Continental, Eugenio had also been developing his business interests. The horse and cart did not appeal to him. He preferred a solid ice-cream motor van. At Giulietta's suggestion he invited Antonio and Vittoria to sell their café, "The Thistle Rest," and come into partnership with him at the Continental. By this time Antonio had brought over his sister Assunta's son, Giuseppe Saracino, from Santa Maria Oliveto. No sooner had the boy arrived from Italy than he was called Josie.

So Antonio, Vittoria, and Josie moved to the Continental, living with the Marzellas in their flat in University Avenue. It was a convenient arrangement, and the new firm was known as Marzella & Cocozza. Another ice-cream van was bought for Antonio, and together he and Eugenio covered the West End of Glasgow including Knightswood while the two women and Josie worked in the café. So it was a time of optimism when everyone hoped to become prosperous.

When Assunta came to Byres Road on Thursday afternoons with Rico, she often saw her friend Giulia, or Assunta Coia might arrive with her "Lambs of St. Anthony" who now included Lucia. The Coias had by this time gone into business in Milngavie. Sometimes another dear friend of Giulietta, Maria Giuseppa Valerio, would arrive all the way from Wishaw, bringing a delicious "clooty dumpling," which she had made on the previous day. The dumpling would be heated in the oven, and they would all enjoy a large piece with a freshly made cup of tea served in Giulietta's Willow Pattern tea set.

For Assunta this was the social highlight of her week. Rico also looked forward to it, for he enjoyed playing with Josie behind the counter, and when he was leaving with his mother to take the subway back to Cowcaddens, Josie always slipped a Jacob's Club Milk Chocolate Biscuit into the wee lad's pocket. It was always consumed in the subway train, and was well swallowed by the time it reached St. George's Cross.

The summer passed and early autumn brought colder, blustery days. One Thursday Assunta decided to visit Erminia Cocozza, Pietro's wife, in Maryhill Road. She would usually walk there with Rico, but it was already getting dark and she thought it better to take the tramcar. It was a journey they had made many times, and Rico was always interested in a large, moving electrical sign on the side of a building at St. George's Cross.

It showed a stout man in a white apron and a large chef's hat frying sausages in a frying pan. By an ingenious system of alternating switches, the white electric bulbs flashed on and off, giving the illusion that the chef's hand was agitating the frying pan, and flickering puffs of savoury smoke seemed to rise from the sizzling sausages. The bottom deck of Glasgow trams still had two long rows of seats allowing passengers to sit facing each other. The tram was not very busy and when Assunta got on with Rico, she sat near the rear platform, while Rico knelt on the seat beside her looking out of the window. Soon they came to St. George's Cross, and Rico looked up at his favourite sign.

Then, as the tram came to a stop, and there was a moment of silence on the bottom deck, Rico turned to his mother and exclaimed loudly, "Look, Mammy, look at that man up there. He's still frying thae bliddy sausages!" amid the tittering of the passengers, Assunta blushed with embarrassment.

Joe and Assunta could never be sure of what their redoubtable infant would do next. He was a daring boy despite his apparent shyness and had a disconcerting habit of addressing his elders as equals. When he was happy, he would break into song quite spontaneously, most often in Neapolitan, rendering the most popular of Caruso's songs.

Sometimes his Aunt Giulietta would come and fetch him on a Monday afternoon and take him with her to the cinema. Although he could not yet read the captions on the films, he appeared to follow the plot and when in doubt did not hesitate to ask. Often he saw the same film twice, for his godmother Vittoria would come for him on Wednesdays or Fridays and, if Giulietta had reported favourably on the film she had seen on Monday, Vittoria would go to the same film. Rico would then tell *her* what the picture was all about. He never fell asleep at the pictures, but sat impassively, studying the technique of the silent films.

When Joe told Rico on his fifth birthday that he had put another five pounds in the bank for him, the boy said, "By the time I am old like you, papà, I shall be really rich."

Joe took him occasionally to a football match, but Rico did not show any enthusiasm for that game, preferring the torrid Hollywood dramas to which his aunt and godmother exposed him twice a week.

One day a famous American movie star, Richard Barthelmess, happened to be in Glasgow. He had made his name in pictures such as *Way Down East* and *Tol'able David* in the early 1920s, but his films were constantly revived as they were popular. When, out of the blue, the famous actor walked into his shop, Joe was astonished and delighted. Barthelmess was fascinated by the atmosphere of the café and willingly accepted Joe's offer of a cup of real coffee. Joe then sat down at the table beside him and talked about his pictures. As they were talking, Rico came over to the table, leant his chin on the edge and, looking intently at Barthelmess, said; "I've seen you somewhere before." The actor was amused and took the boy on to his knee, chatting away.

Rico looked at the actor's face and observed; "Why is it you can really speak? When I see you in the pictures, you move your lips but I cannot hear you."

Barthelmess explained that he would soon be making a new picture in which Rico would be able to hear him speaking. Then he turned to Rico and asked him the stock question; "And what would you like to be when you grow up?"

Rico at once asked, "Are actors rich?" and Barthelmess replied, "Yes, very rich."

"Oh, well then," said Rico, 'I would like to be a rich actor, just like you!"

Rico now began to put aside the games he played and assumed a more useful role in the shop. Small as he was, he insisted upon helping Assunta with her chores in the backshop. He would stand by the door and when he saw a customer enter, he would listen as Rosie took the order and shout through; "One tea and one hot pie!" He would also collect the dirty dishes from the tables and bring them through to be washed. He enjoyed these little jobs and assumed an air of great importance as he went about his duties.

"We have got ourselves a new assistant," said Joe one day as he passed to pick up a pail of ice-cream mixture. Rico heard his father's remark and as Joe drew level with him, making his way back to the freezer, he felt his white apron being tugged and, on looking down at his son, heard him say: "Your new assistant is not being paid."

On a Saturday evening, two obstreperous drunks came into the shop and slumped into one of the seats demanding service. Joe quietly told them to leave. He then went back to the counter, but they continued shouting and began to use abusive language. Rico stood in the backshop doorway and fixed them with an angry stare. Joe went over and told them to get out. One of them lunged out, grabbing Joe by the waist from the side and made to throw him on to the floor. Jake, who was sitting in another seat, rushed up and grabbed the fellow by the scruff of the neck and propelled him to the door. In the meantime Joe had taken the other by the arm and was trying to pull him up to his feet, but he was a thick-set chap and would not budge.

Just then Rico rushed up with a large hatchet and called out, "Leave this bugger to me, Papà, and I'll kill him," and he tried to lift the heavy weapon to strike. He was grabbed in the nick of time by Assunta, and the hatchet fell with a clatter on to the terrazzo floor.

Jake helped Joe to lift the drunk, and they led him to the door and heaved him out.

Later, when Jake was leaving to go home, he said to Joe, "We nearly had a slaughter on our hands tonight!" and he winked slyly at Rico who proudly puffed out his little chest at this recognition of his bravery.

It was 1927 and time for Rico to start school. Giulietta insisted they should send him to a convent school nearby. It was certainly convenient, and the boy soon settled in. He learned quickly but was not outstanding in his written work. Joe, Assunta, Rosie, and Fonzino took it in turn to take and fetch him from the school. Since she could no longer see her nephew in the course of the week, Giulietta would send Eugenio or Antonio to fetch him on Saturday mornings and sometimes he would stay overnight and go home on the Sunday evening. She went on spoiling him in every possible way provided that he learned his prayers and studied his catechism. She was already cherishing the hope that the boy might embrace the priesthood when he grew up. But she never discussed this possibility with Assunta.

As for Assunta, although she appreciated the kindness the boy was being shown at Byres Road, she was not altogether sure it was good for him. Sometimes Giulietta could betray a superior air towards those Filignanesi whose shops were in the less fashionable areas of the city. This attitude also showed in the manner in which Giulietta and Vittoria dressed. Their clothes were of the most expensive quality, their taste impeccable. Of course this added charm to these truly lovely ladies, and both Eugenio and Antonio were extremely proud of their wives.

But Assunta noticed that when Rico spent the weekend at Byres Road, he was less tolerant of his little play fellows in Garscube Road. Usually he and Willie Sneddon, one of Mrs. Sneddon's boys, played together after school. One Monday when Rico came back from school, he made no attempt to go and meet Willie. It was a lovely day and Assunta found him sitting at the table in the backshop musing over his records.

"Are you not going out to play with Willie?" asked Assunta.

"Oh, I can't be bothered," said Rico.

"But it's a nice day and you should really be outside enjoying the fresh air."

"Zia Giulietta doesn't think I should play with boys like Willie."

"What's wrong with Willie, then?"

"Oh, he doesn't wash his face very often, and he doesn't often wear shoes."

"When I was a wee girl in Filignano, sometimes I didn't wash my face unless Nonna Filomena made me do so and on hot days I often ran around in my bare feet."

Rico looked at his mother, and she saw the hint of a sneer on his face as he observed, "You must have been as dirty as Willie."

She drew her hand across his face in a resounding smack that nearly knocked him off his chair. A moment later when her anger had subsided, she was shocked by what she had done. She saw the look of pain in Rico's eyes give way to one of utter astonishment. Her mother had never before slapped him across the face. On the hands and legs, and very often on his bottom, oh yes, but on the face, oh no, never before. And never before had he seen her look so angry. But he did not weep. He rose quickly and made for the door.

"Where are you going?" Assunta called out.

"I'm going out to play with Willie, of course," and he eyed her questioningly to see what response his reply would prompt.

She smiled and said, "That's a good boy. Off you go then. I'll have your tea ready in an hour." He smiled and hurried away to play with his little barefooted, dirty-faced friend.

As the summer months of 1927 were passing, Assunta found she had less energy. She tired easily and began to lose weight. Joe became very worried about her. They had consulted the doctor on various occasions since her illness in 1921, and he had impressed upon them that she had done herself irreparable harm. He advised against having any more children. This was a terrible disappointment for them. When December came with its busy Christmas and New Year season, Assunta found it more and more difficult to cope with the extra work. Joe sold his horse and cart so that he could spend all his time in the shop. Then she started having spasms of pain in the upper abdomen but tried to conceal this from her husband. She did not want to worry him unduly.

One day early in January 1928, Joe had gone to Byres Road to buy some supplies from Eugenio, for Marzella & Cocozza had entered the wholesale trade. Fonzino was on his half-day, and Rosie was working in the backshop while Assunta served at the counter. Even on cold January days, the demand for Joe's ice cream was brisk and Assunta realised she would have to make some more. She went to the cool cupboard in the backshop where the pails of ice-cream mixture were stored and lifted one down.

She felt a jab of pain as she did so and promptly placed the pail on the kitchen table. She would have asked Rosie to carry it to the freezer, but the girl had just gone to the toilet. As she had left the freezer revolving, she lifted the pail and made for the counter. She had taken only a few steps when she felt flaring up inside her the most frightening, overpowering pain. The pail fell from her hand, landing with a dull clatter on its side and spilling the mixture over a large area of the floor as Assunta slumped forward full length and lay face downwards in the thick, sticky, creamy liquid.

When Joe came back from Byres Road, he found the shop closed. Bewildered, he ran into Simpson's to ask what had happened. It was Nancy and Susie who had run to Assunta's aid when Rosie came to fetch them after finding her unconscious on the shop floor. With a struggle they had managed to get her upstairs to the house and had helped Rosie to clean her and get her into bed. Nancy had already run to fetch the doctor. When Joe rushed upstairs, a worried Rosie answered the door.

Assunta lay back in bed, the perspiration pouring from her, her face contorted with agony. Rosie wiped away the sweat with a clean towel while Joe sat on the edge of the bed holding his wife's limp hand, trying his best to comfort her. But she was frequently racked with pain and screamed out. There was a firm knock at the door, and Rosie went to let the doctor in. He hurried through to see his patient.

Joe waited anxiously outside while the doctor thoroughly examined Assunta. When he finished he called Joe and Rosie into the other room and said, "I am going to give her an injection to help her to bear the pain. She must be kept quiet and if she falls asleep, don't disturb her. Her condition is very serious, and I must seek a second opinion. Are you willing to have me call a specialist?"

Joe was only too willing, anything, anything to help Assunta. When the doctor left after giving her the injection, Joe refused to leave her side and sent Rosie down to put a sign in the shop window: "Closed because of illness." When Fonzino came back in the early evening, he wanted to open the shop, but Joe sent him with Rico to Byres Road, and they returned with Giulietta soon afterwards. They found Joe silently weeping in the kitchen, for he really thought Assunta was dying. Giulietta soon got organised and sent Rosie downstairs to cook a meal. Then she made Joe and Rico and Fonzino go down and eat while she sat with Assunta. During the night they took it in turn to sit with her, but she scarcely stirred. She was obviously heavily drugged.

Next day the doctor brought a specialist. They examined Assunta for half an hour, and the low murmuring of their voices was often interrupted by her screams. They told Joe she would have to be operated upon at once. As a result of severe strain, she had done serious damage

160

to her liver. There were other complications resulting from her indiscretion at the time she had given birth to the child. Time was urgent and she would have to be removed to hospital that very afternoon. It was a matter of life or death.

Joe was appalled by the news. The word "operation" conjured up all sorts of fatal terrors, for no one in his family had been in hospital before. The word soon got round the tenement that Assunta was to be removed to a nursing home, for Joe had decided upon the specialist's advice that she should be immediately under his care. At two o'clock a little crowd began to gather at the close entrance. The crowd grew in size, and when two policemen stopped to ask the people to move on, a woman explained that "the wee Tally wummin' frae the ice cream shoap" was being taken to the hospital.

When the ambulance came at two-thirty, the policemen were still there to hold back the crowd, allowing the ambulance men to do their job. When the stretcher bearing Assunta appeared, followed by a tearful Joe, a hush fell upon the crowd broken only by awed murmurs of "Oh, the paer souls," and one or two of the shawled women sighed and shook their heads. As the ambulance drove away, Mrs. Welsh, Nancy, and Susie, who had closed their shops to be there, dabbed their eyes.

Assunta suffered so much before the operation that it did not worry her to find herself in a nursing home. The nurses were kind and attentive. The operation was performed with some complications. The liver had to be stitched and the surgeon decided, in the patient's interest, to perform a hysterectomy. His skill saved Assunta's life. Assunta spent four weeks in the nursing home before being allowed home. A week after the operation, she began to eat again. But she did not care for the food in the nursing home. The nurses were worried by her poor appetite. Her doctor approached her and asked whether she would not prefer some Italian-type food such as spaghetti or macaroni. Assunta became indignant.

"Don't you imagine, Doctor, that we Italians eat only spaghetti or macaroni. We can cook a very large variety of tasty dishes."

The expression on her face was so severe, and at the same time so alive, that the doctor was both pleased and amused as he said: "I can see you are getting better, Mrs. Cocozza!"

Coincidentally, it was while Assunta was still in the nursing home that Giulietta took ill with stomach trouble. She had always suffered from a nervous stomach, but the condition got worse and she had to arrange to see a specialist. Confined to bed for two weeks, she was kept on a starvation diet. It was fortunate that Vittoria was there to attend to her. When next Assunta saw Giulietta, she was dismayed to see how

161

frail her sister-in-law had become in a short time. Giulietta's brother Pietro and his wife, Erminia, also had their share of trouble at this time. Two of their children died in infancy and one of their daughters, Millie, fell into bad health.

By Easter 1928 Assunta was much better, and she was able to resume working in the café. She was warned, however, that she must avoid all heavy work. Joe would have liked to send her home to Filignano for a period of recuperation, but the expenses of the operation had eaten up all his reserve funds. So he continued to gamble, and for once his luck held and he began to win large sums of money. He bought another horse and cart and, as the summer weather continued fair and business was brisk, he realised that, if all went well, Assunta could have her holiday in the following year.

Although she was as cheerful as ever, Joe became aware of Assunta falling into long periods of silence. Something was troubling her. When they were in bed one night, they lay side by side, thinking, unable to fall asleep.

"What's troubling you, darling?" asked Joe.

"Oh, it's nothing, and yet it's everything," she replied.

"Tell me about it," he said.

"Well, it's hard to put into words, Joe, but I just feel a kind of restlessness coming over me now and then."

"Are you tired of living in Garscube Road, Sunta?"

"No, it's not that. It's just that, even after all these years, I still miss my parents. I worry about them as they are not getting any younger. Then I worry about Eugenio, for he too has a problem with Giulietta's failing health. And think of Erminia and Pietro and what they have come through in the past few months. What does it all add up to? What is it all for, all this suffering? And why does God allow it? Is it fair? I don't think so. And do we just accept it all without complaining?"

"I am sure there must be an answer somewhere, at some time," said Joe, not a little surprised that his wife harboured such deep thoughts. There he was, thinking she was worried over petty problems in the shop, when in fact she was pondering the meaning of life. She never failed to astonish him.

"Oh, let's not dwell on these problems, now," he said, leaning over to kiss her goodnight.

"Yes," she said, "but they don't disappear if we simply turn our backs on them."

A few days later, Joe had an exceptionally good stroke of luck on the horses, and he was able to deposit over a hundred pounds in their savings account. That same evening as they were eating, he turned to Assunta and said, "Guess what I am going to do with my winnings from now on?"

"Surprise me!" said Assunta.

"I would like to extend the house at Imperatore."

"What would you add to it?" asked Assunta.

"A new bedroom, just for us. Then we could take a holiday every year in the autumn, just the two of us, like a new honeymoon every time. So much to look forward to."

"Oh, Joe, you do talk a lot of nonsense," she said, "but I like the idea of a new bedroom."

So Joe wrote to their builder friend Peppino di Bona, and plans were made for a new room at the top of the house, with a flat roof above it for a veranda commanding a really superb view of the village. So the year drew to a close on a note of optimism for Assunta and Joe.

Chapter Fourteen

1929 to 1930—Innovations

The year 1929 made an auspicious start in Glasgow when the Coliseum Cinema in Eglinton Street introduced the talking picture to an eager audience with the first showing of Al Jolson's *The Singing Fool* on the 7th of January. Joe, an enthusiastic member of that first audience, was completely enchanted and during the weeks that followed he went to see it over and over again, taking Assunta, Rico, Rosie, and Fonzino each in turn. The film was a great novelty, and Joe would often perform the famous song "Sonny Boy" in the backshop.

Rico acted as his foil and when Joe began, in the best Jolson manner, to sing, "Climb upon my knee, Sonny Boy," Rico would oblige. But when he came to the next line "You are only three, Sonny Boy," Rico would chirp, "No, Papà, I'm only seven."

The song enjoyed a long popularity with the Glaswegians. That was to be expected in a period of sentiment and sentimentality.

It was at this time also that the custom of entertaining in their backshops among the Italians in Glasgow gave way to the regular Sunday meetings at the Fascio di Glasgow. With the rise of Mussolini, the Italians were taking a certain pride in the improvements and developments being made in their native country. Although the Italian Consulate was in the area of Park Circus, the Fascio meetings were held in the Green's Playhouse building in Renfield Street. There on Sunday evenings there were social gatherings, and in the afternoons classes in the Italian language were taught for the benefit of Italian children or adults wishing to improve their knowledge of their native tongue.

Eugenio, Antonio, and Pietro had been quick to join the Blackshirts. They would put on their uniforms after closing the shop on Sundays and go to the Fascio, taking their wives and families for an evening out. Eugenio asked Joe to join the Party, but, although Joe was pleased to learn of the many material improvements taking place in Italy as a result of Mussolini's policies, he was suspicious of all

164

political organizations and declined. This caused a slight cooling of feeling between Eugenio and Joe, and, although it hurt Assunta to see this slight rift, she nevertheless respected her husband's opinion and independent attitude.

She was annoyed, however, when, every time she went to Byres Road, Antonio would observe with a sarcastic smile, "So you haven't yet persuaded compare Joe to join the Party?" Eugenio, on the other hand, never raised the subject and for this she was grateful.

Irena, Joe's sister, found a suitor in Raffaele Ferri, a widower with three children, and the marrige took place in early spring. Joe closed the shop, and they all went to the wedding. In honour of the occasion, Assunta adopted a new hairstyle then popular and appeared with her ears covered in "earphones" woven from the long tresses of her brown hair. They went to the Elsmore Studio and had their photograph taken, Assunta and Joe sitting, with Rico standing between them in his silk shirt and dark blue velvet trousers.

Irena's marriage resulted in the winding up of the café at Parkhead as Leonarda could never have managed it on her own. This gave rise to a new arrangement whereby Leonarda would divide her year into three periods of four months, living in turn with her daughter and two sons. So she would spend four months in Garngad Road where Raffaele and Irena had their business, four in Airdrie with Antonio and his family, and four in Garscube Road with Joe, Assunta, and Rico.

One Sunday evening Eugenio arrived at Garscube Road in his splendid new Chrysler car to insist that Assunta, Joe, Rico, and signora Leonarda go with him to the Fascio where there was to be a splendid production of a play in Italian. They were soon sitting in the little hall in Green's building beside Giulietta and Vittoria, and the flimsy curtains rose on a tiny stage to hush the chattering audience. There then unfolded a very moving melodrama about a brother and sister who had been separated by fate when they were children. As adults they met, not knowing their true identities and, after many vicissitudes, they at last came to know they were related by blood.

The great climax of the play came when the sister, seeing her brother enter and knowing who he really was, called out to him tearfully, "*Ah, Fernando, Fernando, vieni nelle braccia della tua sorella!* Oh, Fernando, Fernando, come to the arms of your sister!" and, as sister and brother embraced, the curtain came down to loud applause. Joe was very amused by this drama, and the final line became a sort of family joke. Occasionally the backshop at 78, Garscube Road would resound with the melodramatic words "*Ah, Fernando, Fernando, vieni nelle braccia della tua sorella!*"

165

When Rico was persuaded by his uncle to attend the Italian classes in the Fascio on Sundays, he recognised the young lady who was his teacher as the one who had played Fernando's sister in the play. When he got home in the early evening, he was sitting eating a plate of spaghetti, which Assunta always made on Sunday, with his father and mother.

As they were twining the succulent strands round their forks, Joe asked, "Well, did you enjoy your Italian lesson today?"

"Yes, I did. It was very amusing. And I recognised the teacher," said Rico.

"Who is your teacher, then?" asked Assunta.

"Fernando's sister," replied Rico with a broad grin.

"What do you mean, Fernando's sister?" queried Joe, at which Rico, skilfully imitating his father's nasal impersonation of the long-lost sister, came out with "*Ah, Fernando, Fernando, vieni nelle braccia della tua sorella!*"

It was Peppino di Bona, now entrusted with the building of the new bedroom in the house at Imperatore, who took over as correspondent that year. His letters came every month, a great source of comfort to Assunta, not only because she rejoiced in the anticipation of seeing the new room, but because she knew Peppino and his wife, Maria, were constantly at the service of her parents. It was Peppino who arranged for day workers to plough and sow the fields, to help Benedetto in the vegetable garden. His daughter, Carminuccia, was at Filomena's beck and call, helping her with the household chores and the feeding of the animals. Strong bonds of affection grew between the Di Bonas and the Cocozzas.

When, in early autumn, Peppino's letter arrived announcing that the new bedroom was ready, Joe saw the look of longing in Assunta's eyes as she read out the news. That night as they lay in bed going over the day's events, Joe turned to Assunta and asked, "How would you like to spend Christmas in Filignano?"

She turned her head on the pillow and looked at him questioningly, saying, "But we couldn't possibly go to Italy at Christmas. The shop is too busy then, and we could not afford to close."

"I wouldn't be coming with you, Sunta. You could take Rico with you."

"But it wouldn't be the same without you, Joe," she protested.

Joe went on, saying, "I would willingly make the sacrifice, darling, because I know it would bring your long period of convalescence to an end and you would come back to me a new woman."

"I don't think I would like to travel to Filignano on my own with the boy," said Assunta.

166

"I happen to know Eugenio and Giulietta are thinking of going back at the end of October."

Assunta knew then it had all been already discussed at Byres Road and Giulietta had made the decision that Assunta and Rico should go with her and Eugenio, for she did not care to be parted from her little nephew, even for a few weeks.

She turned to Joe again and said,

"When you go to Byres Road tomorrow, you can tell Giulietta that I agree!"

Joe smiled. Assunta could get to the bottom of anything. She would have made a good detective.

Next day, as Joe was walking down Byres Road from the Hillhead subway, he saw that both the ice-cream vans were still parked outside the Continental. From the distance he could read the brightly painted slogan above the back door of the second van: "One quality only—the best," and he smiled. Joe had great affection for Eugenio, despite their different opinions on matters political, and he admired his brother-in-law's cleverness.

When he was younger, Eugenio had been a great motor-cyclist and had competed daringly in many races, carrying off a number of trophies. In the end the race organisers had requested him to stop competing and give other contestants a chance to win. That Eugenio was a great organiser was evident in the manner in which he ran his business. His bookkeeping was meticulous, and he had been secretary of the Italian Refreshment Society for a number of years. He even acted as a part-time secretary to the Italian Consul in Glasgow. He also found time to be a motor-car enthusiast and was very proud of his recently acquired Chrysler. As a connoisseur of good music, he had a large collection of gramophone records and loved to give recitals to his friends in the backshop, telling them about the composer and describing the background to the particular item he was playing for their pleasure.

When Joe walked into the Continental, he found himself in front of a beaming Eugenio.

"You're just in time for a demonstration of my latest acquisition," he said, and, taking Joe by the arm, led him into the backshop straight away. He made Joe sit down at the table as he moved over to the shelf above the wardrobe. Joe looked up and saw what looked like a square wireless set with four large, round, black knobs along the front panel. He could not see any loudspeaker in the small cabinet, and he looked questioningly at his brother-in-law, who, by this time had put on a switch and was slowly turning one of the knobs. Eugenio then moved to the cabinet gramophone and slowly wound the spring before placing

167

a record on the turntable. Joe stood up to see what he was doing, and he noticed that the soundbox arm had been removed and replaced with a slightly curved arm made of a brown, shiny substance ending in a small square box beneath which protruded a steel gramophone needle.

Eugenio carefully raised the arm and lowered the needle into the run-in groove on the record. The mighty sound of a full symphony orchestra suddenly filled the backshop with "The Blue Danube Waltz" by Johann Strauss, and Joe looked round, unable to see the loudspeaker from which the strains of the waltz were coming. Eugenio smiled at Joe's perplexity, then he walked slowly over to the wardrobe and pointed to the bowler hat, fixed by its rim on the edge of the shelf above it.

Joe could not believe his eyes, but when he moved closer to the hat he was firmly convinced by his ears. The music was certainly coming from the rounded interior of the hat. When the record ended, Eugenio carefully stopped the gramophone. Then he went over to the hat, unfastened the drawing pins holding it in place, and brought it down to reveal a small circle of metal attached to the centre of the bowl from which two wires went into the back of the square wireless set.

"You have just heard a gramophone record played electrically," said Eugenio. "The impulses are carried from the pick-up" (and he pointed to the square box at the end of the brown arm) "by means of these wires" (and he pulled up two other wires Joe had not noticed before) "to the amplifier" (and he pointed to the square wireless set with the four knobs). "The amplifier receives the signals from the pick-up and converts them into stronger impulses, feeding them by means of these two wires to the bowler hat, which vibrates in the same manner as a loudspeaker cone" (Joe saw a mental image of an ice-cream cone, but that obviously did not make sense) "producing the sound vibrations that create the music you have just heard!"

Joe was left quite speechless by Eugenio's long technical explanation. All he could appreciate was that his brother-in-law had produced a miracle in his backshop. Just then Giulietta brought Joe a cup of coffee.

"Eugenio just likes to dumbfound people with his experiments," she said, "so just drink this coffee and it will settle your nerves."

When Joe had sufficiently recovered from the remarkable musical demonstration, they sat down together and made their plans for the trip to Filignano. Giulietta's main reason for the journey was to consult a specialist in Naples who had made a name for himself with his treatment of stomach disorders. The date for their departure was to be the 20th of October, and the Italan consul himself, Dr. Olivieri, would be travelling with them so they would enjoy customs immunity. There was no limit, said Giulietta, to what Assunta could take home on this special journey.

Joe reflected that there would be a serious limit as he was having to make sacrifices to be able to afford Assunta's holiday. The end of the season had been disappointing as a trade war had flared up between the Ziggis and the Dalredas in Garscube Road. Joe's café happened to be situated between those of the rivals who vied with one another in giving large measure. It was Joe's business that suffered most, caught as he was between the devil and the deep blue sea. In fact, it was becoming so serious that, if the feud between his neighbours did not come to an end reasonably soon, he might be forced to move from the area and find a shop elsewhere.

The day of Assunta's departure drew near, and she wrote to Peppino who passed the news to Filomena and Benedetto. They were overjoyed at the prospect of having their son and daughter home together for Christmas.

The Central Station in Glasgow was especially crowded on the evening of the 20th of October 1929, and, when all the good-byes had been said and many of the ladies began to dab their eyes with their handkerchiefs, the guard's whistle was heard and the train departed, leaving a dejected Joe on the platform ready to face a lonely Christmas without his beloved wife and son. Rico, who had been looking out at this moving scene from the train window, could not help wondering why grown-ups made such a sad fuss on these occasions.

Then, settling down in his corner seat, he found himself face to face with the distinguished-looking gentleman with whom they would be travelling all the way to Italy. Dr. Olivieri spoke beautiful Italian. Although he had attended the Fascio school for a few weeks to learn good Italian, Rico had fallen away, making excuses. He felt that five days of school each week were more than enough and could not see why he should be punished with a sixth. Now he regretted his lack of diligence, for he did not feel fit to converse with this gentleman. In fact he had a strong feeling of inferiority in his presence, which brought on a long fit of shyness.

Every time Dr. Olivieri spoke to him, Rico turned timidly away, closed his eyes, and pretended to go to sleep. Assunta and Giulietta were amused by the boy's performance. He spoke only when Dr. Olivieri went into the corridor with Eugenio to smoke. Assunta wondered just how long Rico's shyness would last.

On the following day, having crossed the Channel, they were travelling on the fast train to Paris. Again Dr. Olivieri tried to engage Rico in conversation, but the boy persisted in his silence. After lunch Rico fell asleep in his corner seat, and as he slept, heavy rain lashed the windows. They were all sitting quietly, Dr. Olivieri as usual directly across from Rico, when the boy opened his eyes, looked at the windows and saw the heavy rainwater. His eyes opened wide as he turned to the consul and said in the broad dialect of Filignano, "*Cazzo e comme chiove!* Hell's bells, just look at that bloody rain!"

Dr. Olivieri, quite overcome with mirth, observed, "I see you have found your tongue, my boy!" Now that his long silence had been broken with such an outrageous exclamation, Rico no longer considered it necessary to maintain his shy atttiude. From that moment he and the consul became the best of friends, and they exchanged confidences, Dr. Olivieri expressing himself in good Italian and Rico in pure Filignanese.

Not wishing to deny himself his music, Eugenio had brought a portable gramophone. When the train made long stops on the journey to Rome, he would play a record to pass the time. Eventually they said good-bye to the consul in Rome. At Venafro they had to hire two taxis to take them to Filignano as Giulietta had so much luggage. Then, when they finally arrived in the piazza, the Di Bona girls, Carminuccia, Mafalda, and Linuccia, were waiting to welcome them and carry their bags. Peppino and Maria were there also and their two young sons, Gaetano and Nicodemo.

As they were making their way up the hill, Assunta glanced up and saw the new room on the top of the house with its flat roof and iron veranda making a lovely terrace. Peppino had done an excellent job, and some day soon she hoped that she and Joe would sleep in that room high up on the hill away from the cares and troubles of the shop. Perhaps, if God was good to them, they could retire there one day and live to a contented old age like Filomena and Benedetto. There they would live together with Eugenio and Giulietta, and how happy they would be when Rico and his wife and children would come to visit them from time to time. Their visits would be frequent, for Rico would have a profession and would be able to afford to visit his parents and his aunt and uncle.

They came round the last corner to approach the gate of the house, and Assunta checked her train of thought. What was all this hopeful daydreaming? Why should her mind be leaping so far ahead into the future at the mere sight of a new room at the top of the house? She had not given way to such wishful speculation for years. Perhaps it was because she was already missing Joe so much.

The reunion with Filomena and Benedetto was a joyful one. A

meal awaited them and, while they ate, Assunta fell silent and let Giulietta give her mother a full account of all the news from Glasgow. When the meal was over, Eugenio and Giulietta went to Bottazzella to visit Luigi and Albina, and Rico went out to find his old shepherd friend Carminuccio. Assunta and Filomena climbed up the stairs to the new bedroom. On Joe's instructions Peppino had bought a new bed in Naples. The intricately carved oak headboard stood out grandly against the freshly whitewashed wall.

From the new balcony, Assunta could look up to the top of Imperatore, and she felt sheltered by the old houses directly opposite. Then they climbed the third stair leading to the new loggia above. It was truly a great moment when they stepped out from the covered doorway of the staircase on to the flat roof and looked across to the mountains in the distance. Assunta felt so free that she experienced the strange sensation of floating in mid-air above this place where she had been born and had happily grown to womanhood amidst the natural elements she loved so much. It was this very ambience that had moulded her spirit, disciplined her body, and trained her heart to be true and sincere.

Filomena stood silently beside her, and they looked down upon the village. She remembered the eve of her departure in February 1915 when she had enjoyed the same scene from the balcony of her parents' bedroom downstairs. Seeing it again now from a higher viewpoint, in a different light, she was fully aware of the progress she had made and how her life had changed so much in fourteen years. A wave of gratitude to God swept over her, and she thanked Him for having guided her to happiness with Joe, for having given her such a good little son, for bringing her safely home to her parents, and above all for granting her the grace of this sublime moment when she could review her life up to that point and recognise she had been exceptionally blessed.

She turned to Filomena who was eyeing her curiously.

"What is the matter, Ma?" she asked. "Why are you looking at me so strangely?"

"I am looking at you because I have never seen you so happy, Sunta," said Filomena.

When Eugenio and Giulietta came back from Bottazzella, they also made the climb up to the loggia on the roof and stood, taking in the breathtaking view. Downstairs Assunta and Filomena were preparing supper while Rico was trying, with little success, to engage his grandfather in conversation.

He had been up to some of his mischief that afternoon with poor Carminuccio. They had decided to play at building houses and had

171

gathered pieces of stone for the purpose. Rico naturally took charge, giving orders to Carminuccio in English. The poor boy repeated the English words Rico spoke without understanding them, and, of course, he did all the wrong things. Rico became annoyed with him and hit him a wallop on the ear. This led to a scuffle and Carminuccio, defending himself against this fierce, little Scot from Glasgow, punched him on the nose. When Rico felt the blood running down into his mouth, he ran to Assunta for help. Poor Carminuccio stood helplessly looking on, feeling thoroughly ashamed as he nursed his sore ear.

Filomena came to Rico's assistance with a basin of cold water and a cloth. In the meantime, Carminuccio told Assunta what had happened. She made the boys shake hands although Rico was not too keen to do so. When Carminuccio went home, Assunta turned to Rico, asking, "Aren't you ashamed of yourself? Why did you start the fight?"

"Carminuccio wasn't doing what I told him to do."

"But you spoke to him in English, didn't you?"

"And what's wrong with that?"

"Carminuccio doesn't understand English."

"Don't they teach him English at school?"

"No, they don't."

"This is a terrible country, where they can't teach boys plain English!" muttered Rico quite unrepentingly. Assunta shook her head.

Over supper Assunta told Eugenio and Giulietta what had happened. Giulietta then reprimanded Rico for his bad behaviour, telling him he should beg God's forgiveness in his prayers that night. Rico looked at his aunt in astonishment, then, turning to his uncle, he observed, "You would think I had murdered the boy."

When they were sitting round the fire after the Rosary, Eugenio asked Filomena to tell one of her stories so that it would be just like old times.

"Make it a happy one," said Benedetto. "We don't want any of your tragedies on this happy evening."

Filomena pondered for a moment, then, clearing her throat she began, "One day a man from Montaquila took his five donkeys to graze in the country. When they had been there all day, he decided to go home, and, mounting one of the donkeys, let the other four go on ahead as they slowly made their way along the pebbled road. The evening was mild, and he began to doze as he sat astride the animal. A little later, when he opened his eyes, he looked at the donkeys and counted them out aloud, saying, 'One, two, three, four. Oh my, I had five donkeys. Where has the other gone? Oh dear, I shall have to go back and fetch the other one.'

"Then, dismounting, he was suddenly aware of his error and said: 'Thank goodness, there are five after all!'

"So he got back up on to the donkey and continued on his way home, dozing again. At a turn in the road, he opened his eyes and, looking ahead, could not see any of his donkeys, for they had already turned the corner and were temporarily out of sight. Alarmed, he called out, 'Where have all my donkeys gone?'

"But, just then, he turned the corner and the donkeys came into view again. At first he was reassured. Then he began counting them, 'One, two, three, four. I have lost one of my donkeys. Where has that blessed donkey gone?'

"At that very instant, the donkey on which he was riding decided to heehaw, and he nearly fell off as he got such a fright. Then, feeling rather foolish, he laughed when he realized all his donkeys were present and correct."

As Filomena ended her story, they all tittered. Then Rico piped up, "But there were really six donkeys all the time, Nonna, weren't there?"

"How do you mean?" asked Filomena, and all eyes turned upon Rico.

"Well, it's very simple," he said. "There were four donkeys in front, and there was the donkey on which the man was riding."

"Yes," said Eugenio, "that adds up to five."

"But then there was the biggest donkey of them all, the man himself, so that made six, did it not?" said Rico triumphantly.

"I'm afraid your son is far too clever for us all," said Eugenio to Assunta.

"Somebody has to be clever in this place where boys don't understand English and people don't know how to count their donkeys," said Rico with an impudent smile.

"That's enough," said Assunta. "Off to bed with you." And she bustled her spirited boy upstairs and came back shortly afterwards to rejoin the family circle round the fire.

Eugenio then brought out the portable gramophone and played some of his records. The old people watched and listened with wonder. It was the first time they had ever heard recorded music.

Between records Filomena kept repeating, "Whatever will they think of next?"

When they went visiting friends in the evening, Eugenio often took the gramophone to give a recital. One evening after supper, when the sky was bright with blue moonlight, he and Giulietta, Assunta, and Rico went to visit the Di Bonas. Eugenio carried the gramophone

173

while he entrusted the records in a special carrying case to his nephew. As they approached the Di Bona house, they could see its four-balconied façade gleaming. Eugenio made them all hush as he quietly went up to the flat ledge beside the main door and carefully placed the gramophone upon it. Then he opened the instrument and beckoned to Rico to bring over the records. As soon as the music started, Eugenio motioned to them and they crept round the corner of the house and hid in a recess between the side wall and the vegetable garden. Meanwhile the tuneful sounds echoed in the still night. The door of one of the lower balconies was heard to open, and Carminuccia came out.

"Who's there?" she called out, puzzled, and she went forward and leaned over to look down from the balcony rail. But she could not see anyone. The music continued to fill the cool, evening air. Next they heard the main door being opened and the two boys, Gaetano and Nicodemo, came out to investigate. When they saw the dark disc on the turntable shining as it revolved, they began to laugh and called up to their sister, "It's Zio Eugenio teasing us with his gramophone!"

The visitors then emerged from their hiding place and, as the strains of the waltz continued, Eugenio took his wife's arm and danced with her on the terrace in front of the house. The rest of the family were by this time on the balconies, and they applauded the dancing couple, charmed by Eugenio's little musical prank.

When they made their way upstairs into the large living-room kitchen, they were startled by the brilliance of the light provided by two carbide lamps sitting on either side of the large mantelpiece shelf over the log fire. At Imperatore they had grown accustomed to the dim light of Filomena's candles, small wick olive-oil lamps, and the one paraffin lamp that sat on the cupboard shelf. The light from the Di Bona carbide lamps was greenish white and cold and made their faces chalky grey.

Maria Di Bona was roasting chestnuts in a large copper pan over the log flames, and she kept emptying them, when they were ready, into a large bowl and passed them round. Still too hot, the chestnuts had to be flipped from one hand to the other until they cooled sufficiently to be peeled. Once the crisp, outer skin was removed, they could be slipped, still hot, into the mouth and they were utterly delicious washed down with a glass of good red wine. Even Rico was offered a glass of wine, but Assunta insisted it should be diluted. The Di Bonas were interested in Eugenio's accounts of life in Glasgow and the elder of the two boys, Gaetano, never took his grey-blue eyes from Eugenio's face. The gramophone was then played, and the evening ended with a grand concert, the most acclaimed item being the *William Tell* Overture by Rossini.

174

The days passed happily, and soon it was the 6th of November and Rico's eighth birthday. A special midday meal was cooked, and Giulietta had baked one of her famous sponges for the occasion. Assunta suggested Rico should invite his friend Carminuccio, so the boy's father took their six sheep to pasture that day. It was a very good meal, and the boys were allowed to drink a glass of diluted wine. They all drank a toast to Rico, and he smiled with grown-up pride. He was now eight years of age. In no time he would be a man.

Ater the meal, Giulietta and Eugenio went off to Bottazzella and Assunta helped her mother to wash up while Benedetto went out for a long tramp up the hill. The boys went upstairs to play with Rico's toys, and Rico showed Carminuccio the comic papers Joe had sent a few days before. Joe always made a small package containing two copies of the *Daily Record*, two comics, and in the centre he would place two bars of chocolate. Rico looked forward to the arrival of the papers every week, and he would stand on the balcony when they were due and look out for the postman. Now Rico let Carminuccio study the comic strips, and he translated the ringed captions for his friend's benefit. Rico was making sure that his friend learned some English.

When they had finished with the papers, the boys went round exploring the house until Rico had a bright idea. He took his friend to the wine cellar, and they explored its dark corners. The strong smell of wine still fermenting in the casks inspired Rico with another idea. He slipped into the house and, when Assunta's back was turned, lifted an empty wine bottle from the cupboard shelf. Then, back in the cellar, he made Carminuccio hold a funnel over the mouth of the bottle and, lifting it up to the large cask containing the good wine they had sampled at dinner, turned the cock and let the wine gurgle into the bottle until it overflowed and spilled on to the stone floor. The boys then drew up two chairs and, sitting down in the manner of seasoned topers, passed the bottle to one another and drank. By the time they had finished their third bottle, the two young bacchanalians were no longer conscious of where they were.

Filomena, going out to throw some crumbs to the hens, was surprised to hear two boisterously sozzled young voices raised in song coming from the cellar. The door was ajar so she moved forward and opened it wide. A very muddled Carminuccio and a thoroughly temulent Rico were sitting back to back on the floor, singing away in torpid, badly slurred voices. A half-empty bottle of wine was flopping loosely in Rico's hand. By the time Filomena fetched Assunta, the boys were in a completely raddled stupor and quite unable to walk when pulled up on to their feet. Their eyes already closing, they were helped one at a time to Filomena's bed where, stretched out side by side on

175

their backs, dead to the world, for four hours they snored their way back to a state of uneasy, troubled, nauseous sobriety.

When Eugenio and Giulietta returned from Bottazzella, an irritated Assunta told them what had happened. Eugenio was amused and he went through to take a look at the culprits as they lay open-mouthed on the bed. Giulietta was shocked and angry, and she took Assunta and Filomena to task for not keeping a more watchful eye on the boys. When Carminuccio's mother, Carmela, worried by her son's prolonged absence, came to inquire, a very ashamed Assunta had to explain what had occurred.

With Assunta's permission, Carmela made her way into the bedroom, pulled her son off the bed so that he fell with a resounding thud on to the stone floor, and, as he sluggishly wakened, she dragged him up on to his feet and, after slapping him soundly about the head, pushed him towards the main door by the scruff of the neck. Rico slept blissfully through this scene, quite unaware of the punishment being meted out to his hapless friend. But his own turn was soon to come. Eugenio pulled him to his feet and led him into the kitchen where Assunta had already filled a large basin with cold water. He was made to wash his face before being marched off to bed by his indignant mother.

On a cold day in December, they heard the sound of pipes echoing from the distance. It was the Christmas pipers, come all the way from Cerasuolo to gather provisions for Christmas while they played the novena before every house in the village. For nine days they would go playing from village to village, and their cart would be heaped high with good things to take home for the festive season. Rico had known only the sound of Scottish bagpipes before. Now the reedy notes of the Cerasuolo pipers conjured up the whole setting of the Nativity in Bethlehem, when so many people came from far and wide to admire and love the newborn child.

The colourful ritual of Christmas with the great climax of midnight mass made a deep impression on Rico, and Assunta, studying his reactions, relived the wonder and enchantment of her own childhood at that time of year.

Early in January, Eugenio suggested Rico should attend the village school. Not only would it keep him out of mischief since he would be occupied from eight o' clock in the morning until noon, but it would bring him into contact with other children and have him appreciate how fortunate he was. As it happened they had all been invited for an evening to the house of the village teachers, don Tito and donna Ida, husband and wife, who had two clever sons. Mario, the elder of the two was studying law, while Sisi, the younger, was a medical student.

176

They set out complete with Eugenio's gramophone, arriving early in the evening at don Tito's house. Rico was overawed by don Tito's severe aspect. He was a small, round man with dark, piercing eyes and a small, square, black moustache. Donna Ida was pleasant, and she smiled and made a fuss of Rico, but he was amused to notice she had a hairy chin and a moustache. Tea was served and donna Ida announced she would now fetch the chocolate cream dish with chou pastries she had especially prepared. A moment later they heard dramatic cries from the kitchen as donna Ida called out, "Oh, the scoundrels! Oh, the thieves!"

Then she appeared in a state of great agitation, carrying a long platter in the centre of which lay the meagre remains of the special dish. Placing it on the table, she explained that those incorrigible sons of hers had been helping themselves when her back was turned. As Mario and Sisi were at that very moment playing cards in the piazza café, they temporarily escaped the weight of their mother's wrath. Donna Ida always seemed to be in the midst of a crisis of one sort or another, as Rico was later to find out.

Attending the village school for the first time, Rico noticed that the walls of the small classroom were covered with pictures of a strong-jawed man wearing a black hat with a tassel. He was respectfully referred to as *Il Duce*. For the benefit of the new pupil, donna Ida gave a special lesson on *Il Duce* and by the end of the hour, Rico understood that this great man was really the modern Saviour of Italy. Donna Ida was fond of giving dictations and at least twice every morning her voice could be heard uttering the magic word, "DETTATO—DICTA-TION."

Jotters were then opened, and pens began to scrape on the lined paper. Sometimes she would set some copying work from textbooks that explained in even greater detail the achievements of *Il Duce*, and, while the pupils were busy writing, donna Ida would disappear to do her shopping at the shop of Maria the butcher, or she would go round to the café for a cup of coffee. The moment she went out, all pens were put down and bedlam broke loose. The boys in the back rows fought, while the girls in the front gossiped. The boys took it in turn to stand by the door in order to warn the others when donna Ida was returning. For Rico it was all a new experience, but he really did not learn very much in the eight or nine weeks he spent in donna Ida's school.

By the middle of February, Assunta was longing to see Joe again. They were all the better for their holiday, and Giulietta had benefited from the treatment of the specialist in Naples.

Many friends came down to the piazza on the morning in mid-

March when they set off on their return journey to Glasgow. The usual tears were wept; recommendations and assurances were exchanged. Having shed most of the contents of Giulietta's luggage, they were now less heavily laden and one taxi was sufficient for their needs to take them to Venafro. Eugenio had given all his records and his gramophone to the Di Bonas as a small token of his gratitude for all they had done and would do for his parents.

As they made their way down the winding road, Assunta summed up the holiday. It had been rewarding in many ways. She had seen her parents happy in the company of their family. Being in close contact with Rico every day, she had been able to study him in all his moods, and a steady relationship had developed between them that had not existed before. Indeed she was now aware of traits in his character that would have to be curbed before he grew much older. She would see to it that he spent more time in his own home when they got back, so that she and Joe could watch him grow as they would want him to, with understanding, firm guidance, and discipline tempered with a reasonable amount of tolerance.

Chapter Fifteen

1930 to 1933—The Move to Wishaw

On their way back to Scotland, they stopped for two days in Paris and visited Antonia and Pompilio who were happily settled in La Villette. By this time they had two chidren, a boy, Dante, and a girl, Ginetta, and it was evident that Pompilio had found his true métier in making accordions. Giulietta had a wonderful time trying out many of his instruments, and she had not lost her skill, for she surprised everyone with the deftness of her touch. It was an eagerly enjoyed visit, and Assunta and Antonia had much to chat about. They promised to keep in touch with one another.

Back behind the counter of the shop in Garscube Road, Assunta soon felt her holiday in Filignano had been a dream. She was perturbed to see the worried look on Joe's face and when she questioned him, he explained that despite a reasonably good season at Christmas, the situation had deteriorated in January and February. There was a marked increase in unemployment, and money was very scarce. To add to their business problems, the Ziggis were still at war with their rivals down the road. Joe's café, caught between them, suffered most. Sales dropped to a very low level. Joe could not afford to pay his staff and first Fonzino, then Rosie had to be paid off. Running the business on their own was not hard, for some days they served less than a dozen customers.

Rico was now in the trying intermediate grade at school, but he was not showing any promising signs. He won prizes for religious knowledge but showed little ability in his other subjects. Perhaps Giulietta's wish for him to embrace the priesthood might, after all, be realised. But Assunta could not really see him in the rôle of priest.

During the Easter period, when Nonna Leonarda was staying at Garscube Road and Rico was on holiday from school, Assunta decided one day to go to Byres Road. The ice-cream vans had already gone out, Josie was behind the counter, and Giulietta and Vittoria were in the backshop when they arrived. The ladies had a visitor. It was Maria

179

Giuseppa from Wishaw who had brought her usual clooty dumpling. They sat and enjoyed a piece with a cup of tea.

In the course of the conversation, it came out that Maria was having problems with her husband Jimmy. They were a childless couple, but had everything to be thankful for. Their lovely café at the bottom end of the town enjoyed a select clientèle, business was good, and Jimmy had even invested in an ice-cream van and was doing a roaring trade. But he had a flirtatious nature, and word had come to Maria's ears that he was in the habit of entertaining attractive girls in his van.

This was a fatal thing to do in a small town like Wishaw and, although there might be no harm in it, Maria Giuseppa with her jealous nature was quite upset. There had been some bitter quarrels between her and Jimmy. Now she wanted Giulietta's advice. How should she deal with her husband? Why, at that very moment as they sat chatting in the backshop at Byres Road, Jimmy might be philandering with some pretty girl in his van!

Giulietta first of all advised Maria to disregard gossip. She should ask Jimmy to his face if he had been seeing any girls. If he denied it, then she should, as a loving wife, trust her husband and believe him. Giulietta was sure, knowing Jimmy, that the stories about him were untrue or grossly exaggerated. To be sure he probably had an eye for a pretty girl. But then so did Eugenio and Antonio. Neither she nor Vittoria took such things seriously.

"You are his wife," she told Maria, "and it is you he really loves." Maria Giuseppa seemed comforted by Giulietta's words, and she said good-bye and departed for Wishaw.

When she had gone, Giulietta was called to the counter to help Josie, leaving Vittoria and Assunta alone.

"You should have been here earlier, *comma'*," said Vittoria, "when Maria Giuseppa was telling us what happened this morning. If it were not so sad, it would be really funny."

"What happened, *comma'*?" asked Assunta.

"Well, it seems that Maria and Jimmy were both working behind the counter, replenishing shelves and sweet bottles, when she accused him of having a girl in his van yesterday afternoon. Of course he loudly denied it, and, one thing leading to another, they began swearing at one another, shouting quite viciously. Then Maria lost her temper and threw a jar at Jimmy and it fell, shattering at his feet. He threw a tumbler at her, but his aim was as bad as hers, and it broke against the glass counter shelf behind her. As they both bent down behind the high counter to pick up the broken glass, they went on calling each other nasty names. Then the doorbell rang and they rose together, all smiles, and, looking at the lady customer who had just come in, chorused together, 'Yes, please?' But the moment the lady had been served, Maria and Jimmy got down again and went on hurling invectives at one another."

Assunta then told Vittoria she had always found Jimmy to be an amusing man but quick to take offence. She remembered a particular incident involving Joe when he was going back to Italy to do his military service. He and Jimmy were travelling together. Now, Jimmy was always well turned out, buying the most expensive of clothes. He took special pride in the hats he selected, which were of the very best quality. He had purchased a very expensive one for the journey to Italy.

As the train was about to depart, he took off his hat and placed it on the seat. Joe was leaning out of the carriage window to say goodbye to his family and, as the train went into motion, he closed it and promptly sat down—on Jimmy's hat, flattening it. Jimmy screamed with real anguish when he saw what Joe had done. He made him rise at once to reveal the poor hat flattened like a pancake.

Refusing to accept Joe's embarrassed apology, he maintained Joe had done it on purpose, out of envy. When Joe tried to reason with him, offering to reimburse him, Jimmy took the hat, opened the carriage window, and petulantly threw it out. Joe had exclaimed, "Oh, my hat!" but Jimmy was not amused.

Vittoria and Assunta were still laughing over Jimmy's hat when Giulietta came back into the backshop.

"What are you two up to?" she asked, and when Assunta went through the story of the crushed hat again for her sister-in-law's benefit, Giulietta said, "Maria Giuseppa and Jimmy certainly are a pair, but I have a terrible feeling, what with her jealousy and his temper, one of these days it will end badly between them." Then she added, "There must be something in the air in the Wishaw area that makes people behave oddly at times."

"What do you mean, Giulietta?" chorused Assunta and Vittoria.

Giulietta went on, saying, "I am thinking of something that took place in Shotts not very long ago, and Shotts is not very far from Wishaw, you know."

She paused until she had their full attention, then began, "Our *compare* Giannino Madella has done well for himself in Shotts. He has a fine café and a large billiard room. An extremely generous man, he never hesitates to help anyone who happens to be less fortunate than himself. Now, about a year ago, he had a visit one day from his *compare*

181

Alfio from Carfin. Alfio was having a hard time trying to pay his expenses, and his unpaid bills were giving him nightmares. So he borrowed four pounds from *compare* Giannino, promising to pay him back just as soon as he could.

"A fortnight later he came back and borrowed another two pounds, and a week after that he was back again to ask for three. This went on for some time until Alfio was owing Giannino more than thirty pounds, with never a sign of him paying any of it back. Naturally *compare* Giannino began to be annoyed at Alfio's persistence and when he appeared again one day, Giannino realised he would have to take certain measures.

" 'Well, what is it this time, *compare?*' he asked.

" 'Oh, *compa*', I have just received an enormous gas bill, and I just don't have the money to pay it. If they come and cut off the gas, where shall I be? Oh, I am really desperate, *compa*', but surely things won't always be as bad as this, and, of course, you do have a note of what I already owe you, and I must absolutely insist you should take a proper rate of interest on the money you lend me.'

"Giannino cut him short, for it seemed he was going to go on forever.

" 'How much do you need, *compa*'?' and Alfio smilingly replied, 'Eight pounds would see me out of my difficulty.'

" 'Very well,' said Giannino, 'just you wait here and I shall fetch the money,' and, leaving Alfio to enjoy the heat of the coalfire, he went through to his little office and took eight pounds from the safe. He came back with the notes in his hand, and, turning to Alfio, said, 'You did say eight pounds, *compa*'?'

"Then, after carefully counting out the notes, he said, 'One, two, three, four, five, six, seven, eight.' While Alfio, his smiling eyes fixed on the money, followed his every move, *compare* Giannino suddenly rolled them into a little bundle and threw them into the flames of the fire. As the notes slowly burned, he held out his hands, and warmed them.

"An utterly unbelieving Alfio looked into the fire. With an incredulous note in his voice, he turned to *compare* Giannino, almost choking as he spoke, 'What have you done, *compa*' Giannino, what have you done?'

"And *compare* Giannino explained, 'Well, *compare* Alfio, it's like this. If I had given you the money, I would never have seen it again anyway. At least, throwing it into the fire, I have been able to heat my hands!'

"A very dejected Alfio quietly took his leave. Needless to say,

182

compare Giannino has not been troubled with him again."

When Assunta got back to Garscube Road later in the day, she found Joe in low spirits sitting behind the counter where he had spent the whole afternoon watching Ziggi's customers filing past with their overloaded ice-cream cones and giant ice-cream wafers, while his own freezerful of ice cream remained untouched. She tried to buck him up by telling him the stories she had heard about Wishaw and Shotts, but he was only half-listening as his problems were uppermost in his thoughts.

The summer wore on, and business was now so bad that the cash drawings for the week sometimes did not amount to ten shillings. Then, on a Friday morning early in October, Eugenio unexpectedly walked in and went up to Joe who was leaning idly on the counter.

Without any preliminaries he asked, "Are you still interested in buying another shop?"

Joe assured him that he most certainly was, and Eugenio went on to explain that Maria Giuseppa had run away from her husband, Jimmy, in Wishaw. The poor chap was in such a state that he wanted to get rid of his shop as soon as possible. He felt so ashamed and feared he would be ridiculed because his wife had gone off with a much younger man, leaving a letter saying they were going to America. Jimmy had telephoned Eugenio that same morning, asking if he knew of anyone who wished to buy a café at a reasonable price. Eugenio immediately thought of Assunta and Joe, knowing of their predicament in Garscube Road.

He now suggested they should go at once to Wishaw. Joe had always believed in fate, and he saw this as a heaven-sent chance to solve his problem. Leaving Assunta in charge, he went to Wishaw with Eugenio.

As soon as Joe saw Belhaven Café at the West Cross in Wishaw, he knew it would have to be his. It was ideally situated at the bottom of the town and looked directly up the main street to the parish church at the top of the hill. Apart from the passing trade guaranteed by its position on the main road, it was surrounded by two-storied tenements on either side while across the road more houses stretched for a considerable distance. Before entering the shop, Eugenio took Joe on a brief tour in the car, and they were satisfied the area was well populated.

The West Cross itself was a sort of Étoile in miniature since six different roads conjoined at its centre, which was marked by a solid iron public convenience beside which was a long metal water trough previously used to water the horses drawing the trams up the main street. Belhaven Café had a double frontage since it had formerly consisted of two smaller shops. Next door was a public house called "The Fit o' The Toon." These were the only shops in this self-contained building, and above them were three houses.

When Joe and Eugenio went in to see Jimmy, they found him all distraught in the backshop while an attractive girl served at the counter. When he saw them, he started to cry unashamedly, pacing up and down in his despair as he ran his hands through his hair. It took some time to calm him down before they could discuss the purchase of the shop.

"I just want to be rid of it," moaned Jimmy, "for everything in the place reminds me of her, and I want to forget her."

He moved over to a cupboard and chest of drawers set against the wall and said, "These are hers. She bought them," and he hit them a mighty kick in his anger. Eugenio made him sit down, reasoning with him. Eventually they got round to discussing the price of the café and when he asked for five hundred pounds, Joe took out his cheque book and, without hesitation, wrote out his cheque for the amount. So the deal was concluded very quickly. An hour later Joe walked into the shop in Garscube Road with Eugenio and announced to a surprised Assunta, "I have just bought us a new shop in Wishaw!"

By early November Jimmy had moved out of Belhaven Café, and Joe had settled in. Assunta remained in Garscube Road helped by her mother-in-law for the time being. Then when the time came to wind up the shop in Garscube Road, Assunta and Joe changed places. In no time Joe had sold off all the shop fittings, keeping only the mahogany-panelled mirrors, which he later installed himself in the Wishaw shop. At last the day came when Joe locked the door of the Garscube Road shop for the last time. Assunta and Rico stood by his side as they had come specially from Wishaw to say good-bye to all their friends in Garscube Road. Tears were shed as they all said good-bye to the Simpsons and Mrs. Welsh, who handed Rico a small parcel wrapped in brown paper and said, "I hope you will spend many happy hours reading this book."

As Rico was still attending the school in Glasgow, it was decided he should stay at Byres Road during the week and go home to Wishaw at weekends. Although Assunta was not too happy about this, she realised it might be harmful to transfer the boy to a new school at that stage. When they arrived at Byres Road to leave Rico, Giulietta was excited as she had just received a letter from Maria Giuseppa in London.

In the letter Maria explained she realised she had done a foolish thing, but what she had done was to spite her husband. She had now paid the young man's fare to America where he could rejoin his parents who had emigrated there some time before. In the meantime she was living alone in a London boarding house but would be returning to Glasgow soon. There she intended to set up a business of her own. As Giulietta was telling Assunta and Joe the news, Rico was already reading the book Mrs. Welsh had given him—*Grimm's Fairy Tales* in a complete edition.

Travelling back to Wishaw by bus later that day with Joe, the sixteen-mile journey seemed long to Assunta. She pondered over the events leading to such an unexpected change in their lives. Fate had stepped in to help them in a moment of crisis, but their salvation was based upon the misfortune of two other people, and she wondered if it was really possible in this life to build one's happiness on the unhappiness of others. She seriously doubted it because it seemed to her to be so monstrously unfair, and this made her very apprehensive. But she shrugged her shoulders philosophically, accepting that all one could do was to make the best of things no matter what lay ahead. In the time she had been married to Joe, they had undergone a number of ups and downs, but they had come through. Perhaps the move to Wishaw might bring good things for them despite the uneasiness she felt deep down within her.

In its décor Belhaven Café reflected the personalities of its previous owners. On entering the shop, one had an overall impression of a brown-and-mahogany interior. Joe had replaced the yellowing mirrors with those from the Garscube Road shop, and they created a feeling of spaciousness. A high mahogany counter behind which a mirror-backed gantry was stacked with bottles of sweets and chocolates, sat squatly on the polished, brown linoleum-covered floor, its width stretching from the low-backed settle seats on the right to the tables and chairs in the sitting room on the left.

In the centre of the counter was an impressive onyx soda fountain crowned on its summit by a large, round electric globe, surrounded at a lower level by glass-shaded bulbs. When lit they created a bright centrepiece. Almost in line with the fountain, where the original partition wall between the two shops had been cut, a red velour curtain marked a line of demarcation between the sitting room, with its round, polished tables and chairs and its two comfortable sofas in the corners of the end wall, and the other side of the shop, with its low-backed seats.

In the corner of the sitting room at the left hand side of the counter was a large acoustic cabinet gramophone. Joe had rather rashly disposed of the horn gramophone in the Glasgow shop, not realising that it would one day be very valuable. On the left side of the counter, an opening with a low, hinged door, had been made to allow access to the sitting room. Behind the door on broad shelves lay Maria Giuseppa's collection of gramophone records in albums. There were operas by Verdi as well as a large number of orchestral and vocal records whose labels announced the illustrious names of Caruso, Galli-Curci, Melba, Ponselle, Gigli, and many other great singers.

The significance of the hanging velour curtain in the centre of the shop did not become apparent to Joe until one day, quite soon after his arrival in Wishaw, he noticed that all the men wearing ordinary clothes and caps always sat in the seats on the right of the counter. Those wearing coats and hats made directly for the sitting room where they sat studying the small menu cards on spring-clip bases on the tables as they waited for service.

The customers in the wooden seats ordered Bovril or Oxo and hot peas while those in the sitting room usually ordered coffee or hot chocolate or Horlicks and chocolate biscuits. Joe decided there and then that he would break down this barrier of class distinction immediately. He went round and drew back the curtain and when the hot pea and Bovril clients came in, invited them smilingly into the sitting room. Some of them were so astonished that they removed their caps and hung them on the clothes pegs on the wall near the curtain.

The coffee and chocolate-biscuit customers did not take too kindly to Joe's new rule at first, casting stern, reproving glances at the Bovril-drinking intruders. They even went so far as to devise a cunning plan by asking Joe to play some of the operatic records, hoping that the serious music would drive the undesirables back to their wooden seats. To their consternation, however, the men sipping their Bovril took great enjoyment in the recital and ordered a second round of hot peas.

In the first weeks in Wishaw, Assunta felt she had moved to a different country. The Wishaw accents were different from those she had grown accustomed to in Glasgow. The people seemed to speak more loudly, and she heard strange words she had not encountered before such as "hapnae" for "haepenny." The open, iron-grilled contraption that drew in the rain water in the street gutters was a "drain" where in Garscube Road it was more colorfully described as a "stank."

But it was not merely a vocabulary problem. She found she had to try and follow two different intonation patterns, the broad vowelled sounds spoken in a very slightly varying monotone by the settle-seat customers, and the more varied, faintly refined but definitely nasal sounds intoned by the coffee clients. These reminded her of the West

End patterns of speech she had experienced in Byres Road.

It was much colder in Wishaw than it had been in Glasgow and the winter of 1930 to 1931 was a severe one. When she rose early in the morning, Jack Frost had done his work on the window panes, and the icy patterns sent shivers running up and down her spine. The heavy frost affected the plumbing and some mornings there was no water to wash with, or the toilet drain downstairs had frozen up. She did not brood over these difficulties and took them in her stride. Nothing in this life was easy, she told herself over and over again, as she carried pailfuls of coal upstairs to kindle the fires to thaw out the pipes, or poured kettlefuls of hot water down the toilet pan until the drainage pipe was cleared.

The Wishawtonians seemed more distant than the Glaswegians, and it took much longer to get on speaking terms with them. The only person in the property who welcomed her during the first few weeks was a kind old lady who lived in the room and kitchen house directly above the café. Her name was Mrs. Docherty, and she was a widow. She assured Assunta she would be only too willing to help her should she require any assistance. The other ladies in the property just smiled weakly and passed without speaking. There were no cooking facilities in the room and kitchen house in the red sandstone building behind the shop where they now slept. All the cooking had to be done in the backshop.

The shop assistant left by Jimmy was called Esther, and she and Assunta got on very well. She was a tidy worker and was well liked by the customers. The shop was busy and thanks to Joe's new rules, the customers began to mix more and soon the coffee drinkers started sampling an occasional cup of Bovril while the capped men brought in their wives for a cup of white coffee. It was a good trading Christmas and New Year, and they began to look forward to better times ahead.

Each weekend when Rico came home from Glasgow, he brought his homework to be done. He would sit at the table in the backshop and rack his brains to do arithmetic or write compositions. But most of the time, he studied Bible history or the catechism. Sometimes he would slip off to the Saturday matinée at one of the local cinemas. Assunta began to wonder why his cinema-going took so long, for he was often away for four hours. It was Nonna Leonarda who informed her one Saturday she had met Rico going into church as she herself was coming out. It was a phase he was going through, Assunta told herself.

Joe had brought his own ice-cream recipe to Belhaven Café, and by the spring of 1931 he was making a reputation in the district. It

187

was still a laborious business, making the ice cream, since the mixture had to be boiled in a ten-gallon, copper-bottomed boiler on the gas stove in the backshop. This had to be done very early in the morning to leave the stove free for tea- and coffee-making when the shop opened at nine o'clock. A local milkman, Johnny Robertson, who had a small dairy in Glen Road very near the café, delivered the milk early in a large churn at the backdoor. So their work routine began before eight o'clock and went on until well after midnight each day. They now had two of a staff, Esther to serve and a charwoman to do the cleaning and scrubbing in the morning.

As summer approached Joe built a small handbarrow to peddle his ice cream round the local streets. Then he had a bright idea and approached the local authority for a permit to have a stance with his barrow at the Belhaven Park gate in Glenpark Street just two minutes' walk from the café. He was given permission on payment of a small annual fee and soon became a well-known figure as he sat on a chair by his barrow outside the park entrance.

When the hot weather came, he bought a fine panama hat and sat it squarely on his head to protect it from the sun's rays. The kids soon started calling him Panama Joe as they queued up for their haepenny pokey hats. During the summer holidays, it was Rico's job to keep his dad supplied with ice cream as he shuttled to and fro from the park to the shop, carrying gallon cans of ice cream. The boy was learning that work was an essential part of living and everyone had to pull his weight.

The busy summer season did not hinder Joe from placing his daily bets. Had he been able to afford the time, he would have loved to attend the local race meetings and see the horses as they ran past the winning post for him. Somehow he had not yet made his fortune gambling although he managed to hold his own. But Assunta could not bring herself to approve of his betting. On one occasion she had laughed heartily over something really funny that had happened.

It was during their last winter in Glasgow when Joe was frequenting the greyhound racing at the White City and Carntyne. There was one dog that was always lucky for him, and its racing name was Little Joe. One evening at the White City, the dog was favourite in the last race and Joe put on a couple of pounds. When the dogs were paraded round the track just before the race, Joe eyed the animal with great admiration as it was in good form and bound to win. When the race started, Little Joe was well ahead of the other dogs and Joe was delighted. He began to shout encouragement in his loudest voice.

"Come on, Little Joe, come on, you beauty, come on, Little Joe!"

As the dogs raced round the bend approaching the spot where Joe was standing, he raised his voice to an even higher pitch, and, as his favourite passed, still in the lead, Joe surpassed himself with a mighty, "Come on, Little Joe!"

The dog, hearing his name called so powerfully, stopped in his tracks. Then, realising probably that the race was well lost, he philosophically decided to relieve himself and, squatting in the very middle of the track, defecated in full view of hundreds of spectators. Joe, aghast, drew back in horror.

Then he heard voices around him muttering, "Where's the bloody fool that scared the dog out of the race?"

Drawing up his collar, Joe beat a hasty retreat lest he be lynched and, with empty pockets, shamefully made his way home. Assunta teased him for a long time afterwards, hoping he would see the folly of gambling and give up the habit. But he never did so. She gave up trying to convince him.

One beautiful sunny Sunday early in May, Joe insisted upon closing early so that they could go for a nice walk. One of Joe's most endearing habits was his ability to drop everything when the occasion demanded. They had been working hard all week, and this was their reward. The three of them set out on the road to Netherton and when they reached the cross, they walked on and came to the Bluebell Woods. The glades were at their loveliest, and they were delighted by the muted chirping of the birds. As they looked up, the pale yellow shafts of lingering evening sunlight painted the leaves with shimmering gold.

Assunta asked Rico to go and gather a bunch of bluebells for her and as the boy scampered off, Joe took her into the shade of a large tree and held her gently against the trunk. His face came close to hers as his hand caressed her cheek. Holding her close he brought his lips to hers. At that moment Rico came bounding back with a bunch of bluebells, and he was surprised to see the lovers kissing under the tree. Then, deciding to be discreet, he ran off to gather more bluebells.

Esther left to get married in the autumn of 1931. Always fortunate in his choice, Joe found another good assistant called Peggy. The autumn season was quiet, and it allowed Assunta and Joe to become better acquainted with their regular customers. His warm ebullience and her calm, polite manner had endeared them to their clients. Assunta was now known as Mrs. Joe. The young set, making their plans for the evening, always put a visit to Mrs. Joe's on their programme. Joe would sit in the bottom seat with some of the boys and play dominoes, while Assunta sat with the girls at the top table, spinning tales about Filignano. Some of the young people were students, and Assunta and Joe had a particular fondness for two boys who sat and had long discussions until well after closing time.

One of them, Jim Thomson, was studying Italian at Glasgow University, and he loved to try out his Italian. He would often ask, "La crema è molto buona questa sera? Is the ice cream very good tonight?" unaware that he was using the wrong Italian word for ice cream.

His friend was Robert Whitelaw, son of the parish church minister. Robert could talk on any subject under the sun, and Assunta, Joe, and Rico would listen fascinated as he discussed ancient history, philosophy, music, art, and Italy, for he was well versed in the latter subject and taught them a great deal about their own country. Assunta often regaled Jim and Robert with delicacies from her kitchen, and they looked forward to eating the delicious pizza and the exquisite lemon-flavoured rice cake she baked from time to time.

Assunta missed Rico when he was at school in Glasgow and looked frequently at the clock on Friday afternoons when he was due to return for the weekend. By this time he had left his pious phase behind him and played with his various pals from Low Main Street when he came home. His young friends never got round to pronouncing his name properly, calling him Reekie. He did not take to this, but put up with it for the sake of their company. If he fell out of their favour because he had not brought a sufficient quantity of sweets from the shop, they could be very cruel and devised a nasty song that they chanted to annoy him. It ran something like this:

> Down yonder green valley
> Where Reekie the tally
> Wis getherin wallies
> Tae mak a wee shop!

Rico now began to show an interest in acting. He organised his own little company among his young friends and devised a play in which he played the principal rôle of the king. The queen was played by a girl called Lizzie, and the courtiers, decked in old curtains borrowed from their mums, were played by the other boys. The play was presented in a narrow part of the backyard behind the house of John Lloyd, who was Rico's special friend.

Old sacks were used to erect a canopy between the border wall and the side of the house. Four rows of chairs borrowed from patient mothers were arranged in front of a low platform made from orange boxes and old planks. An old commode was the throne (an apt choice), and the king and queen were draped in quilts and wore crowns made from old chocolate boxes. The climax of the play was a duel (the swords being safely made of cardboard) between the king and a treacherous nobleman (John Lloyd), and it ended in tragedy as the villain, for once, was victorious. This gave Rico a grand opportunity to writhe in agony before dying bravely, as a king should.

The play, a great success, ran to six performances, each given before a packed house of twelve spectators, (admission was a haepenny, so each performance brought in sixpence) and a seventh performance was planned. But a long-suffering Mrs. Bryce, whose window in the adjoining building looked down into the theatre, had patiently tolerated the noise for six afternoons and could stand it no longer. Just as the final performance was starting, she filled two pails with water and prepared to drown the enthusiasm of the thespians below. But she was spared the trouble by a heavy shower of rain that started at that very moment, penetrating the thin sack roof of the Globe Theatre and drenching the actors and the members of the audience who were obliged to beat a hasty retreat, thus abandoning the seventh performance of their masterpiece.

From that moment Rico decided to relinquish the hazardous career of the theatre and turn instead to the more remunerative profession of the cinema. He plagued his father to buy him a small cinematograph. Joe believed in making his son earn his expensive toys. So, in the summer of 1932, as well as supplying his father with ice-cream refills at the Belhaven Park, Rico had to work three hours every evening in the café. Assunta was very pleased to see how well the boy buckled down to his work. He even seemed to enjoy it. She recognised there was a great deal of herself in her son. He quickly absorbed her thorough methods of work, turning each piece into a kind of respected ritual.

So they all worked hard that summer and the following and earned good money. But by the end of the season in 1933, Joe was exhausted and Assunta, fearing that he would fall ill, suggested he should take a short holiday in Italy. So Joe left at the end of October. Before his departure he honoured his promise made so long before and bought Rico a cinematograph and some rolls of old films.

Eugenio and Giulietta often came out to visit, bringing Rico home on Fridays after school. The boy was not showing any promise in his studies, and Assunta was beginning to wonder whether it would be a good thing to have him change to a school in Wishaw. Wishaw High School would be ideal as it was just two minutes' walk from the café and as Rico was now twelve years of age, it would be the right time to make the change.

Giulietta was outraged as Assunta discussed this with her and Eugenio. The boy must attend a Catholic school and get a good Catholic education. So Assunta backed down, admitting defeat before the overpowering wisdom of her sister-in-law. She loved Giulietta so much she would never have done anything to offend her.

At the end of November, a letter came from Joe announcing his imminent return to Wishaw. He expected to arrive on the evening of the 10th of December. But he would send a telegram when he arrived in London. Assunta telephoned the news to Eugenio and Giulietta and invited them to come out to Wishaw for supper on the evening of Joe's arrival. It would be a grand reunion and *compare* Antonio and *commare* Vittoria, Josie and Pietro Ferri, Vittoria's brother, who was then working at the Continental, would also be very welcome.

"We shall all come on one condition," said Eugenio to Assunta over the line.

"And what is that?" asked Assunta.

"That you bake some of your delicious rice cakes." Assunta promised she would do so.

Chapter Sixteen

1933 to 1934—The Accident

The telegram arrived early in the afternoon of Sunday December 10th and read, "Arriving Motherwell tonight. Love. Joe."

Assunta phoned Byres Road and spoke to Giulietta who told her they would all be coming, except Pietro Ferri who did not like staying up late. So Assunta baked the rice cakes and looked forward to a happy evening. Giulietta decided to take the bus in the afternoon and arrived in Wishaw around four o'clock, just in time to give Assunta help with the cooking. Shortly afterwards it began to get foggy, and there was some ice on the roads. Giulietta phoned Byres Road and advised Eugenio not to risk coming to Wishaw, but he would not listen. He arrived in Wishaw with Antonio, Vittoria, and Josie shortly after nine o'clock. The roads had been bad with patches of black ice, but the big Chrysler held the surface well, only skidding slightly here and there. When he had dropped off Vittoria and Josie, Eugenio went back to Motherwell with Antonio to meet Joe off the London train.

Meanwhile at Belhaven Café, the ladies set the table in the shop sitting room while Josie helped Rico to pin a white bedsheet along the wall, for they were going to have a special film show after supper. By the time the London train was drawing into Motherwell Station, Giulietta, happening to look out, was alarmed to see that the fog was thickening.

"I think we may all have to stay here for the night," she said, and Assunta added, "Well, we can all sleep on the floor!"

Soon there was a loud knock on the back door, and a beaming Joe came in and embraced everyone while Eugenio and Antonio brought in his luggage. Assunta was delighted to see how well Joe was looking. They settled down to their meal, and Joe opened a flask of Italian Chianti. As they were eating, Joe gave a full account of his holiday and he had news for Giulietta and Vittoria of their parents whom he had visited. The talk went on at such length after the meal, while the ladies and Peggy did the washing up, that Rico got tired of waiting to start the film show and lay down on one of the sofas and fell asleep.

Soon it was one o'clock in the morning and much too late for films. Rico was due to travel back to Glasgow with the others so that he could go to school in the morning, but when they saw he was fast asleep, it was decided that he should have the day off. The fog had mercifully lifted, and the visitors took their leave and set off for Glasgow. Peggy roused Rico and took him up to the house, and Joe and Assunta followed soon afterwards. They tiptoed through the kitchen, for Peggy and Rico were already asleep in the recessed beds. Assunta and Joe had just settled in their bed when there was a loud knocking at the front door.

"Who can it possibly be at this hour?" Assunta asked, as Joe went to answer it. She had no sooner spoken the words than she had a premonition that something dreadful had happened.

When Joe, in his pyjamas, opened the door, he was confronted by two policemen. He recognised them, for they were in the habit of popping into the backshop for a cup of coffee when they were on the beat. They told him there had been a bad accident. The Chrysler had gone into a skid at the top of the Beehive Brae in Craigneuk, and it had struck a lamp standard. One of the policemen had brought a car, and he offered to run Joe and Assunta to the scene of the accident. Assunta roused Peggy, told her what had happened, and said they would be back as soon as possible.

When they arrived in Craigneuk, two ambulances were already there. Giulietta and Vittoria, Antonio and Josie were being carried into them on stretchers. Assunta could see no sign of her brother. They were able to exchange a few words with Josie. The others were all unconscious.

Josie murmured, "Poor Zio Eugenio, poor Zio Eugenio," before he also fell unconscious. The ambulances drove away to take the injured four to the Western Infirmary. Assunta turned to one of the policemen.

"What about my brother, Mr. Marzella? Where is he?" Without answering he led her and Joe to a house nearby. As they walked past the car, they were horrified to see the extent of the damage at the front. The doors were all open, and the steering wheel had been pushed back by the impact so that there was hardly any space between it and the driver's seat. Assunta's heart sank and she felt a terrible trembling in her legs. Joe steadied her with his arm and helped her along to the house. In a small, dingy living room, Eugenio had been laid on a sofa and a cushion placed under his head. His eyes were closed, and a thin trickle of blood ran from the corner of his mouth down to his chin.

Assunta heard herself screaming, "Eugenio, Eugenio!" as she fell on to her knees by the sofa. She took her brother's limp hand and kissed it. Then, as the tears streamed down her cheeks, her body began

194

to sway uncontrollably backwards and forwards as the high-pitched lamentations rose from her very depths. Joe stood helplessly beside her, weeping. He looked down on his brother-in-law's ashen face and saw Eugenio's closed eyes. He had fallen into the deep slumber of another world from which he would never awaken.

The arrival of a police doctor brought the trying scene to an end, and Assunta was helped to the policeman's car outside. As they were being driven back to Wishaw, Joe put his arms around her and she buried her face in his shoulder and wept bitterly. Within her the first feelings of irreparable loss were already stirring, creating an unbearable anguish. In this disconsolate state, she was thankful for the warmth of her husband's shoulder against her wet cheek.

Back in the house, they had a sleepless night before them. Joe rekindled the fire in the bedroom while Peggy went down to the shop and made some tea, which she brought up on a tray. Rico was still fast asleep. Assunta could not bring herself to go to bed and sat miserably at the fire wrapped in a blanket. Her tears had dried by this time, but now and again a shrill sob, which she could not suppress, rose to her lips and she shook her head from side to side.

Now Giulietta and Vittoria, Josie and Antonio came into her thoughts. How badly had they been injured? What a tragedy! Then she shuddered as she suddenly realised Rico too might have been in the car. And to think that Joe had been the innocent cause of it all. Her speculations brought her no comfort and as she sat there, she felt her world was crumbling around her. Joe eventually persuaded her to lie on top of the bed, and he covered her with the blanket. He lay beside her, staring at the ceiling.

They rose early and took an early bus to Glasgow after instructing Peggy to bring Rico to Byres Road later in the morning. When Rico woke up, he missed his parents and became suspicious, but Peggy told him they had decided to go early to Glasgow. He thought this very odd and in a disappointed voice asked, "Am I to go to school today after all?"

"No, not today," replied Peggy.

It was all very strange, thought Rico, but then his parents were full of surprises. Perhaps they were going to have another party at Byres Road to celebrate his father's return from Filignano. He could take in his cinematograph, and they could have the film show after all in the backshop that evening. But Peggy would not allow him to take the machine. As they had missed the half-past-eight train for Glasgow at Wishaw Central, they had to walk to the South Station to catch the nine o'clock. Peggy could not travel by bus as it made her sick.

During the entire journey to Glasgow, Rico noticed that Peggy kept looking at him in a strange manner as if she wanted to tell him something but could not. Once or twice she seemed about to speak but changed her mind and coughed nervously. She took a bar of chocolate from her handbag and gave it to him. This was extremely odd! He was never allowed to eat chocolate so early in the day.

Arriving at the Continental with Peggy, Rico was surprised when the door was opened by Pietro Ferri. When he saw Rico, he threw his arms round the boy and began to weep. Rico knew then that something terrible had happened. He looked round the shop where people were standing in small groups with bowed heads speaking in low tones. He heard a voice say, "Crushed by the steering wheel—killed outright—the others are all in hospital. Poor Giulietta will never survive this tragic loss."

Rico turned wildly to Peggy, "Where are *Ma* and *Papà*? Why don't you tell me what has happened?"

Peggy took him by the hand and made him sit down on one of the sitting room seats. Then, quietly, she told him what had happened.

In the Western Infirmary, Assunta and Joe were waiting to see Giulietta and her relatives. They were led into a small side room and found her lying in a bed, her face a tragic mask, her eyes fixed on the wall opposite the bed.

Assunta sat beside the bed and took Giulietta's hand, murmuring, "Oh, Giulietta, my poor, dear Giulietta!"

To Assunta's astonishment, Giulietta, still in a state of shock, turned and looked at her very coldly. Then she said something very strange.

"I have lost both flesh and property."

"I don't understand, Giulietta," said Assunta.

"Eugenio has not left a will," went on Giulietta, "so, by Italian law everything will go to his parents and *you* will be the one to benefit." Assunta was outraged by Giulietta's words. That her first thought, stunned as she was, should have concerned Eugenio's estate horrified her.

Then Joe spoke, "Don't you worry on that account, Giulietta, for Assunta and I have no intention of depriving you of what is yours. We are not interested in Eugenio's estate."

Even allowing for the fact that Giulietta was not herself just then, the tremor in Joe's voice betrayed his anger and indignation. Giulietta then realised she had spoken hastily and, to make amends, began to cry. But her sister-in-law's words had troubled Assunta and now left her disillusioned.

Assunta and Joe were further dismayed when they saw Antonio

and Vittoria, for their attitude was unmistakably sullen and resentful. Assunta was truly dumbfounded that in the midst of such a tragedy—her brother was gone and nothing would bring him back—these people seemed to be more concerned with the disposal of his estate. From this time her feelings could never be quite the same towards Giulietta and her brother, Antonio. By neglecting to make a will, Eugenio had raised a veil of suspicion and distrust between his wife and his sister.

The funeral of Eugenio Marzella was one of the largest ever witnessed by the Italian Colony in Glasgow. After a solemn requiem in St. Peter's, Partick, the hearse, followed by two carloads of wreaths and flowers and more than fifty cars full of mourners, made its way slowly to St. Kentigern's in Lambhill on the icy December morning. A weeping Antonio, released from hospital, led mourners to the open grave and looked on dazedly as the coffin was lowered into it. It was not usual for women to attend funerals in those days, but Assunta had insisted upon being there. When the others were making their way back to the cars after the short funeral oration, she lingered by the grave and cried. Eugenio's death marked the end of a significant period in her life.

When Giulietta came out of hospital, legal papers were drawn up in which Assunta renounced all claims to her late brother's property. After the signing at the lawyer's office, Assunta was taken to Byres Road where she was warmly welcomed with reassuring smiles from Giulietta and Vittoria. But Assunta could not feel the full warmth of affection she had always felt before for her sister-in-law and when Giulietta, over a light meal, began discussing her plans to have an elaborate tombstone erected over her husband's grave, Assunta scarcely listened.

For Giulietta the supreme moment of renunciation and submission in Christ's period of probation on earth had occurred in the Garden of Gethsemane when he was faced with the reality of the sacrifice he was required to make. It was then he had questioned whether the bitter chalice lying immediately before him might not be turned away. Giulietta desired to have a white marble statue of Christ in that particular attitude sculpted in Italy. He would be kneeling holding the chalice in his right hand while his eyes would be raised in supplication to his heavenly Father.

Assunta, knowing her brother had never been seriously religious, considered Giulietta's plan excessive, but she said nothing. She looked at Giulietta and thought, *This stone she wants to erect is really for her own comfort, so why should I begrudge her this little thing when she has lost so much?*

She pitied her sister-in-law so much at that moment that she put her arms around her and hugged her, saying, "I am sure Eugenio would be honoured by such a stone."

After her brother's death, Assunta went less frequently to Byres Road. She was kept in touch with all the news by Rico who was still attending school in town. Early in 1934 Assunta noticed he was going into another of his devout moods. He seemed to spend most of the time reading the Bible, and the walls of the alcove of his bed were covered with sacred pictures replacing the photos of film stars he had previously pinned there.

Giulietta had evidently renewed her campaign to make her nephew a priest. He went to confession every week and communion every morning. Assunta was not happy when she observed a tendency in him to be very toffee-nosed towards others, while his "goodness" positively oozed out of his saintly pores.

"We shall have to do something about Saint Rico quite soon," she said to Joe one night. "The air of holiness around him is making me sick, and I feel I could almost begin to dislike him."

"He is at an impressionable age," Joe reassured her, "and he will soon grow out of it, I am sure."

Their circle of friends in Wishaw had broadened. Among their regular customers each day for a jugful of ice cream was Miss Jean Patrick who lived with her uncle and aunt, Mr. and Mrs. Martin in a solid old house called "Dimsdale" in Low Main Street. Mrs. Mary Martin had a splendid rhubarb patch in her rambling garden behind the house, and when the rhubarb was in season, she would send large bundles up to Assunta. The Martins were a very polite and gracious couple. One day when Jean and Assunta were talking about the washing and drying of clothes, Assunta told her she had problems in getting all her clothes dried in the backshop with its single pulley. Jean immediately suggested Assunta could take her washings down to the Martins' back garden and hang the clothes out there. So twice every week Assunta went down to "Dimsdale" with basketfuls of wet clothes, and Mary and Jean would help her to hang them out on long lines where they could flap about in the sunlight. Thus a strong friendship grew between them, and Assunta enjoyed sitting for a few moments chatting with her friends on the sheltered garden seat, set in a pleasant little arbour surrounded by flowers and shrubs. Sometimes Nonna Leonarda would accompany Assunta and while the Martins chatted with Assunta, the old lady kept the lawn free from dandelions, which she zealously plucked and took home to cook.

Assunta's visits to the Martins helped to assuage the pain she still felt over Eugenio's death. She missed Rico when he was at his aunt's in the course of the week and Joe, sensitive to her sad moods, bought her a canary in a cage and hung it high on a bracket above one of the shop windows. The bird was a good whistler, and its bright song in the morning cheered Assunta as she went about her work in the shop.

Then one day a stray, grey kitten wandered into the café, and Assunta decided to keep it. After feeding it with fresh milk, she made it a bed in a suitable corner of the backshop and prepared a boxful of sawdust, which she bought from the little butcher shop across the road, for the kitten's toilet. She then named the furry little creature Baldassare, after the famous but naughty puss who stole the ham from the *pignatta*. Baldassare grew into a handsome cat, and he would take up a position on top of the end-seat partition near the backshop and gaze haughtily at the customers as they sipped their coffee or spooned their ice cream.

Unfortunately Baldassare began to take too great an interest in Dickie. Assunta caught him fixing the little yellow bird's cage with a wicked gleam in his eyes. But a well-aimed whack on the rump with her broad hand quickly brought the offending puss to his senses. Assunta kept a vigilant eye upon him, for she knew cats can hypnotise birds and she did not want anything to happen to Dickie. Baldassare evidently sensed his mistress's thoughts and judiciously renounced his evil intention. There was no doubt he was a wise cat.

Despite the pleasantness of the summer days that year, Assunta could not completely dispel the sadness tearing at her when she thought about Eugenio. Joe determined to seek a remedy soon. She was suffering from a double-edged problem. *That* he could see. On the one hand, she was missing her brother with whom she had been so close, and on the other, she felt she was drifting away from her son who was coming under Giulietta's influence more and more as the weeks passed. Joe soon found a solution. A year in Filignano would solve their problems. In the company of her parents, who were getting so much older, Assunta would find an affection and sympathy so necessary to heal the wound in her heart. Rico would benefit from the change of environment. Joe would see to it that the boy led a healthy life working with his grandfather on the good land. It would knock the nonsense out of his head and help to mould his character.

Joe acted quickly. He wrote to his cousin Alduccio in Collemacchia and arranged to rent the shop to him and his wife, Rosa, for a whole year. Alduccio's reply came quickly, accepting Joe's offer. Assunta showed enthusiasm for the plan, and they arranged to leave for Italy just as soon as Alduccio and Rosa arrived. Giulietta was disconcerted by their plan and suggested they should go without Rico, as a year abroad would seriously disrupt his schooling. But when she caught the look in Assunta's eyes, she realised that nothing would persuade her to leave Rico behind. As Assunta was not in a mood for festivities, they delayed their departure so that they arrived in Filignano after the feast of the 8th of September 1934.

Chapter Seventeen

1934 to 1935—A Year in Filignano

On the long journey home to Filignano, Assunta was tormented by dark thoughts. She had a strong, premonitive feeling this would be the first and last time that the three of them would be together in the place dearest to her heart. With the prospect of being with her parents again, she tried to dispel the lingering depression that had preyed upon her since Eugenio's death by telling herself she must do everything in her power to make their year in Filignano a truly memorable one. It would be a time of contentedness upon which they could look back with pleasure in the dark days of the uncertain future lying before them.

As she fell into long, pensive silences, Joe tried his best to cheer her. He would take her hand and press it gently, and she would turn to him and smile. Away from the bustling activity of the shop, Rico saw his parents in a different light. He had always known they were deeply in love, and now he was touched by the tenderness they showed one another.

At long last Assunta stepped on to the welcoming soil of her native village and, as she stood there in the piazza, she breathed deeply and savoured the ripe scents of autumn she had missed so much. The trees had not yet completely shed their leaves, and they glittered in variegated russet tones against the pale blue sky. A feeling of security warmed within her, for it was here her roots lay. But as they walked up to the house, she became dejected again. Eugenio would never more tread upon this pebbly road. Never again would he see the gentle pattern of the simple life through the natural cycle of the seasons in Filignano.

In the first few painful moments of their arrival outside the house, the wound of her grief was reopened when Filomena came out to meet her, throwing her frail, languishing arms round her daughter's shoulders with a kind of frantic desperation.

Her voice rising as she sobbed, the old lady called out her son's name, "Eugenio! Eugenio *mio!*" over and over again in an uncontrollable dirge rising from the deep pool of sorrow within her. They stood for a long time locked in a painful embrace, trying in vain to allay the sharp pangs of their distress with tears. Joe and Rico looked on in silence. Then Assunta, glancing over her mother's shoulder, saw her father, a small, forlorn figure, sitting on the log seat outside the wine cellar, aimlessly swatting flies in the warm September sun.

She gently moved away from Filomena and went over to sit by his side. Joe, Rico, and Filomena went into the house, and Assunta turned to her father and asked, "How are you, ta'?"

He had aged so much in such a short time! Now he turned to her and his eyes, small and sunken, looked at her questioningly. Then he spoke, "But you, who are you, lass?"

"Don't you know me, ta'? I am Sunta, Sunta, your daughter." There was a plaintive note in her voice.

A small spark of recognition gleamed in the old man's eyes as they quickly brimmed with tears and, his voice breaking, he asked, "And Eugenio? Where is Eugenio?"

But the early, heart-rending moments of their reunion passed, and soon Assunta began seriously to carry out the resolution she had made during the journey to Filignano. She took over the household tasks from her mother, and the work filled her hours. By and by her concern gave way to a bitter-sweet resignation, soothing her troubled mind. Early in the morning, when she went out to feed the hens, Severina the goat, granddaughter of Chiaruccia, and the pig, the sounds of the animals brought vivid sensations of memories recalling her happy girl-hood, and she began to smile again. She took to visiting old friends, insisting that Filomena should accompany her.

Joe went along with Benedetto on his excursions to the wood, helping him to bring home logs. As for Rico, he found himself again in donna Ida's school after an interval of several years. Early on Sunday mornings, he would go with Assunta down to the market in the piazza. He plied her with questions as they walked along together, and it gave her great pleasure to answer them. The close, fond relationship they had once enjoyed was thus being renewed, and Assunta noticed that he was losing the wan, pious look that had so troubled her because she felt it did not become him. His appetite was prodigious, and he thoroughly appreciated the wholesome, natural food his mother and grand-mother prepared each day.

In no time, encouraged by Assunta and Joe, he made friends with the village girls and boys. They played together, went to the *macchia* to gather firewood and, on rainy days, stayed indoors to read. But the wine cellar was strictly out of bounds!

What particularly delighted Assunta and Joe was the boy's readiness to confide in them and the enthusiasm he was displaying in adapting to the rural life of Filignano. He willingly rose at the cock's first call and helped his grandmother and mother in the kitchen. When it was time for school, he would run up the hill to fetch Nicandro, son of Elmerinda, one of Assunta's girlhood friends, now a widow, and Carminuccio who was still tending his father's sheep after school.

In the piazza outside the school, they would meet Elio, the joiner's son, and Minicuccio, the son of Maria the butcher. Minicuccio was a rare phenomenon, a likeable bully, a fellow of wild, mercurial moods often reflected in his dark, fiery eyes. He could be hostile and demanding one moment and incredibly friendly the next. His relationship with Rico was a strong one, alternately warm and belligerent. When they sat together at the back of the class, they exchanged heavy thumps and kicks under the desk when donna Ida turned her head to look out on to the piazza. Out of school they walked around arm in arm like bosom friends.

Every evening over supper Rico eagerly recited the day's activities, giving a full account of his frequent clashes with Minicuccio, or his long debates with Nicandro, who, although he was younger, was already showing signs of becoming a philosopher-politician. Elmerinda's house had an imposing veranda looking over the pebbled road leading up the hill. When Nicandro, in oratorical mood after reading some speech by *Il Duce* in the newspaper, took up an imposing stance at the very edge of the loggia, he would launch forth in a mighty tirade against Italy's enemies, his voice echoing down the length of the road as he firmly stuck out his chin.

To add emphasis to certain points in his oration, he would punch the coping-stone before him on the low wall surrounding the veranda. One day, in the middle of a fiery speech, he hit the stone with such vehemence that he split the flesh of his little finger. The climax of the sentence he was calling out with such stentorian bombilation was unexpectedly punctuated with a blasting scream of pain, and the speech was brought to a sudden close.

The Di Bona family came to visit often, and the bond of affection between them and the Cocozzas grew even stronger as the weeks passed. Assunta was amused to see that Rico was beginning to take an interest in one of the girls, Gina. She was a slender, delicately featured girl with grey-blue eyes and shining brown hair. She had a very expressive little face and a bubbling, very appealing, musical voice. Rico always sat as close to Gina as he could on those evenings when the Di Bonas came to visit, and they would all gather around the fire.

One evening Gina was called by her mother to help Assunta to fetch some biscuits and she rose quickly, forgetting to disentangle her hand from Rico's. Rico lost his balance and fell from the chair where he was sitting on to the floor. Amidst the mirth, Rico was not amused and he blushed in his confusion. Later that evening, when they were going to bed, Joe remarked to Assunta that their son, with his new romantic interest, was no longer in danger of embracing the priesthood. Assunta smiled.

The winter wore on, cold but dry, and they spent a great deal of their time visiting and being visited. From time to time, they were warmly welcomed by Giulietta's parents at Bottazzella, and they also went often to see *commare* Vittoria's parents, Edoardo and Giusta Ferri in the large *palazzo* at Valle. Assunta wrote faithfully to Giulietta and Vittoria with news of their parents. Christmas passed quietly as Assunta was not yet in a mood for festivities, although Rico made the effort and built a crib in the arched niche of the stair landing where Assunta's Holy Child had been so revered by her grandmother. When she looked at the new manger surrounded by low glimmering candles, Assunta's thoughts went back nostalgically to grandmother Vittoria. She too was no longer with them.

In January the pig was slaughtered, hams cured, and sausages made. In the middle of February, Joe decided to take Assunta with him on a trip to Casamicciola where they could take the baths. They were gone for two weeks, and Joe benefited very much from the treatment on the island. Assunta herself was in brighter fettle. But it was Rico who finally succeeded in driving away the last traces of lingering sadness, bringing an end to her long period of mourning. With his pranks and wit, he distracted her and her merry laugh returned.

One evening, as they sat as usual around the fire, Filomena was trying to patch an old skirt. Her eyes were failing, and she always had difficulty in threading the needle. Annoyed with herself, she turned to her grandson and asked him to thread it for her. Taking the needle and thread, he obliged.

Then, as he handed back the threaded needle, he remarked, "Good gracious, to think you have grown so old and you still haven't learned to thread a needle!" Assunta laughed so heartily that she nearly choked, and Joe gave her a light thump on the back to help her clear her throat.

They were just settling down again when Rico went on, "What a family this is! Old ladies who have never learned to thread needles and husbands who beat their wives for laughing!"

Assunta went into an uncontrollable fit of laughter, and her affliction spread to the others until the tears were running down their cheeks.

Only Benedetto did not laugh. He sat in his corner and muttered, "This place is becoming a madhouse!"

Rico was fascinated by his grandfather's clothes. One morning he was first to get up and, stealing quietly into his grandparents' bedroom, quickly lifted Benedetto's clothes, and put them on in the kitchen. He had some difficulty with the hide sandals, but managed to squeeze his feet into them. Then, proudly, he scampered up the hill to show off in front of Nicandro and Carminuccio. By this time Filomena, Assunta, and Joe were preparing breakfast, but Benedetto did not seem to be making any move to rise. When Filomena sent Assunta through to rouse him, he was lying wide awake and explained that he could not get up as his clothes had disappeared. Just then Rico came back, and Filomena and Assunta were amused to see how well his grandfather's clothes fitted him. Assunta took him by the ear and led him into the bedroom.

When Benedetto saw his grandson in his clothes, he said, "In this house it would appear that the first to rise in the morning gets dressed!"

But the incident established a new rapport between Benedetto and Rico, and the boy took to accompanying his grandfather on his excursions for firewood on those days when he did not need to go to school. He also began to be interested in the working of the land and could often be seen hoeing by Benedetto's side in the vegetable patch. Rico began to stretch and lost the fat he had been carrying when they arrived in Filignano. There seemed to be no end to his energy, and he consumed vast amounts of food. He had never been so well in his life. This pleased Assunta.

One morning Joe could not find his open razor. He surprised Rico, face lathered, trying to shave.

"Time enough for that in a year or two," he said, taking the razor away from the boy's hand.

Rico was now as tall as Minicuccio, and their friendship was as hearty as ever. They decided they should become *compari*. This involved them in a little ritual that took place at the holy water font in the church. First they had to kneel at the back of the church and pray for one another. Then, after crossing themselves, they took up their position in front of the font in the presence of their two witnesses, Nicandro and Elio. They each dipped their right hand into the holy water and, while their fingers were still dripping, firmly shook hands.

Then Minicuccio said to Rico, "*Gesù Maria, compa'*," and Rico responded, "*Gesù sempre, compa'*."

They then embraced and left the church arm in arm. They were now *compari* for life. As such, they had the right to ring the church bells on Sunday mornings or feast days. This introduced Rico into the magic world of the belfry, and Minicuccio taught him how to ring the bells. Two were rung using only the clappers by hand. But the largest of the bells was swung by a rope with heavy counterweights. It was a noisy, exhilarating experience, and the bells were never so well exercised.

Filomena liked to store her eggs in the large chest containing wheat grain in her bedroom where it was cool. Every morning, when the hens laid, she collected the eggs in a basket, took them through to the chest, and buried them in the grain. Rico observed and took note. As a growing boy, he was always hungry and one day Carminuccia Di Bona, Gina's sister, showed him how to pierce the shell of an egg with a needle and suck the white and the yolk. At first he thought he would not like the raw taste. To his surprise he really enjoyed it. So, when he felt hungry between meals, he would sneak into Filomena's bedroom armed with a needle, burrow in the wheat grain, lift out an egg, pierce the shell and suck. Then he replaced the empty shell in the grain.

Came Easter Sunday morning, and it was time to make the Easter omelette. Filomena went through to fetch the eggs, and it did not strike her that they were unusually light. Then, when she began to break shell after shell to find nothing inside, she cried out in dismay: "Who has been at these eggs?" and Rico, who was sitting innocently on the settle, looked at his grandmother and said with complete conviction, "Not me!"

Next day a lock was put on the chest, cutting short the activities of the mysterious egg-sucker.

Easter brought warm, sunny days, and they all went out to work with Filomena and Benedetto in the fields, weeding, digging, and hoeing. It was about this time that Severina the goat gave birth to kids. It was the first time Rico had seen an animal in labour, and he was fascinated by the skill with which Filomena delivered the kids. One of the little animals took to Rico and followed him everywhere like a little dog. It grew rapidly, balancing on its long, shaky, spindly legs. It was a delightful creature, and Rico became very attached to it. As it followed him around, it would utter its funny little dry, staccato whimpers.

One day it followed him up the stairs and settled in a corner of the room. The window was open, and Rico heard Nicandro calling for him outside. Forgetting the kid, Rico ran down to meet his friend who was talking with Assunta. The kid, hearing Rico's voice through the open window, jumped on to the sill and looked down. At that moment Assunta's eyes were drawn to the window and she uttered a cry of dismay as the kid, anxious to rejoin his master, leapt out of the window and landed painfully with a shrill squeak on his spindly legs, which were fortunately sufficiently pliable to absorb the shock of the fall. Assunta lifted the poor creature and nursed him gently in her arms, delicately stroking his poor legs. But he had suffered no injury, and shortly afterwards was prancing once more at Rico's heels as if nothing had happened.

Rico began to spend more and more time at the Di Bona house with Gina and her sisters, Indina and Carminuccia. His heavy crush on Gina made him the butt of jokes and teasing on the part of Minicuccio and Nicandro, but Rico did not seem to mind. Being in the Di Bona house so often brought Rico into frequent contact with the Di Bona boys, Nicodemo and Gaetano, and sometimes he would accompany them to the site where they were building or repairing a house, and he found it interesting to help them, working with heavy stones and lime. His clothes often got into a mess.

A strong bond developed between Rico and Gaetano. It was a sort of hero-worship on Rico's part, for the boy was much older than him. Gaetano spoke with a very quiet voice, and he had interesting stories to tell about the old days in Filignano, tales his grandfather had told him when he was a boy. It was a happy time of varied activity for everyone, and soon Joe decided on a second visit to Casamicciola. Assunta would have liked to bring Rico along with them, but he refused, preferring to remain in Filignano.

Before they left for Casamicciola, they took part in an interesting ceremony. Rico had never been confirmed and when it was known that Monsignor would shortly be coming to Venafro to perform confirmations, Filomena insisted her grandson should take advantage of this opportunity to complete his Christian education. Peppino and Maria Di Bona came to ask if Assunta would honour them by being godmother to their daughter Indina who had become very attached to her. Assunta was delighted to agree.

Rico was then asked if he would like Peppino and Maria to be his godparents. Perhaps foreseeing certain difficulties in that it might not be possible for them to be godparents and father- and mother-in-law if he married Gina, Rico came up with the bright idea that he would like Gaetano to be his young godfather. It did not seem to occur to him that there might be a problem later on, in having a godfather as a brother-in-law! The Di Bonas were surprised but intrigued by Rico's suggestion, and on the following evening Gaetano appeared to ask formally if he could be godfather to Rico.

A few days later, at a colourful service in the Venafro church, the two godchildren, Indina and Rico, were confirmed by Monsignor in the presence of their respective godparents. The bonds between the two families were thus further strengthened. After the ceremony they went to a photographic studio where they were photographed with an ancient plate camera in daylight. When the photos were collected later, they caused much merriment for they looked as if they had been taken in the early days of the camera, all soot and whitewash, their faces frozen in vacant expressions.

When they left for Casamicciola, Joe and Assunta decided to spend two days in Naples to revive happy memories of their honeymoon, staying at the same inn as they did in 1921. The owner, Signor Alfonso, much mellowed with age, recognised them, for his years had not impaired his memory, and he gave them the same room that they had used before.

Next morning they decided to visit Mount Vesuvius. It was a dramatic experience. They took the funicular to the top and reached a point where the molten lava was flowing down in rivulets. The dark, red, steaming liquid looked very ominous. People were throwing coins into the lava, and a man with a long-handled iron ladle fished them out and laid the pieces of liquid with coins embedded in the centre on the ground to cool and harden. Assunta and Joe each threw in a coin, and the man with the ladle told them to return later when they could collect their lava souvenirs.

When they reached the top to look down into the crater, they were overawed by the hellish spectacle below them and not a little frightened. The plutonic, fiery, ebullient mass gurgled deep down in the heart of the crater, emitting strong, smoky fumes filling the air with sulphur. They did not gaze long but drew back with relief and made their way down to where their lava-surrounded coins lay waiting for them.

After lunch they went to Pompeii and sauntered through the ruins. As they passed through the ancient streets with the fragments of houses, shops, and temples around them, it dawned on Assunta that, centuries before, these places had been teeming with human beings, alive and happy, going about their business. These cobbled streets had echoed with the music of children's voices and the rumbling of chariot wheels as they rolled along the smooth stone tracks. Now there was only silence. And with this silence, she felt a strange, comforting feeling of calm coming over her. She sat down beside Joe on a low wall, and they did not speak. A soft, warm breeze encircled them and for a lingering moment, they felt they could sense the presence of the Pompeians who had all died at the same time in that very place one day in the year 79.

The two weeks in Casamicciola were over and when they returned to Filignano, it was to find that Rico had been up to more mischief. He had scandalised the old ladies of Imperatore by taking a bath in a large tub on the loggia on a hot day. In the morning he rose early and drew buckets of water from the cistern. He carried these up to the tub, two at a time, until the tub was nearly full. The intense heat of the sun warmed the water and when he felt it would be comfortable, he stripped off and plunged in just as Zia Adelaida came to her window in time to see this pagan spectacle.

The old woman came rushing down to complain to Filomena who, working in the vegetable garden below the house, could not witness her grandson's scandalous behaviour. By the time the old women came round to the loggia, they were astonished to see three naked bodies bobbing up and down in the tub, splashing good water all over the place. Rico had invited Nicandro and Carminuccio to pop in.

Needless to say, Rico caught a chill as a result of his daring but execrable exploit, and he had been confined to bed for three days with a terrible fever. His poor old grandmother was at her wits' end when she heard him screaming during the night. In his delirium he claimed to see vampires at the foot of his bed. It was all too obvious to Filomena that someone had put the evil eye on the boy. How else could his irrational behaviour be explained? Bathing in tubs, indeed. So she exorcised the evil influence herself by placing wheat grains in a bowl of water by the boy's bed and when the malevolent grains came to the surface, she plucked them out and threw them into the flames of the fire downstairs. Next day Rico was up and about, as if nothing had happened.

Assunta and Joe shook their heads when poor Filomena excitedly gave them this pitiful account of their son's bad behaviour. He had to be punished, for this time he had gone too far. So he was forbidden to visit the Di Bonas for a whole week. For seven long days, he would not see his lovely Gina. But they had not reckoned with that young lady's ingenuity. Indina came visiting every day with little gifts of *biscotti* and cakes. And when Assunta was not looking, she would slip a letter from Gina to Rico. Then, before Indina went home, Rico went upstairs to his room and penned a frantic, heartbroken note to his sweetheart. Thus the little go-between was kept very busy that week. In reality Assunta was very amused by the bathtub incident, but she had to show respect for her mother's outraged feelings.

"I wonder what Giulietta would think of her little priest now?" Joe said to Assunta.

"I don't think she would be amused," replied Assunta.

Strangely enough a letter came from Giulietta on the following day, saying she was coming to Filignano to join them for a short holiday. It was now near the end of July, and Giulietta expected to leave Glasgow early in August. They could then all travel back together in September. Giulietta thought of everything. She was a good organiser. But how would she react to the change in her nephew? Assunta thought of writing to her to warn her. Then she thought better of it and decided to let matters take their own course.

As it had been a hot summer, the harvest was early, and Rico and Joe rolled up their sleeves and helped to cut the wheat. For the first time in years, Assunta carried large sheaves of corn on her head from the fields to the *aia* beside the house. The Di Bona girls all came and helped, and Assunta became better acquainted with Gina. The more she talked with the girl, the more she liked her. It would do no harm to encourage Rico's sentimental attachment to her and perhaps, one day, it could ripen into a more permanent relationship.

When the harvest was all gathered, they held a party on the *aia*. It was a lovely evening. The moon shone brightly in a dark purple, velvety sky in which the stars also shimmered, and the warm night air spread the perfume of the freshly cut wheat in stimulating wafts to whet the appetite of the workers for the sausages and wine and sweet cakes spread out on the long trestle tables at the end of the *aia*. The music from an accordion accompanied the dancing and Raffaele, Nicandro's older brother, sang to appreciative applause, his voice echoing mellifluously across the valley.

When the party was at its height, Joe took Assunta by the hand and led her into the house and up the three flights of stairs to the loggia above their bedroom. There they could look down on their guests whose chattering, happy voices rose up to them in merry waves. They leaned against the iron railing and turned their eyes to the distant Mainarde mountains, whose sharp outlines, highlighted by the moon, stood out against the sky. Breathing in the fine night air, at first they did not speak. Then they heard the strains of Assunta's favourite song "Maria, Mari'" as Raffaele turned his handsome face up to the two figures on the loggia. Joe placed his hand over Assunta's as the song reached its passionate climax.

When the dancing was resumed, they moved to the front of the loggia where they could look down on the village without being seen by their guests. The sound of the music was less pronounced there, and they could quietly contemplate the moon-bathed landscape. It was Joe who broke the silence.

"I wish it could always be like this, the three of us here in Filignano." He paused, then spoke again. "I feel so happy it seems too good to be true."

"Yes, it would be fine," agreed Assunta, "but we can't live on beautiful dreams."

"But we *can* have a dream, can't we?" said Joe.

"There's no harm in that, Joe," said Assunta.

They fell silent again, enjoying the silvery enchantment of the moment. Then he drew her to him and kissed her softly on the lips with long, lingering tenderness. Assunta closed her eyes and for the briefest of instants she felt she was no longer in that place at that time. It was as if she and Joe had been swept into another dimension in which they alone existed, no longer two beings but a single one to remain there forever. The universe around them no longer existed, but *they* did within a living element composed of the ecstatic vibrations of their love.

When she opened her eyes, Assunta had the uncanny sensation of having died and returned. In the years that followed, she could never forget that transcendent experience with Joe on the loggia at Imperatore.

Giulietta arrived a few days later, bringing presents for everyone. She had shed much of the sadness and self-pity troubling her after Eugenio's death and was more resigned to her widowhood, finding help in the comforting ministrations of the church. Filomena welcomed Giulietta with a few tears but she was now resigned to Eugenio's loss, and the reunion with her daughter-in-law was not so painful for her as it had been with Assunta.

It did not take long for Giulietta to realise that her nephew had moved well out of the circle of her influence. She saw so many changes in him of which she strongly disapproved. His parents were too easygoing, she thought. And, having good eyes in her head, she soon knew what was going on between Rico and Gina. This was really the limit. Such precociousness! What were Assunta and Joe thinking of? Were they wanting to see their son married at the age of fourteen? What nonsense! Something would have to be done about it.

One day, when she was going to visit her parents, she asked Rico to accompany her to Bottazzella. They took the high road leading past the Di Bona house. Signora Maria was leaning on the balcony as they approached. Now, Eugenio and Giulietta had been godparents to young

Gaetano when he was confirmed some years before.

"*Gesú Maria, comma'*," called out Maria, and Giulietta gave the required response, "*Gesú sempre, comma'*."

Maria then invited Giulietta and Rico to come up for a short visit, so they went in for a moment. When the ladies began to chat, Rico got bored and he wandered off in search of Gina. Giulietta observed him out of the corner of her eye as he was slipping away. She called out, "Don't go too far, Rico, for we shall soon be leaving."

The minutes ticked past, and Rico did not come back. When Indina appeared, Giulietta asked her if she had seen Rico. The girl told her he had gone up to the vineyard to help Gina who was gathering grapes. Giulietta was not pleased. At the end of half an hour, Rico was still absent so Giulietta excused herself and left. She told signora Maria to tell him, when he came back, to go home.

"Tell him also I am very angry with him," she said meaningfully. Signora Maria smiled. She knew what was annoying her *commare*.

When Rico eventually returned with Gina, carrying a large basket full of ripe grapes, his aunt's stern message was conveyed to him, and he rushed off along the road to Bottazzella and soon caught up with her. He apologised for his behaviour and said he had acted unthinkingly. He looked so crestfallen that she could not help smiling, her face brightening with affection. She decided to try another tactic as they walked along and asked him about his work in school.

Then she asked, "Do you really like living in Filignano?"

"I like it so much, *zia*, that I would really love to stay here and not go back to Wishaw," he said.

"But what would you do here? You know your parents want you to make something of yourself. Have you lost all notion of one day being a priest?"

Rico smiled, saying, "I don't think I was cut out to be a priest, *zia*. And besides, I think I would like to get married here!"

"So you would like to marry Gina?" asked Giulietta.

"Yes," answered Rico, "but not right away. We could really wait until next year!"

Giulietta nearly exploded when she heard his words. She could have laughed and cried at the same time.

"I'm afraid that is something you will have to think about very carefully, my lad," she said, "because I don't think you could support a wife on what you would earn here as a farmer and you surely would not expect your father and mother to slave away in Wishaw in order to support you and your wife here?" Rico flushed as his aunt's voice fell shrilly on his ears, but he did not answer her question.

In the evening, after supper, Giulietta told her nephew to go to bed as she had some matters of a private nature to discuss with his parents. When Rico had retired, she turned upon Joe and Assunta like a virago and lashed them mercilessly with her tongue, giving them a full account of her conversation with the boy in the afternoon. They were so taken aback by her tone that they sat in silence when her outburst had come to an end.

Then Assunta finally spoke up, saying, "The boy is just going through a necessary stage in growing up. It's puppy love. But I certainly would not discourage him, for she is a nice girl and they get on well together."

"Utter nonsense," said Giulietta, "and you know as well as I do he would be marrying beneath him. The girl is not good enough for him."

Then Joe spoke up. "Apart from disagreeing with everything you have been saying," he said with emphasis, "I don't think it is a matter that really concerns us. It's his problem and he will have to work it out. Once he is back in Scotland, he will realise after a year or two whether his intentions are serious."

"You may have difficulty in persuading him to go back to Wishaw," said Giulietta in a peeved tone.

"We are still his parents," said Joe, very pointedly, "and I am sure he will do what we tell him." Filomena and Benedetto made no comment, but the old man caught Assunta's eye and winked. She smiled.

The rest of the month passed quickly as the grape harvest kept them busy. As the day of their departure for Glasgow came near, Rico was nervous and listless. He had tried to talk his parents into letting him stay in Filignano until Christmas. They refused. He said they would be missing the Feast of the 8th of September. Could they not stay for another week or two? Joe explained they had made an agreement with Alduccio, which must be honoured. They had to be in Wishaw by the 5th of September. Rico shrugged his shoulders and sulked. Assunta felt for the boy and tried to cheer him up with vague promises. He could write to Gina and Gaetano. Perhaps next year he could come back to Filignano in the autumn for a short holiday and enjoy the September Feast. She knew he had a resilient nature and would soon settle down when they got back to Wishaw.

On the morning of their departure, there was a large turnout of friends to see them off in the piazza. The Di Bonas were there in full strength, and there was much affectionate hugging and kissing. As the taxi, driven by Michele, brother of Maria the butcher, moved away down the white, dusty road to Venafro, Rico buried his face in his hands and wept bitterly. Joe put his arm round the boy's shoulder to comfort him. Assunta and Giulietta dabbed their eyes. Joe and Assunta exchanged a bitter-sweet smile. A happy year had come to an end.

Chapter Eighteen

1935 to 1936—Halcyon Days at Mrs. Joe's

They arrived in Wishaw with only a day to spare before Alduccio and Rosa were due to depart for Filignano. There was very little stock-taking to be done, as they had let supplies run low. Their bags were already packed, and they left on the following day.

Joe now set about reorganising the shop and made some altera-tions. The old counter was replaced by one of modern design. A new "iceless" freezer was installed in the body of the counter, which un-fortunately entailed the removal of the onyx soda fountain. The cabinet gramophone was taken up to the house and replaced by the very latest HMV radiogram with an automatic record-changer. The instrument was placed in the sitting room and attracted a flock of new customers who came to listen and marvel at the complicated mechanism that dropped the records one at a time on to the turntable as the pick-up arm swung over to alight neatly on the run-in groove of the record. By pressing a little bronze button on the front of the polished mahogany cabinet, the record could be rejected and the next in the pile played. Assunta was satisfied that Joe was continuing the tradition of clever innovations in the field of recorded music in which Eugenio had so skilfully specialised at the Continental.

Now it was time to consider the subject of Rico's further education. The boy was not keen to return to the Glasgow school. One of their regular customers was a charming deaf lady who taught mathematics at Wishaw High School. She came in often to buy ice cream and lived in a cottage in Glasgow Road. She wore a hearing aid and always carried a small battery pack. Joe asked her into the backshop for a chat and explained his problem. He would like his boy to be educated at Wishaw High. She promised to speak to the rector. Two days later Joe received a message sent by hand from the school. He had a short friendly interview with the rector. Rico started attending the school on the following Monday. From that day he never looked back. Not only did he find the atmosphere in the school congenial and friendly, but he sensed right away that here he would be accepted. This had not been the case in Glasgow. At Wishaw High the teachers took an interest in their pupils, and the classrooms buzzed with an air of busy contentedness. Going to Wishaw High was fun. School in Glasgow had been misery and hell.

Gina's letters arrived regularly from Filignano. At first Rico received them with eagerness, and Assunta saw him intent on writing long replies. But as the weeks passed, it became all too apparent his love was waning, for his replies became shorter and shorter. His ardour was being dampened by his new interests at school.

One day he turned seriously to his mother and said, "I think I probably did the right thing, I mean, not getting married in Filignano. Perhaps there is more to life after all than love and marriage!"

"Then you should write to Gina and explain how you feel," said Assunta. He took his mother's advice. By the spring of 1936, the correspondence had come quietly to a close.

On Easter Sunday morning, although the shop was open for the sale of chocolate Easter eggs and ice cream, Joe always liked to have a cooked breakfast when he would serve a large omelette containing sliced Filignano sausages and dried mint. Rico asked his dad if he could have the privilege of making the Easter omelette, as he was beginning to fancy himself as a cook. Joe gave his consent, and Rico went ahead with his cooking while his parents served the Easter morning customers. He switched up a dozen eggs, adding dried mint and a measure of salt together with a large spoonful of olive oil. Then, having sliced the sausages, he put them to fry in the big frying pan over the gas flame. When the sausages were cooked, he added the beaten eggs.

Then, as he shook the pan, he decided to raise the gas. Some of the oil spilled and caught fire. Soon the frying pan was in flames and Rico, struck by panic, lifted it and ran to the counter shouting, "Papà, papà, the omelette is on fire!"

Joe took the pan from him, rushed to the sink, dropped the pan into it with a clatter, and turned on the tap. With a great deal of hissing, the fire was extinguished. Joe then made Rico clean up the mess and scrub the pan until it shone again.

"Now go and help your mother and Peggy," said Joe. "I'll make the omelette. But we'll let you try again next Easter. Perhaps by that time we shall all have acquired a taste for flaming omelettes!" And, as Rico disappointedly joined Assunta and Peggy, they heard Joe strike up "Maria, Mari' " as he prepared to make the omelette.

As business improved, happy times came to the foot of the town.

With its distinctive, roomy openness, it was an attractive area. The squat, solid building in which Belhaven Café and the atmospheric pub known as "The Fit o' The Toon" were situated looked directly up the steep hill of Wishaw Main Street.

The pub had changed hands and was now owned by a hearty, ruddy faced, corpulent gentleman called Cornelius McGowan, known to all his clients as Conn. It was a large, roomy bar, painted pale green, with pillars supporting the ceiling. A fire burned in the grate behind the bar. Conn presided at the high mahogany counter, entertaining his clients with great eloquence. Should a stranger, happening to be passing through the town, break his journey for a refreshment at "The Fit o' The Toon," he would find himself engaged in interesting conversation with "mine host." He was a mine of information on local history. If he took a particular fancy to the stranger, he would give an account of the history of the pub, explaining how it had once belonged to one of the greatest wrestlers in the world, Sandy Bain, who had toured Africa and Australia with the great Hackenschmidt. If the client continued to show interest in Conn's report on Sandy Bain, he would move to the far end of the counter and rummage for a while among some shelves to produce, with a certain reverence, a dusty old ledger. After blowing on it to remove the surface dust, he would bring it over, lay it on top of the counter and, opening it at random, present it for appraisal. There before him the traveller's eye would see records of barrels and hogsheads of "sixpenny whisky" written by Sandy Bain in the finest copperplate. Conn would then remark that for a champion wrestler to be such a superb penman was a most remarkable thing.

Conn was something of a penman himself, for one of his favourite pastimes was writing indignant letters to the local or national press. He would discuss possible solutions for the urgent problems of the moment. In a short time, he had become something of an institution and many came to seek his advice over their refreshments. Good counsel was offered willingly and with pleasure. And when a relieved client, after acting upon his advice, came back to inform Conn that all had gone well, the stout counsellor beamed as if to say, "I could have told you it would!"

The Cocozzas got on well with their publican neighbour, and they often exchanged pleasantries. Assunta and Conn always happened to wash their shop windows at the same hour each morning. They would emerge from their respective doorways with sweeping brushes and give the pavement a good sweep. Then out came the large pails of water and the long-shafted window brushes. After soaping the windows, they would throw a pailful of water over the glass. One morning they were working away at adjoining windows, unaware of one another's movements, so absorbed were they in their task. As a result they aimed their pails of water simultaneously. The spray from Assunta's window drenched Conn while that from the pub window drowned her. A dripping Conn called over to a soaked Assunta, "Next time we should bring our bath towels, dear!"

Behind the "Fit o' The Toon" was an auction sale room run by the McNamara brothers. It attracted many clients on Saturdays, which made the café and the pub busy. On warm, summer days, when the double doors at the front and the side doors lay open for ventilation, the voice of the auctioneer with its rising and falling singsong tones echoed round the West Cross, while old pieces of furniture, carpets, second-hand mirrors, cutlery, musical instruments and china chamber pots were offered to the highest bidder.

At the corner of Low Main Street and Glen Road on the right of the café was one of the most important establishments in the area, Peat's, general outfitters, suppliers of carpets, beds, bedding and linoleum and—pawnbrokers. The three brass balls, placed high on the outside of the building, shone resplendently, calling all who were in pecuniary need to come and pledge their precious belongings. The main door led into the body of the shop where curtain materials were stacked in bolts behind the counters, while the floor area was covered with stand hangers bearing suits and dresses, coats and frocks, and tall rolls of variegated linoleum stood all around like marble columns supporting the roof of this small temple of trade. Upstairs, new furniture could be inspected, beds and bedsteads, dressing tables and wardrobes in great variety. The rear entrance to these fine premises in Glen Road consisted of a small wooden door leading directly into the "pawn." There the high counter was divided into three compartments, affording a degree of privacy for those who came to pledge.

The manager of Peat's was a handsome, fair-haired man in his early thirties, and he had a staff of several young lady assistants. One of these, a vivacious, pretty girl named Mae Marshall, was one of Assunta's most regular customers. She had a very sweet tooth and was constantly nipping over from the "pawn" to the café for a quarter of sweeties or ice cream. Now Mae liked her ice cream soft, newly made, still revolving in the freezer. So she made a special arrangement with the Cocozzas. They bought all their dish towels and dusters from Peat's. When the ice cream was nearly ready, Assunta or Joe would stand at the backshop window that looked over to the side window in Peat's. When Mae passed the window, they signalled to her that the ice cream was ready. Mae would then snatch some dish towels and tell the boss she was going over to the café.

Commercial travellers in chocolates carried interesting sample trays in those days. When a traveller called with some interesting new lines, Assunta would signal to Mae and she would dart over to sample them. One day an expensive new item on display was Chocolate Brazils at one shilling and threepence a quarter. That was a lot of money to pay for a quarter of chocolates.

So Joe turned to Mae and said, "If you like them, we'll stock them, but who will buy them when they are so dear?"

Chewing the gorgeous sample, Mae said, "I'll buy them." So they were ordered.

With her bright, breezy personality, Mae endeared herself to Assunta and Joe, and a warm friendship developed. Joe who was, as ever, very fond of the lassies, never failed to give Mae a "wee squeeze" under Assunta's watchful eye, every time the girl came into the shop. Sometimes she would pop in for a cup of coffee when she had finished work and would sit in the backshop chatting with Assunta.

Assunta would often remark with a smile, "Oh, I wish I had a wee girl just like you, Mamie, ma wee Mamie."

When there was a lull in trade, Assunta would often look over to Peter Hislop's, the grocer across the road. His van would be parked at the shop door, and he would come out in his white coat and his bunnet, a lit cigarette dangling nonchalantly from his lips, and load his van with orders all meticulously arranged in individual cardboard boxes for delivery to his customers. If she raised her eyes, Assunta would be likely to see old Mrs. Hislop, Peter's widowed mother, a stoutish grey-haired lady with a charming smile, sitting out on the window sill cleaning her windows. The staff in the Hislop grocery consisted of Peter, his mother, and Miss Dickson.

They offered first-class service with a personal touch, stocking the finest groceries, excellent ham, and fine barrel butter that was skilfully battered into shape before being placed on the scales. A beautiful black cat presided at one end of the counter. The staff worked long hours, and Peter had been known to make his deliveries very late in the evening, while the little lamp in his office at the rear of the shop was often seen to burn after midnight. For that reason he came to be known as "The Midnight Grocer."

The whole area of the West End formed a friendly, neighbourly community, and Assunta felt very much at home. She knew all her customers by name and listened behind the counter to their troubles and their joys. The "tennis crowd" from the club at the bottom of Low Main Street usually ended their day in the café. But when they came at the last moment in large numbers, Assunta and Peggy were hard pressed to serve them, so the girls would take trays and help to serve the others and afterwards they would give a hand with the washing-up. Assunta loved to have all these young people around her, and she took a very personal interest in them. She was witness to their romances and their heartbreaks and was at hand to give them her moral support.

Among the regulars was a pale, grey-blue-eyed girl with delicate features called Betty. She had a very tiny, squeaky voice and was very shy. When the bright, gay young people gathered to chat over a cup of coffee in the end seat, Betty looked on, smiled occasionally, but hardly ever spoke. Assunta kept a sympathetic eye on the girl, wondering what she could do to bring her out, for she felt drawn to wan, timid, wee creatures.

Then, one evening, she noticed a change in Betty. Her eyes had an unaccustomed glow, and her attention seemed to be attracted to a handsome young man called Jim Daly, who was sitting in the next seat. Jim was not only good-looking, with his dark wavy hair and brown eyes, but he was a loquacious young man with a warm personality. He was studying to be a lawyer and often had long arguments and discussions with Jim Thomson and Robert Whitelaw.

Betty sat with her girl friends and looked on admiringly, never speaking. Assunta was sure the girl had a heavy crush on Jim Daly, while *he* was scarcely aware that she existed. Many of the girls clustered round him, and he could take his pick. Every night he accompanied a different girl home, while poor Betty looked on with envy.

He happened to come in before his friends one day and sat down beside Assunta in the first seat and chatted. In the course of their conversation, Assunta let it slip that he had a serious, unknown admirer. He raised his eyebrows in surprise at the idea of having aroused the interest of someone he did not know. A moment later, Betty came in and when she saw Assunta sitting with Jim, she hesitated. But Assunta called her over and introduced the young people. Then she made an excuse and rose, leaving them alone. Not realising that Betty was his unidentified admirer, Jim chatted away, asking her about herself, and he was rather flattered that she blushed so much when he spoke to her. He suggested they take a stroll down Glen Road as it was a sunny evening. When they had gone, Assunta complimented herself at having played Cupid.

She did not see them again for a few days, but it came to her ears that Jim had taken to Betty and they had been seen going out frequently. He had even taken her to a dance at the university. Assunta kept Joe informed of the progress of this little romance and one afternoon, when Betty came in on her own and ordered an ice, it was Joe who served her.

As he put the ice down before her, he said, "I hear you have a handsome new boyfriend, Betty?"

And she, in her thin voice answered his question with another, "Who wiz tellin' ye?" which sounded so funny that Joe could not help laughing. Now, Assunta and Joe had a naughty habit of inventing nicknames for their clients. From that moment poor Betty was known as "Who wiz tellin' ye?" uttered in a high-pitched voice.

Most of the other members of the regular "gang" also had their sportively familiar names. There was young Jim Wilson who loved to finish off partly consumed drinks or ices. He was known as "*Lecca-piatti,*" that is to say "Plate-licker." One of the regular street-corner leaners, who somehow always managed to have a tear in the seat of his trousers, was gleefully dubbed "*Curofor,*" which, literally translated, means "Bum out."

Jim Turner was one of the most musical of their young clientage. He was a tall, smiling, freckled lad known to his friends as Gem. A great devotee of the famous Bing Crosby, whose films were then enjoying a great vogue, Gem could not only sing delightfully, emulating his idol, but he could imitate the great crooner's skill as a whistler. It was Gem who persuaded Joe to buy some Crosby records. Issued under the black-and-gold Brunswick label, they each cost two and sixpence.

When the evening recitals began on the radiogram, the selections were varied to suit many tastes. Beniamino Gigli's rendering of Puccini's "Che gelida manina" would be followed by Gracie Fields singing about Sally in her alley. Roy Fox, Jack Payne, and Ambrose and their orchestras would play selections of the popular tunes of the day, while Bing Crosby would raise his attractive baritone in Hoagy Carmichael's "Stardust" or a selection from the film *Mississippi,* including "Soon" and "Down by the River." When Crosby came on, Gem harmonised to make a melodious duet. But in no time this became a veritable trio when Dickie the canary, high in his cage, took up the challenge and joined in, matching the intricate pattern of Gem's whistling. Under Gem's influence, Rico became an enthusiastic Crosby fan, and it soon became obvious to Assunta that her son was dipping into the shop till, for the collection of Crosby records began to grow very rapidly.

She whispered her suspicions to Joe. When the shop closed and the customers had all gone, Rico would sit with his father in the top seat and help him to count the day's drawings. While Joe counted the one pound and ten shilling notes, Rico arranged the coins in wobbly columns, the half-crowns in eights, two-shilling pieces in tens, shillings and sixpences in precarious twenties, and tiny threepenny pieces in round loose mounds of forties, while the pennies were in squat, solid twelves and the haepennies in steady twenty-fours.

One evening when they had finished counting, Joe asked Rico, "Now, how much of this money is mine?" Surprised, Rico fixed his father with a questioning look.

"What I mean," explained Joe, "is how much money have you seen fit to leave for me today or how many Bing Crosby records have you managed to smuggle in?"

Cornered, Rico grinned and answered, "Only two today, Papà."

"I don't like boys who dip into tills," said Joe. "When you want something, you have only to ask."

"I'll remember that, Papà," said Rico, smiling again.

Two days later he tugged at his father's coat and asked, "Can I have two and sixpence, Papà?"

"What's it for?" asked Joe.

"A new Bing Crosby record has just come out." Now Joe hated Bing Crosby.

"Don't you think we have suffered enough of that bloody man's groaning?" asked Joe.

"But Papà, you promised. Can I have two and sixpence?"

"No," said Joe.

In the afternoon Rico borrowed half a crown from the shop till and made a hurried trip to Mitchell's record shop. When he returned with the record, he hurried round to the back and up the stairs to the house and placed it on a shelf in his wardrobe.

The old cabinet gramophone had never been used since it was taken up to the house. Now Rico would disappear upstairs frequently and if the house window was open on warm days, the sounds of Bing Crosby's latest records could be heard echoing in the passageway behind the shop. When Assunta heard the music one day as she was going out to the toilet, she realised at once what that rascally son of hers had been up to. She mentioned it to Joe. He was in a bad mood that day as his horses had not been running in form.

He stormed up to the house and went in just as Rico was lifting another Crosby record from a pile of some twenty others on the broad window sill. Then he snatched the record from the boy's hand and threw it out of the window. It landed in fragments on the ground below. He went out and walked angrily down the stairs. Just as he came to the spot where the broken record lay in jagged pieces, the twenty other records came flying out of the window and he was forced to raise his arms to cover his head as they landed all around him, breaking on the ground. It dawned upon him then that his son was as bad tempered as he was!

Assunta found the incident diverting, although Rico did not speak to his father for a week or two. She tried to persuade Joe to give the boy a regular amount of pocket money each week so that, if he wanted to buy something, he could have the pleasure of saving for it. But Joe would not heed her advice, and Rico went on filching half-crowns from the till. At the end of a few weeks, he had managed to replace all the records he had thrown out of the window.

As the summer was ending, the room and kitchen house directly above the shop fell vacant when Mrs. Docherty died. When they moved into it, they found the greater noise of the traffic disconcerting until they got used to it. One evening shortly after they had moved, Robert Whitelaw and Jim Thomson came into the café. They were in a very discursive mood, and they talked and talked long after closing time. Joe finally had to ask them to leave. Jim suggested he could accompany Robert down to the Manse and they could finish their discussion on the way. In the meantime the Cocozzas made their way up to the house and were soon in bed.

As it was a warm night, Joe raised the front window a few inches before getting into bed. Ten minutes later, he and Assunta heard the sound of two familiar voices approaching from Glen Road. It was very obvious, as Jim and Robert passed beneath the window, that their long discussion was still being pursued. Robert was now accompanying Jim down to Shieldmuir where he lived. As the night wore on, they passed several times down to the Manse, up from the Manse, down to Shield-muir, up from Shieldmuir, and, as they spoke loudly, their voices echoed over the West Cross and disturbed Joe every time they passed.

By this time it was after three o' clock in the morning, and Joe was getting more and more annoyed. He lay awake listening for their steps, and sure enough, he could hear them approaching again from the distance while their voices resounded in the night air. Just as they were drawing level with the window, Joe leapt out of the bed, lifted the sash and roared down at them, "Are you two buggers not going to let us have any sleep tonight?"

They looked up and grinned broadly as they apologised for keeping him awake. Then Robert turned to Jim and said: "I'll leave you here, old man. We can go on with our discussion tomorrow, I mean, later today."

He shook Jim's hand and set off down Glen Road, after giving Joe a friendly wave and a broad smile, while Jim set out for Shieldmuir. Joe shook his head, went back to bed, and soon fell asleep.

Occasionally, when his gambling fever rose to a high pitch, Joe could not resist going to the local race meetings. Assunta did not like this at all. It meant the loss of a whole afternoon's drawings with the horse and cart. One day Joe was determined to go to Lanark races. Assunta was just as decided that he would not go. It was Peggy's half day, and Joe should be helping her in the shop until Rico came home from school. No, her punter husband was not going to have his way this time.

At lunch time Joe ate his meal hurriedly. Then he went up to the house and changed into his good suit. He came down soon afterwards with his light raincoat over his arm.

Assunta asked, "Now, just where do you think you are going, Joe?"

"I'm going to Lanark to the races."

"You can't leave me here on my own."

"You'll manage quite well until Rico comes home."

"If you step out of that door, Joe, I warn you I shall put on my coat and go to Glasgow."

"But what about the shop?"

"If you can forget about the shop to go to the races, so can I."

"You wouldn't really close the shop if I went to Lanark, Sunta, would you?"

"Just try me and see!"

Joe made to embrace her as he made his way out of the backshop, but she stepped aside and pushed him away. He walked out and made his way to the Lanark bus stop across the road. Assunta stood behind the counter, looking out, and she could see him standing with his *Noon Record* spread out before him. It was time to teach him a good lesson. She slipped on her coat and hat, put some money in her handbag, closed the main doors of the shop and locked them, and, without even glancing in Joe's direction, began walking down Glasgow Road and crossed over to go down to the Glasgow bus stop.

Joe, his nose still buried in his paper, did not actually see her leaving the shop. Then, glancing up to see if his bus was approaching, he was startled to notice that the shop doors were closed. Looking down Glasgow Road, he then saw Assunta, with her handbag under her arm, casually sauntering down to the other bus stop as if she had not a care in the world. He angrily crammed the *Noon Record* into his coat pocket, ran across the road, and began to walk rapidly down Glasgow Road to catch up with his wife. Then, as a bus passed him, he began again to run. When he saw the bus stopping, he panicked, for he was not sure if she would board it. But, as the bus drew away, he sighed with relief, for she was still standing at the bus stop.

"What do you think you're doing?" he panted, as he came up to her.

"I'm going to Glasgow to buy a few things," she replied in an impudent tone. Then she went on, "If you can throw away your money at the Lanark races, I'm sure I can afford to spend some on myself." Joe took her by the arm.

"Come on, Sunta, let's go back," he said with resignation. They walked slowly up the road, and Assunta took the shop keys and handed them to him. He opened the doors. They went in. Assunta hung up her hat and coat and put away her handbag. Joe went up to the house and changed back into his working suit. Then he came down again, took up his position behind the counter, and did not speak. He did not speak to his wife for a week. But he went on betting.

Soon after this little clash, Peggy left to get married and they were obliged to find another assistant. A young, unemployed grocer's assistant with a bright personality was Joe's choice. His name was Frank, and he was very smart in the shop. As business went on improving, it soon became necessary to have an additional help, a charming girl who was slightly deaf called Mary. As it was their turn to be hosts to Joe's mother, Leonarda, who was now affectionately known as Narduccia, Assunta found herself with a very full backshop when it came to mealtimes as the year 1936 drew to a close. Mary was a very clean worker and a good cook. She could make an excellent clooty dumpling and as the colder days came, this delicacy was very welcome.

Assunta's visits to Byres Road were few and far between and though she saw Giulietta and *commare* Vittoria from time to time, there appeared to be less communication between them. Giulietta had now become completely immersed in the role of the resigned widow, turning more and more to the devotional consolations of the church. The Xaverian Missionary Fathers were frequently entertained to lavish meals in the backshop at Byres Road, and Giulietta, Antonio, and *commare* Vittoria were extremely generous in their donations to help the good work of the missionaries.

Giulietta was keen to introduce the Fathers to Assunta and asked them to call upon her sister-in-law if they happened to be in Wishaw, but, although she was devout in her own way, Assunta was shy about entertaining the priests in her small backshop and did not encourage their visits. Apart from Easter and Christmas, she did not feel the need to attend mass on Sundays and Rico had followed her example. Joe, on the other hand, went to mass every Sunday, and he was not worried by the apparent backsliding of his wife and his son.

Giulietta and Vittoria had always taken great pleasure in dressing fashionably, spending large sums of money on clothes of the highest quality. When Vittoria's birthday came round, Antonio decided to treat both his wife and his sister to new fur coats. Two magnificent pony-skins were purchased from Karter's in Sauchiehall Street, and, when Joe and Assunta paid a short visit to the Continental one chilly afternoon, they were treated to a fashion parade in the backshop. Joe congratulated *compare* Antonio on his good taste, while Assunta admired the elegance of the ladies. Vittoria was about the same height as Assunta, and she insisted that her *commare* should try on her coat. At first Assunta was not too keen, but encouraged by Joe, she agreed. When he saw his wife in the fur coat, he was so impressed that he decided there and then to buy her one just as soon as he had a lucky week on the horses.

He accordingly placed his bets with great care and in no time at all, his winnings having risen substantially to more than two hundred pounds, he took the bus to Glasgow, went directly to Karter's, and ordered a pony-skin coat for Assunta.

About three weeks later, a box bearing the Karter stamp was delivered by van to Belhaven Café, and when a puzzled Assunta opened it and parted the many layers of tissue paper, she was astonished to see a fur coat. At that precise moment, with perfect timing, Joe came beaming into the backshop, fully expecting his thrilled wife to throw her arms around his neck in gratitude. But her reaction was quite unexpected.

She smiled and said, "I think you meant well, spending good money on this expensive coat, Joe, and I think it was a very kind thought, but you should have told me beforehand and I could have saved you the bother. It's much too extravagant and far too grand for me, and I would rather you had spent the money on something useful. So just take it back to the shop where you bought it and ask them to refund the money!"

Joe was flabbergasted. He took the box from her, flew upstairs to the house and into the bedroom, and threw the coat in its box on to the top of the wardrobe. Then, livid with rage, he gave the wardrobe a good kick, which resounded through the floor and could be heard by a slightly apprehensive Assunta behind the counter downstairs. He then kicked the wardrobe again, even more wildly, so that it swayed back and struck against the wall, while Assunta winced as she heard the noise above her. When Joe came downstairs some time later, he ignored her and did not speak.

Oh, my God, she thought, *now he is in one of his huffs again. I have really done it this time!*

After the midday meal eaten in complete silence, Assunta washed the dishes. Then, seeing Joe still sulking behind the counter, she told Rico to wash some pails before going back to school. Making her way upstairs, she went into the bedroom and there she saw the box containing the coat, sitting at a crazy angle over the edge of the wardrobe top. Taking a chair, she gingerly lifted it down. She took out the coat and laid it out on the bed.

It looked even more expensive than *commare* Vittoria's. She really did not care for it. It had a very special collar made from another type of fur to contrast with the pony-skin. It was very lustrous, and she did not know what kind it was as she was not at all knowledgeable on the subject of furs. In fact, she felt there was something very distasteful about wearing the furs of dead animals. But the peace of her home was at stake. So she slipped on her best dress and shoes and put on the coat.

Glancing into the long wardrobe mirror, she was startled at her reflection and asked herself aloud, "Who *is* that overdressed, rich-looking woman looking at me?"

Then she made her way downstairs, hoping none of the neighbours would see her, and entered the backshop. Rico was still scrubbing pails at the sink and when he turned and saw his mother, he nearly dropped the one he was holding.

"Go through and tell your father to come in for a wee fashion show!" she said.

A moment later, a delighted Joe was admiring his beautiful wife as she took a few restricted paces up and down the rather crowded floor.

Assunta threw him a hypocritical smile and asked, "Do you think I am in the fashion now?" Then she added, "Thank you, darling, for the lovely present."

The ice was broken. Joe threw his arms around her, nearly smothering her in the fur collar. Then, glancing into the long mirror on the backshop partition, they broke into merry laughter when they saw what an incongruous picture they made together, she in her expensive pony-skin and he in his long white apron! By now the backshop was full, for Mary, Frank, and Rico were all there applauding.

Yet, once the coat was carefully hung in a special cloth cover with moth balls in the wardrobe, Assunta was very rarely to wear it. She just did not care for fur coats!

Chapter Nineteen

1937 to 1943—A Time for Dying

In the early days of 1937 the letters from the Di Bonas brought bad news from Filignano. Filomena was very ill. The doctor had been consulted but had been unable to diagnose her illness. Although she was still able to hobble about the house, her legs, covered with varicose ulcers, were very painful. Peppino Di Bona had arranged for Zia Adelaida, who lived nearby, to stay with the old people and look after them, and he was paying her a wage. Assunta was very worried, and Joe assured her that he would not hesitate to send her home if Filomena's condition did not improve. In the meantime she awaited each postal delivery with dread.

As if she did not have enough on her mind, trouble arose between Rico and his father. Although he had made some progress in his schoolwork in French, science, and English, Rico's performance in mathematics, Latin, and history left a great deal to be desired. Joe criticised him for spending too much of his time at the cinema or listening to Bing Crosby. This led to quarrels, and Assunta was very upset by these angry scenes.

But Robert Whitelaw took a great interest in the boy and helped him with his history studies. Then Joe arranged for a mathematics teacher to give Rico private tuition. But a busybody informed Joe that his schoolboy son had been seen taking several girls to the cinema. There were more bitter scenes between father and son in the backshop. Assunta told Joe to be less interfering, but he was determined that nothing should hinder his son's education. Since the boy's singing voice had not fulfilled its earlier promise, it was obvious he would never be a great singer. Joe decided that Rico should have the chance to go to university and prepare for the teaching profession. Rico, who was more inclined to seek a career in films on the production side, resigned himself to his father's plan for the sake of peace.

The social life of Belhaven Café went on as usual with its evening radiogram concerts, games of dominoes, educational discussions led by Robert Whitelaw, and the late night selection of "hits" on the radio when the young people, unwilling to go home, lingered to hear the Elsie Carlisle version of "Let's Put Out the Lights and Go to Sleep!" In fact it became a final singsong in which all the young set joined in, as they made their way out to go home, and their voices could be heard ringing along the street when it was nearly midnight:

No more money in the bank,
No cute baby we can spank
What's to do about it?
Let's put out the lights and go to sleep!

Then one morning in February, the dreaded letter arrived from Filignano. Filomena was bedridden, and the doctor offered no hope for her recovery. Joe quickly made the necessary travel arrangements, and Assunta found herself again in Filignano on the 11th of March. She was shocked when she saw her mother lying in the large bed. She was so tiny and frail, her small eyes protruding from her emaciated face. Yet she still had pinkness in her cheeks. There was also a great change in Benedetto. He was terribly bent and when he tried to walk with the aid of a stick, he tottered from side to side as if he would fall. Zia Adelaida had been looking after Filomena and Benedetto with care and affection. Her son Alessandro brought the firewood, which Benedetto was no longer fit to gather.

Assunta and Adelaida tried their best to nurse Filomena back to health, but, as the weeks passed, it became obvious that she would not rally, and she sank gradually into a completely helpless state. They took it in turn to sit with her each night.

March passed and April came with its promise of spring, but the improvement in the weather did nothing to help poor Filomena as she drifted slowly into death. In the final stages of her illness, she could barely speak. Her once lovely eyes, enlarged in her wasted face, never closed, fixed on Assunta as she sat beside the bed. When the final agony began, the priest was sent for and the last sacraments were administered. Outside, in the large kitchen, the women of the neighbourhood, led by *commare* Maria Di Bona, knelt reciting the Rosary.

As Assunta, Benedetto, and Adelaida sat by the bed, Filomena looked at her daughter, then turned her head slowly to the window. Assunta knew she wanted her to open it and did so. She could see now from the serene expression on Filomena's face that she was quite beyond pain. The sounds of life drifted into the darkening room, and beyond the murmuring of the praying women in the kitchen could be heard the occasional bleating of the goat. Filomena turned to Assunta and smiled. Then she made an effort to raise her arms as Assunta, falling on her knees, leant forward and took her poor mother into her arms. Filomena looked into Assunta's face and murmured, "Eugenio . . ."

Then her eyes closed and it was over. It was such a beautiful, peaceful end that Assunta could not weep. But when she had gently laid her mother's body back against the pillows, she murmured in a singing voice, "*Mamma bella, mamma bella, bella mamma me'.*"

When Assunta arrived back in Wishaw, it was to find Joe was having trouble with his legs. For the time being, he was forced to give up his ice-cream round. The horse was still being stabled at the Martins, and every day Joe would limp painfully down to attend to Nellie's needs. The pain made him irritable and when Narduccia came to stay, he was inclined to be short with his mother when she indulged in her usual complaints. The old lady had become soured in her old age, looking at the world with a jaundiced eye. Perhaps she resented being shuttled around between her daughter and her two sons. The fact that Joe and Assunta got on so well aroused her hostility, and at times she could be very sarcastic. She would sit in her corner seat in the backshop by the fire and pass comments upon her daughter-in-law's work.

One afternoon Assunta was washing pails in the sink. Narduccia followed her every move, remarking more than once that her son's wife was much too fussy. Was it really necessary to rinse so often? Then, when the pails were put away and Mary brought in dishes to be washed, Narduccia went on baiting her daughter-in-law. She sat staring at Assunta with her arms folded, shaking her head. Then, obviously bored, she let out a deep sigh, making a very strange sound, rather like a prolonged, "Ooooooooofa!" Then she went on, saying, "Such a fuss over the washing of a few dishes, for first they must be rinsed, then soaped, then rinsed again, not once mind you, but twice or even three times." Assunta felt she was going to scream. The old woman was really getting on her nerves.

Joe, at the counter, could hear the rise and fall of his mother's voice and was well aware of what was going on. Mary took in a small stack of tea plates. Assunta lifted them one by one and washed them.

"That's right, my dear," moaned Narduccia, "just take your time. Soap each one and rinse three times. You'll be standing at that sink all day and all night."

Something snapped in Assunta's head. She lifted a second pile of dirty tea plates and hurled them into the sink where they broke with a dull clatter. In the heavy silence that followed, Narduccia was struck dumb. Then Joe stormed into the backshop and turned upon his mother in a fury. He said things to her no son should ever say to his mother.

229

Assunta then turned upon Joe and reprimanded him in harsh terms for daring to talk to his mother in such a manner. Tempers flared and Assunta, turning to the ledge next the sink, lifted another stack of plates and hurled them on to the floor while Joe, despite his sore legs, stamped angrily into the counter. In the meantime Narduccia had slipped into her coat and, taking a large paper bag and a knife, went off to Belhaven Park to gather dandelions. When calm reigned again and Assunta had swept away the broken dishes, Joe came sheepishly into the backshop to apologise to his wife. Some time later they were standing side by side looking out of the backshop window when they saw Narduccia coming across the road carrying the large paper bag crammed full with fresh dandelion leaves.

"Narduccia is bringing us her peace offering," said Joe.

Early in July, Giulietta was obliged to go to Filignano when her parents died, within days of one another. When she returned to Scotland at the beginning of August, she came to Wishaw to assure Assunta that Benedetto was being very well cared for by Zia Adelaida and the Di Bonas. Since the Bottazzella house where her parents had lived was now unoccupied, Giulietta told Assunta that she had decided to move her furniture there from Imperatore.

Then she came out with a very pointed question. "Am I still entitled to *my* share of the Imperatore house, and, if so, would you be willing to buy it so that I could use the money to improve my house in Bottazzella?"

Again Assunta was astounded, as she had been when Eugenio was killed, that in the midst of her grief, Giulietta's thoughts should be dwelling on mercenary details concerning property. It was time to set her sister-in-law right.

"According to Italian law, it is quite clear, my dear Giulietta, that you are not entitled to a single stone of our house at Imperatore. If you have been allowed to live there since Eugenio's death, it was as our welcome guest. If you want to move to Bottazzella, please do so, although no one is asking you to leave Imperatore. But don't expect *me* or *Joe* to pay for improvements to *your* house."

Quite taken aback, Giulietta caught the next bus back to town where she told her brother Antonio that his little scheme to extort money from the Cocozzas had not worked. This incident broadened the rift between Assunta and Giulietta.

Although Joe had resumed part of his ice-cream round by the end of the summer, Assunta could see he did not have his former energy, and she felt a holiday in Filignano would do him good. When Giulietta heard of Joe's intended trip, she decided to join him, as she still had some matters to settle concerning the estate of her parents. So a small company of seven travellers set off for Italy. Along with Giulietta and Joe, there was young Silvio Ferri with his cousin Ettore Fiorentino, a very droll gentleman from Bellshill who loved to give recitations of the poems of Robert Burns. There was also an Italian lady with her daughter, a rather spoiled girl, who made the journey unpleasant because of her constant complaints. But Joe derived much benefit from the brief holiday and, when he came back at the start of the festive season, the Cocozzas enjoyed a happy family Christmas.

Joe bought Rico the cine-camera the boy had been wanting for so long. Rico lost no time in shooting his first films in the snow-covered streets. By this time he was in his fourth year at Wishaw High and had made up his mind to specialise in French and German. He found German difficult, but it offered an interesting challenge. He spent many hours reading German poetry. This seemed to rouse an interest in the music of Wagner, and the early days of 1938 brought new musical sounds to the café as the Valkyries rode each day through the sitting room while the mournful tones of Isolde's "Liebestod" stilled the late evening chatter of the patient customers. Joe was not very enamoured with this kind of music, and he began to wish his son would revive his interest in Bing Crosby.

Rico longed for a proper little room where he could show his films, and he was wily enough to persuade Joe to cut off a section of the backshop and construct a small store room, sandwiched between the counter gantry and the rest of the backshop area. This room measured roughly four and a half yards by three, but the storing shelves were placed very high and beneath them Joe panelled the partitions and stained them. A screen was erected at the bottom end, with miniature footlights operated by a small dimmer switch. A projection port was cut out from the back partition and suitable glass inserted. Then a special hinged shelf was installed to support the projector behind the port so that the whirr of the machine could not be heard in the miniature auditorium. Following his late uncle's example, Rico bought an amplifier, loudspeaker, and turntable. The speaker was placed under the screen on the top of Joe's desk, while amplifier and turntable were operated from the backshop. Thus the films could be shown with an appropriate musical accompaniment.

By this time Rico had also acquired a motor-driven 9.5 mm Pathé Projector, which could take large reels of film. The next step was to acquire some films. The ideal place was Frank's at Glasgow Cross, and there Rico spent many hours examining stacks of second-hand films. In a comparatively short time, he was able to purchase some of the

231

great classics of the German cinema, the Wagnerian influence still being strong. The screen in the store room Bijou in Belhaven Café was enriched with the presence of Leni Riefenstahl's *The Blue Light*, a beautiful film shot in the Dolomities, Pabst's great film of *Faust* starring Emil Jannings as Mephistopheles, and Murnau's great flying classic *The White Hell of Pitz Palu* not to mention a varied selection of Chaplin comedies as supporting items on the programmes. Rico worked out elaborate scores to accompany the films from his growing collection of records, and his wondering audiences of four or five people had their ear drums shattered by the strains of Sibelius's *En Saga* as Leni Riefenstahl dramatically fell off the mountain top at the end of the film.

The experience of this intense interest in the cinema on the part of her son opened up a whole new world for Assunta. She enjoyed the artistry with which the films were presented and began to see depths in her son that she had never suspected existed. Perhaps the cinema was to be his profession, and he would one day find a place in the film industry. While Joe could only agree with Assunta, admiring his son's skill, he nevertheless insisted that a university education would give Rico the cultural background he would require for such a career.

In the spring of 1938, Giulietta went on a pilgrimage to Lourdes. She seemed chastened by the spiritual experience and brought Assunta a small metal statuette of the kneeling Bernadette Soubirous with the figure of the apparition standing on a rock. The musical mechanism played "Ave Maria." Assunta was moved by Giulietta's gesture and embraced her affectionately. Then they sat down to a cup of tea and had a heartfelt talk that did much to restore the harmony they had enjoyed together in the happy days of the 1920s. Without actually saying she had been wrong, Giulietta, by her attitude, was giving Assunta to understand that she regretted the disagreements that had estranged them in recent years.

Assunta now became reconciled to the sad fact that she would only rarely see old Italian friends. The sixteen miles between Wishaw and Glasgow seemed to create an insurmountable gap. She missed the Coias who had settled in Milngavie and often thought of "The Lambs of St. Anthony," wondering how they had grown up. She did not often get the chance to make the long journey to Garngad Road to visit Joe's sister Irena, who now had a family of her own, or to Airdrie to visit Genevina and Antonio. They were all so occupied with their businesses that they were losing touch with one another. The Filignanesi met only when someone married or somebody died.

So the weeks and months flew past, and the year 1939 brought international tension. People sensed that a war was coming, and they

232

apprehensively determined to enjoy life while they could. It was an attitude that encouraged business, and the summer of 1939 was one of the busiest they had experienced since they came to Wishaw. Joe did a roaring trade with his ice-cream cart while Assunta's sleeves were rolled up from early morning until late at night in Belhaven Café. But the busy summer was coming to an end and, as August drew to a close, gloomy headlines in the newspapers announced another crisis. On September 1st Germany invaded Poland. Britain declared war on Germany on September 3rd.

For the first few months, the war seemed a remote phenomenon and people went on with their daily routines, as best they could. But as time went on, Joe became very disquieted and anxious. He sensed that something frightening was about to occur. When his customer friends discussed with him the possibility that Italy might come into the war on the side of Germany, he grew exasperated and strongly denied any such contingency. Then, in the late afternoon of June 10th, when he was on his round at the far end of Waverley Drive, one of his lady customers came out to tell him pointedly that Italy had declared war on Britain and France.

Dumbfounded, Joe could not believe his ears. There must be some mistake. Then, when the full realisation of what he had just heard dawned upon him, he broke down and, burying his face in his hands, wept bitterly. The lady left very sorry for him and quietly suggested he should make his way home. He thanked her and urged Nellie into a trot. The little bells on her harness jingled in panic as she almost stampeded down the road, urged on by her frantic master. Joe imagined he felt hostile looks thrown at him from the blurred windows speeding past him on either side of the road.

Assunta had already heard the bad news and had closed the shop. Rico helped his father to unload the cart, and Joe took the horse and cart down to the Martins' stable. When these good people heard the horse's bells, they came out to commiserate with Joe and assured him that he should not worry as they would stand by him no matter what happened. Above all he was not to worry about Nellie. They would attend to the horse.

When Joe was making his way painfully up the road to the shop, he was insulted and spat upon by some of the more ignorant inhabitants of the street. When he came into the backshop, he fell into Assunta's arms and cried out his heart. Rico looked on helplessly in dismay. It so happened that both Mary and Frank were off that day, so the three of them sat in the backshop wondering when a knock at the door would announce the arrival of the police, for Joe was certain they would all be interned. Then he went through mechanically to remove the cash from the till and locked everything away in his desk beneath the cinema screen in the store room.

Outside they could hear the loud voices of people walking past. Someone banged his fist against the shop door and shouted, "Rotten Tally traitors. Rotten Tally bastards."

Assunta laid the table and put out some food and when they were sitting toying with their forks, unable to eat for fear, there was a knock at the back door. Assunta started and Joe made to open the door, but Rico stepped in front of him and bravely opened it himself. To their relief it was Robert Whitelaw. He told them to go on with their meal and did his best to reassure them that they would not be taken away. Then Jim Thomson arrived and Assunta made coffee.

As they talked, the hum of voices in the street increased and when Robert climbed on to a chair to look outside from the top of one of the shop windows, he was alarmed to see that dozens of people had gathered on the pavements outside and were taking up positions all round the area of the West Cross, leaning on the iron railings, talking among themselves. Some were pointing to the café and shaking their fists, their eyes glaring with hatred.

Robert took Jim aside into the sitting room and told him quietly that he did not like the way things were going at all. So they decided to go out by the back door and have a walk round to investigate. Then, telling the three frightened Cocozzas they would shortly return, they went out and walked casually round the corner into the main road. As they sauntered around, they kept their ears alert, overhearing some alarming remarks.

"Jist wait till it's daurk and we'll smash the windaes an set fire tae the———shop."

"They shid be dragged oot an lynched."

"The polis wull nae intefere if we dae it, they're———enemies an we'll git thum, the bastards."

By this time there were over two hundred bystanders gathered round the whole area of the cross, and their voices grew louder and louder. Robert went into the telephone callbox and phoned the police. The officer on duty was not interested, saying that all the foot patrolmen were out and they already had some trouble at the other end of the town.

Jim and Robert made their way round to the back door and knocked three times. Joe opened to let them in. He had been looking out of the shop window, and his face was ashen with fear.

"They look as if they would like to murder us," he said quietly so that Assunta and Rico would not hear.

"Now don't you worry, my friend," said Robert. "Jim will remain here with you while I go to the police station for help. Try to keep calm until I come back."

When Robert had gone, they sat quietly near the fire, listening as the menacing noises grew in volume outside. Someone walking past the backshop window hit a pane with his fist and shouted obscenities. Joe put up the heavy wooden shutters. A few seconds later, the top pane was shattered by a bottle or stone. Then they heard someone with a stick drumming an ominous tattoo on the iron railings in front of the shop. Assunta began to weep again. Her face was flushed, and she felt that her whole world was collapsing around her. A wave of rage at the sheer injustice of it all swept through her.

An hour passed like an eternity. They kept hearing thudding noises and reverberations as objects bounced off the plate-glass windows of the shop. Joe fetched the steps and took down the bird cage. Poor Dickie had been fluttering with fright every time the windows were struck. Baldassare, who ordinarily would have kept one interested eye on the cage, now sensing danger, ignored Dickie and curled up in his bed by the fire where Rico could lean over and stroke him reassuringly.

It was getting dark. The drunken voices of boozers could be heard singing in slurred tones. Suddenly there was a loud knocking at the shop door and Joe went through, followed closely by the others. They heard Robert's voice.

"Open the door, Joe. It's all right."

When the door was opened, Robert came in followed by a police inspector and four policemen. The inspector was well known to the Cocozzas, having spent many a pleasant hour over a coffee or an ice in their backshop. He told Joe that he would like them all, for their own safety, to make their way up to the house. His men would form an escort. Assunta quickly gathered some food in a basket, while Joe collected the cashboxes from his desk. The four policemen went outside and moved back the rabble standing on the pavement. Jim took the canary's cage and Rico the cat, and the terrified company made its way round the corner, guarded by the four policemen and the inspector. The louts standing just outside the shop began to shout and jeer, and some of them spat. The inspector turned on them and gave them a piece of his mind. But this only subdued them for a moment.

As they made their way up to the house, Assunta was conscious of the curious eyes of her neighbours staring at them from the surrounding houses. When they reached the landing outside the house,

Mrs. Irving, who lived next door, came out and touched Assunta's arm, smiling reassuringly. Assunta weakly returned her smile. The policemen saw them safely to the door and went back to patrol the streets, but the inspector remained behind and went into the house with them.

In answer to their tremulous questions, he assured Joe and Assunta that they would not be interned. He would see to it that his men would patrol the area all night and they would be safe. When he left, he shook Joe's hand and said he would be back on the following day. The blackout curtains had been drawn, and they sat in the kitchen. Assunta kindled the fire as it was getting cool. Robert and Jim talked with them until midnight.

When they had gone, Joe put out all the lights and tiptoed to the front window to peep out into the street below. Most of the would-be lynchers had disappeared, but there were still about fifty men and women who lingered, waiting for something to happen. Then Joe heard the voice of the man who had spat at him when he was coming up from Martin's stable. This was a man to whom Joe had done many a good turn, often lending him money when he was in need. He turned now to some of his fellow layabouts and shouted, "Whit are ye————waitin' fur? Smash the————windaes. That shop is stowed wi' fags."

At one o'clock in the morning, they tried to settle down for the night. They did not undress but lay on the tops of their beds, Rico in the kitchen, Joe and Assunta in the bedroom. They tried to close their eyes, but the persistent buzzing of the angry voices in the street kept rising to them and they could not sleep. Around two o'clock in the morning, they heard the bell-like sound of shattering plate glass as the window directly beneath the bedroom was smashed. A few moments later, the other window met the same fate. Assunta buried her face in Joe's shoulder and wept bitterly. In the early hours of the dawn, they heard the banging of a joiner's hammer as the windows were boarded up. They were to remain so for some time.

True to his promise, the inspector called next day. He tried to persuade them to be brave and reopen the shop as soon as possible. They must carry on normally as if nothing had happened, and he was sure they would have no difficulties. He would see to it himself that they were well protected. Many of the other Italians in the town were being interned that day. When Joe asked why he was not being taken away, the inspector told him they knew he was not a member of the Fascist Party. But he and his wife would have to register as enemy aliens, and their movements would be restricted. They would not be allowed to travel more than five miles from Wishaw. In a few days they should report to his office where they would be issued with special alien identity books.

When Mary and Frank turned up next morning at their normal time, Assunta hugged them both. It was decided to leave the shop closed that day. Mary and Frank could cook their meals downstairs and bring the food up to the house. Assunta got Frank to telephone to Byres Road, and a very distraught Giulietta informed him that both Antonio and Josie had been taken away for internment. Frank gave Giulietta the Wishaw news. Assunta realised how fortunate she was that Joe had not been interned.

One day two weeks later, two detectives came into the shop and advised Joe that he would have to get rid of the radiogram as it contained a valve amplifier, and, since he was an enemy alien, it would be possible for him to use the equipment to transmit information to the enemy. Peter Hislop had agreed to store all their cigarette stocks in his warehouse as there was always the possibility that the café might be burgled. When cigarettes were needed to restock the gantry shelves, Frank went over to collect them from Peter. Now Peter and Frank carried the heavy radiogram over to the house above the grocer's shop where it would be safely stored. Rico was very bitter about this great loss and observed, "They are even depriving us of our music."

A few days before his son's eighteenth birthday, Joe paid a visit to Mitchell's Record Shop and purchased a small HMV portable, spring-driven gramophone. It was hidden away until the morning of the 6th of November when Rico was pleasantly awakened by the sound of music. Joe had set the gramophone on the table beside his son's bed, and for once he decided to put up with the moaning Mr. Crosby. Since the old cabinet gramophone had finally expired, Rico was overjoyed by his father's present.

"Papà thinks of everything," he said.

It was a difficult time, but Assunta and Joe gradually came to terms with their problems. Joe sold the pony and cart and worked by Assunta's side in the café. With his reassuring presence, she felt safer when they were subjected to insults from customers who resented Italy's part in the war. At first business was very poor. Then, as time passed, their regular customers began to drift back. But Assunta was on her guard, feeling she had lost the special intimacy she had once enjoyed with them. It was as if an invisible veil of distrust had risen between them, which it would take much time to rend.

Although Rico had not been very enthusiastic about returning to school, when a note came from the rector requesting Joe to send his son back, the boy took his books and went. The start of 1940 saw him preparing to sit for his Higher Leaving Certificate.

Supplies became scarcer, restricting the shop's turnover, but this did not seem to worry Joe unduly. The sad fact was that Italy's participation in the war had broken his heart and his spirits were low. His health suffered as a consequence. He was thankful he had not been separated from Assunta and Rico, yet he felt that his life had changed and nothing would ever be the same again as it had been in the happy days. Assunta tried to cheer him, but he fell into long, silent, despondent moods.

A letter from Filignano, finding its way through Switzerland, came to announce the death of Benedetto. Assunta was inconsolable. She felt she should have been by his side when the end came.

Thanks to the help given him by Robert Whitelaw, Rico succeeded in passing his Highers, and he applied for a place at Glasgow University where he hoped to study French and German. His parents were pleased when he was accepted. Life was moving swiftly, events rushing relentlessly on. As the restrictions on their movements were lifted, Joe and Assunta began to go visiting, renewing old friendships. Most of the male Italians in Scotland had been interned, many of them on the Isle-of-Man. The tragedy of the ill-fated ship *Arandora Star* made widows of many of the Italian women. It was difficult for them to be reconciled to their tragic loss in the strangely embarrassing atmosphere of subjection in which they found themselves as enemy aliens.

When Rico began his studies at the university in the autumn of 1940, his mother suggested he should stay one or two nights every week with his aunt and godmother. Living in their top flat in University Avenue, at night when there were air raids, the two women were terrified, but felt safer with someone else's presence in the house. One night when the sirens sounded, Rico was amused by the spectacle of his Aunt Giulietta in her long nightdress parading round the flat, sprinkling holy water all over the rooms to ward off the German bombs.

The winter passed quietly, and Rico settled down to his studies. Joe insisted that his son should study Italian. In the absence of the Italian professor, Ernesto Grillo, who had also been interned, the Italian Department was being supervised by Mr. Archibald MacKinven, a tall, thin, very learned gentleman with a long nose that ended peculiarly in a small, vertical, perfectly square plateau. It was this perhaps that contributed to the rich sonority of his deep voice when he read out his lectures on Dante, quoting dramatically from the *Divina Commedia*.

In the spring of 1941, Joe fell desperately ill. The local doctor was not very sympathetic in his treatment of the patient. He diagnosed heart trouble and advised him to lose weight, placing him on a strict diet. But Joe had already been losing weight, as he had lost his once-prodigious appetite. He became so ill that it became necessary to admit him to a nursing home near Charing Cross in Glasgow. Rico visited his father every day, but Assunta could only go to the nursing home once a week. Joe did not take to being there, as he had never been in a hospital before, and the nurses were very hostile towards him. One night, in an air-raid, the window of his room was shattered by a bomb blast. No one looked in and he lay in a cold draught all night. By morning he had caught pneumonia.

On April 10th, when Joe was still in the nursing home, Narduccia, who was living with Antonio and his family in Airdrie, was discovered dead in her bed by her granddaughter Dalfina. She was buried quietly in Airdrie a few days later. Joe was so desperately ill that Assunta sought the doctor's advice as to whether she should tell her husband about the bereavement. The doctor advised against it. By the end of April, Joe had improved only slightly, but he was by this time sick of the nursing home and the rude nurses, and, against the advice of the doctors, he insisted upon being taken home.

One day when he was sitting up, feeling a bit better, he turned to Assunta and said, "I can't understand why my mother has not come to see me. I have had many visitors since I came home, but there is no sign of my mother. Is she ill?"

Assunta quietly told him about Narduccia's death. He cried bitterly for several hours and could not at first bring himself to forgive his wife for not telling him before. But, once he was well enough to leave his bed, the bitterness wore off and he was less resentful, realising that Assunta had acted upon the advice of the doctor.

One day late in May, Joe decided to visit his mother's grave. Before leaving for Airdrie, he went to the local fruit shop and made a special purchase. When he, Assunta, and Rico arrived at Narduccia's grave, Joe fell on his knees, lamenting the loss of his mother. Then, drying his tears, he took the large brown paper parcel he had brought from Wishaw and unwrapped it to reveal a large basket of fruit crowned with a fine bunch of black grapes. Placing this offering on the grave, he said, "These fruits were what she liked."

At the June diet, Rico passed all his examinations and his parents were very pleased. They noticed, however, that he was becoming less willing to help with the shop work. When the new session began in October 1941, this attitude became even more apparent. The old conflicts flared up between Joe and Rico, and Assunta found herself often playing the role of peacemaker. Some weekends Rico did not even come home, making the excuse that he had too much studying to do.

By this time most of the young customers of the café were away on national service. Robert Whitelaw was in the navy, Gem Turner and Jim Daly in the army, while Jimmy Leccapiatti, the famous plate-licker, was in the air force. Assunta and Joe found it necessary to extend their catering facilities, as troops on the move often called in for snacks. Sometimes foreign soldiers were stationed temporarily in the old distillery in Glasgow Road. Once a company of Polish soldiers remained there for a few days.

The local girls lost no time in entertaining these attractive men and one of Wishaw's most glamorous young ladies, Rina Baillie, a model who had won several beauty competitions, came in one evening accompanied by a Polish officer. They sat until well after closing time. Now, when late customers had to be shown out during the blackout, they were escorted through the backshop to go out by the back door. In the darkness, the two iron poles supporting a landing above were a constant danger. Many a customer had walked into them, banging their brow very painfully against the unyielding iron. When Rina and the officer rose to leave, it was Assunta who led them politely to the back door.

Then, as she opened it cautiously, she turned to Rina and warned, "Watch that pole in the dark, dear."

Rina, mistaking Assunta's warning as a reference to her escort, turned indignantly and said, "I'm surprised at you, Mrs. Joe. You know I'm not that sort of girl!"

The winter of 1941 to 1942 passed, and Belhaven Café found itself with a reduced staff, for both Frank and Mary left to join the forces. The Cocozzas had to depend on the part-time help of several married ladies. Mrs. Irving came down every day to help with the dishes. Mrs. Reid, who lived across the road, did the cleaning and scrubbed the floors.

The summer of 1942 was a warm one, and often Joe, feeling exhausted, would walk slowly down to the garden of the Martins and sit for an hour or two conversing with them. One afternoon they closed the shop, and both went down to the garden. Rico happened to be home, and he brought out his cine-camera and made a short film of his parents chatting with Mr. and Mrs. Martin and their niece, Jean. In the setting of the rambling garden, Assunta took a good look at Joe and it came to her that she was losing him. His clothes were hanging on him, and his eyes bulged slightly in his wasted face. Their doctor was of no help. He was a snobbish man who was not interested in enemy aliens. The regulation heart tablets he prescribed did nothing to ease Joe's condition. As Assunta lay awake at night listening to his laboured breathing, she knew he would not be long for this world.

On those days when the weather was mild and Joe could scarcely draw a breath, he would hang over the iron railing outside the shop and exchange a few words with his betting friends. Despite his condition, his interest in the horses was still high. His favourite bookie was a Mr. Thomson of Carluke, and Joe would phone his bets using the public telephone outside the café. When he was unwell and confined to the house, Rico would phone the bets for him.

As the awful war dragged on, Joe became more and more dejected and sad. He could never be reconciled to the fact that Italy had turned against Britain, and his double loyalty gave rise to conflicts within him, for he had a strong love for the country that had given him his living.

When the autumn of 1942 came, cold and dismal, and the leaves began to fall, Joe took to his bed. His appetite grew poorer, and Assunta found it difficult to get him to eat. Yet every day he studied the *Noon Record*. Although Assunta had always been opposed to his gambling, she was thankful now that it took up his attention.

Fruit was scarce and one day he took a strong craving for a fresh lemon drink. There were no lemons to be bought in Wishaw. Assunta phoned Giulietta, begging her to try the shops in Byres Road. But there were no lemons in the West End shops. Giulietta arrived in Wishaw next day and, opening her handbag, brought out a small, shrivelled lemon she had come upon at the bottom of her fruit basket. The skin had lost all its yellow and had turned into a dullish, russet brown.

Assunta took the precious fruit and cut it carefully in two. It was very juicy. She squeezed and squeezed and poured all the juice into a cup. There would be no more than a full tablespoonful, she thought. Then she picked out twelve little pips that were lodged in the squeezer and put them in another cup. She placed this cup on a shelf in the kitchen cupboard and promptly forgot about it. From the juice of the lemon, she managed to make four drinks that Joe greatly enjoyed over the next three days. He blessed Giulietta each time that he took a quenching sip.

It was a cold, gloomy Christmas, and Joe was glad Rico was home for the vacation. The boy was doing so well in Italian that Mr. MacKinven had asked him to teach the elementary class as there was a staff shortage. His son was becoming a teacher, thought Joe. But was *he* going to live long enough to see him graduate? He doubted that very much.

The year 1943 began wearily. The food situation was bad. Everything was rationed. Fresh milk was in short supply, and it was impossible to make good ice cream. The handling of sweet coupons was another nuisance, and there was even danger in touching some of the

241

filthy books that were being tendered over the counter. Paper work was on the increase since countless forms were required to be filled in. Yet, when Assunta entrusted this work to Joe, it gave him something to do and he felt he was being useful. A regular stream of visitors came to the house, and many of Joe's gambling pals would come and sit with him and chat. A special concession was made by the police, and Joe was allowed to purchase a small electric radio so that he could listen to the racing results in the afternoons.

As the university session drew to a close, Rico, who now travelled every day to and from Glasgow, kept his father company as he pored over his books preparing for examinations. Joe's legs were badly swollen, and he was often breathless. Some days the swelling subsided, and he would feel better. One day when the uncaring doctor called on his fortnightly visit, Joe, delighted that the swelling in his legs had gone down, turned to him and, lifting his trousers, said, "Look, Doctor, see what an improvement there is in my legs."

The doctor looked down, then raised his eyes and with a supercilious grin, remarked, "Don't worry, old chap, they will be as swollen as ever by tomorrow."

Under his breath, Joe cursed his malevolent doctor. Next day his legs were again badly swollen.

The 14th of May was a Friday, and Rico had gone up to the school to visit some of his favourite teachers. In the early afternoon, Assunta went up to the house with a cup of tea for Joe. She found him gasping for breath as he sat in his chair. His face was ashen. Alarmed, she rattled on the water pipe in the kitchen that resounded in the backshop downstairs and Mrs. Reid came up to see what was the matter. Joe seemed to be sinking.

Assunta begged her to fetch the doctor who lived nearby in Glen Road. Mrs. Reid ran to the doctor's house, but it was his wife who answered the door. The doctor was not in, she was told, and would not be back until the evening. Just then Mrs. Reid saw Rico coming down from the school. She ran to meet him and told him his father was dying. He started to run and when he reached the house, rushed up the stairs. Opening the door he hurried through to the bedroom. To his relief, Joe was standing, leaning against the mantelpiece, apparently none the worse for his attack.

Assunta, happy that Joe had survived the terrible fit, was pummeling the cushion for his chair so that he could sit again. Rico went up to his father and, throwing his arms round his neck, broke into uncontrollable sobs. Joe held the boy in his arms for a time and, catching the look in Assunta's eyes, held the boy back and said, "I'm all right now, but I'm glad this happened. I was no longer sure that you still loved me, but now I know that you do." So the rift between father and son, which had troubled Assunta for so long, was finally mended.

On the following day, Rico phoned Joe's bets as usual to Mr. Thomson in Carluke. It was a sunny day and the shop was busy, but Joe was still not well enough to go downstairs. Rico placed his father's chair on the landing, and Joe sat out in the sun wearing his famous panama hat. Many passersby waved up to him, and he smilingly acknowledged their greetings. Perhaps the bitter times were coming to an end. That same night Assunta was relieved to see that Joe slept very peacefully. She thanked God that the worst was over and Joe was finally beginning the long journey to recovery.

Next morning Assunta and Rico rose early and, after studying for a while, Rico joined his mother in the shop and helped her to prepare for the day's business. At lunch time he took up his father's meal. Then he remained with Mrs. Irving in the shop to let his mother go upstairs. Time passed and Assunta did not return. The rattling of the water pipe in the backshop sent Mrs. Irving up to the house to see what was wrong. Rico became uneasy. The poor woman returned, her cheeks flushed, to tell him to close the shop at once and go upstairs as his father was very ill indeed.

When Rico entered the bedroom, he found Joe sitting on the edge of the bed with his legs dangling helplessly over the side. Assunta was weeping. Joe's eyes were already glazed and unseeing, and the horrible sound of the death rattle filled the room in laboured lamentations. Assunta went down on her knees and placed her arms round his waist, trying desperately to hold on to him, pleading with him not to leave her.

"Don't go, my darling, please don't go," she whimpered. Scarcely had she uttered these words than his eyes turned upwards and a last, desperate groan broke from his lips. Then he was gone. Helped by Mrs. Irving, Assunta and Rico moved him round until he lay on his back.

"Ah, Giuseppe, Giuseppe," moaned Assunta, and her eyes, opening wide, looked questioningly at Rico. He took her gently by the shoulders and made her sit down by the fire.

"It's all over, Ma," he said, "and he can't suffer any more."

The doctor arrived and Mrs. Irving showed him in. He merely glanced at Assunta, who was quite beside herself, went to the bed, looked at the dead man and said, "Yes, he is dead."

Rico went into the kitchen with the doctor who wrote out a death certificate. Then, leaving Assunta with Mrs. Irving, he went to the undertaker to arrange the funeral. And Assunta sat, staring vacantly at Giuseppe on the bed, knowing he was no longer there. She sobbed and shook her head from side to side. Her hands trembled and she felt cold. Mrs. Reid now came in and she and Mrs. Irving tried to persuade Assunta to lie on Rico's bed, for it was apparent to them she was in a state of shock. But she refused to leave the bedroom and began to weep.

Rico telephoned Byres Road, but when his Aunt Giulietta came onto the line, all he could say was, "Papà, papà," before he broke down. Giulietta knew at once what had happened and she tried to calm the boy, but her own voice betrayed her emotion and so they both stood silently crying.

The undertaker brought the coffin early in the evening and it was set up on trestles near the window. The Marsellas, who lived across the road, came to offer assistance. There was John and his wife, Rosa, and their aunt, a dear little lady called Pace, who had never married, and who had been a good friend to Assunta for some time. They all knelt and recited the rosary. As their voices rose, Assunta's thoughts went back to Imperatore and the evenings when they sat and prayed round the fire, she and Filomena, Joe and Benedetto. Now they were gone, Filomena . . . Benedetto . . . and Joe. But she could not really believe he was gone. Was it really posssible? Was this all just a horrible nightmare? Would she awaken to find him still there beside her in the bed, breathing easily as he had done on the Saturday night?

Next day Rico made his way to the local Catholic church to arrange for the funeral. When he rang the bell of the chapel house door, it was opened by the canon himself, a tallish man, slightly stooped, with grey hair over a stern face. When Rico explained his mission, the old man asked him to describe his father. Rico did so.

"Your father was a Mason," said the priest, "so he cannot be buried with the full rites of the church."

"I beg to differ, Father," said Rico. "My father was not a Mason. You are perhaps confusing him with someone else."

"Don't argue with me, boy," said the irate priest, "your father was a Mason, and that is the truth."

Quite taken aback by the vehemence of the old man, Rico asked helplessly, "Then what are we to do?"

"For your mother's sake and for your own, I shall permit a mass to be said, and Father Donahue may accompany the hearse to the grave, but the coffin may not be brought into the church during the mass," said the canon. Rico felt an uncontrollable rage at the old man's words and he could have taken him by the shoulders and shaken him to rid him of his stubbornness, but he controlled himself and walked away, crushed and humiliated. How could he tell Assunta when he got home that the local church would not accept his father's body?

When, with his lips trembling, he told his mother of his conversation with the priest, he saw a sudden fire in her eyes.

"I might have known something like this would happen," she said.

"*He* was the one who went to mass every Sunday when he was fit. You and I were the backsliders. So they are punishing *him*. I have a good mind to ask Mr. Whitelaw, the minister, to conduct the funeral service." But Giulietta, who was standing close by, was quite shocked by Assunta's words and she tried to persuade her, for the sake of appearances, to agree to the arrangements suggested by the canon.

"All right," said Assunta, "I shall go through with it, but they will never see us again," and she looked significantly at Rico.

The funeral was a wretched affair. The hearse was left standing at the church door, while a bitter Assunta knelt grinding her teeth with rage during the mass. Joe was buried at St. Kentigern's in Lambhill. A dry-eyed Assunta, listening to the meaningless murmuring of repetitious prayers at the graveside, felt physically sick at the sheer injustice of it all. Then her attention was distracted by the plaintive singing of birds, and she blessed them for offering their little chorus. It seemed to her to be more appropriate to the occasion.

When they were riding back in the taxi, she and Giulietta, *commare* Vittoria and Rico, the tears came and she wept bitterly. Then, turning to the ladies, Assunta suddenly hissed, "The rotten, ignorant hypocrites!" And, looking Giulietta straight in the face, she added, "Don't ever talk to me about priests again."

Chapter Twenty

1943 to 1960—Marking Time

For the first few weeks after Joe's death, Assunta went about impercipiently, keeping herself busy with chores that were not always necessary, feeling that life was after all quite meaningless. The horror of his last moments were nearly always with her, and she kept hearing his desperate, agonising, dying gasps. She scarcely ate and grew very thin. When she thought of the incidents following his death, she was horrified.

When she went to bed each night, she could not sleep. She tossed and turned in her agitation, her arm stretching out over and over again to feel his body that was no longer there beside her. Then she would curl up into a little ball of grief and cry. Her weeping was subdued and she whimpered like a wounded animal until the tears stopped and her throat was dry and painful with the strain. In the early hours of the morning, she would fall into a fitful slumber that did nothing to refresh her for the hard day of work ahead. That summer she leaned very heavily on Rico and, so well aware of her grief, he did his best to please her, seldom going out. Curiously, she stopped thinking of her husband as Joe, reverting to his Italian name Giuseppe.

People can be very cruel, and when Giuseppe's will was published, a lady customer, who lived close by in Low Main Street, came into the shop to make a purchase. As she was being served, she looked meaningfully over the counter at Assunta and said, "You'll be all right now, with all the money your husband has left you."

"What do you mean—all right?" Assunta asked with a wounded note in her voice. "How can I be all right without him? Do you think a little money can make up for his absence? If you do, then I hope some day you will find yourself in my position and you will realise then how unimportant the money really is!" The lady was sorry she had spoken and hurried out of the shop.

One night, completely worn out, Assunta fell asleep as soon as she got into bed. She dreamt Giuseppe was standing in the room. He came close, took her hand and spoke, "You must always sleep in this room, Sunta, for it is here I shall come for you."

"When, Giuseppe, when?"

"Within a short time that is really not in time,
within a short time that is really not in time,
within a short time that is really not in time . . ."

His voice faded with his image into the distance of another dimension.

Although she was comforted by this strange dream, Assunta went on mourning for Giuseppe. Rico began to take her to task, trying to persuade her to be more cheerful and to stop neglecting herself. In her stark, black, shapeless clothes, she was beginning to look like an old woman, he told her. But she paid little heed to his remonstrations. She dreamt more and more and reached a point where she looked forward to going to bed in order to dream. Since she was now resting, her appearance improved and the roses came back to her cheeks. Her deep mourning finally came to an end when she had two dreams in one night.

In the first dream, she was again a little girl in Filignano, and she was going with her parents to work in a field some distance from the village. When they arrived, she was so tired that she lay down under a tree and fell asleep. She must have slept the whole afternoon for when she awoke, Filomena and Benedetto had gone home, leaving her behind. How could they have forgotten her? She began to cry, for she did not know the way back to the main road. Presently a woodman came by and, seeing her in distress, offered to guide her to the main road. On the way they talked, and she learned he was Gaetano Cocozza. When he had seen her safely to the road, she started to walk home and turned once or twice to see him standing smiling at her with his axe slung over his shoulder. He waved to her. Even as she dreamt of this incident from so long ago, she remembered that it was only many years afterwards she had discovered Gaetano Cocozza was Giuseppe's father who had died so young. He had died so young! Giuseppe too had died so young!

She turned on her side and began to dream again. This time she was sitting beside Giuseppe in front of the kitchen fire at Imperatore, and they were alone. He was telling her the story of Violetta Coia whose husband, Carmine, had died when he was only thirty years of age.

He went on, "In the morning when they came to fetch the coffin, Violetta was hysterical with grief. She stood at the window directly above the house door, beating her breast and screaming with anguish. Then, when she looked down and saw the front of the coffin emerging from the doorway, she leaned forward and pulled her long black hair out in handfuls, throwing the strands down so that they fell on top of the coffin. She actually drew the very blood from her scalp."

And, as Giuseppe turned to look at Assunta, she saw, to her surprise, that he was smiling despite the sadness of what he had just been telling her. He spoke again, saying, "I don't want you to be pulling out your hair for me, though it is no longer auburn as it was when I first set eyes on you and fell in love!"

As the dream faded, Assunta awoke smiling. The sun was streaming in through the window, and in the early morning air she could hear the birds twittering outside. She knew then that she was to stop mourning for Giuseppe.

Later that same morning, she came upon the cup containing the twelve pips from the last lemon Giuseppe had enjoyed so much. When her good friend Tom Shortland of Glen Road next came in for his ration of sweets, she showed him the seeds and, as she knew his life centred round his garden and his greenhouse, where he grew marvellous flowers and plants as well as the most delicious tomatoes, she asked whether it would be worthwhile planting the seeds. He looked at them and fingered them.

"Yes, we'll have a try," he said.

Early in the previous year, he had given her some tomato plants and she had placed them in the shop window where, with the full warmth of the early morning sun they flourished, producing a healthy crop of tomatoes. With the help of Tom's green fingers, Assunta was sure she would soon have a lemon tree to remind her of Giuseppe.

The time for Rico's final examinations came. He was worried and nervous, and it was now Assunta's turn to encourage him, as he struggled through them. But he managed to pass, and soon afterwards Assunta found herself attending the graduation ceremony along with *commare* Vittoria and Giulietta. As they watched Rico walking on to the platform to be capped, she felt that Giuseppe was there beside her, as proud and happy as she was at that moment.

No sooner had Rico graduated than his army papers arrived. So, she was going to be on her own now! She shrugged her shoulders resignedly. She had been through worse trials. Even this prolonged war must sometime come to an end.

Rico's first posting was to the Pioneer Corps and he was sent to Buxton. There, he assured his mother in his weekly letters, he was having a grand time building Nissen huts. He spent the whole, cold

248

winter of 1944 in Buxton before being posted as an interpreter to an Italian prisoner-of-war camp at Belle Vue in Manchester. Assunta looked forward with great anticipation to his regular letters in which he described in vivid detail the ups and downs of life among the prisoners. He seemed to feel that the work he was doing was useful, and she could sense he was happy and making many friends among the Italians. By this time she had had the telephone installed in the back-shop and was able to look forward to Rico's call every Sunday evening.

Above all, Assunta kept herself busy and, although goods were scarce, she improvised and managed to do a good trade. When apples were in season, she would make candy apples using some of the shop's sugar ration. She also concocted other delicacies using cornflakes and melted chocolate, which she sold "off the ration" to eager customers. A new manager had been appointed in the Royal Bank at West Cross and, when Rico came home on leave, he became very friendly with this gentleman as they were both interested in good music.

The manager took an interest in helping Assunta with the shop books and discovered the poor soul had not been making adequate claims for shop expenses for her tax allowance and was consequently overpaying to a considerable tune. He soon set the situation right and Assunta was able to start saving money, placing some in the bank. The rest she deposited instinctively in an old biscuit tin that she hid at the back of a shelf in the backshop.

One morning Tom Shortland came in with a lovely little lemon plant. Twelve had actually grown from the seeds, but they had all died except two. He would keep one himself in his greenhouse. The other was for Assunta. She placed it in the window beside the tomato plants and watered it faithfully. For a few weeks, it seemed to thrive. Then one cold morning she came down to find it was wilting. It died in the course of the week. Assunta felt she had lost a friend. When she told Tom, he said, "I'll give you the other one but not until next year. By that time it will be indestructible, believe me."

The year 1945 began with vague hopes that the war might soon be over, and for the first time in years Assunta felt optimistic and found herself singing one day. As Easter approached, she telephoned Giulietta and Vittoria and made a daring suggestion. Rico had been pleading with her for some time to go down to Manchester and meet his prisoner friends. Why should they not close their shops for a week and have a holiday? Giulietta and Vittoria thought it was a grand idea, and a week later the three of them were on the Glasgow-Manchester train laden with all sorts of good things they had baked and cooked.

They were going to be staying with a Mrs. Collins who had befriended Rico on the day he arrived in Manchester when she saw him marching along the road to the camp near her house carrying his rifle and his kit bag. Mrs. Collins walked with the aid of a stick, and she was one of those rare people who are good through and through. Her large, smiling, luminous eyes revealed the kindness of her heart and the nobility of her soul.

A fever of excitement and anticipation swept through the camp of 126 Italian Labour Battalion on the morning when the visit of the three Italian ladies from Scotland was due. Indeed it was a special occasion for a gunless guard of honour stood drawn up at the camp gate, while British and Italian officers and NCOs stood ready to welcome them. Rico had borrowed the large Chevrolet, which served the camp, to drive round to the Collins house to pick them up.

When they drove in through the gate, there was a great cheer. Then, when the ladies stepped out, there were loud sighs of nostalgia and admiration as the Italians remembered their mothers back in Italy. Many a sentimental tear was shed, and when the ladies had been introduced to the officers and NCOs, the men who formed the camp personnel also surged forward to shake hands.

Someone called out, "*Viva le tre mamme!* Hurrah for the three mothers!" and although only Assunta could legitimately claim the right as a mother, Giulietta and Vittoria smiled with pleasure, acknowledging the greeting. So the "three mothers" were taken on a triumphal tour of the camp, calling at the tailors' shop, the cobblers' shop, the bakery, the pasta factory, and the kitchen. Then they were treated to refreshments in the British Officers' Mess before proceeding to the quarters of the *capo campo*, or camp leader, and the Italian officers one of whom, to Giulietta's awed surprise, was a close relation of His Holiness the Pope, as Rico told his aunt. What the cad did not tell her was that the captain, despite his connection with the Holy Father, was an agnostic.

In the course of the week, the three mothers made a tour of the hostels in the Lancashire area where the prisoners were stationed, and they were thrilled by the reception they received everywhere from these home-starved, affection-hungry men. The climax of their visit was a special show given in their honour at the camp in Manchester.

After a concert performed by the camp orchestra with their great singer Raffaele Turco, a cook who hailed from Naples, a special guest appearance was made by the Percivals and Rico. Now the Percivals were well known to the Italian prisoners in England, Scotland, and Wales, for they had given of their services for more than two years touring the various camps with their music. Arthur Percival, second violinist and sub-leader of the Hallé Orchestra, performed with his wife, Winifred, pianist and singer, who had been born in Fiume and was bi-lingual. Rico and groups of prisoners from the camp had often been invited to their charming house, *Fiumara*, in Victoria Park. A warm friendship had sprung up between them.

When the curtains were drawn for the second half of the show and raised a moment later to reveal the Percivals, there was thunderous applause. Then Rico came on to the stage and sang a few Italian songs to their accompaniment, ending with Assunta's favourite "Maria Mari'." A hearty singsong brought the show to a close, and the "three mothers" were then escorted to the stage where they were presented with bouquets of flowers. It was this visit to Manchester that dispelled the last of the sadness from Assunta's heart.

On the 7th of May 1945, the Germans surrendered at Rheims, bringing the war in Europe to an end, and Assunta began to look forward to Rico's return home. For a time this was delayed as he felt it was his duty to remain in Manchester until all his prisoner friends had been repatriated.

Assunta was disappointed and then, to add to her despondency, she lost her pets. Baldassare, her cat, was killed one day by a passing car when he was crossing the road to meet the fish man. A week later Assunta, coming down to open the shop one morning, missed Dickie's welcoming trill. The poor little feathered friend was lying dead on the bottom of his cage. She put the cage out and decided she would have no more pets. Yet every morning she still went out to feed the birds at the back of the property. When one feels most deserted, a new friend always appears.

One of Assunta's most regular ice-cream customers was Mrs. Marshall, who lived with her husband, Willie, and her daughter, Betty, in a cottage house in Glen Road. The Marshalls had lost their son, Stuart, a flying officer in the RAF who had been shot down over the Channel. Rico had always been on good terms with Betty who was one of the most attractive girls in Wishaw. He always referred to her as "Cleopatra."

Mrs. Marshall, coming in one day for ice cream, found Assunta in difficulties, as her part-time assistant had failed to turn up. Without waiting to be asked, Mrs. Marshall slipped off her coat, donned an apron, and in no time was busy clearing dishes from the tables and washing up in the backshop. This was the start of a very long friendship, for Mrs. Marshall came out once or twice every week to help in the evenings. But she would not accept any payment for her help. Bored at home, she found the activity in the café stimulating.

The year 1946 did not see an end to rationing, and it was hard work trying to make reasonable profits on a limited turnover. Then, at long last, in September 1946 Rico was demobilised. Assunta was overjoyed to have him home, but after the first few days he showed no signs of settling down. He was cross and restless and felt confined in the shop. He was also very impatient with the customers and could give them the sharp edge of his tongue. This she could not forgive, and told him so in so many words. He shrugged his shoulders, put on his jacket, and went out. When he returned an hour later, he was tipsy. Assunta was displeased. She made him drink some strong coffee, then, when she had a moment, she sat down at the table in the backshop and spoke to him.

"I see you have picked up some bad habits in the army, my boy. But when you come home to me, you leave your bad habits behind. Do you understand?'

Rico looked at his mother and smiled blearily. "Yes, boss, you're the boss, boss," he said.

Later in the day, when he had sobered up, he was exploring the shelves in the backshop when he came upon the old biscuit tin containing her hard-earned savings.

"What's this, Ma?" he called out. "Have you been holding out on me? Stashing the cash away when I was away fighting for you, eh?"

"Just put that tin back where you got it," she said, "That's for a rainy day."

"No time like the present then," said Rico as he looked out of the window and saw it was pouring outside, He sat down at the table, emptied the tin, and counted the contents. There were over seven hundred pounds in single-pound notes and fivers. Rico whistled.

"You must have known I fancy buying a car, Ma." What could the poor woman do? He was as stubborn as his father when he had a notion for something. So she let him have the money, and he bought a second-hand car with which he had nothing but trouble. When he got rid of it after two months, he sold it for two hundred pounds. So he squandered his mother's hard-earned money on a piece of junk. Yet she was not angry with him, just disappointed because he was so pig-headed. Having been in the army, he now thought he was a man. But he had a long way to go, she thought.

Antonio and Josie were now home in Byres Road, and Josie was still not showing any sign of taking to himself a wife. *Commare* Vittoria was an incorrigible matchmaker. She had tried more than once to find a suitable match for Rico, arranging "accidental" meetings in the backshop of the Continental with eligible young Italian ladies, such as

Lucia Coia, daughter of Parisio and Assunta from Milngavie. But without success. Now she was determined to find a wife for Josie. So she went off to Filignano with him, and the search began.

In no time she had found the very person for Josie, a charming, lovely girl called Antoniella Cocozza, one of a large family, all girls. She was really very beautiful with her large, smiling brown eyes, and when her lips parted, they revealed a perfect set of even, pearly white teeth. Now Josie was not exactly good-looking, but he was a likeable, steady chap and Antoniella took to him. The marriage was quickly arranged and on the 29th of January 1947 was celebrated with a bright nuptial mass in the church at Filignano.

When the happy couple were brought to Glasgow by their triumpant Aunt Vittoria a few weeks later, Antoniella was already carrying her first child. A great reception was held in the Ca'doro in Union Street, and it was one of the very rare occasions when Assunta and Rico had a day out together. It was a very jolly affair and Antonio, as usual, having had too much to drink, gave a spirited recital of Italian songs. Assunta was delighted to see many old friends she had not met for years.

Used to the varied routine of his work in the army, Rico became more and more bored with the café. He tried to persuade his mother to sell out and move to a small house somewhere but she would not hear of it. Then, in the spring of 1947, they received an unexpected visit from Mr. Archibald MacKinven. He wondered whether Enrico would be interested in an assistant-lectureship in the Italian Department at the university.

Rico was pleased to accept the offer. His appointment was due to start in the autumn. So he decided, before assuming his new post, to have a few weeks in Italy and, selfishly leaving his tired mother to cope as best she could with her limited staff, he bought a 16mm cine-camera and went off on a grand tour of Italy. There he visited many of his former prisoner friends who had been repatriated and were successfully taking up the strands of their lives.

When Rico returned a few days before starting at the university, she observed a great change in him. He seemed more considerate and was very subdued. Something had evidently happened to him in Italy that left him so chastened. But Assunta did not pry. She just observed and formed her own conclusions. One thing she knew for certain. Such submissiveness in him could only mean one thing. He had been or still was in love.

One morning in April 1948, Tom Shortland arrived with the other lemon tree. He felt the time had come for it to be tended by its mistress.

Assunta placed it carefully in the shop window where she was still growing tomatoes, taking care not to water it too frequently. It thrived in the summer of 1948, and it gave her immense pleasure to see it growing each week. It was a link with Giuseppe who was, as always, constantly in her thoughts. Twice a year she made the journey to his grave in Lambhill, yet she never really felt near to him there. His presence was still strongest in the room where she slept, and he still came frequently into her dreams—happy dreams of times past and those still to come. For she never doubted they would be together again.

In the autumn of that same year, Assunta and Rico were obliged to buy the property in which the café was situated. Had they not done so, they would have been forced to get out. The whole transaction was completed within a month, and Assunta could not help thinking they had perhaps acted impulsively. They now owned the whole property comprising the pub and the café and the houses above them, the small block of houses behind, the auction room where the McNamaras still did business, and all the ground down to the next feu. Rico assured his mother that he had some big plans in the offing.

"I wonder what he is up to now?" she asked herself. She was not long in finding out. Rico saw the purchase of the property as an opportunity to realise one of his most cherished dreams—to own his own little cinema and make his own films. With tremendous energy he set about fulfilling his plan. The McNamaras were asked to find other premises, and soon remarkable renovations were begun in the old auction room. In a few months, it was speedily converted from a dingy, bare, rather evil-smelling hall into an attractive little cinema. The décor was simple but effective, set off by lavish velvet curtains mounted on the proscenium. The auditorium housed over a hundred tip-up seats, and the projection room was equipped with the finest American 16mm projectors and a good-quality amplifier. Beyond the projection room, a cutting room was fitted out for film editing, and an adjacent committee room also served as a book library containing dozens of volumes on every aspect of the art of the film.

While these wondrous activities were being carried out, Assunta kept slaving behind the counter to earn the money to pay for her son's extravagances, for he had already managed to spend most of the small fortune his father had left. But Assunta did not mind. As long as she was able to work, she was perfectly contented. Besides, she really enjoyed the ceaseless activity and the constant coming and going.

Then Rico gathered together some cine enthusiasts and formed a film unit. Films were planned and quickly put into production. The actresses and actors were recruited from the café customers, some of whom were already playing an active part in local amateur dramatics. A film society was constituted. Enrolments were promising and soon there were more than two hundred members. Like a veritable tornado, Rico moved in and out of this small hive of artistic animation, burning the midnight oil to write scripts for films or to prepare lectures. Assunta looked on and never stopped wondering. She knew that his frenzy of action was a self-imposed distraction to relieve the sadness that still gnawed at his heart, for she could see it in his eyes in unguarded moments.

Within a year, Rico made a name for himself as an outstanding and imaginative producer of fantasy films, winning many national awards. The telephone never stopped ringing. It was like living in a little Hollywood. In the midst of it all, Assunta kept sensing her son's loneliness. Her participation in his film world was confined to the late hours when the shop was closed and everyone else had gone. Then he would take her round to the cinema and instal her comfortably in the back row to see the run-through of the film for the following night's show. The lights dimmed and the MGM lion roared from the screen to announce a classic musical or a great Garbo drama. Assunta enjoyed these midnight matinées,and it was even more exciting when she was the first to see the completed version of one of Rico's new films.

It struck her that most of the films had a dreamlike quality, and, although she could not always follow the complicated structure of the sequences, she was most sensitive to the moods he created, which, to her great concern, still revealed the lingering sadness he harboured for someone he had obviously lost. Still she never questioned him, hoping he might one day confide in her and, when he came to reveal what had been troubling him for so long, she would be able to help him get over it.

By this time, despite her earlier resolution, Assunta had three new pets. There was a magnificent Russian-blue cat whom Rico called Szostakowicz. Assunta just called him Szosti. Then there was a tiny female kitten, also grey, who never grew. With her squeaky miaowing soprano, she simply had to be called Toti after Toti Dal Monte. One day Rico arrived with an Alsatian pup, and Assunta told him at once to take it back. Then, when he put the little creature on the floor, it looked up plaintively and produced a little puddle. This she could not resist, and the pup was allowed to stay. He was called Ric.

Everything seemed to be happening fast. Assunta found a new shop assistant, a young woman who had been a nurse. Her name was Ninnie. Assunta changed it to Minnie. A good worker, Minnie had great patience with the customers. She had a gift for putting cheeky boys in their place with some well-aimed sarcasm. Her rather loud, piercing voice, trained to be heard in a busy ward, commanded respect. Minnie was to remain with Assunta for many years, although she and Rico could not agree and fought incessantly.

The café regulars of the 1930s and 1940s had now been succeeded by a postwar generation of teenagers, but some of the "old gang" were still present. Jim Thomson played a very active part in the film unit and film society, acting in some of Rico's films. Robert Whitelaw was practising medicine away from Wishaw, but, when he came to visit his parents, he never failed to call on Assunta, always greeting her with the same words: "How are you, Assunta my dear? You are looking more beautiful than ever."

Assunta's pets were a source of joy for her. Ric had grown into a fine dog, a very gentle creature and he would sit on the shop step allowing himself to be stroked by the passersby. Szosti was jealous of the dog and would have nothing to do with him. Toti, on the other hand, loved the warmth of the dog's body and often curled up near his tummy and slept blissfully. When Ric was taken for a walk down the glen, he would grab Toti by the skin of the neck and take her along, dangling contentedly from his large mouth. One day a lady walking up the road screamed when she saw the tiny cat hanging from the dog's mouth, mistaking her for a grey rat.

But Ric took a painful skin disease and, despite all the care and attention given him by a caring Assunta, the condition did not improve. He became very thin, his ribs standing out, his poor doggy face covered in sores. Assunta found him one morning in his bed in the corner of the living room, showing very little sign of life. The vet was called but shook his head when he examined him. He gave him an injection. Ric slipped quickly away. Assunta wept sorely.

Rico had now enlarged the house upstairs considerably. Taking in the flat next door, he made a nice home decorated in a very Continental style. Yet Assunta refused to cook upstairs, preferring to use the back-shop. A glass-covered porch was built on the landing outside the flat, and in one half a toilet was installed. The other half formed a small square vestibule, and it was here that Assunta decided to house her beloved lemon tree. Under the warm glass, caressed by the sun's rays, the tree grew luxuriantly, its lustrous, vivid green leaves weaving a pleasant pattern of colour and in the warm weather exuding the slightly acidic perfume of the lemon.

The years 1950, 1951, and 1952 passed all too quickly, and one day Assunta received a letter from Filignano. It was from her old friend Antonia's sister, Gaetana. Gaetana had a daughter called Palma who was anxious to come to Scotland to work. Would Assunta be interested in employing the girl? Since Rico now slept in his own bedroom at the other end of the flat, there was a spare bed in the kitchen recess. This gave Assunta a great idea. It would be marvellous to have Antonia's niece living with her. She would take Gaetana's daughter in and give her as good a training as Giulietta had given her so many years before.

A few weeks later, Palma Valente arrived in Wishaw. She brought with her three large suitcases, two of which were crammed with parcels of cheese, sausages, ham, and dried fruit. She wondered why, in such a busy train, she had enjoyed the whole compartment to herself from London to Glasgow, but when the cases were opened, the strong odour of goat's milk cheese spread through the flat and the windows had to be opened wide. Rico arranged to distribute the carefully labelled parcels to Palma's relatives in Lanarkshire as quickly as possible.

Eighteen years of age, Palma was a typical, unsophisticated, southern Italian beauty with marked African features and traits. Although she was not stout, she was very full in the chest and her thick-set body sat on spindly legs ending in two large feet. She had a very strong neck, having carried heavy weights on her head since she was a child. She bubbled with laughter and high spirits and when she spoke in a rather nasal, adenoidal voice, she reminded one of Luise Rainer, the great Jewish MGM star. Indeed her features were not altogether unlike Rainer's. She had the large, questioning, brown eyes, but the oval face had been cast in a rougher mould.

She was brimming with energy, and nothing troubled her when it came to heavy work. She washed and scrubbed, heaved and carried, and was quick to follow Assunta's instructions. But she had one rather disconcerting habit. She would insist on carrying things on her head. When serving the sitting room, she would balance a tray with two cups of coffee on her head all the way from the backshop and set it down with panache before her astonished customers. Once she made a public spectacle of herself by carrying three bags of provisions down the length of the main street, one in either hand and the third on the crown of her head.

At first her English vocabulary was limited, but she learned rapidly. She had indeed picked up some meaningful expletives from the Americans who had passed through Filignano and, as the boys in Belhaven Café could not resist teasing her, she would lose her temper with them and call them all sons of bitches. Once she used a stronger expression that shocked Assunta. A conspiracy was hatched to soften this bad habit. Rico told her that if she really wished to insult someone, the worst word she could use was RASCAL. He then passed this information on to the boys. One evening when Jim Thomson and a quiet, mischievous lad, Ian Paterson, had been teasing the life out of the poor girl, she flared up and turning on them, gave them a mouthful ending with "You, you, you bloody RASCALS!" at which Jim and Ian threw up their hands in horror, their faces aghast. Palma smirked with great satisfaction and, catching Rico's amused eye, nodded thankfully as if to say, "That should shut them up, once and for all."

Perhaps because she had such big feet, Palma could not resist buying shoes. Almost every week she bought pair after pair. She always had at least half a dozen pairs down in the shop and kept changing them in the course of the day. With her funny little ways, she was a constant cause of merriment and Assunta was happy that she had her. Assunta paid her a good wage and opened a bank account in her name. Deposits were made regularly every week. Palma approved of this arrangement. She was saving a dowry for herself. For she was determined to get a husband. That had been her main reason for leaving Filignano where a girl could be considered old at twenty-two. She now had four or five years to save for a husband.

One day Palma had spent the whole morning cleaning the flat before coming down to eat. After lunch she took over from Assunta who went upstairs to rest for an hour as her varicose veins were troubling her in the hot weather. When Assunta unlocked the outer door of the vestibule, she made to greet her lemon tree, as she always spoke to it, but to her horror the tree was not there. She thought at first Palma had put it in the living room, but it was not there. She looked in the kitchen. No tree. In her bedroom. No sign of it. Leaving the outside door open, she rushed downstairs, through the backshop into the counter and, grabbing Palma by the shoulders, whirled her round and asked, "The lemon tree? What have you done with my lemon tree?"

Palma had decided it was an unbecoming nuisance in the porch and had taken it round to the refuse area behind the cinema, where the dustbins were. Assunta could have slapped the girl. She grabbed her by the arm and propelled her to the back door, out into the narrow passage round to the dustbins. Thank God, the tree was still there! A frightened Palma was now shedding tears. She had never seen her aunt look so angry before. She was made to carry the tree back up to the porch, and when it was again safely in its place, Assunta turned to her and warned, "Don't you every lay a finger on my lemon tree again or I shall kill you!" From that day Palma treated the tree with respect.

When Minnie came to work one morning, she was accompanied by a fully grown Alsatian dog. She knew how much Assunta missed

Ric. This dog was much darker than Ric and had a fiercer aspect. His master, a friend of Minnie, wanted to be rid of the dog. Would Assunta be interested? She was not really very keen and was hesitating.

At that moment Rico walked in, took one look at the dog and exclaimed, "That's the very dog I need for a new film I am planning to shoot in a few weeks!" That was how Rinty found a new home at Belhaven Café.

A letter arrived one day from Siena. After reading it, Rico went pale and quickly disappeared upstairs. Having seen his reaction, Assunta knew something was wrong and she followed him. He was not in the living room. She knocked at the door of his bedroom. He called to her to come in. He was sitting at the window, gazing out. She could see he was very upset. The letter was still in his hand. She sat down beside him and took his arm, trying to comfort him without asking the reason for his distress. They sat in silence for a considerable time and occasionally he sighed deeply.

"Is there anything you want to tell me?" asked Assunta. He sighed again and his lips trembled, but still he could not bring himself to speak. Assunta rose to leave him but, as she reached the door, he called her back and made her sit again beside him. Again she took his arm. Then, plucking up courage, he began, painfully, to blurt out his long, sad story.

In the summer of 1947, he had fallen in love with a girl in Siena who was engaged to a wealthy industrialist. She returned his affection, and they went away together to Florence. Her father had followed them there, and there had been an angry scene between him and Rico. Gloria had gone back to Siena with her father, and Rico had not seen her again.

Assunta now knew why she had found Rico so changed when he returned from Italy in the autumn of 1947. But why was he so upset now? What news was in the letter he had just received from Siena? He explained that he had recently written to his friend Luciano Turi in Siena, asking for news of Gloria. Now Turi had written to say that Gloria had never married her wealthy fiancé. She had fallen into bad health and died in a sanatorium in the autumn of 1948.

While Assunta did not resent Rico's filming activities, she was disappointed that each year, when the café was at its busiest, he would leave her to go off to Italy or France for weeks on end. The loneliness of her summers was relieved only by the sheer pressure of work and the friendly presence of Palma by her side. Rico's film fever grew more acute, and in 1955 he gave up his post at the university to devote himself more and more to film production. Whenever Rico took a decisive step in his life, he liked to celebrate by treating himself to something very special.

Now he bought an expensive MG sports car. He insisted on taking Assunta out for a spin every week, leaving Minnie, Palma, and Mrs. Marshall in charge of the shop. One day they went on a long trip to sunny Dunbar. His mania for speed asserting itself, Rico pressed hard on the accelerator pedal and Assunta, glancing at the speedometer, saw that they were doing 110 miles an hour. She turned to him casually and remarked, "I *know* you are doing more than 50 miles an hour!" Rico nearly choked.

Despite Rico's frequent suggestions, Assunta never again relished the idea of a holiday in Filignano. She felt if she went there, her memories of it would be spoiled, for the house on Imperatore had been badly damaged in the war and many of her old friends including the Di Bonas, Peppino and Maria, had perished during the bombardments that ruined many houses in the village. But Giulietta went back to Filignano often. Without consulting either Assunta or Rico, she arranged to have repairs done to the house to make it habitable. Then, upon returning from her holiday, she went out to Wishaw to ask Rico to pay for the repairs. Since he had not been consulted beforehand, he refused. This caused some bad feeling between him and his aunt, but Assunta did not intervene.

At the start of 1958, Giulietta fell ill. She died on the 29th of May. Her funeral reopened some of the grief in Assunta's heart. Their lives had been so intertwined that Assunta could not help feeling, as the coffin was lowered into the grave beside Eugenio, that a part of her own life was coming to an end.

That summer, Assunta's health took a turn for the worse. She spent some weeks in bed with varicose ulcers. When she was able to get up again after treatment, she found her energy had gone. Everything she did required a great effort on her part. She felt she was beginning to wind down.

Then, as 1958 was ending, Palma became very restless. She had not yet managed to find a husband, and, when she formed an attachment with a lad from Cleland, Assunta did not approve because she knew he drank. So Palma decided to go back to Filignano where, even at the age of twenty-three, she would find a man on the strength of her dowry. She left with two large cases filled with clothes and a large trunk packed with chocolate and shoes. On her way to Italy, she decided to stop in Paris for a few days to visit her Aunt Antonia.

Four weeks later she sent an urgent request asking for all her money to be transferred to a Paris bank, as she was going to be married. In her letter she enclosed a photo of her fiancé, a very handsome young man. Assunta and Rico were delighted she had done so well for herself and made the necessary arrangements for the transfer of her money. Soon some snapshots of her wedding arrived, and it was evident from the broad smile on Palma's face that she had found her ideal man. Assunta, taking a closer look at the groom's face, thought she detected a sinister expression in his eyes. She shuddered as she put the snap away.

The year 1959 was a very trying one for Assunta. Her health was poor, yet she could not bring herself to consider the possibility of giving up the business as she could not imagine the West Cross without its Belhaven Café, in which, to her disappointment Rico was not interested. He, too, had struck a bad patch. With the increasing popularity of television, all was not going well with the film society. The inevitable eventually happened, and the society had to be wound up. For years Rico had been trying to break into professional films, but, although he had worked in an assistant capacity on some productions in Italy and France, it had not amounted to anything of a permanent nature. Yet he went on prolifically turning out his own films, which not only involved him in considerable expenditure, but, in Assunta's opinion, became more and more impenetrable. He was so determined to be serious, she thought, when in actual fact his best films were comedies. But could she tell him this? She might as well talk to the walls.

One morning when she awoke, Assunta could not get up. When Rico came stumbing into the kitchen about an hour later, she called out to him for help. He ran downstairs and telephoned for the doctor. After examining Assunta, the doctor spoke to Rico and told him she was suffering from complete exhaustion. She would require to stay in bed for two weeks at the very least. So Rico had to roll up his sleeves and work in the café. To add to his troubles, Rinty, who still had a very wild streak in him, developed a nasty habit of tearing children's clothes. If he saw a pair of boys fighting on the pavement outside the shop, he would jump up to separate them, tearing their trousers. It became a costly business, replacing torn trousers every week.

So Rico brought the dog upstairs where he would lie faithfully by Assunta's bed and whine, complaining about the doleful treatment that was being meted out to him. Assunta made him sit up and talked to him, telling him he was being punished for tearing so many trousers. He seemed to understand. When Minnie came up with her tea, she told her to take the dog back down to the shop as he had promised to be good.

Minnie murmured, "They're all nuts in this house!" before leading Rinty away.

But Rinty kept his promise. He stopped tearing boys' trousers. He took to chasing cars and motor-bikes instead. It was so much more fun. One day he barked and chased a motorcyclist and the poor chap, unnerved, ran into a lamp standard. Fortunately he escaped unhurt, but Rico had to pay for a new headlamp. A week later Rinty made his last chase and was injured under the wheels of a bus. That was the end of poor Rinty.

Assunta and Rico now knew they could not continue to run the café. They made it known to *compare* Antonio, who was in contact with so many Italians, that they were anxious to sell the business. But it was difficult to find a purchaser. Plans had been passed by the local council for road improvements at the West Cross, and the future existence of the property was very much in the balance. So prospective buyers came, made enquiries, and lost interest.

Then one of Assunta's goddaughters, Lita Furetta, came visiting out of the blue with her husband, Alfredo, and their young daughter. Assunta had not seen them for years. They wanted to buy the shop but would like to rent it first for a trial period of two years. In that time the fate of the building would be decided by the local authority. Assunta and Rico accepted their proposal, and it was agreed that the Furettas would take over at the beginning of April.

Rico could not miss the chance of making a film about Belhaven Café before it changed hands. So a few weeks of the winter of 1959 to 1960 were spent in making a comedy starring Assunta as Mrs. Joe, the stern proprietrix of the café, who had to put up with the erratic behaviour of two lazy, young scallywags, Gerry and Norman, who applied for the part-time job advertised in the shop window for shop assistants and general washer-uppers. Although she was physically exhausted, a brave Assunta struggled through this trying experience, turning in a neat performance as herself. Gerry was played by a quiet, shy lad called Gerald Scanlan, whom Assunta naturally renamed Gerry Scandal, while Norman was played by the mischievous son of a very dear friend of Assunta, who lived in the local housing scheme known as Wishawhill. Norman's mother, whose maiden name was Giorgina Cocozza, had been twice married, Norman being the son of the second husband.

Many years before, Giuseppe had been approached by Giorgina's father, Vincenzo Cocozza, for a loan of money as he was having difficulties in making ends meet in his little café in Craigneuk. Giuseppe had very willingly lent him the money, but, as times were hard, only part of the debt had been repaid when Vincenzo suddenly died. Soon after her father's death, Giorgina happened to call at Belhaven Café one day, and she sat and had a cup of coffee with Giuseppe and Assunta. In the course of their conversation, Giuseppe mentioned the money that was still owing to him. Giorgina, naturally, had not known about the loan. But she was a young woman of integrity. She asked Giuseppe how much was outstanding.

When she was told, she said, "Well, I couldn't possibly offer to pay back such an amount in cash, but I feel my father's debts should be honoured. Would you consider employing me so that I could pay you back?"

As they were needing extra help, Giuseppe and Assunta accepted Giorgina's offer with pleasure. So she spent the better part of the summer repaying Vincenzo's debt. Giorgina was one of those rare people who restored one's faith in the human race.

The first three months of 1960 passed and soon it was time for the Furettas to move into Belhaven Café. Although Assunta no longer had misgivings about giving up the business since, after all, it was her own goddaughter who was going to be there, she did have anxious moments wondering what lay before her and Rico in an uncertain future.

When the stocktaking was over on the last evening of March, Assunta, Rico, Lita, Alfredo, and their little girl sat in the backshop for a last cup of coffee. Mrs. Marshall had left as soon as the shop was closed, taking a last affectionate look round the Kiddies' Corner where she had spent so many happy hours filling the sweet bottles with boilings and slipping the occasional Carluke Ball into her mouth. Minnie had already left some time before to return to her nursing.

When Assunta handed over the keys of the shop to Alfredo and Lita, she felt a flutter at her heart. Then she put on her coat, and Rico took her arm to help her upstairs as she seemed quite overcome. They heard the Furettas driving away as they slowly made their way up the long stairs. When they reached the landing, Assunta turned to Rico and asked, "Do you think we have done the right thing?"

Chapter Twenty-one

1960 to 1977—Going Away

Next morning Assunta was awakened by the smell of freshly-made toast. Then Rico appeared with a breakfast tray.

"Good morning, Susie," he said. He had taken to the irritating habit of calling her Susie, a name she detested.

"How does it feel to be retired?" he went on.

"You mean tired!" she answered, as she sat up to take the tray from him. But the light breakfast of tea and buttered toast was welcome, and she settled down to enjoy it. She could hear Rico bustling around in the kitchen, humming contentedly to himself. He was so glad to be rid of the café, she thought, but he might yet live to regret the step they had taken.

That first day in the house was strange. It marked the start of an entirely different routine, a way of life to which she was not accustomed. To have time to sit and eat undisturbed was an unusual luxury. Then there was the silence. She missed the constant ringing of the bell in the shop every time the door opened to admit a customer.

Rico, noting her preoccupation and mistaking it for depression, suggested that they should go out after lunch. So, for the first time in many years, mother and son walked together up the street to do some shopping. She saw many changes and everywhere new faces and strange people. There was a time when she could have walked the whole length of the street and known everyone she met. A dozen times they were stopped by old customers. They were all greatly surprised to see Mrs. Joe out shopping.

When they came home, she prepared the evening meal while Rico set the table. When they had eaten, he helped with the dishes before going out. Then she found herself alone. Walking idly round the rooms with a duster in her hand, she paused to look out of Rico's bedroom window. It was a fine evening, and people were coming and going in the street. She could hear the ringing of the till in the café. This gave her an idea. She would pop down and give Lita a hand. She would not offer to serve at the counter. If only Lita would allow her to wash some dishes in the backshop where she felt so much at home!

When she knocked at the back door, it was a strange girl who answered. Lita had lost no time in employing new staff. Then she came forward herself with an enquiring look. Assunta explained she had come down to give some help. Lita rather grudgingly let her in. Assunta sensed a certain hostility in her goddaughter's attitude.

There was a large pile of unwashed dishes, and Assunta started to work. But Lita never came through to speak to her godmother, and Assunta was embarrassed at having to make trite conversation with the girl who brought in the dirty dishes. So Assunta spent a very uncomfortable hour in the backshop and when she had cleared the dishes, she told the girl to inform Mrs. Furetta that she was going upstairs. As she made her way up to the house, she felt deeply mortified and her lips trembled as she put the key in the lock and let herself in. Fortunately Rico was not long in coming home, and she put on the kettle for a cup of tea. She did not tell him she had been downstairs.

Next morning when Rico was going for his newspaper, Lita called out to him from the shop door saying she wanted a word with him. When he came back from the newsagent's, he found himself standing before an angry Lita.

"Your mother," she began in an indignant tone of voice, "thinks she is still the mistress of this shop. She came down last night and took over in the backshop. Well, I want you to tell her *I* am now the mistress and she is not wanted here."

Rico looked at her cynically. He had known her for some time and in a moment of doubtful taste had even engaged in a mild flirtation with her some years before. Marriage had not changed her. She was still shallow and unfeeling.

"I'll give my mother your message," he said quietly and turned on his heel. When he told Assunta about the short exchange with Lita, she nodded sadly and muttered, "I won't trouble her again, you can rest assured."

Lita prided herself on her great cleanliness, but one morning Assunta saw a crate full of empty, dirty milk bottles lying at the back door. When she looked out from the landing later in the day, the dirty bottles were still there in full view.

Most of my customers will not know I have given up the shop, she thought, *and they will imagine I have left these filthy bottles outside.*

When she thought no one could see her, she slipped downstairs, lifted the heavy metal crate, and carried it up to the kitchen where she washed the bottles one by one before carrying them down again and placing them neatly beside the back door.

So the sunny days of the summer passed lingeringly for Assunta, and she spent her time in the house cleaning and washing with her

Beatty washing machine or rinsing out dusters at her white enamel sink situated directly above the one she had used for so many years downstairs. She never took off the floral aprons that she loved to wear. Indeed she felt quite undressed without her apron. Standing at the sink, she would wave out to old customers who happened to be passing.

When friends called she was always asked the same question, "How does it feel to be retired?" and she came out with a new reply: "It's just a change of sink!"

At first, many of her former customers would come to visit her, telling her how they missed her in the shop, and she would make them a cup of coffee. She baked every week and they all relished her delicious rice cake and the *Gnocchi dolci*, crisp, biscuity, lemon-flavoured bows fried in deep olive oil. She called them "knocks." But as the weeks passed, her visiting customers slipped away until her only regular visitors were Mrs. Marshall and Mrs. Martin and Jean. In the evenings she would sit, still wearing her apron, with her legs stretched out on the sofa and read. She enjoyed the gossip that passed for news in the daily papers and spent a great part of her mealtimes discussing what she had read with Rico. He realised that his mother was becoming a mine of useless information on all the crimes and scandals in the country.

As autumn drew near, Assunta began to wonder when Rico would decide what he was going to do with his life. His filming activities were drawing to a close as he was not getting any work. Then, one day, fate took a hand. He happened to meet the secretary from Wishaw High School, when he was out shopping, and she asked if he could help out for a couple of weeks teaching French, as a teacher had been taken ill and they could not get a temporary replacement. Rico accepted.

At the end of the two weeks, he was asked to stay on. Assunta was pleased as he was near home and could come back for lunch every day. Some of his colleagues from the school came to visit, and soon there was a regular coming and going of visitors, which Assunta enjoyed. None of her Italian friends came to see her with the exception of the Marsellas' aunt, Miss Pace Macari, who lived with her niece across the road. She and Pace were such good friends, and they could spin each other tales about the old country, speaking the dialect.

The winter of 1960 to 1961 passed uneventfully and then one day early in February, Rico, who had been to Byres Road, brought the sad news of the death of their old friend Parisio Coia of Milngavie. A week later a long letter from Antonia in Paris came to shock them with the tragic news that Palma was dead.

After her marriage in Paris, Palma had kept in touch and when her first child was born, she sent a snapshot of the baby with his father.

266

Antonia explained in her letter that all had not gone well between Palma and her husband who had turned out to be an idler, a drunkard, and a womaniser. Once Palma's dowry had been spent, he lost interest in her and neglected her. The poor girl had been obliged to find menial work picking rags in a paper factory. Then, when she was carrying her second child, her husband came home one evening dead drunk. They quarrelled and came to blows. Struggling on the landing outside their house to escape his angry fists, Palma tripped and fell down a flight of stairs. She was taken to hospital where she gave premature birth to a deformed child before dying shortly afterwards.

☆ ☆ ☆

On evenings when she was bored by television, Assunta would ask Rico to bring out his projector and together they would look at a film he had made in Filignano and another in Capri in 1955. Such a host of happy memories crowded in on Assunta when she saw these films that she was uplifted for days afterwards. By this time Rico had left Wishaw High and was doing a course at Teachers' Training College. The course ended in the summer of 1962, and he was then appointed to a lectureship in a college in Glasgow.

As the months passed, Assunta lost all notion of time. The weeks dissolved into months, and all her old Italian friends were fast disappearing. Josie Saracino, Giulietta's nephew, died at the early age of forty-seven, leaving his wife, Antoniella, with two children, Eugene and Assunta. In the summer of 1962, Giuseppe's brother Antonio and his wife, Genevina, both passed away. Early in 1963, *compare* Antonio went into his last illness and died on the 19th of March. In June of that same year, Assunta Coia followed her husband, Parisio, to the grave. Each time she heard of someone dying, Assunta felt more and more cut off from the happy past.

Rico seemed happy in his job in Glasgow. He was now in his early forties and still showed no inclination to marry. Assunta had taken to throwing him broad hints, for she would not always be there to look after him. Her advice fell on deaf ears. Every summer, he flew over to Paris and had the time of his life, for he always came back bursting with good health and high spirits. He never went to Italy. His record collection obsessed him as much as ever and his taste was unusual to say the least, for Assunta's eardrums were sometimes subjected to the most awful modern sounds that passed for music. He would spend hour after hour with his tape recorders, recording, editing, arranging, re-playing, fascinated by the terrible noise he produced on the machines. When Assunta could stand it no longer, she would put on her coat and go down to visit Mrs. Martin and Jean.

The café had by this time changed hands, for the Furettas left after the redoubtable Lita had managed to alienate most of the customers by her impudent and tactless behaviour behind the counter. A lady, who had been widowed during the war when she lost her husband on the ill-fated *Arandora Star*, took over and rented the shop for two years. Assunta was again free to go down to the backshop where she was invariably made welcome by the kindly Mrs. Jean Marsella and her charming daughter, Esther.

☆   ☆   ☆

The years passed in a monotonous pattern, but Assunta was not bored so long as she had her son beside her in the winter months. She was most alone in the summer when Rico went off to Paris. Then the time dragged, even though she filled it with reading or sewing or embroidering. She could often sense Giuseppe's presence within her, and this made her happy. The character of the West Cross was slowly changing.

Conn McGowan, the ebullient owner of the "Fit o' the Toon," was dead. When Peter Hislop, who had married late in life, died suddenly of a heart attack one day in 1965, Assunta was very shocked. It was shortly after his death that his widow gave up the grocery business, and the shop was sold and made into a launderette known as the Launderama. The large pub on the corner across from the café, once known as Quinton's Bar, was converted into a licensed hotel known as the Commercial. Peat's the pawnbrokers gave way to a shop specialising in car parts called Route 6.

Assunta saw all these changes gradually coming about as she sat at her window. And in the evenings, the drunks would go tottering on their way home and the young lovers walked down the street hand in hand like infatuated children. Sometimes as she lay in bed on warm nights with the window open, voices drifted up from the street, snatches of conversations, laughter, crying and swearing. Often she was outraged by the obscenities uttered by young voices. She began to wonder what the world was coming to. Yet the last thought in her mind was any desire ever to move from the West Cross. How could she leave the house above the café when it was there that Giuseppe would come for her when her time came?

Commare Vittoria died in September 1966. The era of the Continental in Byres Road had also come to an end. Antoniella, Josie's widow, had opened a restaurant at the bottom end of Byres Road across from the Western Infirmary. It was called "Ristorante Roma," and she and her children were the only ones left to carry on the tradition of good service established so long ago by Eugenio. Assunta felt drawn to Antoniella, for she was an indefatigable worker like herself and made enormous sacrifices to educate her children, just as she and Giuseppe had done for Rico.

When Assunta sat quietly in the living room some evenings with Rico while he was preparing his work, she was inclined to reminisce. One evening she talked about the early history of her family, going back to her great-grandparents. Rico pricked up his ears. Much of the information she was giving was entirely new to him. He interrupted her and asked her to follow him into his room. He made her sit at a small table behind a microphone and record all she had just been telling him. She talked for an hour and then they sat back and listened to the tape. Yet it did not occur to Rico just then that this activity could become a regular thing, allowing him to build a store of valuable material that might one day be of historical interest.

One afternoon, Assunta received an unexpected visit from Mrs. Brown, whose son Gavin had been projectionist in the little cinema downstairs in the days of the film society. Mrs. Brown continued to visit her regularly every Thursday, and sometimes she and Assunta would take long walks and gather dandelion leaves when they were in season. Mrs. Brown was a fount of information on local affairs and she could trace the family tree of all the well-known Wishaw families. The conversation never lagged when she was in the house, and Assunta came to look forward to her Thursday visits when the time just seemed to fly.

Now a regular pattern of visits was established. Mrs. Hislop, Peter's widow, came on Wednesdays, Mrs. Brown on Thursdays, and Mrs. Martin and Jean on Fridays. Assunta did not have time to be bored, and she did not mind Rico's frequent absences quite so much. Then Antoniella Saracino began to visit every month, and she always arrived laden with good things. She was an excellent baker and brought delicious egg sponges, spinach pies, and other mouth-watering delicacies. She and Assunta always chatted in Filignanese. On a very special day, Lucia Coia, now married to Silvio Ferri, called with her children, Angela, Nick, and Aldo, and they went over old times and relived the happy moments they had known at Byres Road.

Working at her Beatty washing machine one day in the summer of 1968, Assunta suddenly felt jabs of pain in her right leg and had to stop and sit down. When she tried to rise, the pain returned, and when Rico came home, she had to struggle to go and open the door. When he saw the state she was in, he called the doctor who diagnosed phlebitis. She was confined to her bed for four weeks.

It was then Rico had the idea of having her record her anecdotes on tape. The recorder was installed in her bedroom and the microphone placed on the table by the bed. A recording session was held every evening. This served two useful purposes. The tapes preserved her vivid recollections of the anecdotes and stories she had heard from her mother, and they re-established a strong bond of communication between Assunta and Rico. Listening to Assunta, Rico began to perceive depths in his mother he had never bothered to look for before.

On her seventy-fifth birthday, they made a special recording in the form of a long conversation. It was strewn with nostalgic recollections, and Assunta went back to her early years in Byres Road, Garscube Road, and Wishaw. What impressed Rico was the lack of resentment she showed for those people who had been unkind to her. Now that the unpleasantness of her experiences was over, she could look back and see the humour in them. Assunta was mellowing.

One day when Mrs. Hislop was making her weekly visit, they were talking about their lives and how they had slaved behind counters for so many years. Mrs. Hislop smiled and asked Assunta, "If you had your life to live over again, would you do it differently?"

And Assunta answered, "No, I would do it just the same!"

Inevitably a slow deterioration in her health set in after her seventy-fifth birthday in May 1970. She had no desire to go out, and was unable to cope with the heavy housework she had been doing for years. Confined as she was to the flat, her windows assumed greater importance for her and she looked out to observe the behaviour of a new generation that had come up since she left the café in 1960. She did not really approve of the cuddling and kissing that she saw among the bright young people on the pavements of the main street, as they flaunted their adolescent passions for all to see.

"This is a new world," she told herself philosophically, "and there is nothing we can do about it!"

At the back of the flat, in the glass-covered porch, she still attended to her beloved lemon tree, which had grown considerably over the years. In the morning, after watering it, she would go out on to the landing and throw food onto the roof for the birds.

She made a special friend of one little bird, and on sunny mornings, she would take a cushion and sit on the top step of the stair. When the bird saw her sitting there, he would flit down and land on the bottom step. Then, as she threw him an odd crumb, he would make his way up to her step by step until he was pecking away at her feet. All the time he would be chirping, "Cheep, cheeeep, cheeeeep!" and Assunta would comment, "Yes, it's all right for you, my wee friend, to say 'cheap, cheap, cheap,' but tell me, what's cheap nowadays with coal at fourteen shillings a bag when we used to pay eight pence a bag in 1915!"

Some mornings, if Assunta was tempted to lie in bed later than usual, the little bird would fly round to her bedroom window, look in, tap with his little beak on the pane and chirp, as if to say, "When are you going to get up, Assunta?"

☆   ☆   ☆

The café had changed hands many times and the new owner, who took over in August 1970, decided to convert it into a fish-and-chicken bar. Neither Assunta nor Rico were particularly enamoured with this idea, but they were reluctant to interfere with anyone's right to earn a livelihood. When permission was sought for the change of use, they signed the document giving their consent, on condition that every pre-caution would be taken for the proper extraction of cooking fumes so that no unpleasant odours would filter up to the flat. But the stipulation was not honoured, and shortly afterwards, the strong, pungent odour of burning fat began to infest Assunta's bedroom and the kitchen. Complaints were made but they fell on deaf ears.

Now, one of Assunta's greatest comforts on winter nights was her coal fire in the kitchen. It was there she would entertain her friends, and she would spend the last part of her evening before retiring, en-joying the warm glow of the coals. Unfortunately the greatest source of smell from downstairs was the fire, as the flue was adjacent to the one being used for extraction by the fish-and-chip bar. Rico decided the fire would have to be removed. A battle of wills began, but Rico was insistent and Assunta had to give in.

A fireplace specialist, recommended by Gavin, Mrs. Brown's son, appeared with his assistant on Assunta's doorstep one morning. His name was Harry Lennox, and he was one of those rare persons who still respected the feelings of others, especially old people. He could see by the pained expression on Assunta's face when she greeted him with "So you have come to remove my old friend?" that she was very attached to her coal fire.

He did his best on that sad day when Assunta was compelled to

271

say good-bye to her "old friend" to make the parting as painless as possible. Resorting to the simple expedient of making her talk about herself, he asked her question after question about her life in Italy and in Scotland. By the time "old friend" had been broken into small pieces and removed, Assunta found she had gained a new friend in the person of Harry Lennox.

Naturally she could not call him by his real name. She knew him as Larry Lennon. He became a frequent visitor, dropping in at odd times on the way to or from his various jobs, and Assunta was always ready to brew him a strong cup of tea, pitch black, which he thoroughly enjoyed. It was Harry who modernised the kitchen with luminous white tiles on the walls to give Assunta more light. The work brought him into frequent contact with the Cocozzas, and they welcomed him and his family as warm, sincere friends.

The constant coming and going of so many of Rico's acquaintances, colleagues, students, authors, actors, and actresses made life interesting for Assunta and broadened her horizons. Although her eyes were beginning to fail, she continued with her embroidery and spent many hours in her reclining chair, sewing designs and flowers in a bright variety of colours on table cloths, tea cloths, and chair backs. Her appreciation of music kept growing, and she spent many hours listening to the radio. She especially enjoyed film scores that Rico played each time he brought home a new record.

"I see you have brought a new pancake," she would say, and then listen attentively when he played the record. The two favourites she asked to hear again and again were the lovely score by Richard Rodney Bennett for the film version of Thomas Hardy's *Far from the Madding Crowd* and the unusually tuneful numbers composed by Leslie Bricusse for the musical version of James Hilton's *Good-bye, Mr.Chips*. It was about this time that Rico introduced her to large print books from the library, and she developed an interest in literature.

When she came to difficult passages in the texts, she would press Rico for an explanation and he would take the book from her and read the passage aloud, explaining every shade of the author's intention as he went along. In a sense it was ironical that Assunta's cultural interests should be growing just when her health was beginning to fail. Her favourite television programmes were those dealing with wildlife although she loved to see her favourite films of the 1930s when they were revived. A very special favourite was *David Copperfield*.

Since she was often confined to bed for long spells, Rico had so

272

arranged her bedroom that, by leaving the door open, she could glance to the right and see the working area of the kitchen reflected in her dressing table mirror. This was a good idea, as it gave her a keen interest to watch Rico's every move when he was preparing something special for dinner or trying to bake a rice cake. She would call out to him when she thought he was not doing it as *she* would have done it.

The summer of 1972 was notable for the arrival of a guest from France. Antonia had written asking if her granddaughter Patrizia could come on a visit for a month, as she had been studying English in her French school. Assunta looked forward to welcoming her old friends' granddaughter, and it was arranged that Patrizia should sleep at Mrs. Brown's house where she could also have breakfast. She could then spend the rest of the day at Assunta's and have her main meals there.

In her mind's eye, Assunta had pictured a girl such as Antonia had been when they were both young. She was to be disappointed. The sixteen-year-old girl who arrived from Paris wearing heavy make-up trying to look older than her years did not conform to Assunta's image. She tried her best to be kind to the girl, but there was no communication between them. Patrizia was very difficult to please and no matter what Assunta or Rico prepared, she refused to eat more than a mouthful. It was a very worrying month, and Assunta was glad when it came to an end and the girl went back to Paris. A day or so later, Mrs. Brown came upon dozens of sweet and chocolate wrappers hidden under the mattress of the bed in which Patrizia had slept. This explained her apparently poor appetite. She had put herself on a special diet of sweets and chocolate!

In December 1973, after a year of ups and downs, Assunta fell ill and was removed to a local hospital. After a few days of tests, the sister in charge of the ward informed Rico that his mother had a tumour. She might suffer a great deal of pain, and then again she might not. But she was being sent home to die. Should the pain become unbearable, she would be readmitted to hospital. In the meantime she was being discharged, as there was a shortage of beds. A detailed report would be sent to her doctor within a few days. The news was a terrible blow to Rico.

Assunta was brought home. Although she was in some pain, she did not complain. She could put up with anything so long as she could be at home in her own room. Rico made no mention to her of his conversation with the sister, and, as the weeks passed, the doctor did not receive any report concerning a tumour. It was all a mystery, and no one seemed to know just what Assunta was suffering from.

In the spring of 1974, she began to suffer from bouts of breathlessness. A large oxygen cylinder was installed beside her bed, and she obtained a measure of relief from it. But she came to rely upon it too much and sometimes had to be given oxygen during the night. An electric bell was placed at her bedside, and she would ring it several times every night. Rico lost a great deal of sleep and became irritable. So they both came under strain. She was worried because she realised she was becoming a burden to him, and he was worried because he was finding it increasingly difficult to cope.

He arranged for a woman to sit with her during the day when he was at work, as she required constant attention. Then, when he found it impossible to get a night's sleep, he employed a night nurse three nights a week. It was an unrelieved period of misery and pain, and Assunta grew more and more frail. The flat assumed the atmosphere of a small hospital in which they were both confined. Only when visitors came, was the gloom temporarily dispelled. Mrs. Brown's visits on Thursdays were very welcome, for she would arrive around lunch time and stay until late in the evening. While she sat with Assunta, Rico worked on a thesis he was writing, which had become a form of escape for him. As he worked at his typewriter in his room, he could hear the steady rise and fall of Mrs. Brown's voice at the other end of the flat.

By the autumn of 1974, with the prospect of a heavy teaching session before him, Rico knew something would have to be done. He carefully explained to Assunta that he had two alternatives. Either he continued to nurse her, in which case he would have to give up working, or she could agree to go into hospital for a few months, at least for the duration of the teaching session. Her lips trembled when he faced her with this terrible choice. But she knew what she must do.

"Whatever you say, Rico," she said with a sad note in her voice.

Assunta opened her eyes. Where was she? This was not her room. Where was Rico? She had tried to press the bell button by her bed but could not find it. She looked round the small, dimly lit ward. There were three beds against the wall opposite, all of them occupied. Now she began to recollect. Rico and Mrs. Brown had come with her in the

274

ambulance. She had refused to be carried and walked down the stairs to the vehicle. She had to show them she was not as ill as they thought. Perhaps, when they saw how well she really was, they would relent and take her home after a few days. But here she was now lying in a small ward with five other old women. Old women. *My God*, she thought, *am I really getting old*? Her body felt old, but *she* didn't. The only way to get out of this place was to get better. She would show them!

☆   ☆   ☆

At visiting times it was customary to wheel the patients into the dayroom. Assunta did not like this practice. There was no privacy amidst the hubbub of the dayroom. So she asked the nurse if she could stay sitting in the ward. There she sat alone, waiting for the sound of Rico's step in the corridor. She could easily discern his heavy tread. He would always be overweight. At last he arrived with a tray of fruit. Sitting beside her he asked how she felt.

"I'm getting better," she said. "When can I come home?"

"But you've only been here a week," he said.

"Seems more like a year to me," she observed and went on, "I'm going to tell you something. Some of the old dears in this ward are not all there. If I stay with them much longer, I'll go round the bend as well!"

Rico laughed. "It's surely not as bad as that?" he asked.

"No, it's worse!" said Assunta.

☆   ☆   ☆

Depressed as she was by the hospital, Assunta's condition grew worse at first, but after a few weeks, she began to improve. Rico encouraged her, telling her he was trying to have her transferred to Wishaw Hospital where she would be so much nearer home.

"Then perhaps I could come home?" she asked in that particularly plaintive tone she could assume so easily when she wanted to touch him. For, although she was sure of his affection, when she lay alone in the hospital bed, she could not help feeling rejected and unwanted. She felt she had nothing in common with the older women in the ward who were all of them living in varying stages of confusion. Confusion. That was the common word in the hospital. When the old ladies tried to reach out to express the fantasies that were the only remnants of the beautiful moments in their lives, they were "confused."

275

When Rico tried to be kind to one of the ladies in Assunta's ward, who had expressed an interest in pictures, by bringing her an art book, the sister took him aside and told him not to bring any more as the old lady was confused. And confusion can be contagious. Rico began to regret he had put his mother in that awful place.

Christmas Day 1974 was a very sad one for Assunta and Rico. No one had bothered to tell him at the hospital that the patients would be allowed to wear dresses for the Christmas celebration, so he had not brought a dress beforehand. To his dismay, when he arrived for the afternoon visit, he could not find Assunta in the ward. When he was directed to the dayroom, he could not see her there. He asked the sister where his mother was. She pointed to a forlorn, pitiful little figure in a horrid, black dress that was not hers, sitting sadly, jammed between two other women, in a corner of the room. When he sat down beside her, he could see tears in her eyes.

"They made me put on this awful dress," she said, "and I know it probably belonged to someone who died here."

Rico was mortified. He took her hand and squeezed it. She held on to his, tightly, unwilling to let go. If he had a car, he would have taken her home there and then at that very moment. The contrived air of jollification around them wounded them. Some of the nurses were tipsy. It was all so humiliating.

Soon afterwards Assunta was transferred to Wishaw. It was a brighter, cottage-type hospital and the nurses were cheerful, sympathetic, and understanding. Assunta seemed much happier, and she was making great progress in preparing herself to go home. The only thing that worried her was the fact that she was occasionally showing signs of losing her customary alertness when she yielded to the soporific effect of the sleeping pill that the night nurse insisted upon giving her each evening. She decided she would have no more of them. When the nurse turned her back, she would spit the pill out into her hand and keep it there until the nurse had gone. Then she would slip it into the waste bag by the bed. She was determined to be clear in her mind at all times. Otherwise she might as well be dead.

The teaching session was drawing to a close, and Assunta began to look forward to going home. One day in the middle of April, Rico came to visit her and in the course of their conversation, he let it slip that he was going to have a holiday. He was going to France for a few weeks. Assunta's ears pricked up.

"When are you going?" she asked.

"Just as soon as we close for the summer," he replied.

"But I thought I was to be coming home in May," she said.

"Well, you know, Ma, I simply have to get to Paris to do some work on my thesis. It's been dragging on for so long, and I simply must try to get it finished this summer. I'm sure you wouldn't mind, would you? You seem to have settled so well here and you are content, and they do look after you, don't they?"

Assunta did not answer. She was so utterly disappointed and not a little angry. So he was breaking his promise to her for the sake of a miserable thesis. She would show him.

For the next two weeks, Assunta became the most difficult patient in Wishaw Hospital. She defied the nurses' orders, went constantly to the toilet unaided, fell twice when she slipped on the ward floor, refused to eat, and became more and more distant and withdrawn. Rico was annoyed when he saw how thin she was becoming. When he spoke to her, she barely replied, and the long silences were filled with apprehension. Sometimes she would look at him accusingly and ask, "Are you looking after my lemon tree?"

At the end of an afternoon visit, the sister asked to speak with Rico. She told him his mother had become impossible. She was disrupting the smooth running of the ward. He would have to arrange to take her home as soon as he went on holiday. So Assunta had her way, and Rico cancelled his trip to Paris.

It was Larry Lennon and his son, young Harry, who brought her home. Mrs. Brown and Rico were waiting to welcome her. Rico had prepared a good lunch. Despite the cancellation of his plans, he was very happy that Assunta was coming home. It was a warm, sunny day in May just a week before her eightieth birthday. The banging of the metal gate downstairs announced her arrival. Larry and Harry formed a comfortable chair for a very frail Assunta by linking their arms. They carried her upstairs. Mrs. Brown and Rico came out on to the landing.

"Welcome home," said Mrs. Brown.

Assunta placed her feet on the landing, stood up and said, "Am I really here?" Then she brushed past Rico and Mrs. Brown and walked into the kitchen where the tree, with its lovely bright green leaves, stood beside the washing machine, silhouetted against the white tiles. She stretched out a shaking hand and lightly touched one of the leaves.

"Hullo, lemon," she said. "I'm back!"

And indeed she was and had not the slightest intention of going back to hospital. This she made very clear. In the first few days she was back at home, Rico observed some subtle changes in her personality. She seemed very distant at times, as if she was letting him know she had been hurt. Falling into long silences when she was sitting in the special geriatric chair he had bought for her so that she could enjoy the comfort of a back support, her eyes seemed to focus on some indefinable distance beyond the confines of her room.

When Rico sat beside her and asked, "A penny for your thoughts?" she would start, turn round, look him straight in the eyes, and say, "They're not worth a penny!"

Whether it was simply that she was really getting old, or that the drugs she had been given had affected her, Rico detected childlike traits in her behaviour. Her voice had altered, growing thinner and higher pitched so that it sounded like the voice of a little girl. And she sometimes behaved like a little girl who craved affection. When she went to bed at night, she insisted on a goodnight kiss. Yet she had always considered this sort of thing as being sloppy. If her back was painful and he offered to rub it, kneeling by the special hospital bed that had replaced her own, she would lean her cheek against the top of his head and keep it there until he had finished. Rico, touched by her helplessness, gave her all the affectionate attention he could. As the summer wore on, she began to lose the starved look and her spirits rose.

Assunta liked to hold court on Wednesdays. Since her return from the hospital, the numbers of Wednesday afternoon visitors had increased. Mrs. Hislop came regularly and sometimes Mr. and Mrs. Madden who lived nearby or the Marsellas from the other end of the town dropped in. Assunta would preside in her upright chair, fitted with a special tray that also acted as a barrier to prevent her from getting out of the chair without aid. While Rico made tea for the visitors, Assunta would tell them stories from Filomena's repertoire.

One Wednesday afternoon, Rico, glancing through from the kitchen now and then, saw Assunta, as she spoke, stealing glances at her reflection in the long dressing-table mirror by the window, where she could see herself in profile.

When the visitors had all departed, he asked her, "What was all that business with the mirror today? It's not like you to be looking at yourself in mirrors. What was it all about?"

"I'm glad you mentioned it," said Assunta, "for I knew I had something to ask you."

"I'm all ears," said Rico, and Assunta went on, saying, "Well, you know how you have recorded all these stories I have been telling for so many years. When I go away, people will be able to hear me telling them on tape. But it struck me today, as I caught a glimpse of myself in the mirror, they won't be able to see the wonderful expressions on my face as I speak."

"Yes, that's true," said Rico, "but just what are you driving at?"

"You remember the other evening when we were watching 'Tomorrow's World' and they were showing one of these new video camera things. Don't you think it would be a good idea to get one of those and then I could be seen as well as heard on the tapes?"

"But do you realise how much such a camera would cost?" said Rico.

"Probably a couple of thousand pounds!" said Assunta.

"And how do you expect me to afford that?" asked Rico.

"You're always getting bank loans for one thing or another. Just get another one and buy a camera!" This really knocked the wind out of Rico's sails.

But Rico gave in. He had not used a cine-camera for years. He got a bank loan and bought a Super-8 Sound film camera just before Christmas. Assunta got her wish and had the satisfaction of seeing the "wonderful expressions" on her face as she told her stories.

Their happiness at Christmas was spoiled by the untimely death of Antoniella Saracino who finally succumbed to the dreaded cancer that she had suffered for so long and so bravely. Assunta was deeply saddened by the loss of her friend, her last link with her loved ones in Byres Road.

Rico gave up any idea of sending Assunta back to hospital when she improved so much in the winter of 1975 to 1976. But he was obliged always to have someone who could be with her while he was at work in Glasgow. After trying various home-help ladies, he eventually made enquiries and came up with one who had retired from the service and was looking for a part-time post. The morning she arrived, when Rico answered the door, he found himself looking down at a petite, plump little lady with greying hair and bright, very mischievous grey-blue eyes.

"I'm Mrs. Grimes," she said. "I've come to look after your mother."

And she was true to her word. Jenny Grimes, whom Assunta quickly renamed Jean, was the very person to look after her. Always hearty and cheerful and often boisterous, she gave Assunta the affectionate attention she required. She had a naughty sense of humour, and there was never a dull moment when she was in the house. Assunta found her a suitable Italian name when she was not calling her Jean. The name "Curcetta" or Shorty was given because of her short legs.

Jenny's arrival marked the start of a happy summer, for Assunta seemed to be on the mend. In May, Assunta lost her old friend Mrs. Martin who had been preceded to the grave some time before by her faithful niece Jean. Assunta felt she would soon not have any old friends left. The thought of dying herself never seemed to enter her head and, despite certain physical disabilities, she was feeling well enough to go on forever. She was contented in a happy routine from which she derived much enjoyment and fun.

Rico managed to get her to sing again, and on her eighty-first birthday she recorded some songs with him. Shortly afterwards she sent Jenny down to the late Mrs. Martin's garden for some rhubarb one day. Rico had been to the dentist that morning and when he came home, he made some delicious lemon custard. He then served it in the kitchen with the stewed rhubarb and a very ripe banana that was about to depart. Now Assunta and Rico had often engaged in spontaneous mock operas. The rigid rule was that everything had to be sung in the best operatic style. Rico now placed his stereo tape recorder on the table and while he, Assunta, and Jenny enjoyed their rhubarb and custard with the departing banana, they sang. Rico edited the recording, adding some concrete music and recorded a BBC 3-type announcement at the start. The one act no-opera was announced as the latest work of a well-known composer and it was given the title of "Custard and Rhubarb with Banana." It was a great success with visiting friends.

Rico applied for a wheelchair and twice took Assunta out round the town. But she did not take kindly to the idea and asked him to send it back. Then, one day, he managed to take her out in the car, and they visited cousin Dalfina and her husband, Tony Franchitti, in Motherwell. They sat out in the little garden at the back of the house, feeding the birds, and enjoying the sunshine. Rico filmed it all. They were not to know it was to be Assunta's last outing.

One afternoon, Rico came home with a triumphant smile spread across his face.

"I wonder what he has been up to now?" said Assunta to Jenny. He did not speak but went to the refrigerator where he always kept a bottle of Asti Spumante. Opening it with a loud pop, he poured the wine and offered a glassful to each of the ladies before taking one himself. Then he turned to them and said, "Before I propose this special toast, I must ask you both to bow to me, for I have just been made a *cavaliere* by the Italian Government."

280

Assunta looked at Jenny, winked and commented, "What a clown my son is!"

Assunta looked very well during the rest of the summer but, as the first days of autumn approached, she grew listless and began to suffer spasms of pain in the bowel. With the pain came dark premonitions. Yet she was determined to live every fine moment to the full. In the morning, she would lie awake listening to the dawn chorus outside her windows. The echoing footsteps of a solitary man on his way to work gave a human touch to the natural music. Later, when the children were making their way to school, she would listen eagerly for the prattle of their shrill voices. One in particular attracted her attention. It was a little boy called Billy Boyd, who always whistled merrily in tune as he walked smartly under her window, and every morning he had a different tune to offer. She clung to all these sounds of life, savouring them, and took ever more interest in the street scene every day.

Rico had no sooner resumed his work in October than Assunta took to her bed. A long period of agony began for them both. The bowel condition grew worse week by week. A kind neighbour, Theresa Murphy, brought a commode, and this was a tremendous help as Assunta became too weak sometimes to walk to the toilet. Rico was more and more disquieted by her suffering, but she kept refusing to take painkillers. The doctor was very solicitous and understanding, calling as often as he could and prescribing mild sedatives. On those days when Rico did not have to go to work, he was in full charge at home. As the weeks passed, Assunta could see he was under unbearable strain. She began to pray that she would soon die.

When she could not eat the good food Rico had prepared, he grew irksome and lost his temper, saying terrible things that he regretted afterwards. One day he had gone out of his way to prepare broccoli, one of her favourite dishes. She interrupted him constantly to be helped on to the commode. When the meal was ready, he was just about to bring in her tray, when she asked to be helped down again. Then, when he had lifted her back into bed, he brought back the tray. She nibbled without appetite at the greens, then asked him to take away the tray as she could not face the food. It had taken him much effort to prepare the meal. Something in him snapped. He lifted the tray and threw it on to the floor. Then he lifted a glass and shattered it in the sink.

Assunta, alarmed, began to shriek with fear, "Please, please, please, Rico, calm down, can't you see I'm dying?"

When Rico heard this, he lost all control. "Dying, dying, you are always dying, but you don't bloody well die!" he screamed out. Then he added, "It's I who am going to die, for I am going to put an end to

281

it right now. I've had enough!" and he took a chair and lifted it over to the window. Then he opened the window and, standing on top of the chair, lifted a foot on to the sill, shouting, "I'm going to jump out of this bloody window!"

Assunta at once called out, "Don't jump, don't jump, who'll look after me?" Rico paused, then he turned his head slowly round, looked at her, and burst out laughing. In a flash she had made him see the ludicrousness of the melodramatic frenzy he had worked himself into.

Christmas passed and a grey 1977 began. Assunta continued to suffer great pain, yet she tried to control herself so that Rico would not see how much she was suffering. But at times she could not suppress the cries that rose to her lips when she felt a flame flare up inside her, burning her up. When she cried out, he would rush to the bed and hold her. And she held onto him as tightly as she could until the spasm was over. Then she would look at him and always say the same words, "You are my strong arm."

As long as he was at home, she was calm, feeling safe, but when she was left with Jenny, she was scared in case she should die when he was not there. And when at last he came home and the evening meal was over, he would sit beside her and she would never take her eyes from him as he sat correcting or reading. When he had gone to bed, she would take her rosary beads in her hand and ask God that she might be allowed to die in her own room where Giuseppe had promised to come for her. The priest, who had befriended her when she was in hospital, came on the first Friday of every month to give her communion.

One Friday, when the priest had gone, she had a long discussion with Rico on spiritual matters. He asked her pointedly if she really believed in life after death. She answered with humour that, since one could not be sure, it was as well to be on the safe side and pray, just in case. But Rico knew that she did believe and had always done so. She took this opportunity to tell him exactly what was to be done when she died. She wished to be buried in her wedding dress in the lair where Giuseppe lay in Lambhill. The funeral was to be simple, and she did not want any wreaths. She hated wreaths. Her death was not to be announced in the papers. If the priest should insist, a short service could be held in the house, but she had no desire to be taken to the local church that had refused Giuseppe the full rites to which he was entitled.

"When I have gone away," she added, "I would like you to invite all those good people who have been kind to me and make them a nice meal, the sort of meal I used to make when I was able. And when you are all sitting there eating, you can play some of my tapes and listen to me. You may even talk about me, if you like, so long as you don't say anything bad about me!"

One day early in February, when she had been in great pain all morning, she called out to Rico, who was working in the kitchen, "Ah, Rico, Rico, I'm afraid I have not long to go, Son." He went through to chide her for talking such nonsense. When the doctor examined her later that afternoon, he shook his head when Rico was showing him out.

"You must try and persuade her to go into hospital," he said, "for she is far from comfortable here."

Rico told her what the doctor had said, but she only muttered, "I'll do my best, Son, to die soon, here, in my own room."

But each day she got worse, and the constant physical strain of lifting her in and out of bed was telling on Rico. For him it was an endless nightmare, and he could not suppress the fits of screaming that racked him when his nerves snapped. And all this time Mrs. Brown never failed to come on Thursdays and sit with her. If she fell into an uneasy sleep for a short time, when she opened her eyes, she could see Mrs. Brown's fixed earnestly upon her, watching her every move, ready to give assistance when it was needed. Then, in the end, she was obliged to submit to the doctor's injections to kill the pain. But she begged him to stop them, and he left some strong tablets to make her sleep.

On the evening of Sunday, the 27th of February, Assunta, by a miracle, enjoyed an evening free from pain. She even recorded a story on tape. Rico had baked pizzas and Assunta, showing a remarkably keen appetite, devoured a large portion. Then she asked for another piece. She had not felt so well for a very long time. Rico's spirits rose to see her enjoying her food with so much relish. Surely, at last, she was going to get better! Assunta, savouring the tomatoes and herbs in the pizza filling, was reminded of those pizzas Filomena had baked so long ago. How much water had flowed under the bridges since those happy days!

The evening was cold and Rico opened the doors of the coal stove that supplied hot water to heat the entire flat. It had been installed in Assunta's bedroom so that she could occasionally enjoy the live flames, for she still missed her "old friend" of the kitchen. Now the flickering flames from the coals brought back more memories of Imperatore and, when Rico came to sit beside her, she began to reminisce.

283

Her eyes glowed with happiness as joyful moments from the past surfaced in her mind. When it was time for her to go to sleep, she did not need a sleeping tablet. As Rico leaned forward to kiss her on the forehead, she put her arms round his neck and kissed him on the cheek.

"Thank you for a lovely evening and a delicious supper," she said, "and bless you for being such a good son."

The first part of the night passed peacefully. Shortly after two o'clock, Rico rose to go through to the kitchen for a glass of water. When he reached the doorway, he was surprised to hear moaning and, hurrying through to the bedroom, was horrified to find Assunta lying helplessly on the floor beside the bed. To avoid disturbing him, she had tried to get to the commode and had fallen. She must have been lying on the floor for some time as she was icy cold when Rico lifted her into the bed. He covered her and quickly made a cup of tea for her. Then he filled two hot water bottles and put them in beside her. But she kept shivering, partly with fright, and he rubbed her arms and hands to restore the circulation. He stayed by the bed for the rest of the night.

When the doctor came to see her on the Tuesday morning, he told Rico she would have to be sent to hospital. He promised to try to have her admitted to Strathclyde Hospital in Motherwell. Later that morning he phoned to say Assunta would be going in on Thursday.

With the help of Mrs. Brown and Jenny, Rico did everything possible to make her comfortable and ease her pain. She asked for her dressing table to be moved over so that she could see her lemon tree in the kitchen. Her appetite was very poor, but she tried valiantly to eat some of the food put before her. On the Wednesday, just as she was about to have her lunch, a small plateful of pasta and milk, she turned to Rico and asked unexpectedly, "What has become of the cine-camera you bought?"

"It's in my room," he answered.

"Have you any films?" she asked.

"Yes, I have," he replied.

"Then put one in the camera and film me while I eat," she commanded. After placing the tray on the bed, Rico set up the camera, as she had requested, and made a short film. She looked quite pitiful as she tried bravely to swallow the food, but she was determined to finish the film. At one point, when she seemed to be distracted, Rico called out from behind the camera, "Hello!" and Assunta, looking straight into the lens, said with emphasis, "Hello, . . . and cheerio!"

On the morning of Thursday, 3rd March, Rico was trying desperately to please his mother in every way he could. He prepared a tiny portion of roasted cheese, to which she had always been very partial, for her breakfast. She ate and enjoyed it. The ambulance that was to take her to the hospital was not due until two o'clock in the afternoon. But the doorbell rang at ten o'clock, and Assunta's heart missed a beat. She listened anxiously as Rico answered the door, and she could hear the muffled tones of a conversation. Then Rico appeared to explain that an ambulanceman had called, mistaking their house for that of her friend Pace Macari who lived across the road. What a coincidence. She and Pace were both being admitted to hospital on the same day.

Then the bell rang again. Assunta said, "This is becoming a busy house!"

It was Theresa Murphy, "The Lady of the Commode," as Assunta always called her, come to see how she was. Theresa had no sooner departed than Jenny arrived, followed by Mrs. Brown. Assunta felt she was getting every attention on her last morning at home, and she smiled as she listened to their reassuring chatter. She knew she was not going to get better despite all their assurances. Yet they went on talking, promising that she would surely be home in time for Easter.

Then Jenny said good-bye, and while Mrs. Brown helped Rico in the kitchen, she leaned back on her pillows. She had not slept all night, still hoping that Giuseppe would come for her there. Then she complained of feeling cold, and Rico heated the special white cloth she liked to wear over her hair in bed. As he placed it round her head, its heat was very comforting and she looked at him gratefully and murmured, "Aaaaaaaaaah!" with great satisfaction.

Rico began to prepare lunch and as a special treat, he fried a few chips in olive oil. These were her favourites. Mrs. Brown fussed round her, raising her pillows to make her more comfortable. She lay back and took a good look round her room, her eyes lingering over the objects she had gathered over the years. There they all were, each one recalling a special occasion: Giulietta's statuette of Bernadette of Lourdes, the musical boxes Rico brought her from Italy, Mrs. Hislop's Manx cat and Jersey jug, her wedding photograph on the wall beside the stove, and above the stove itself the large hand-coloured photograph of baby Rico when he was only nine months old.

Many a time he had threatened to take it down and hide it in the attic, but she had always told him, "Leave it there so I can always keep an eye on you!"

She sighed as she realised she would probably never see them again. Then it was time to eat, and she enjoyed the small handful of chips with a tiny grilled steak and some fried green peppers. When she had eaten, she asked to be helped to the toilet, and Rico and Mrs.

285

Brown each took an arm and supported her as she made her way through the kitchen. When she reached the lemon tree, she paused and looked at it for a long time. Then she turned to Rico and said, "Don't forget to give my lemon tree its drink every week—no more than a pint of water."

When the ambulance arrived in the middle of the afternoon, she was carefully wrapped in warm blankets. She did not want to be taken down on a stretcher, so the ambulance men brought a special chair and carried her down the stairs. Assunta had never shed tears when she had gone to hospital previously. Now she knew this was the last time she would go down the stairs, and she wept.

The little side room in the hospital was clean and airy. Rico and Mrs. Brown had gone, and she was quite alone. She could hear the coming and going of nurses and orderlies in the corridor. Above her in some other ward the sound of children's voices. A nurse looked in frequently, taking her pulse, easing her on the high pillows supporting her. The nurse kept talking to her addressing her as "Gran." When she came in again, she asked, "What would you like for your tea, Gran, scrambled egg or fish?"

Assunta looked at her and raised one eyebrow. "You keep calling me 'Gran,' Nurse," she said, "but I am not a gran." Then she added meaningfully, as an afterthought, "Not unless that little bugger has been up to something, behind my back."

The nurse hurried gleefully to tell Sister what Mrs. Cocozza had just said, and it was duly reported to Rico when he came to visit.

With each day that passed, Assunta grew weaker. Her eyes began to fail, but her sense of hearing became more acute and she could easily distinguish the heavy tread of Rico's shoes in the corridor and knew when he was about to arrive. Many visitors came and went, and she was pleased when Rico's old sweetheart, Gina, and her sister, Indina, made the effort of coming all the way from Glasgow, where they had been living for many years, to see her again. She even had a visit from a nephew she had not seen for many years. Now that she was dying, they were all coming to see her.

By the beginning of the third week in hospital, she began to be unsure of where she really was. One evening Rico brought Jenny to visit and, after a few minutes, Assunta, thinking she was at home, turned to her and told her to put on the kettle for a cup of tea.

Mrs. Hislop came to pay a last visit. Then on Saturday, the 26th of March, Rico brought Mrs. Brown in the evening. Assunta seemed utterly exhausted, and they did not stay long. She was scarcely able to speak, but as they were about to leave, she turned to them and said feebly, "I am going away."

The nurse left the door of her room open so that she could call out if she required attention. She could not have wished for more loving care than these angels in white were giving her, and she loved them for it. That night she suffered excruciating pain and her muffled screams brought the night nurse to administer the heavily doped sleeping tablets that would give her temporary relief. In the early hours of Sunday morning, she lay listening to the birds singing in the trees outside her room. The nurses came and washed her and changed the soiled bedsheets. The sheer humiliation of it. She who had never dirtied a bed in her life.

Morning drifted slowly into afternoon, and she lay there horribly twisted. Her body was slumped forward so that she seemed deformed, and her dulled eyes stared unseeingly from their sockets. But she still knew where she was and was well aware of what was happening. For she was going now, that she knew with certainty.

The pains in her feet and legs had disappeared. But she was not really comfortable, even though she had no pain. She would have wanted to smooth the white sheet overlapping the light blanket in front of her, but she had not the power to move her arms or her hands. The creases in the sheet, so close to her face, irritated her. No one knew how to iron any more. The old skills were disappearing one by one.

She could not swallow, and the mushy mess the nurse had tried to feed her lay in a mass in her mouth, making it difficult for her to breathe. When would Rico come? The minutes trailed past more and more slowly. She could see the vague outline of the doorway in a grey mist, and now and then she could hear the reverberating steps of the nurses in the corridor. Then, at long last, she heard the steady, heavy tread of Rico's shoes and sighed with relief. When he appeared she could not see him clearly as he hung his jacket by the door, but when he drew near to the bed, he came into clearer view, emerging from the mist that so mysteriously persisted at the far end of the room.

He kissed her on the brow and spoke comforting words. Then, with a paper tissue, he cleaned out the mess from her mouth, brought some water in a glass and, holding a steel basin under her chin, made her rinse out the rest of the nasty stuff. Her mouth was pleasantly refreshed, but the effort exhausted her and she sank back helplessly on to the raised pillows behind her and closed her eyes for a few moments. He went on talking, moving nervously round the room while she listened.

He drew up a chair and sat by the bed just as she opened her eyes again. Now she could see him clearly, the mist having disappeared completely, and she noted he was wearing a new shirt and a horribly bright tie. He really had no taste in ties, she thought.

He saw her looking at the shirt and remarked, "Yes, it's a new shirt. Do you like it? It's pure cotton," and he gently lifted her right hand and placed it on the sleeve to let her feel the softness of the material.

She grunted approvingly to let him know she liked it. Then she gazed up into his eyes to catch his attention and, as he answered her look, she moved her eyes down quickly to the terrible tie, then raised them to the ceiling and puffed her mouth to let him know it was really more than loud, that awful tie. She heard him chuckling. As he continued to sit, she felt his warm hand closing over hers and, soothed by the contact, closed her eyes and fell into a very light slumber, so happy to have him all to herself.

She was awakened by music. Rico was softly humming the tune of her favourite "Maria, Mari'," and it evoked such a host of pleasing memories that she smiled at him gratefully as she opened her eyes. He smiled back, knowing she must be thinking of Giuseppe. Then he rose, put on his jacket, and said he was going home. He would be back early in the evening, he assured her. She nodded. He leaned over and kissed her again on the brow. Making an effort she raised her right hand with difficulty and managed to brush his cheek lightly with her fingers. He took her hand and kissed it before laying it down. Then he left the door open as he made his way out to the corridor, and she heard his steps fading away. She closed her eyes again and sighed.

Now life began by degrees to ebb from her. Her feet and legs lost all feeling, her arms became numb. She was breathing with great difficulty, yet the strain did not seem to be troubling her. Out of a memory that was now ever so faint, she heard children's voices singing:

> When I was young, each morning I saw the sun rise
> High in the blue sky smiling upon me,
> Giving me strength to be brave and good
> And enrich my life with the warmth of giving love.

Now I am old and I see the sun is setting.
Soon I shall yield to the softness of my night.
And I ask myself, was I ever brave and true?
Yes, I filled my life with love, in loving you.

Nurses were coming and going in the little room attending to the dying woman, but she was no longer aware of their presence. Her eyes were closed, and she could feel all around her and within her all those she had known and loved. They were and would always be a part of her and she a part of them.

When the telephone rang, Rico's heart jumped, for he knew before he lifted the receiver that it was the hospital. He raced down to the car and, driving like a madman, arrived at the hospital ten minutes later. The Sister met him in the corridor and murmured apologetically, "I'm very sorry, it's too late now. She just threw her arms round my neck a few moments ago and passed away."

"Can I see her?" asked Rico.

"In just a moment," said the Sister.

She had slipped away when he was not there. Suddenly he felt quite alone and lost, as only a child can feel alone and lost. The Sister came to show him into the side room. Assunta was lying stretched out on the bed. The colour had drained from her cheeks, and already her features were assuming the ivory smoothness of a statue. The Sister left him alone, and he stepped forward to look down on his mother's serene face where a smile still lingered around the lips. He leaned down to kiss her brow, still faintly warm. The tears came to his eyes and in a pitiful voice bearing strong traces of the lamentations he had heard as a boy at funerals in Filignano, two words escaped instinctively from his lips and he repeated them as he wept, over and over again, "*Mamma bella, mamma bella, mamma bella!*"

The countless particles of all she had experienced during her probation on earth were clustering round her for the last time, clinging to her in warm waves of love, before drifting away to precede her into that other element where she was now being irresistibly drawn. And

289

now, wonderfully, unexpectedly, and yet inevitably, she was standing once more on the high loggia at the top of the house on the Hill of Imperatore. Giuseppe put his arms around her as she raised hers to meet the embrace that would make them one forever. . . .